Praise for J.

"Historic. Romantic. Riveting. Rich and multi-layered, *Crucible of War* is the epic continuation of an unforgettable series. Joan Hochstetler gives us a rare glimpse into America's past, leaving the reader enriched and wanting more. I highly recommend this amazing book and series!"

—LAURA FRANTZ, AUTHOR OF *The Colonel's Lady* AND *Love's Reckoning*

"We have given this series to all of our family so that they will understand the foundation of this country and the freedoms they enjoy. If you haven't read it yet, you should. You will relive the sacrifices, romances, and pain experienced by past patriots. You will understand what you have benefited from when you experience this trip through history as written by Joan. It is historically accurate fiction, and a very engaging and interesting read. I can't wait for the next book to come out!"

—JOHN E. ANDERSON, SGM RET., U.S. ARMY INTELLIGENCE & COMMUNICATIONS COMMAND

"J. M. Hochstetler weaves a tapestry rich in detail, a riveting story of adventure and intrigue in a time when men and women made choices that wrenched the heart, but honored God. An engaging new chapter in the on-going saga of how an enduring nation—and an equally enduring romance—were forged in the *Crucible of War*."

—LORI BENTON, AUTHOR OF *Willa,* FORTHCOMING FROM WATERBROOK MULTNOMAH, AUGUST 2013

Crucible of War

THE AMERICAN
PATRIOT SERIES
~BOOK 4~

J. M. HOCHSTETLER

Charlotte, Tennessee
37036 USA

Crucible of War

Published by Sheaf House®. Requests for information should be addressed to:

Editorial Director
Sheaf House Publishers, LLC
1703 Atlantic Avenue
Elkhart, Indiana 46514

jmshoup@gmail.com
www.sheafhouse.com

Library of Congress Control Number: 2012939631

ISBN: 978-1-936438-07-5 (softcover)

All scripture quotations are from the King James Version of the Bible.

Cover design and interior template by Marisa Jackson.

Cover art: "Battle of Eutaw Springs, September 8, 1781". Painting by Don Troiani, www.historicalimagebank.com. Used by permission.

Maps by Jim Brown of Jim Brown Illustration.

12 13 14 15 16 17 18 19 20 21— 10 9 8 7 6 5 4 3 2 1

MANUFACTURED IN THE UNITED STATES OF AMERICA

This book is dedicated to the men and women of our first Greatest Generation who pledged their lives, their fortunes, and their sacred honor to establish a new nation. Through their noble heroism they secured for future generations the great ideal of liberty and justice.

Blessed be the Lord, my strength,
Which teacheth my hands to war,
And my fingers to fight;
My goodness, and my fortress;
My high tower, and my deliverer;
My shield, and He in Whom I trust;
Who subdueth my people under me.
PSALM 144:1–2

But I will remove far off from you the northern army,
and will drive him into a land barren and desolate,
with his face toward the east sea.
JOEL 2:20

An award-winning author and editor, J. M. Hochstetler is the daughter of Mennonite farmers, a graduate of Indiana University, a professional editor, and a lifelong student of history. Her contemporary novel *One Holy Night* was the Christian Small Publishers 2009 Book of the Year and finalist for the American Christian Fiction Writers 2009 Carol Award.

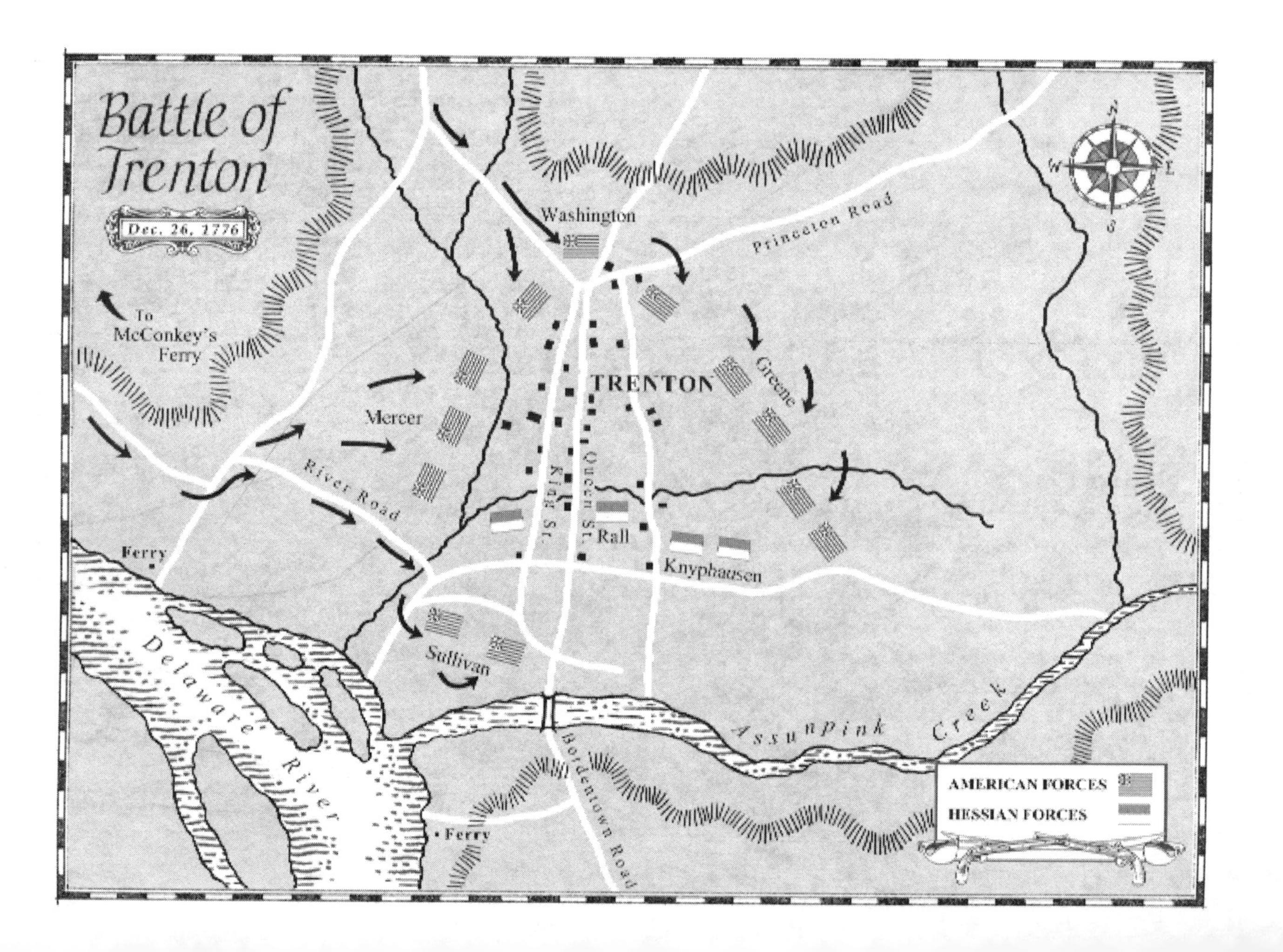
Battle of Trenton
Dec. 26, 1776
To McConkey's Ferry
Washington
Princeton Road
TRENTON
Greene
Mercer
River Road
King St.
Queen St.
Rall
Knyphausen
Ferry
Sullivan
Delaware River
Assunpink Creek
Bordentown Road
Ferry
AMERICAN FORCES
HESSIAN FORCES
N
W
E
S

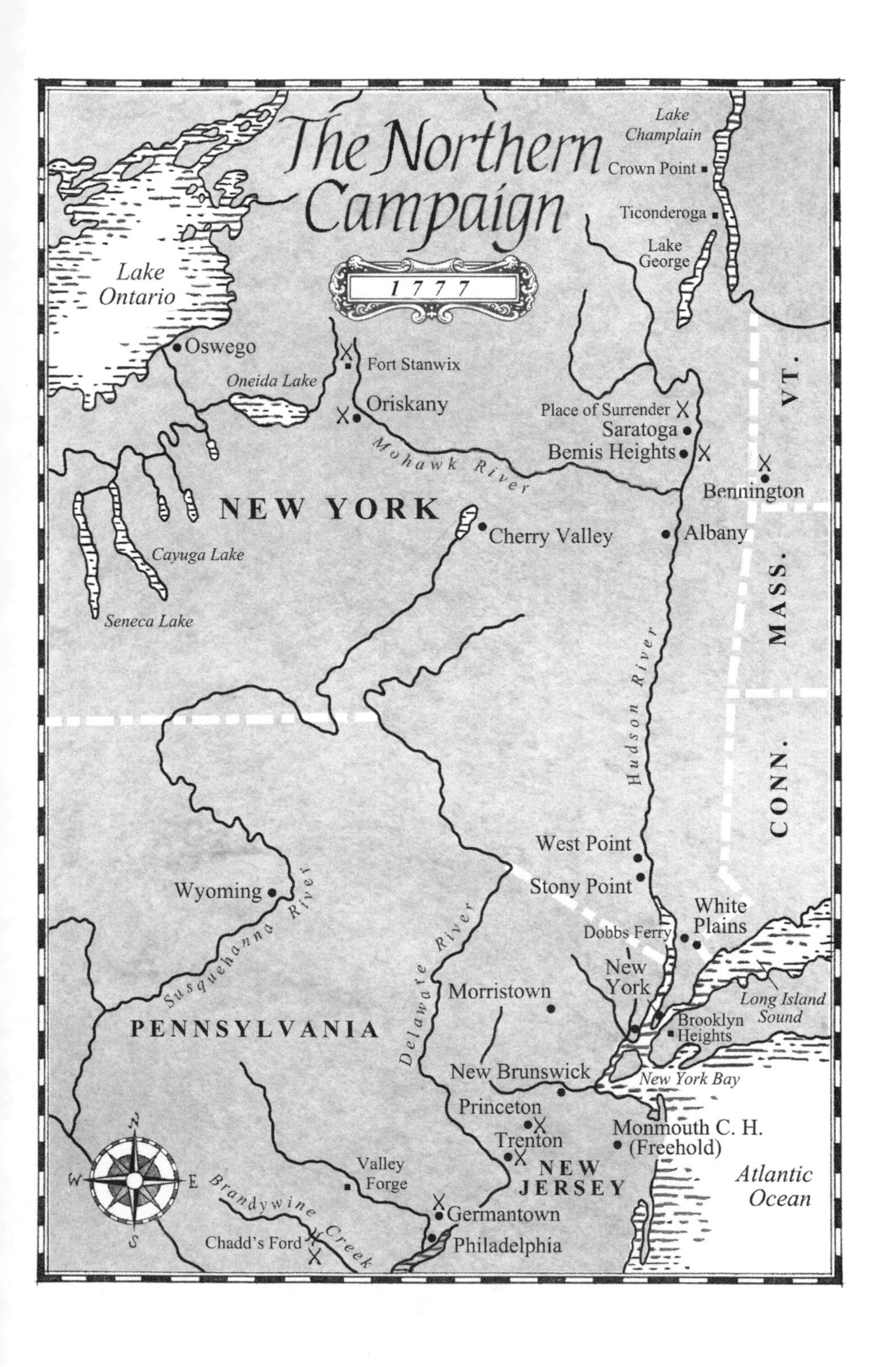

The Northern Campaign
1777
Lake Champlain
Crown Point
Ticonderoga
Lake George
Lake Ontario
Oswego
Fort Stanwix
Oneida Lake
Oriskany
Place of Surrender
Saratoga
Bemis Heights
Mohawk River
VT.
Bennington
NEW YORK
Cherry Valley
Albany
Cayuga Lake
Seneca Lake
MASS.
Hudson River
CONN.
West Point
Stony Point
Wyoming
Susquehanna River
Delaware River
White Plains
Dobbs Ferry
New York
Morristown
Long Island Sound
PENNSYLVANIA
Brooklyn Heights
New Brunswick
New York Bay
Princeton
Trenton
Monmouth C. H. (Freehold)
NEW JERSEY
Atlantic Ocean
Valley Forge
Brandywine Creek
Germantown
Chadd's Ford
Philadelphia
N
E
S
W

OTHER BOOKS BY
J. M. HOCHSTETLER

DAUGHTER OF LIBERTY
The American Patriot Series, Book 1

NATIVE SON
The American Patriot Series, Book 2

WIND OF THE SPIRIT
The American Patriot Series, Book 3

ONE HOLY NIGHT
(2009 Christian Small Publishers Book of the Year)

FORTHCOMING VOLUMES IN THE AMERICAN PATRIOT SERIES

VALLEY OF THE SHADOW, Book 5
REFINER'S FIRE, Book 6
FORGE OF FREEDOM, BOOK 7

In previous volumes . . .

BOOK 1, DAUGHTER OF LIBERTY

EASTERTIDE, APRIL 1775. In the blockaded port of Boston, Elizabeth Howard, the beautiful daughter of Tories, plays a dangerous game as the infamous courier Oriole. Hunted by the British for smuggling intelligence and munitions to the Sons of Liberty by night, she flirts with British officers by day to gain access to intelligence the rebels so desperately need.

But she hasn't counted on the arrival of Jonathan Carleton, an officer in the Seventeenth Light Dragoons. To her dismay, the attraction between them is immediate, powerful—and fought on both sides in a war of wits and words. As the first blood is spilled at Lexington and Concord, Carleton fights his own private battle of faith. And the headstrong Elizabeth must learn to follow God's leading as her dangerous role thrusts her ever closer to the carnage of Bunker Hill.

BOOK 2, NATIVE SON

BRIGADIER GENERAL JONATHAN CARLETON has pledged his allegiance to the cause of liberty, his service to General George Washington, and his heart to fiery Elizabeth Howard. But when Washington takes command of the American forces, he orders Carleton to undertake a perilous journey deep into Indian country and persuades Elizabeth to continue her work as a spy.

Captured and enslaved by the Seneca, Carleton is stripped of everything but his faith in God. At last rescued by the Shawnee, he is taken into deep Ohio Territory and adopted as the warrior White Eagle. When he rises to become war chief, he is drawn unwillingly into a bitter war against the white settlers who threaten to overrun the Shawnee's ancestral lands.

Meanwhile, as General William Howe gathers his forces to attack the outmatched Continental Army at New York City, Elizabeth despairs of ever learning Carleton's fate. But as the western frontier explodes into flame, the name of White Eagle begins to spread beyond the borders of Ohio Territory.

BOOK 3, WIND OF THE SPIRIT

ELIZABETH HOWARD SCRAMBLES for crucial intelligence—and her life—as the fateful confrontation between the Americans and the British explodes at the Battle of Brooklyn. Her assignment leads her into the very maw of war, where disaster threatens to end the American rebellion. Yet all the while her heart is fixed on Brigadier General Jonathan Carleton, whose whereabouts remain unknown more than a year after he disappeared into the wilderness.

With Washington's army driven out of New York and the patriots' cause on the verge of extinction, Elizabeth is reunited with Colonel Charles Andrews. She joins him on a desperate journey to find Carleton before the British can capture and execute him for treason.

Far out on the western borders, Carleton, now the Shawnee war chief White Eagle, is caught in a bitter war of his own. Forced to lead raids against the white settlers encroaching on Shawnee lands, he walks a treacherous tightrope between the alluring widow Blue Sky, the vengeful shaman Wolfslayer . . . and the longing for Elizabeth that will not give him peace.

Chapter One

AN HOUR EARLIER the level of misery had finally surpassed the worst Brigadier General Jonathan Carleton had suffered as a slave of the Seneca.

Things hadn't improved since then.

"I've spent merrier Christmases," Colonel Charles Andrews shouted, his voice barely audible above the wind's blast.

Carleton directed a wry glance at the two Shawnee warriors who hunched on either side of him, silent and grim-faced, blankets hooded over their heads beneath their heavy bearskins. Shifting from one foot to the other in the effort to restore a measure of circulation, he drawled, "Not to worry, Charles. Once we make the New Jersey shore we've but to march a mere ten miles to reach Trenton."

"A cheery prospect, considering that, if anything, this infernal storm's getting worse."

Squinting through the Stygian gloom against a driving sleet that threatened to scour the skin from his face, Carleton assessed the faintly blacker line of the frozen New Jersey shore still some distance ahead. Their progress was agonizingly slow, and at every moment the water's surge drove jagged ice floes against their clumsy vessel, threatening to either stave it in or capsize it. Or both.

The rising nor'easter that had plagued the Continental Army all the way to McKonkey's Ferry, increasing in intensity while they embarked on a fleet of heavy black Durham boats, ferries, and other sturdy craft, showed no signs of diminishing and every sign of worsening. Its shriek whipped away the creak of oars, the slap of water and thud of ice, the stamp of horses' hooves against the ferry's planks, and the animals' occasional agitated squeals when their footing lurched beneath them.

"At least we will not drown—as long as we manage to reach shore," he returned in the Shawnee language.

"No," Andrews grumbled in the same tongue. "We will freeze to death instead."

Red Fox, the older of the Shawnee brothers, grunted. "If the Long Knives defeat our British fathers in spite of Moneto's mighty north wind, then our people will do well to change their allegiance."

Carleton's adoptive cousins, the warriors had also been his trusted lieutenants during the previous summer and fall in the Shawnee's war against white settlers pushing into Ohio Territory. Until Carleton had been unwillingly drawn back to the life torn from him eighteen months earlier when he'd been captured and enslaved by the Seneca.

He clenched the freezing fingers of one hand around his mount's reins, with the other clung to the ferry's rail to steady himself against its pitch and yaw. "You speak wisdom, my brother."

"No matter the outcome, we will have much to report to the council at *Pooshkwiitha,* the Half Moon," Spotted Pony noted.

Red Fox's eyes narrowed with a shrewd light, and he gave a curt nod.

Carleton returned to his contemplation of the gradually nearing shore, striving vainly to still his shivering. Although he held nothing but the utmost respect for the skill of Colonel John Glover's regiment of sturdy Marblehead mariners, he'd believed even they would need a miracle to convey Washington's corps of 2,400 seasoned Continentals across the swift-flowing, ice-choked Delaware in a raging blizzard. Never mind doing so rapidly enough for the army to push south to Trenton in time to attack the isolated Hessian garrison before dawn.

In spite of the worst the heavens could throw at them, each passing moment gave evidence that a miracle might well be delivered. Straight ahead, the riverbank steadily assumed a clearer shape in the faint glow of ice and snow.

"What do you think of Ewing's and Cadwalader's chances of getting across?"

Before Carleton could respond to Andrews's question, the ferry collided with a massive ice floe. The colonel staggered against his squealing horse, losing the reins as he clutched at his hat to keep it from being torn away by the gale.

While the Shawnee quieted their own skittish mounts, Carleton captured the reins of Andrews's bay, and with the colonel's servant, Briggs, helped to steady the animal. "Much depends on their determination," he shouted, handing Andrews the reins. "They'll likely encounter worse ice downriver near the falls."

The vision granted Carleton on the ride to the ferry flooded into his mind. Again he saw the cloud of fire and smoke twining up from the dark earth and towering into the heavens ahead of General George Washington as though leading the rebel army on. Such a visitation had led the ancient Hebrews out of Egypt to the land of promise. The memory warmed Carleton more than a raging blaze and hardened his resolve.

"Whatever comes, we've the greater power on our side," he said, more to himself than the others.

Andrews leaned closer to study his face in the uncertain light of the guttering torches held aloft by the sailors guiding the vessel. After a moment the colonel straightened and, his expression easing, followed

Carleton's calculating gaze toward the dim shore that loomed ahead of them.

⊛ ⊛ ⊛

" 'HAST THOU ENTERED into the treasures of the snow? Or hast thou seen the treasures of the hail, which I have reserved against the time of trouble, against the day of battle and war?' "

Jeremiah Wainwright let fall the heavy draperies and turned from the window, where he had been observing the lash of the storm across the bleak landscape outside. He directed a glance at Elizabeth Howard and her aunt, his deeply lined face reflecting his usual good humor.

"According to Job, 'twould seem the Almighty has unloosed his storm against one side or the other in this conflict. Or perhaps both," he amended dryly.

"It's certain both sides are to suffer from it," Tess Howard returned, her expression reflecting her concern as she extended her hands toward the fire.

Wainwright's wife, Lydia, gave Elizabeth a kindly nod. " 'Tis a blessing thy headache relieved enough for thee to partake of at least a little dinner after all."

For a moment Elizabeth listened to the moan of the wind and the pecking of sleet and snow against the glass, while strong gusts shook the stone house. She had been gone for less an hour on her clandestine ride to meet Carleton before his brigade left for the ferry. With no one the wiser, on her return she had slipped back into the inn through the rear passageway, narrowly avoiding the young servant girl, Chastity Bridewell.

After creeping soundlessly up the back stairway to shed buffalo robe and boots and tidy her hair and clothing, Elizabeth had joined the others downstairs. Now, although the hour neared midnight, they still lingered, basking in the warm glow of the parlor's blazing fire, reluctant to seek their cold beds.

"I'm sure it was no more than the cold and strain we've all been under," she said.

"No doubt taking some nourishment helped," Tess agreed, reaching over to pat her hand. "Your eyes are brighter, and the color has come back into your cheeks."

"It's well the army has come so close to thy home in Philadelphia that thou and thy native friend might join thy brother here," Wainwright noted.

Elizabeth threw him a veiled glance, hastily reviewing the story she and Tess had concocted with Colonel Stern on their way to the inn after their arrival at the rebel camp the previous night. She had the uncomfortable feeling that he harbored some suspicions of their tale, though at the same time she sensed only good will on his part.

"We were most delighted, as you can imagine."

"Regardless of the storm," Lydia put in, smiling.

Tess laughed. "We didn't anticipate such severe weather, but once on the road we were determined not to turn back until we obtained our goal."

"Blue Sky was so eager to see Charles that we couldn't delay our visit longer," Elizabeth agreed.

"She is anxious for her husband?"

Elizabeth followed Lydia's glance toward Blue Sky, who poised on the edge of a wing chair like a bird about to take flight, her unhappy, longing gaze fixed on the black panes of the window nearest her. "Charles also worries constantly for her welfare as she doesn't yet speak English well," she explained. "Thankfully we each have learned enough of the other's tongue in the past two months to communicate what is needful. But she and my brother are only recently married, and it's hard for them to be parted."

"Especially in such danger and at the time some celebrate as the day of our Lord's birth," Wainwright put in, raking his fingers through the greying hair that fringed his brow. "Remember, my dear, when thou wast newly with child the first winter of our marriage, and I'd been carried off by our British brethren to supply their army in the war against the French?"

"Well I do," answered his plump wife, raising her plainly capped head from her sewing to give him a warm glance. "I feared I'd not see thy face again, nor ever would our child."

Smiling, Elizabeth noted their unadorned clothing and serene faces before focusing on her surroundings. The gracefully proportioned room's furnishings were tidy and comfortable, as were those in the rest of the spacious building. The simplicity of the inn's accommodations reflected the religious convictions of its devoutly Quaker proprietors, thus no decorations of the season enlivened the space.

The celebration of Christmas was also strictly banned in Boston and in all of New England due to the region's Puritan heritage. It was not so here in Pennsylvania, and after briefly witnessing the revelry of the troops from the Middle and Southern States in the camp the previous night, Elizabeth found herself longing for such happy distractions to ward off the anxious thoughts that set her heart in turmoil.

Deep in thought, she started when Chastity pushed aside the grey wool blanket that hung over the door and entered, rosy-faced from the cold, with an armload of wood for the fire. The servant girl was perhaps sixteen, slight but sturdy, her pretty face and lively demeanor at odds with her Quaker dress and cap. Through half-closed eyes, Elizabeth watched the girl pile the split logs on the hearth, then stamp the snow from her boots and shake out her shawl before kneeling to build up the fire.

Although a draft seeped around the edges of the windows, Elizabeth's woolen jacket and heavy stroud petticoats, bolstered by the warm leggings concealed underneath—all acquired during her stay among the Shawnee with Carleton—kept the chill at bay. Heavily swathed in her woolen traveling garb, Tess appeared cheerful as well, but Blue Sky, clothed as warmly, seemed too distracted to note any discomfort.

"To what tribe belongeth thy friend, Eliza?" Wainwright glanced from Tess to Blue Sky, one eyebrow raised.

"The Shawnee," Tess responded. "I confess that when my nephew first brought her to us I had reservations about his taking a native woman as his wife—which I know to be uncharitable. We doubtless all have our prejudices, and I admit to mine. But she has become like a daughter to me. She also is a child of God, and I warrant there could be no better helpmeet for Charles, nor one he could love the more."

Elizabeth surmised that her aunt, known to the Wainwrights as Eliza Freeman, also sensed their hosts' hesitation at harboring an Indian in their home. She raised her cup and studied the depths of the wintergreen tea, by now gone cold, pleased at how neatly Tess had directed the conversation to safer ground.

"She is a believer, then?" Lydia cast another curious glance at Blue Sky, who appeared to take no note of their conversation.

Elizabeth took a sip of the cold tea. "I know you believe in the inner light," she said with a smile, "and if anyone has it, Blue Sky surely does."

"The love of God shows no preference," Lydia murmured, returning her attention to her sewing.

"Thou art right in that, good wife." Wainwright reclaimed his seat by the fire. "But tell me, what think you of General Washington's driving forward this desperate venture on such a night? Does he not take a dangerous gamble?"

Elizabeth returned her cup to its saucer on the small table beside her, considering how far they could trust their hosts. "He does, but judging from what Charles told us, he has no choice. Since the army was forced out of New York, their fortunes have sunk so low that the support our glorious cause once enjoyed has declined in proportion. And the largest part of the army is set to disband with the closing of the year if something is not quickly done. It's a desperate gamble indeed, but unless they meet with success soon, all may be entirely lost."

"You're an anomaly among your brethren," Tess pointed out. "My understanding is that Quakers do not believe in war and killing, and yet you give support to the rebellion."

Their hosts exchanged a sharp glance. Returning her attention to her sewing, her round face sober, Lydia completed her seam. Mouth pursed, she knotted the thread and snipped it off with her scissors.

Wainwright's breast rose and fell in a deep sigh. "We have two sons in the conflict, and—"

"Are about to be read out of our meeting because we support their decision," Lydia finished for him. "We may not agree with Isaac and Joseph in all things, but in matters of conscience thou must follow the inner light thou art given, even if it leads contrary to that given to others."

"What regiment do your sons serve in?" Tess asked.

"Isaac is an aide to General Greene. Joseph is with the artillery under General Dickinson posted this side of the river, directly across from Trenton."

Elizabeth regarded their hosts with sympathy. "Colonel Stern told us that you've . . . transmitted intelligence to the General."

"Thou art also spies, I think," Wainwright countered.

Elizabeth met his piercing gaze with a steady one. "It isn't safe for us to confide more in each other than civility warrants, Jeremiah. Were you—or we—to be captured . . . " She let the words trail off.

Wainwright rose and returned to the darkened window. Drawing the shutters closed against the storm, he faced Elizabeth, his expression thoughtful.

"Thou speakest well, Jane Andrews . . . if that indeed be thy name. Thou and Colonel Andrews, though brother and sister, differ greatly in appearance, he being light of coloring and thou dark—though thy complexion be as fair as his," he conceded.

Elizabeth smiled. "Our father was widowed before he married my mother. I resemble her, and Charles his own mother."

Wainwright directed his keen glance to Tess. "I take it thou art this child's maternal aunt."

"I am," Tess returned, expression and voice equally calm. "Sadly my sister died in childbirth, but that gave me the joy of rearing both Jane and Charles. He is as dear to me as if he were my own nephew, and so I consider him to be."

"Forgive me if I am too direct in my curiosity. It interests me greatly that thou hast with thee a Shawnee maiden who is married to an officer of the rebellion. Members of her tribe are not common in the eastern colonies, thus I cannot help but wonder where they met. I'm not ignorant of the border wars—" He raised his hand to silence Elizabeth's exclamation. "I've heard the name White Eagle, and it occurs to me that perhaps thy brother is he."

Elizabeth shot Tess a quick warning glance.

"Or perhaps White Eagle is another," his wife interjected firmly. "Cease, husband. Thou art too curious for the circumstances."

"Thy admonition is well spoken, Lydia." Appearing crestfallen, Wainwright conceded, "Truly, I'd not know the particulars. Considering our dangerous roles, the less we know of each other, the better for all."

Elizabeth became aware that Chastity had lingered overlong in building up the fire. Finished, she rose with what Elizabeth thought to be reluctance and turned to leave the room.

"Wouldst thou bring more hot tea, child?" Lydia indicated the teapot. "What little is left has long gone cold."

"The water is already on the boil, mistress," Chastity said primly. "I'll be but half a minute." Taking the teapot, she left the room.

When she had gone, Elizabeth turned her attention to Blue Sky, whose head was bent over hands clenched so hard the knuckles whitened. Her eyes were closed and her lips moved, though she made no sound.

"Our desperate state may soon find some improvement, however," Wainwright continued, brightening. "Thou knowest, dost thou not, that Benjamin Franklin left for Paris back in October to join Silas Deane and Arthur Lee in negotiating a treaty with the French?"

Tess leaned forward eagerly. "Rumors have it that France is already supplying us secretly, and that the Dutch and Spanish may also soon join in the war against Britain."

"Don't forget the British have spies in every court," Elizabeth reminded them. "They must be well aware of who's supplying and advising us. I daresay they'll bring pressure to bear on our secret allies until they're forced to end their support . . . or bring it into the open."

They all looked up as Blue Sky sprang out of her chair and began to pace up and down, distress evident in every taut line of her body. "I should have gone with him!" she cried in Shawnee. "Golden Elk should not make me stay here when he—"

Elizabeth rose and flew to her adoptive sister. Taking Blue Sky's hands in hers, she said, "Do you not think my heart also aches to be with White Eagle? But Golden Elk was right. The storm is too great for a woman to endure, and the battle will be worse. How can they attend to their duties when they are burdened with worry for us? Would we not become a hindrance and so endanger them?"

"How are they to bear this storm any more than we?" Blue Sky protested in anguish. "If they should die—"

It was what Elizabeth most feared but had resolutely barred from her consciousness. Clinging to Blue Sky's hands, she said, "We must hold them up in prayer. It is the most powerful thing we can do. Moneto will care for them. Surely he will preserve their lives." Her reassuring words sounded hollow in her ears, but to her relief they seemed to calm Blue Sky.

Hearing movement behind her, Elizabeth turned to see that their hosts regarded the two of them with wide eyes and raised eyebrows. As did the servant girl standing in the doorway holding back the blanket that covered it with one hand and the steaming teapot in the other, a strange look on her face.

None of them understood what she and Blue Sky had said in the Shawnee tongue. Yet Elizabeth feared that she had revealed more than she ought by speaking it with a fluency she had denied.

IT WAS PAST MIDNIGHT when the ferry bumped and ground against the shallow bank, jarring men and horses alike. Carleton and his companions wasted no time quitting the vessel. Once disembarked, they mounted and worked their way through a milling Massachusetts regiment that appeared to be in exceedingly high spirits in spite of the storm. With good-humored banter and curses, the men jostled for position around sputtering fires fed with fence rails and any broken branches and underbrush that could be found in the vicinity, whether dry, wet, or green. Soaked through and shaking with the cold, they beat frostbitten hands together and stamped their cracked and bleeding feet to keep them from freezing completely.

From around one campfire, someone raised his voice in a lusty chorus, quickly taken up by his fellows, while laughter and catcalls offered counterpoint to the singers.

Sir William, he, snug as a flea,
Lay all this time a-snoring;
Nor dreamed of harm as he lay warm
In bed with Mrs. Loring.

"Let's pray that Howe remains snug abed with his paramour a while longer," Andrews said with a grin. "At least long enough or us to have our way with the garrison at Trenton."

Giving a short laugh, Carleton spurred Devil forward. "To our good luck, General Cornwallis is on his way home to England for the winter. I've a great deal more regard for his abilities and activity than I do for our newly knighted Sir Willy."

They hadn't gone far before Elizabeth's cousin, Captain Levi Stern, intercepted them. "Pa needs to talk to you," he shouted over the howling wind.

Motioning them to follow, he reined his horse around and led the way through a snow bank into the lea of a shadowy copse of trees that mercifully afforded some shelter from the elements. They found Colonel Joshua Stern, the regiment's commander and Elizabeth's uncle, huddled with Major James Smithson of the Rangers over a sputtering, smoky fire of green wood torn from the surrounding trees and rotted branches pried loose from the frozen ground. Both greeted Carleton's party with noticeable restraint as they dismounted.

"Are the men and horses all disembarked?" Carleton enquired of the major.

Smithson nodded and blew on his chapped fingers. "I left the captains to get 'em into line and call roll," he growled. "We encountered a problem I thought you should know about."

Carleton scrubbed the sleet from his face with his gloved hand. "What's gone amiss?"

Smithson shifted uncomfortably, darting glances between Carleton, Andrews, and the Shawnee warriors. "Well, sir, the men ain't takin' kindly to servin' with colored troops."

Stern's mouth tightened. "Captain Moghrab and his company are all excellent horsemen, and the general and I agreed they're better suited to his brigade than mine."

"Colored men ain't the equal of—"

"I'll be the judge of that," Carleton cut him off.

"Even the Gen'l don't want blacks serving—"

"Because he fears a slave uprising." Carleton waved his hand in dismissal. "All these men are freemen, and His Excellency will discover they'll fight, and fight well. Anyone voice objections to serving with Indians?"

Smithson gave a curt nod. "'Them savages ain't any better'n the coloreds, if you ask me—"

"I didn't. Those who object have but to endure it until we return to camp. Then anyone who considers himself a better judge of a comrade's competence and devotion to duty than his commander will be immediately excused from serving in the Rangers and will be transferred to the infantry, where he may serve with those of equal station."

Major Smithson's eyes widened and his jaw dropped. "Sir, you can't—"

"Try me." Teeth gritted, Carleton brought his face close to the major's. "If you believe yourself superior to another man simply because of the color of your skin, you'd better be prepared to prove it in battle."

AFTER GOING OVER THEIR ORDERS in detail with his officers, Carleton reviewed his brigade with approval mingled with caution. While in Virginia, Andrews had recruited three troops of light cavalry and two troops of light infantry, with their support personnel, outfitting them in buckskin hunting shirts and breeches, knee-length boots, and cocked hats, and equipping them with sabres, carbines, and pistols. For the night's work, Carleton had detached his two best mounted troops, fit, ready, and eager for duty.

A number of the Rangers were personal acquaintances from Carleton's youth, men he had grown up with, but who seemed strangers to him now because of the intervening years when he had lived in England, and then among the Shawnee. Yet he was surprised that the anguish, anger, and alienation he had struggled against since leaving Grey Cloud's town eased as he interacted with them. The familiar habits of discipline and command, whether of warriors or of soldiers steadied him, and a welcome confidence dispelled the turmoil of emotions.

The pleasure several of his former acquaintances expressed at his presence would not let him forget the treacherous ground he stood on, however. He and Washington had discussed the possibility of somehow concealing from the British his return to command the Rangers, but had quickly concluded that it was a practical impossibility to keep the news from leaking out. If he were taken prisoner, his fate would be a hasty—and very public—execution, and Washington had made it clear that Carleton was to take every precaution to avoid capture. Considering the high price on his head, however, that would be a task easier to assign than to accomplish, and Carleton determined not to worry about it.

What concerned him more at the moment was the undercurrent of tension among his men. Doubtless some measure of disquiet was due to the attitudes Smithson had expressed. Yet Carleton sensed there was more to it.

Officers and rank and file alike were well aware that the majority of the army's enlistments would expire on December thirty-first. And almost to a man the soldiers were determined to return home regardless of any inducements to stay.

And who could blame them? They were worn out with the fatigues of marches and battles, often deprived of even the basic necessities of existence. At home their women and children suffered hardship, struggling to maintain farms and businesses in their men's absence. They had already endured more than anyone should be expected to, and if they stayed, only more sacrifice lay ahead of them.

Their departure would reduce the Continental Army to a shadow of 1,400 men, a force so small that the British would brush it aside like a flea. That had to concern newly enrolled troops, such as his Rangers, as well. Washington had to make a bold stroke without delay or the game would be up once and for all. With nothing to lose and everything to gain by going on the offensive, their commander had decided to strike before the end of the year in hopes that success might persuade many of the men to stay, while also hardening civilian opposition to Britain.

To the rebels' good fortune, after driving Washington's corps out of New York, through New Jersey, and across the Delaware into Pennsylvania, British General William Howe had inexplicably neglected to follow up his advantage by pushing on to capture Philadelphia. Instead he had closed the campaign in mid December and given leave to General Charles Cornwallis to return to England. Then the British commander in chief had retired to New York to receive the red ribbon of a Knight Commander of the Bath from his sovereign and while away the winter with his mistress, leaving his army scattered in a string of lightly manned garrisons spread across the eastern half of New Jersey under the command of General James Grant.

The relative isolation of the southernmost outposts, especially the three forward positions along the Delaware, offered possibilities too tempting for Washington to resist. Posted six miles downriver at Bordentown on the river's eastward bend lay a detachment of Hessian grenadiers, Jägers, and artillery under Colonel Carl von Donop. Several miles below, Lieutenant Colonel Thomas Sterling commanded the

Forty-second Highland Regiment and a grenadier battalion at Black Horse.

But it was the exposed northernmost position at Trenton, on the opposite side of the river from the rebel camp, on which Washington had fixed his sights. And twelve miles behind it, the strongly manned garrison at Princeton, where Grant had established his headquarters.

Since fleeing across the Delaware in early December, Washington's army had more than doubled in size to 6,000 effectives, bolstered by the arrival of a remnant of captured Colonel Arthur Lee's brigades, General Horatio Gates' corps, and two brigades under General John Sullivan, which for once gave Washington an advantage over his nearest opponents.

Fourteen hundred Pennsylvania and New Jersey militia had increased that advantage. Although sorely lacking in clothing and equipment, they harbored rage enough to overcome those minor deficiencies. After initially declaring their loyalty to the king in exchange for promises of protection, the residents of New Jersey had instead been subjected to widespread senseless murders, the ransacking and plunder of their homes and churches, and the wanton rape and abuse of their wives and daughters by the occupying British and Hessian troops. Over the past weeks the eastern New Jersey militias had risen in violent revolt. Driven past the breaking point, they had swarmed to Washington's standard in droves, determined to visit retribution on their tormentors.

In a council of war held little more than twenty-four hours earlier, Washington had outlined a daring plan to do just that, one that would take advantage of the Christmas celebrations for which the Germans were famous. That night, the twenty-fifth of December, while Colonel Johann Rall's three Hessian regiments were assumed to be still engaged in revelry, General John Ewing was to cross just below the town at Trenton Ferry with 800 Pennsylvania and New Jersey militia and seize the bridge across Assunpink Creek to prevent the Trenton garrison from escaping to the south. Meanwhile, Colonel John Cadwalader was assigned to cross the river at Burlington with a combined force of 1,800 Pennsylvania Associators and Continentals to prevent von Donop's detachment from coming to Rall's aid.

At the same time, the main American column, commanded by General Nathanael Greene and personally led in the attack by Washington, would strike Trenton. The men had been ordered to observe a profound silence until reaching the outskirts of the town, and no one was allowed to quit his ranks on pain of death. If they achieved success against Trenton, Washington hoped to lead the combined force in an immediate move against Princeton and Brunswick.

The countersign for the day was Victory or Death.

CARLETON FOUND forty-four-year-old General George Washington wrapped in his cloak and seated on a wooden box, brooding over the ruin of his plan. His back to the wind, the General's mulatto slave, Will Lee, hunched over him, turbaned head bent, face impassive as he tried to shelter his master from the driving wind and snow while clutching the reins of his mount and the General's tall white gelding, Blueskin.

Nearby, heavily cloaked, hats secured to their heads with wool kerchiefs, Washington's aides, handsome, broad-shouldered, young Irish Colonel John Fitzgerald and twenty-four-year old George Baylor, stared pensively across the Delaware. Barely visible through the driving sleet, the random assortment of vessels still fought their way through the jagged ice floes to deliver another load of troops to the New Jersey shore.

Generals Greene, Sullivan, Mercer, and Stirling clustered around their commander. Stamping their feet and clapping their hands to maintain circulation, they milled restlessly about, clearly eager to move forward before they all froze. Washington resolutely ignored them.

Dismounting, Carleton exchanged curt nods with the other officers before saluting. "We await your orders, Your Excellency."

Washington glowered at him. "Curse this storm! We are already three hours behind schedule, and as the last of the artillery will not be brought over for at least another hour, there is little chance of our reaching Trenton before dawn. My first concern was to maintain secrecy until the moment of attack, but there is no hope of ensuring that now."

"This storm will afford us a great measure of concealment," Carleton pointed out. "Surely Colonel Rall won't expect an attack in such weather."

"Having been the instrument of our defeat a time or two already, I doubt he considers us a threat of any consequence to begin with," Fitzgerald noted.

"All to our advantage," Carleton returned with a smile. "Sometimes our best plans go awry for a reason,"

Washington grimaced. "You believe Providence has blessed us with defeat and followed it up with a blizzard for our benefit?"

Carleton raised an eyebrow. "Judging from my own experience, I'd not put such measures past the Almighty."

Washington gave him a keen look, an unwilling smile tugging at the corners of his mouth. "I have had a few such experiences myself," he conceded. "As I recall, one of them brought us together."

Carleton bowed. "So it did, Your Excellency."

Rising, Washington drew himself up to his full height and shook the snow from his cloak. "As soon as the last of the artillery arrives, form your men into column," he barked to his officers. "Tell the others to do the same. We cannot afford to linger one minute more than necessary."

When they made to move off, he raised his hand. "Any time you must conscript goods, you are to assure the owners that the army will pay a fair price for them. And remember that in all circumstances women and children are to be tenderly treated. I will personally see to it that those responsible for any cases of abuse are severely punished."

Scanning their faces, his eyes narrowing, he added, "If we do no better than the king's men, we shall not deserve the loyalty of our fellow citizens—or the blessing of God."

Chapter Two

SHIVERING IN THE DRAFT that seeped around the edges of the window, Elizabeth drew her buffalo-hide robe tighter around her shoulders and leaned her head against the icy pane, grateful for the thick, dark cascade of waist-length hair that provided an additional layer against the cold. On the floor beside her, the single candle guttered, its fragile flame casting a small circle of dim light against the deep shadows of the room.

Eyes closed, she concentrated on the nor'easter's unabated blast, straining consciousness through the night and the storm, down the long miles that separated them, to where he was. Yet all her mind could encompass was a dark, empty void.

Instead, the memory of their last moments together stole her breath and ignited a fire in her breast—the passionate kisses, tender caresses, and breathless endearments all the more precious for their brevity. She bent double with rising fear that clenched her stomach in a sharp physical ache. Her words of reassurance to Blue Sky earlier in the evening now seemed most hollow.

Every fiber of her being cried out to follow wherever he went, no matter the violence of the storm or the death and destruction that surely lay at night's end. She knew she could not survive even an hour against such a gale, yet in that moment reason fled.

For he was gone into unimaginable danger. Again. So soon after their all too brief reunion. Whether he or any of those she loved would return alive—

Fearfully she thrust the thought from her. A light snore drew her eyes to the drapery-shrouded four-poster bed where she had left Tess lying curled beneath a pile of comforters. Brushing away tears, despising the weakness that had overcome her, she glanced over her shoulder at Blue Sky.

Protesting that a Shawnee woman would never find comfort on such a soft mattress, she had foregone the bed to sleep on the rug beside it, wrapped in blankets and covered with a bearskin. After a time of prayer with the Wainwrights, Blue Sky had brightened and declared that Moneto had shown her that their men would be safe and that the army would meet with great success. When the three women retired to their chamber to continue their petitions, she had quickly fallen asleep, too weary to keep her eyes open any longer. In repose her features had lost the strain that had shadowed them ever since Andrews's brief visit at nightfall.

Elizabeth had at first been giddy at Blue Sky's prophecy, feeling its truth in her spirit. But now, alone, with everyone else asleep, her emotions plummeted. It felt as though she wrestled with the Tempter, striving against the voices of doubt and fear that mocked her with the harsh conditions Washington's bedraggled army faced.

And the painful reality Carleton faced in the midst of it: Drawn back against his will to a people and a war no longer his own—why? Because of her.

No, more than just that, she reminded herself. He had been called back by an even more powerful force than earthly love and felt it keenly, though it wrenched his heart.

Yawning, she turned back to the window and rubbed her eyes. They felt hot and grainy as though someone had thrown sand into her face.

With her fingertips she widened the circle her forehead had melted through the frost on the windowpane and strained to catch a glimpse through it before it froze over again. Against the unbroken blackness outside she could see only horizontal sheets of wind-driven snow buffeting the glass.

From downstairs she heard the tall case clock strike the first quarter after three. Would the night never end? The cold seeped into her limbs from the unyielding pine planks of the floor on which she sat. By now she was so stiff from her vigil that every movement pained her. Yet the irrational fear that if she gave in to sleep, her inattention would result in the destruction of Washington's forces—as though she alone were responsible for their protection—would not let her rest.

Nor would dawn bring relief. Carleton had warned that should the army succeed in taking Trenton, Washington might well decide to attack Princeton without delay. Although he had promised to send word as quickly as possible, it might be a day or more before reports of the battle could reach them.

If they were still there. For Pete had orders to convey her and Tess across the Delaware and back to New York as soon as the river was passable. Thus they might wait in suspense even longer, not knowing whether their men were alive or dead—or worse, prisoners subject to the unmerciful abuse meted out by the Hessians.

Like Carleton's, her role was clearly laid out, and neither of them could shrink from it. With the last of her strength, she clung to Blue Sky's calm assurance that their success was already assured.

God had brought her and Carleton back together, after all, when she had thought it impossible. If the Lord had accomplished this, then He would accomplish all he purposed for their lives without fail. He would lead them forth to their destiny just as he had brought the Israelites out of Egypt to the land of promise, calmed the stormy sea that threatened to capsize the disciples' boat, and preserved Paul even through shipwreck.

None of these things had depended on human effort, but on the One who had created them and governed all that existed. Those He called, God would protect.

By slow degrees peace fell over her soul like a mantle, strengthening her. And into her mind crept the words of the psalm.

He that dwelleth in the secret place of the Most High
Shall abide under the shadow of the Almighty.
I will say of the Lord, "He is my refuge and my fortress:
My God; in Him will I trust."
Surely He shall deliver thee from the snare of the fowler,
And from the noisome pestilence.
He shall cover thee with His feathers,
And under His wings shalt thou trust:
His truth shall be thy shield and buckler.
Thou shalt not be afraid for the terror by night;
Nor for the arrow that flieth by day;
Nor for the pestilence that walketh in darkness;
Nor for the destruction that wasteth at noonday.
A thousand shall fall at thy side,
And ten thousand at thy right hand;
But it shall not come nigh thee.
Only with thine eyes shalt thou behold
And see the reward of the wicked.

"Lord God," she whispered, throat tight, "surround them with a wall of fire. Be a shield and bulwark to them. Keep them in the shadow of your wings, give them good success, and bring them safely back to us again."

True to Washington's calculations, it took another hour to transport the last of the artillery across the ice-choked river.

Twenty-six years old and taller even than Washington, Colonel Henry Knox was a great, fleshy man. Apparently impervious to the weather, he moved rapidly, considering his girth, bustling from one gun carriage to another, urging his artillerymen and the civilian drovers to greater haste in hitching the draft horses to the trails. It was by the sheer force of personality and an exceedingly powerful bass voice, Andrews decided, that Knox was able to restore a reasonable degree of order to what had begun as a scene of complete disarray.

Knox's party was soon joined by Colonel Glover, his short, stocky form impeccably attired despite the storm in a spotless blue coat adorned with silver lace. Accompanying him was a large contingent of Marblehead fishermen, a considerable proportion of them black, all easily recognizable in woolen caps and short blue jackets over white shirts and tarred trousers. After considerable consultation between the two officers and what seemed an interminable struggle, the gun carriages were at last in their places and ready to roll.

Andrews scraped the frost off his pocket watch, squinting in the torchlight to make out the time. His gut tightened. It was nearing four o'clock, and General Matthias de Roche-Fermoy had only minutes ago ridden off at the head of his command, under orders to secure the roads between Trenton and Princeton. They were four hours behind schedule now, with no hope left of reaching Trenton before dawn.

Returning the timepiece to his pocket, he spurred his horse forward to rejoin Carleton at the head of the brigade. Studying his superior and friend, Andrews reflected that no one who did not know Carleton intimately would discern the subtle tension and grim determination that shadowed his face and the taut line of his body. Appearing perfectly at ease, he gave no outward evidence that the night's outcome concerned him—or that he chafed against the strictures of a role he had been left no choice but to resume.

Andrews, however, knew full well the cost of Carleton's decision to leave his Shawnee kindred and rejoin Washington in the fight against Britain. And he wondered how long Carleton could hold at bay the savage bonds of the Shawnee before the brooding soul of the war chief White Eagle reawakened.

Andrews wondered, too, at his own wholly unanticipated ties to the tribe. At the memory of his and Blue Sky's wedding night, his blood heated. He had not thought it possible to love a woman as he did this young Shawnee matron he had known for barely two months. When he had held her in his arms for the first time, it had been as though his past melted entirely away and only a joyful future remained.

But now worries crowded in. Would he survive the battle to return to her? And then what? How could he safely keep her with him in the midst of war? Yet it was already impossible for him to conceive of separation from her.

Suddenly stricken, he studied Carleton's impassive countenance. He appeared not to note Andrews's scrutiny, and the colonel wondered whether he thought of Elizabeth. No matter how thorny their circumstances, Andrews and Blue Sky at least could find comfort in each other. What must Carleton and Elizabeth feel at being forbidden to marry?

Andrews's bonds to Blue Sky, and through her to the Shawnee, constrained him far more than he could have imagined when he had chosen her as his bride and been adopted by the clan's sachem, Grey Cloud. In ways he could not have anticipated when he and Elizabeth set out on the journey to find White Eagle the previous fall, he now fully comprehended the terrible dilemma Carleton had faced at their sudden, unanticipated arrival.

For day by day, as Andrews's devotion to his bride grew along with his admiration for Red Fox and Spotted Pony, he wrestled with the same warring allegiances. And already he doubted which side would ultimately win his soul.

THE COMMAND TO MOVE OUT passed hurriedly along the army's ranks, shouted from officer to officer against the gale. Before ordering his troops to mount, however, Carleton first gathered the men around him. Soberly he led them in a prayer of repentance, asking for forgiveness for their sins and a renewed determination to live according to God's laws to His honor and glory, and ending with a plea for protection and mercy on this march and in the coming battle.

At his command the Rangers mounted, with Captain Isaiah Moghrab's troop taking the van. After the confrontation with Smithson, Carleton had resolved to make a point, and judging from the scowls of many of the men, he had succeeded.

Shrugging off their disapproval, he ran his gloved hand over the polished stocks of the fine French carbine and brace of Spanish pistols in his saddle holsters, protected from the weather by the folds of a thick blanket, then lightly touched the exquisitely forged pommel of his British-made sabre. The familiar feel of masterfully crafted wood and steel pleased him.

His weapons had been taken from him by the Seneca at his capture, but while outfitting the brigade in Virginia, in the confidence that Carleton would someday return, Andrews had appropriated these from the Jamestown warehouse Carleton had inherited with his uncle's import business. And so he had, though it had been against his will.

The image of Elizabeth was never far from his thoughts, but now he pushed it aside, determined to keep all betraying emotions at bay and allow only the duties of the coming hours to occupy his mind. To play the role, as Elizabeth had urged that desperate day at Fort Pitt when he had come perilously close to snatching her up in his arms and riding back to his people hell-bent, the fate of the Long Knives be damned.

Her grace had saved him yet again. And he had made up his mind to submit his proud heart to whatever destiny the One who held their first allegiance called both of them.

While the long column formed up along the riverbank behind its screen of sentries, leaning into the nor'easter's relentless blast, he glanced back over his shoulder at the broad expanse of icy black water they had just crossed against all odds. And he found himself praying it would not be the only miracle that blessed them that night.

WELL IN THE COLUMN'S VAN rode a small detachment of cavalry, hurrying ahead to seize the junctions of Scotch and Pennington roads north of Trenton and take prisoner anyone going in or out of the town. It was commanded by Captain William Washington of the Third Virginia Regiment, a distant cousin of the General, with slight, eighteen-year-old Lieutenant James Monroe as his subordinate.

Also heading southeast was another advance party of green Jersey recruits under Captain John Flahaven of the First New Jersey Continentals. They would follow the Delaware and block the lower portion of River Road.

Behind these outriders, General Stephen's Virginia infantry regiments led the main column, with orders to attack the Hessian pickets on Trenton's outskirts and storm any strongholds that offered resistance. They were guided by a number of mounted men from the area with hard, set faces, who, on hearing of the crossing, had flooded in to volunteer their services against the hated Hessians.

Following a narrow track that led northeast, rising steeply from the river through a darkly shadowed wood, the column marched full into a violent hailstorm. Heavy rain and squalls of sleet and snow more intense than any they had yet encountered lashed them and soaked to the skin men the campfires had just begun to dry out.

Carleton twisted in the saddle to look back. Along with the bobbing light of scattered lanterns, torches stuck into the exhalters of the field pieces sparkled and sputtered in the blowing sleet, casting circles of dancing light and shadow across the ghostly pines that overarched the road, branches already so thickly coated with ice and snow from the previous week's storms that in places the steady accumulation bent them nearly to the ground.

Something about the spectral trees and the wind's deep moan as it roared through the forest impressed him with a deep sense of foreboding. The shadow of a long-forgotten memory hovered at the edge of his consciousness, but he could not grasp it, had a discomforting sense that it was better he did not.

They had gone barely a hundred yards, breaking with difficulty through the drifting, sleet-crusted snow only to find the roadbed beneath a greasy quagmire of mud. The march ground to a crawl as time and again the heavy gun carriages sank to their hubs in the mire, forcing the entire column to halt while weary soldiers dragged them free to lumber forward another short distance.

Brushing away the haunting shades of the memory, Carleton fixed his mind on the task before him and ordered his brigade to the road's edge. The infantry units behind them followed their lead, trailing back in long files interspersed with gun carriages, supply wagons, and riders.

After fighting their way a mile and a half to a crossroads where loomed a solitary tavern under the sign of the Bear, they turned onto Bear Tavern Road with considerable relief. It bore southeast, directly toward Trenton and mercifully ran oblique to the wind. Though whipped by bands of hail, sleet, and snow broken by occasional brief lulls, they were at last able to move at a faster pace along the higher land.

Carleton alternated between sinking into a drug-like trance and jolting back to painful consciousness whenever his stallion plunged through a deep drift with a snort and groan before plodding doggedly on. Returning from riding back down the line to check for stragglers, Andrews drew up beside him.

"If there's a hell, this is it!" he shouted over the blast.

"Although the temperature's not what I'd expect," Carleton returned dryly, "I can't contest your conclusion."

Andrews guffawed. "The devil works in mysterious ways."

Carleton marveled that he had heard not a single complaint from the men. They continued to move stoically forward with as much speed as they could muster, heads down, bearing the storm with astonishing composure. Yet as he focused on the road ahead, he couldn't help wondering whether any of them would have the strength left to fight when they reached their goal.

If they reached it.

Grimacing, he reflected with black humor that he had made a habit of getting himself into impossible situations. First, as General Thomas Gage's aide he'd found himself unwillingly fighting on the side of the British at Lexington and Concord—while serving as a spy for Washington. Then he'd been arrested for treason and almost hanged before Elizabeth Howard, as the patriot courier and spy, Oriole, had rescued him in a daring raid on the British gaol.

He'd almost been recaptured on the journey to New York to join up with Washington, who had then refused him permission to marry Elizabeth. Instead Carleton had been assigned to travel to the western frontiers to negotiate with the Indian tribes for their support of the rebels in the war against Britain. All too predictably he had been captured and, worse, enslaved by the Seneca.

It was an experience he never wished to repeat, but one, he acknowledged now, that had taught him much and strengthened him immeasurably. And at last, by God's grace, he had been reborn. A party of the Shawnee among whom he had spent much of his youth, had rescued him, taken him to Ohio Territory, and adopted him into the Kispokotha clan as the warrior White Eagle. As their war chief, he had led the fight against the white settlers bent on stealing Shawnee lands.

It was there Elizabeth had found him, a miracle that still astounded him. Yet she had become the instrument that had torn him from his people and brought him unwillingly back to rejoin the Americans in their fight against the British. And now they'd been wrenched from each others' arms once again, while he rode toward a battle whose outcome was uncertain at best.

Would they never enjoy the blessings of peace as husband and wife? The Shawnee council had forbidden them to marry, and even if their objections could be overcome, Washington's opposition still remained in effect.

Carleton clenched his teeth and stared into the raging tempest, overcome by a tide of longing and fear. Did she wait for him back at the inn? Or had she melted into the army's ranks in disguise to even now ride somewhere behind him, safely out of his notice?

Safely? No safety would be found here. Hardened soldiers were having difficulty enough enduring the brutal weather and would face battle at their march's end. Surely even Elizabeth would not be so foolhardy as to make the attempt to join them. Yet at thought of her daring escapades as the rebel spy Oriole, he worried. And smiled at her bravery.

Remembering how often in that dark night among the Seneca he had prayed to die, he was humbly grateful. For God had preserved him through that terrible storm that He might bring her back to him.

The ways of the Almighty are higher than the ways of humans, Carleton concluded. Always He tested severely, for His own good ends, those He called to serve His unseen purposes.

As on this night and in this storm.

⊛ ⊛ ⊛

HE HAD NOT THOUGHT it possible for the weather to get any worse. He'd been wrong. It seemed as though the heavens suffered no lack of invention when it came to torment. Even through his thick leather gloves, his fingers throbbed and burned like fire from the cold, and every joint ached.

Concern that both gunpowder and weapons were by now so wet it would be difficult, if not impossible to fire when they finally encountered the enemy was second only to worry about the men. Unlike his well-equipped Rangers, few of the rank and file had adequate clothing, and what little they did have was thoroughly soaked, their sleet-roughened rags freezing stiffly to the wearers' bodies. Many were altogether barefoot, while the more fortunate limped along with bloodied feet bound in rags. It would be a miracle if they did not all suffer from frostbite.

As though heaven's Furies determined to make their situation ever more desperate, the column ground to a sudden halt at the edge of a deep ravine. Directly front of them the ice-slick road fell steeply to a rocky stream the local guides called Jacob's Creek. It was impossible to see to its bottom, but as he reined Devil around to peer into the defile, Carleton could hear the surge and roar of water surely a hundred feet below.

In moments artillerymen and drovers scurried to unwind drag ropes and unharness the horses. Mooring the ropes around the trunks of large trees, they began to slowly lower the wagons and gun carriages into the ravine.

Carleton dismounted. Ordering his men to do the same and to lead their mounts down the incline, he warned them to take special care for their footing.

"At this rate it'll be full day before we reach our goal—if we even do," Andrews muttered.

Isaiah led his mount up beside them, his dark countenance creased with concern beneath the misshapen hat and woolen kerchief that muffled his head. "The horses be sufferin' as much as the men. No one be able to bear this much longer."

"We Shawnee do not fight in such conditions," Spotted Pony grumbled. "Even our women have better sense than to ride out in a storm. I tell you, the Long Knives have lost their minds."

Thinking of Elizabeth's and Blue Sky's pleas to accompany them, Carleton rolled his eyes. When his gaze met Andrews's, both choked down laughter.

Huddled beneath his bearskin and blanket, Red Fox grinned. "They are crazy, but clever like a fox. If we do not believe we can do this, then neither will the British. We will take them by surprise and vanquish them."

Andrews translated the warriors' words for Isaiah, and an unwilling smile played over the black man's face. "At least we ride. The infantry . . . " His mouth tightening into a hard line, he shook his head. "Men be freezing in their tracks."

Judging from the shouts coming from the other side of the creek, the loads that had already been lowered were being hauled up again. A guide offered the unwelcome news that there was a smaller ravine just beyond the top of the far slope that was even steeper.

To all appearances unperturbed, Washington rode up and down along the column, ceaselessly urging his men forward. As he approached them, without warning his horse slipped on the icy slope, squealing as his hind legs slid out from under him.

His mouth gone dry, Carleton watched as Washington caught the horse's mane in a firm grip and jerked his head up, at the same time shifting back in the saddle. For a tense moment the big stallion floundered, then he found secure footing and righted.

Letting out his breath, Carleton began to feel his way cautiously down the slope, keeping Devil on a short rein.

ON THE OTHER SIDE of the ravines they came to a high, level stretch that rose by gradual degrees. Once again they were exposed to the full force of the bitter gale that swept across the highlands in alternating curtains of snow, sleet, and rain broken by brief lulls. The road seemed to stretch before them without end, and increasingly men began to straggle and lag behind.

When Carleton doubted they could go much farther, the road dropped into a long slope leading to the outskirts of Trenton. Now the drovers were forced to haul back on the drag ropes with what remained of their strength to prevent the gun carriages from tearing loose and rolling downhill, crushing the horses beneath them.

Finally reaching a crossroads where the slope leveled out, they entered a small village amid a lull in the storm. Unhappily Carleton noted that the contours of land and buildings had begun to emerge more distinctly and at a greater distance through the blowing veil of snow.

"What time is it?" he called to Andrews.

The colonel pulled out his watch and rubbed the glass clear. "It's five forty-nine—not much longer till dawn."

Carleton beckoned to one of the guides leading the column. The man drew his horse to Carleton's side.

"Where are we?"

"Birmingham," the man responded, rubbing heavy-lidded eyes.

"How far to go?"

"We're 'bout halfway."

Carleton waved the man off and turned back to Andrews and the two Shawnee, who had reined their mounts up beside them. "We are halfway there," he said curtly in Shawnee.

Their faces set in hard lines.

Ahead of them, Stephen's Virginians came to a halt before the black bulk of a large house. Shadowed riders came up from behind at a quick trot. As they drew level Carleton recognized Washington and Greene and their aides.

"Soldiers, keep by your officers. For God's sake, keep by your officers!" Washington repeated as they passed by, his deep voice urgent.

They pulled up at the head of the column. Motioning Andrews to follow, Carleton led the way forward. As they came to the column's van a man and woman with several children, all bundled in heavy coats and shawls, emerged from the house and hurried toward them, carrying baskets and jugs. Leaning against the force of the wind, they stopped beside Washington's horse.

"Your servant Benjamin Moore, Your Excellency," the man called out, lifting one of the baskets for Washington to take.

His wife pressed close to offer a pottery jug, while the children distributed food and drink to the other officers and aides. Carleton and Andrews gratefully accepted the food they were offered.

"Sir, I thank you," Washington said with quiet dignity. "We have had a long, cold ride, and we have yet miles to go."

"I wish we had food and drink enough for all your men," Moore responded. "We have looked eagerly for this day, and you have our prayers for protection and success. May the Almighty ride with you."

For a moment Washington regarded him soberly. "Thank you, my good fellow. Your prayers are more welcome than food and drink and will do us more good."

The senior officers gathered round. While they shared the food among them, bolting down bread, cheese, and slices of cold meat, Carleton mentally reviewed the maps of Trenton their local guides had provided, along with detailed descriptions of the terrain and important landmarks. He was also personally familiar with the place, having frequently passed through on his travels between Virginia and Massachusetts during his earlier years in the colonies.

The town's consequence was that it and lay at the head of navigation on the Delaware River was an important stop on the King's Highway between New York and Philadelphia. About a hundred houses, churches, and businesses, including numerous mills and iron furnaces, nestled among the wooded hills in the crook of the Delaware and Assunpink Creek, and four well-traveled highways bisected the area.

Angling down from the northwest through the low ground along the Delaware, River Road carried a busy traffic of goods and travelers from the local ferries to Trenton's marketplace and mills. Above the town to the north, Pennington Road and the King's Highway, also known as Princeton Road, converged and were intersected by Trenton's two main streets, King and Queen, which ran parallel downhill to the river. Extending to the Assunpink on the south side of town, Queen Street crossed a sturdy stone bridge and merged into Bordentown Road.

When the food had been devoured, Washington went over their assignments one last time. Major General John Sullivan's First Division of mostly New England troops under brigadier generals Arthur St. Clair, John Glover, Paul Sargent, and Joshua Stern, would continue their advance straight ahead along River Road, entering Trenton from the northwest along Water Street. After consulting with one of the guides, Washington ordered Sullivan to halt for a few minutes at the crossroad leading to Howell's Ferry so the Second Division, which had the longer march, would have time to get into position.

For a moment he stared into the distance, frowning. "Nothing has been heard from Ewing and Cadwalader, I take it." When several of the officers shook their heads, he said, "The ice may have prevented them from getting across the river. It is imperative, then, that you move quickly through the town and seize the roads below it to prevent General von Donop from coming to Rall's aid."

He turned to Carleton. "Detach one of your troops under Colonel Andrews's command to accompany Sullivan's column. You and the remaining troop will stay with the Second Division."

Carleton touched his fingers to the brim of his hat, as did Andrews. "Sir."

Washington turned his attention to the tall, affable former Quaker, Major General Nathanael Greene. The Second Division, consisting of the brigades of Adam Stephen, Hugh Mercer, and William Alexander, Lord Stirling, would take the longer, slower route, attacking Trenton from the north. To get there, they would first travel northeast away from the river, then turn southeast and follow Scotch Road to where it merged with Pennington Road a short distance above the town.

"According to our intelligence, one of Colonel Rall's outposts lies just below that juncture. It is there we begin the attack," Washington concluded. He pulled out his watch. "Set your watches by mine, gentlemen."

The officers hastily fumbled beneath their coats and blankets to retrieve their timepieces. The wind was again beginning to rise, and the cold deepened.

"It is now . . . " Washington paused, scrutinizing the watch face. " . . . six-fourteen."

With the others, Carleton and Andrews reset their watches.

"The attack is fixed for eight o'clock sharp," Washington emphasized. "Make sure you are in position in good time. It is vital both divisions begin the attack at the exact same moment. Strike with great speed and force. We must deny Rall the opportunity to mount a counterattack."

Just then a soldier ran up to Glover, who leaned down from his horse to confer with him. After a moment, Glover straightened.

"Your Excellency, my men have checked their weapons, and even our best-secured arms are wet and not in condition to fire."

"We're in the same case," Greene said. "Snow and sleet have melted into the cartridge boxes, and our powder is wet through."

"What's to be done?" Sullivan demanded.

Curbing his restive mount, St. Clair growled, "There's nothing for it but to push on and charge."

"Few of the men have bayonets," Stirling pointed out.

His jaw hardening, Washington brushed aside the objection. "Advance and charge."

GRAPESHOT SCREAMED through the trees, rattling in the leaves and branches like hail. As debris sprayed over her, Elizabeth instinctively ducked behind a boulder. Trembling, she sought the dim shadows of the men crouched to each side, all but obscured by drifting gun smoke.

From the corner of her eye she caught the flaming scarlet of Catchfly. Everything around her had been obliterated, but like a small, steadfast beacon of determination, the wildflower clung to the trampled earth, its petals gleaming like brilliant flecks of blood.

Without warning, solid shot ripped into a tree in front of her, cracking it in half with a deafening roar. The thunder of its fall shook the earth. Bloodied, she clawed free of its branches, her ears ringing, while the multiplied crack of gunfire sent musket balls through the air, whining like hornets.

"Sammy!"

Shocked by the sound of her own voice, she watched in suspended horror as Isaiah's elder son crumpled to the ground, gasping, clutching at the crimson fountain that spurted from a gaping wound in his chest. Yards away and out of her reach, he stiffened and writhed, straining for breath.

Unable to move, she stared in horror as by swift degrees the youth's face contorted, his dark skin turning bronze, his curly black hair lengthening and straightening into a blond mane, while his face distorted into Carleton's visage. He turned his head, piercing grey-blue eyes seeking hers in accusation and appeal. Then he slumped back, his body shaking, at last lay limp and still.

Levi jerked her to her feet and spun her to face the oncoming grenadiers. "There's nothing you can do for him! Fire!"

Jonathan! No . . . no! she cried. But no sound came from her throat.

HEART RACING, BREATH SHORTENED, Elizabeth jerked to consciousness. She was bathed in sweat, stiff and sore from lying on the floor's cold planks. As though from a great distance she heard the case clock downstairs toll six times, while, unabated, the sound of the wind's shriek filled the room, the world.

Disoriented, she forced herself upright and looked blankly around her, fighting through the oppressive aura of the dream. Blue Sky had gone, and the door of the bedroom stood slightly ajar. Hearing the rustle of covers, Elizabeth glanced at the bed, where Tess abruptly sat up and pulled aside the hangings to poke out her head, hair and shift askew.

"Are you all right?" she said, her words slurred with sleep. "I thought I heard something. Where's Blue Sky?"

Unable to speak, Elizabeth turned back to the window. The tentative light of early dawn filtered through the thick coating of ice that obscured the panes with fanciful designs.

Nothing could be seen outside. And beneath the howl of the storm . . . silence.

Chapter Three

INVISIBLE BEHIND THE STRENGTHENING SQUALLS of the storm, the sun's red orb lifted above the obscured horizon. Although the dark clouds and stormy weather made it impossible to see very far, the leaden skies brightened faintly, bringing the landscape near at hand into more distinct focus.

An hour earlier the two divisions had separated, Sullivan's marching straight ahead along River Road. Andrews's detachment, including Spotted Pony and Isaiah's black troop, had ridden away with them.

Greene's Division, with Washington in the lead, had forged away to the left. Approximately three-quarters of an hour ago, they had turned onto Scotch Road, where they made faster progress.

Washington rode ceaselessly along the line of march, calling out to his men, "Press on, boys! Press on!" And without complaint, they all marched doggedly on.

Ten minutes after sunrise they approached the juncture of Pennington Road, where Captain Washington's detachment had set up a roadblock. Huddled together under guard amid a copse of trees in the lea of a rise, a motley group of what appeared to be local residents sheltered beneath a few blankets. They were mainly men, but Carleton could see a couple of women among them.

"Is it just me, or is it not fit for man or beast to be abroad?"

he said to Red Fox. "What are all these people doing out in such a storm?"

The Shawnee warrior met his astonished gaze with an amused one. "It appears even the Long Knives' women are crazy."

"I can't vouch for the sanity of our own."

Red Fox guffawed.

Behind them, Smithson said, "Sir, as your second, I need to know your commands and what our situation is. Pray, speak a civilized language instead of this barbaric tongue."

Carleton rounded on him. "You'll receive all communications relevant to you—in the king's English."

Smithson gave him a dark look. Considering the man through narrowed eyes, Carleton hardened his determination to cut off any challenge to his authority without hesitation. His experience with the shaman Wolfslayer had taught him most thoroughly that to give quarter to an enemy, especially in one's own ranks, led only to disaster.

A cry from the head of the column drew him around. Squinting through the driving rain and sleet, Carleton made out a substantial party of armed men striding toward them through the fields from the direction of Trenton.

He drew on the reins and raised his hand. Behind him low commands traveled the length of the detachment, and the brigade pulled to an abrupt halt. Washington swept by at a gallop with Greene on his heels.

Reaching under the folds of the blanket draped over his thighs, Carleton pulled his carbine free from its holster, from the corner of his eye saw Red Fox draw his rifle at the same time.

Blocked by Washington, the group's leader came to a halt and saluted. "Victory or death, your Excellency."

Carleton relaxed and felt those around him do the same. "One of ours," he murmured.

Red Fox gave a curt nod.

In a slow Virginia drawl the man said, "Capt'n George Wallis, reportin', Your Excellency. Gen'l Stephens's regiment."

Noting that the muscles in Washington's jaw hardened, Carleton urged his stallion forward to his commander's side.

"You men were not assigned to the advanced parties," Washington said. "What are you doing here?"

"Sir, them dirty Hessians kilt one o' our men a few days back, and the gen'l sent us to teach 'em a lesson. And that we did, sir. We took one o' their outposts last night, kilt four and winged 'leven, near as we could figure. The whole garrison turned out after us," he concluded with a broad grin, "but we give 'em the slip. We finished our business and are at your command, sir."

Everyone in the vicinity started as Washington tore his cocked hat from his head and slapped it hard against his thigh. "By God, you've accomplished nothing but to place the Hessians on the alert!"

"But, sir—"

Tightlipped, Washington reined his horse around. His eyes fell on Lieutenant James Monroe.

"Bring General Stephen here at once."

Snapping a salute, the lieutenant spurred his mount back down the line.

"Steady, sir," Carleton said in a low tone.

Washington gritted his teeth. "If we weren't on the way to battle, I'd cashier the man this instant."

"I'd not blame you."

Carleton knew that Stephen had been a thorn in Washington's side ever since he had been Washington's second in command during the Seven Years War, which ended a couple of years before Carleton left for England for a few months and ended up staying a decade. Judging from their interactions during the past couple of days, the rivalry between the two men had not diminished in the intervening years.

In a short time Monroe returned, the general at his heels.

"Did you order this company to cross last night and attack the Hessian outposts?" Washington demanded, his tone icy.

Eyes narrowed, Stephen stiffened. "I did, sir. The Hessians attacked and killed—"

"I made it abundantly clear that everyone was to maintain the most absolute secrecy until we reached our goal. Thanks to your efforts, that is no longer possible. You, sir, have put the enemy on their guard."

Stephen regarded his furious commander with a sneer. Wallis's shoulders slumped, however; he was clearly crestfallen. His compatriots shifted uneasily from one foot to the other.

"My apologies, sir." Chagrin tinged Wallis's voice. "We was just followin' orders. Didn't mean no harm."

With obvious effort, Washington turned his back to Stephen and fixed the captain in a kindly gaze.

"I would be pleased, sir, if you and your men would join my column."

Wallis gave a hasty salute. "We'd be honored, Your Excellency."

His face tense, the muscles in his jaw working, Washington nodded to Wallis, who hastily effaced his party into the column. Leaving guards behind in charge of the prisoners, Captain Washington's detachment joined the column's van, and they rode on, each man keeping his opinions to himself.

DURING THE NEXT QUARTER HOUR scouts rode in at intervals to report on the location of Hessian guard posts that encircled the town from River Road to Princeton Road, roughly a mile out from its center. Below the town, another guarded the bridge over Assunpink Creek and the lower ferry landing. At first light, Carleton knew, a dawn patrol would ride out and shortly thereafter the night sentries posted between these outposts would be relieved by a contingent of day pickets. Numerous soldiers would be out and on the move just as Washington's force approached.

Once again the storm temporarily subsided, and by degrees a stormy, ominous light gave greater depth to their surroundings. In moments more, the marching column approached an isolated farm surrounded by woods.

Carleton rode in the van with Washington and Greene, and as they came even with the house, he saw a man in the side yard, chopping wood. Evidently startled by the tramp of feet and rumble of gun carriages, he looked up, eyes widening, then dropped his ax and gazed down the column's length, openmouthed.

Washington reined his stallion to a halt by the fence and called, "Can you tell me where the Hessian outpost is?"

For a moment the man stared at him, dumbfounded. Then, alternately glancing toward his house and back at them, he began to edge toward the side door.

"He's afraid," Carleton said to Colonel Fitzgerald, who rode beside him. "He must think we're British."

Fitzgerald quickly called out, "You need not be frightened. It's General Washington who asks the question."

Instantly the man's countenance brightened. "They're staying at Mr. Howell's cooper shop," he said, pointing to a small building little more than half a mile farther along the road. "A patrol come back in not a quarter of an hour ago."

"Have the day pickets come out?" Washington prodded.

"Yes, sir. They passed by just before the patrol come back, and I ain't seen 'em since."

Washington touched his fingers to the brim of his hat. "Thank you."

He hastily gathered his officers around him. "If the day pickets have gone out, the storm has concealed us from them. We must not delay, but strike immediately and hard."

Dividing his column into three units, he sent General Mercer's New England and Maryland troops off to the right and Fermoy's Delaware brigade to the left. Stephen's Virginians and Stirling's Delawares would form the center of the attack, with Captain Washington's detachment and Carleton's Rangers leading the charge behind Washington and Greene.

At the head of his column, facing the road before them stiffly erect, Washington raised his sword, then brought it forward. "Advance and charge!"

Mercer's and Fermoy's detachments broke rapidly away to each side at the same instant Washington spurred his horse in the direction of the cooper shop. Carleton urged Devil forward, feeling the thunder of his Rangers close behind.

As the divisions spread out across the fields to grapple with the unknown, his gut clenched with the tension that fairly crackled through the bedraggled column, energizing men and horses who were bone weary and nearly frozen to break into a loping run.

Chapter Four

FROM THE BROW OF A GENTLE RISE, Andrews gazed thoughtfully down the narrow track that beckoned the column. Under the stormy sky, daylight had strengthened enough that he could clearly make out a small frame house a quarter mile ahead, fronting River Road. An equal distance beyond it, well back from the road, a stone mansion lay wrapped in a misty veil of blowing snow.

Sullivan's division lay concealed in the woods behind him and the other outriders. From his advanced position Andrews could see no sign of life anywhere in the vicinity. Shortly after they had separated from Greene's column, however, one of Captain Flahaven's scouts had intercepted them to report that a strongly manned Hessian outpost was stationed in the mansion, with a picket post in the frame house. Following the scout, they had ridden up to Flahavan's position with all caution.

"Do you see any movement?" Andrews asked Spotted Pony.

His gaze keen, the warrior studied the fields and woods spread out before them, then pointed to the barely visible coil of wind-whipped grey smoke that wreathed the mansion's chimneys. "Only the smoke from that house."

Andrews turned to Flahavan. "You say that stone house is General Dickinson's home?" he said in English.

Nodding, the captain curbed his mount and indicated a point across the river. "He commands our batteries over there."

Andrews shaded his eyes with his hand. Through the trees that lined the riverbank, almost obscured by swirling snow and sleet, he could just make out the dull glint of cannon barrels a short distance south of them on the opposite shore.

"Then I hope his family's found other accommodations."

Colonel John Stark drew his mount up beside them. "To dislodge the enemy, Philemon will blow the house away, if need be," he growled. Eyes narrowing, he glanced at Spotted Pony, then back to Andrews.

Tall and wiry, with high cheekbones and a prominent nose, Stark commanded a New Hampshire brigade as tough and wily as their colonel. He had no great love for Indians, Andews knew, and he ignored Stark's stare.

"You made good time," Flahavan noted.

"This infernal cold is good for something, at least," Andrews returned dryly. "The mud finally froze enough to give the gun carriages better traction and speed us on our way. Knox refused to leave behind one gun."

As General Sullivan eased his mount from behind the trees sheltering the rest of the column, all three officers saluted. Without speaking, Spotted Pony kicked his horse's flanks and disappeared through the trees, heading back to the Rangers. Andrews glanced after him, frowning.

"The night sentries pulled back in just before you arrived, sir, and the day pickets rode out in that direction." Flahavan pointed off to his left toward Pennington Road. "Haven't seen hide nor hair of 'em since. I guess they're in no hurry to come and play—with us, at least. Greene's column may have the honors."

Sullivan's handsome patrician countenance eased to a tight smile. "Then we'll have to provide incentive for them to return to their proper station." He pulled out his pocket watch and squinted at it. "It appears we're right on time, gentlemen. Form up your men and on my order advance and charge."

⊛ ⊛ ⊛

ANGLING ACROSS THE OPEN FIELDS straight at the cooper shop, Washington brought his stallion to a long trot, closely trailed by Will Lee and General Greene. To all appearances the three men were oblivious of the storm's renewed assault that without warning descended from the thick clouds blotting out the sun. The stinging rain, snow, sleet, and roaring wind at their backs would blow full into the faces of the enemy, while providing cover for the attackers.

Neck and neck with Captain Washington, Carleton gave Devil his head and drew one of his pistols from its holster, praying his weapons were dry enough to fire. Unloosing the hair-raising ululation of the Shawnee war cry, Red Fox held course with him, brandishing his rifle over his head. The thunder of hooves heralded the charge as they closed on the nondescript building in a rush.

They were yet some yards distant when the door of the cooper shop swung open and a Hessian officer emerged. As he looked calmly around, he suddenly stiffened, staring in their direction.

Beside Carleton, Red Fox shouldered his rifle, aimed, and fired in one smooth motion. A puff of snow exploded from the building's wall an inch from the man's head. Immediately Carleton heard the crackle of a volley from behind him, and a burst of musket balls swarmed past to strike the snow and the building directly ahead.

"Der Feind! Heraus!"

The officer's scream reached him faintly above storm's howl, instantly whipped away by the gale. Within seconds, a strong body of Hessian soldiers tumbled out of the building, juggling their weapons while they frantically pulled on coats and scrambled to form ranks.

With the multiplied crack of muskets all around him, the familiar rush of exhilaration, fear, and reckless determination rose in Carleton's breast, flooding away all other consciousness, sweeping him forward in its tide. Instinct took over, and as the Hessian soldiers returned an unsteady volley, he aimed and pulled off a shot, saw a man fall, then instantly shoved the pistol back into the holster and tore free its mate.

SULLIVAN'S COLUMN was barely on the move when a single shot echoed from the picket house. It was quickly answered by Andrews and the others in the van, then the column deployed rapidly across the road and the snowy fields to each side.

Other than Stark's well-equipped New Hampshiremen and a couple of companies in Stern's regiment, few had bayonets and most of their muskets were too wet to fire, Andrews knew. But at the deep-throated boom of Dickinson's artillery, Sullivan's troops unloosed a great roar and. brandishing their weapons, pressed forward to overrun the picket house.

Directly ahead of Andrews, a company of Hessian Jägers streamed into view from the far side of the stone mansion and hastily formed up in the road. Others sprang to service the battery next to the house or scrambled for shelter behind trees and fences. In seconds a rolling musket volley discharged at point blank range.

A ball from one of the Hessian six-pounders screamed past, fearfully close. Andrews swore and jerked on the reins, dodging the ball by inches. Spotted Pony and the soldiers all around them did the same, but none fell nor did anyone slow his pace.

At that moment, from the river's opposite bank, Dickinson's artillery roared to life, spewing solid shot through the trees. One exploded through an outbuilding next to the house while others dug deep furrows in the snow banks, casting up geysers of earth and debris.

At his side Andrews saw that a savage light illumined Spotted Pony's visage. Teeth gritted, Andrews drove his spurs hard into his own mount's flanks, sabre upraised, and together they closed on the Hessian force at a mad gallop.

From short yards away, eyes blurred by stinging snow and sleet, he made out the terrified faces of the enemy, felt the ground quake beneath the hooves of the horses and the feet of more than a thousand charging men. At the last moment, the Hessian force broke and parted before them like waves before a ship's prow.

CARLETON HAD COME UP beside Washington, and for several strides they rode head to head, the main body of the Rangers coursing around and behind them. Suddenly the deep, repeated boom of artillery reached them from their right, in the direction of the lower River Road, and they exchanged a look of satisfaction and relief. Sullivan's division had entered the fray right on time.

Now the infantry surged forward, a guttural roar echoing from thousands of throats while they raced toward the enemy as though the night's travail had never been. In an irresistible tide they were almost upon the Hessian pickets when Carleton saw the outmatched foe break and scatter, turning tail to run pell-mell back toward the town.

At the same instant, borne on the wind, the urgent rattle of kettledrums beating the call to arms reached him. Suddenly a stronger force of Hessians appeared through the trees, running forward to envelope the retreating pickets. Carleton fired again and replaced his spent pistol with the carbine.

He was conscious that around him several of his Rangers fell, but beside him Red Fox kept pace, his war club raised, and they drove together toward the Hessian line, heedless of danger. Under the press of the charging Continentals, the enemy began to give ground, firing from behind trees and hillocks, houses and outbuildings, while they withdrew grudgingly toward the high ground on the town's north end. Washington reined his stallion around to face his oncoming column, ignoring the musket balls that scoured the air all around him.

"On, boys, press on! We have them now!"

THE ENTICING AROMA of the hot breakfast Lydia and Chastity spread before them made Elizabeth's stomach growl. But the food might as well have been ashes. She could hardly choke down a bite, and she saw that Tess also hardly tasted her meal.

Blue Sky, however, ate with a good appetite. "There is nothing to fear. You will see. Moneto has spoken it," she assured them with cheerful confidence.

Smiling, she glanced through the dining room window to the front porch, where Elizabeth and Tess had found her in the pale, cold light of dawn. Wrapped in her buffalo hide, her long, black hair flying in the gale, she had stared serenely into the sweeping snow in the direction of the Delaware, little more than a mile distant, head cocked to catch any sound. But the three of them had discerned nothing save the moan of the wind and the pecking of sleet against the building.

Elizabeth leaned her throbbing head on her hand and absently stirred the now cold egg yolk with her fork. "My head knows you are right, but my heart . . . " Tears filled her eyes. "Why is faith so hard at times, yet so easy at others?" she asked Tess in English.

She was interrupted by Lydia, who bustled in with the teapot, followed by Chastity carrying another platter of ham still steaming from the fire. " 'Tis so for all," Lydia said as she circled the table to refill their cups. Stopping at Elizabeth's chair, she rested a gentle hand on her shoulder. "I myself spent the watches of the night praying mightily for God's hand of protection over our boys."

"Do you believe dreams can portend the future?" Elizabeth asked, her voice muffled.

Tess set down her teacup and gave her a keen look. "Your uncle Joshua would say that dreams are no more than the shadows of our fears."

"Thy dream was an unhappy one?" Lydia prompted.

Blue Sky clasped Elizabeth's hand. "What is it, Healer Woman?"

Elizabeth fought back tears. For a moment she hesitated, overcome by the irrational fear that to give voice to her dream would call it into being.

At last she choked out, "I saw Jonathan . . ." Shaking, she turned to Blue Sky and whispered hoarsely in Shawnee, "I dreamt . . . that White Eagle died in the battle."

Blue Sky's fingers tightened over hers. "The evil spirits would steal your peace, that is all. White Eagle is under Moneto's protection, as are Golden Elk and all the others. Do not fear, my sister."

Just then the clock in the passage began to toll the hour. The dining room door burst open, and Wainwright hurried inside, his clothing heavily frosted with ice. Stamping clumps of snow from his boots, he lifted his hand for silence.

"Do you hear it?"

When they all regarded him in puzzlement, he motioned for them to wait until the clock finished striking eight times. As the echo of its deep tones dissipated into silence, Blue Sky sprang from her chair and bolted for the front door, Elizabeth running after her, with Tess and the Wainwrights close behind.

Buffeted by the gale, they stood rapt at the edge of the porch, straining to make out the distant, wooded line of the Delaware in a world obscured by misty whiteness. Then Elizabeth drew in her breath and pressed her hand hard to her breast.

Muffled by the roar of the wind and the hiss and seethe of swirling snow, the repeated, reverberating boom of cannon fire reached them through the dark dawn.

The deafening scream of solid shot hurtling overhead and the crackle of rifle and musket fire echoed from the wooded hills. Oblivious of the musket balls whining past, Carleton fired his carbine, then tore free his sabre and spurred his stallion.

Increasingly now he passed brilliantly uniformed Hessian soldiers sprawled in the snow. A few tried to crawl out of the path of the oncoming Americans, but more lay motionless, the snow around them stained scarlet.

Washington and Greene led the way into the town at a quick trot, while the First Division's right wing slanted farther eastward across the fields in the direction of Princeton Road. Brushing aside the detachments that opposed them, the main column quickly seized the high ground at the juncture where Pennington and Princeton roads intersected Trenton's two main streets, King and Queen.

While Mercer's brigade streamed past to enter the town through backyards and alleyways, Knox urged his artillery to the brow of the hill. In furious haste the gunners began to drag cannon, howitzers, and mortars into position to sweep the streets that converged directly below.

Carleton signaled his detachment to halt, then motioned to Red Fox to accompany him. Together they rode forward to join the officers who clustered around their commander.

From their vantage point Carleton could see the entire town spread out below. The storm had momentarily eased, and through the trees and buildings to his far right, he caught the dull glint of the ice-clogged Delaware and the movement of Sullivan's division advancing rapidly in the face of stubborn opposition.

Farther off to the south wound the wooded line that marked the narrower tributary of Assunpink Creek. Carleton could just make out the bridge immediately below the town, the only crossing for some distance because of the mill pond on its east side. A Hessian force appeared to be in possession, and he could see both soldiers and occasional knots of civilians streaming across the bridge to disappear through the trees.

Leaning close to Red Fox, he pointed out the advance parties of Sullivan's division, now flooding into the lower reaches of the town. "Find Golden Elk and Spotted Pony," he said in an undertone. "Tell Golden Elk the bridge over the creek is in the hands of the enemy."

Without speaking, the Shawnee warrior kicked his horse's flanks and plunged down the slope.

Keeping an eye on a sizeable body of Hessians assembling at the lower end of King Street, Carleton hastily reloaded his pistols and carbine. At closer range, in front of an expansive white frame house, a Hessian artillery unit raced to harness horses to their gun carriages, while in front of them a small band struck up, the blaring strains of a martial tune adding its clamor to the already deafening cacophony.

Everywhere enemy soldiers milled about in confusion, driven by screaming officers. Broken units scurried to meet both Mercer's detachment and Sullivan's oncoming column, which poured through house lots laying down a withering fire or attacking with fixed bayonets. Others, singly or in small groups, sought concealment or escape by any means available.

By now the small detachment of Hessian artillery had brought their guns around. With a deafening explosion, solid shot arced upward and plowed into the hillside just below Carleton. Squealing, Devil backed away and began to rear, but Carleton tightened the reins and quickly brought him under control.

The enemy gunners scrambled to adjust the elevation of their pieces, and before the American batteries could respond, more shots tore by. One struck the leading horse hitched to a three-pounder and knocked it on its back. The animal lay thrashing in its death throes, a gaping wound in its belly spurting gouts of crimson blood onto the snow. Cursing mightily, rawboned sixteen-year-old Sergeant John Greenwood tore off his battered hat and struck it across his thigh, then stalked forward to stare down at the helpless creature in outrage.

"Leave it, man!" Carleton shouted, reining Devil around. He ducked as another shot whined past to splinter a nearby caisson.

"Fire!" Knox's stentorian voice bellowed from behind him.

Immediately the American six-pounders and howitzers roared to life. In spite of the drenching the guns had received, blazing rounds of solid shot, grapeshot, and canister screamed overhead and descended in a pure arc to sweep the entire length of the narrow streets below like a giant broom, bouncing along the cobbles and smashing into buildings, blowing through walls, windows, and roofs while explosions of debris cast deadly missiles in all directions.

Enemy gunners dodged and fled in panic as both men and horses fell beneath the onslaught. With the volley, the town's remaining inhabitants, men, women, and children, precipitously abandoned their homes to stumble into the streets. Their terrified screams drowned out the voices of the Hessian officers, who vainly struggled to bring their men into formation.

Grimly Carleton watched the town center disintegrate into a scene of complete chaos while the American forces converged from three sides at once, firing from inside and behind buildings and any available cover. In the storm's renewed violence, the gunners under captains Thomas Forrest and Alexander Hamilton bent to shelter their field pieces with their bodies in the effort to keep powder and touchholes dry, all the while keeping up a blazing fire.

Drifting smoke from musket and cannon volleys mingled with wind-whipped sleet and snow, quickly obscuring friend and foe alike. Explosions of musket and artillery fire, iron crashing through brick and stone, the rending splinter of wood and glass all echoed in the narrow lanes, punctuated by the shouts and curses of the combatants and the cries of the wounded and the town's terrified residents, raising an inconceivable din that rose to the heights with appalling clarity. Carleton became aware that he had pressed his hands over his ears against the racket and noted with a grimace that those around him had instinctively done the same.

Although he managed to keep his expression stoic, the sights and sounds were wrenching, almost too much to bear. His stomach clenched with the same roiling nausea he had experienced more than once on discovering Wolfslayer's depredations during raids against the Long Knives.

Without warning, the thought of Elizabeth, suppressed until now by sheer force of will, struck him forcefully. He found himself longing for her with an intensity that took his breath away.

Is it all worth it, Beth, all the killing, the wanton destruction? In the end, is what we gain greater than what we lose?

There seemed no answer.

GREENE POINTED IN THE DIRECTION of a grove of trees on the town's near east side. "That must be Colonel Rall at the head of that large body of grenadiers."

Taking the spyglass Washington offered, Carleton studied the strong Hessian force that streamed through what appeared to be an orchard and the open field beside it. At their head rode a burly figure in ornate uniform whom Carleton guessed to be the Hessian colonel, fifty-year-old Johann Rall.

"They're moving to flank us." He returned the spyglass to the General. "If we try to drive them off, the way's clear for them to retreat to Princeton Road."

"Then let's flank them instead," Greene suggested, his hands clenched on the pommel of his saddle.

Washington's visage hardened. "My thought exactly. General Carleton, alert Hand and Haussegger to the enemy's movements. Order them to circle around between the enemy and Princeton Road, and place your Rangers wherever they will do the most good. Under no circumstances must Rall reach Princeton."

Carleton saluted, forcibly suppressing the tumult of emotion that threatened to overcome him. "He shall not, sir, if I've any say in the matter."

Greene motioned the youngest of his aides, Isaac Wainwright, forward and ordered him to accompany Carleton as a messenger. The muscular young captain joined Carleton with alacrity.

Carleton led the way down the rear slope of the hill, then along Princeton Road. Within moments they located the far left wing of the American force. When they tracked the two colonels down, Carleton explained the danger, pointing out the orchard south of the road, visible through the storm's veil as a slightly darker smudge against the low, wooded hills marking the distant line of the Assunpink.

"If he tries to break through to Princeton, he won't get far," Hand growled, the set of the balding Irish doctor's jaw reflecting stubborn determination.

Hand's veteran Pennsylvania riflemen in their black hunting shirts and Haussegger's mixed Pennsylvania and Maryland German regiment were quickly in motion, with scouts ranging eagerly ahead to probe the Hessian position. They swept around to the east under cover of a strong squall of sleet and snow, Carleton leading his Rangers in advance of the infantry. As they crossed Princeton Road, a couple of scouts intercepted them.

"There's a strong force of the enemy moving out of the orchard and advancing on that hill," the first reported breathlessly, pointing to the promontory off to the right where Carleton had left Washington and Greene.

"Let's cut 'em off and show 'em what we're made of, boys!" Hand shouted, already in motion.

The column surged after him to form a battle line on the high ground overlooking the orchard. Squinting through the heavy snowfall, Carleton noted with approval that they had a clear line of fire on the enemy's flank.

The crash of the Americans' volley was quickly supported by a musket and artillery barrage from the heights. Pinned in a deadly crossfire, the Hessian force recoiled in confusion, men toppling like dry hay before a scythe. In advance of the American line, Carleton could not hold back a pang of admiration for the Hessian colonel, who stood in his stirrups waving his sword in spite of the musket balls that hissed all around him.

"Alle was meine Grenatir sein, vorwerds!" Rall screamed.

With the clamor of drums, fifes, and bugles, the grenadiers reversed their march and began to fight their way back into the town, their brilliant battle flags snapping bravely in the wind. They strode without wavering into a hail of fire from Sullivan's and Mercer's oncoming brigades that steadily thinned their ranks.

SENT BY SULLIVAN to secure the bridge, in a fierce rush Glover's and Sargent's regiments, with Andrews's detachment in the van, burst upon the strong Hessian detachment holding it. The enemy force scurried across the graceful span, leaving their dead and wounded lying where they fell.

Glover indicated the enemy force now occupying the high ground on the far bank. "If we hold that position, we can block any attempt by the enemy to either counterattack or escape. We have the advantage of numbers, and I say we take it."

Turning to Andrews and Spotted Pony, Red Fox swept his arm toward the northeastern border of the town. "The Long Knives' warriors hold the ground there."

Andrews translated for Glover and Sargent, adding, "If we cut off Bordentown Road and at the same time extend our lines along the creek, we'll have the town completely encircled."

Giving him a determined nod, Sargent immediately ordered his Continentals to advance across the bridge. Supported by a withering fire from the Rangers and Glover's troops, they quickly spread out along the far bank, driving the Hessians before them and taking prisoner any who lagged behind.

A REMNANT OF RALL'S REGIMENT staggered back into the town center through a withering crossfire. As he closely pursued the dwindling force up King Street, Carleton realized the Hessian colonel meant to recapture the cannon his men had abandoned under the American barrage from the heights.

Ahead of him, he saw a compact body of Virginians and New England gunners, who had evidently come to the same conclusion, tearing madly down the hill toward them. Dismounting, he ordered his troop to do the same and directed Smithson to post them among a large contingent of Mercer's, Stirling's, and St. Clair's soldiers who were firing from inside the doors and windows of shattered houses and buildings on each side.

As they dispersed, Carleton raced forward at a crouch, one pistol leveled, the other stuck in his sash. He wove his way from cover to cover until he reached the broken Hessian detachment's left near a barricade of boards the enemy gunners had thrown up around their field pieces.

At the same moment the American phalanx he had seen approaching, led by Captain Washington and Lieutenant Monroe, charged straight at the grenadiers who were frantically loading the guns. In the melee, Washington went down. Monroe urged his corps forward, only to take a musket ball in the chest. He staggered and fell, blood spurting from the wound.

Hearing a shot from overhead, Carleton glanced up. In seconds the barrel of a musket protruded from an upper window of the house behind him, and an old woman leaned out to pull off another shot. He turned back in time to see one of the Hessian grenadiers stagger, then sink to his knees. Beside him a captain wheeled and fired over Carleton's head, the shot followed by the old woman's strangled cry.

With musket balls and grapeshot pelting the air on every side, Carleton reflexively aimed and fired at almost point-blank range, dropping the captain in his tracks. Several paces away, he saw Colonel Rall rein his mount around to reach out to his fallen subordinate.

Jaw clenched, Carleton tore his second pistol free of his sash, cocked and leveled it in one smooth motion, and squeezed the trigger. As though he observed the action from a great distance, he heard the pistol's sharp report and felt its brief recoil. A spurt of fire and white smoke belched from the end of the barrel.

Rall jerked powerfully, eyes widening, mouth gaping open like a fish out of water as a crimson stain spread rapidly across the side of his uniform. For a moment suspended, he fixed Carleton in an astonished gaze, transferred it to the smoking pistol in his hand.

At that moment a rifle shot rang out from across the street. The bullet tore through the colonel's side below the first, and as his mount half reared, he reeled and fell forward, clutching at the saddle's pommel, while several of his men sprang to catch him.

Feeling nothing but the bitter cold that numbed his limbs, Carleton searched above the melee for the shooter and caught a glimpse of Red Fox lowering his rifle. From the other side of the barricade he heard Sergeant Joseph White scream for his men to take the Hessian guns.

Under savage assault, the enemy again broke, pelting down a cross street. One of their mates, braver than the rest, stubbornly continued trying to load one of the cannon. His face contorted, the sergeant leaped toward him, his sword raised two handed above the man's head.

"Run, you dog!"

Beneath his tall grenadier's hat, the man's face drained of color, and he ran.

In seconds the American gunners dragged the gun around and dropped in a canister of shot and touched the match to the touch hole. With a deafening explosion, shrapnel whirred through the air in the direction of the retreating grenadiers.

Now additional American units poured down from the high ground at the head of the street. Among them came General Washington, calling out, "March on, my brave fellows! Follow me!"

At the head of Mercer's, Stirling's, and St. Clair's units, his troop had by now reached Carleton. Grabbing Devil's reins from a private, he shouted, "Mount up!"

As the men scrambled into their saddles, Red Fox appeared like an apparition out of the haze of smoke and snow.

"You showed up at an opportune moment," Carleton snapped as he swung into the saddle. "Where've you been?"

Red Fox allowed an enigmatic smile. "Helping Golden Elk take that bridge."

Carleton motioned his detachment forward to pursue the retreating Hessians. "I'm glad you made yourself useful. And I'm glad you're back. There's more to do."

❋ ❋ ❋

RALL'S SHATTERED REGIMENTS staggered back to the orchard east of town, where they were soon surrounded. By the time Carleton and Red Fox galloped up at the head of the Rangers, the disoriented Hessians were surrounded by units from Stephen and Fermoy's commands, who had advanced within fifty paces, keeping up a hot fire while officers from Haussegger's regiment called out in both German and English for the enemy to ground their weapons and surrender.

Colonel Baylor, Washington's aide, rode forward to convey terms of surrender to the senior Hessian officers. Thc Hessians conferred, then finally issued orders. One by one the soldiers began to reluctantly lay their colors on the snow and ground their weapons, their expressions registering humiliation, resentment, and relief.

Carleton pulled out his watch. The hands pointed to 8:57. The battle had lasted a little under an hour.

While the American and German troops mingled, Carleton ordered his detachment to wait and spurred his stallion back up the hill. He found Washington close by Knox's batteries, conferring with Stirling as they studied the action slowly dying down in the town center.

Carleton drew his stallion to a halt next to Captain Forrest and motioned toward the sweating soldiers loading their guns with rounds of canister. "That won't be needed now. They've surrendered."

"I just now noticed that." A broad grin creased Forrest's face. Turning to Washington, he shouted, "Sir, they have struck!"

Washington glanced toward him, eyebrows raised. "Struck!"

The captain waved his arm in the direction of the orchard below. "Their colors are down."

Washington stared at the units milling in the orchard below, his face brightening. "So they are. Put your men at ease, captain."

The rattle of musketry reached them from the direction of the creek. Leaving Stirling behind, Washington motioned Carleton to follow, and they spurred their horses toward the sound of the gunfire.

About halfway down the hill, they came upon several Hessian soldiers assisting a wounded officer into the Friends' meetinghouse. At the same moment, Sullivan's aide, Major Wilkinson, with Andrews and his detachment on his heels, galloped up from the direction of the bridge. Saluting, the two officers reported the surrender of the last of the Hessian regiments.

For a moment Washington brooded over the battlefield, then he grabbed Wilkinson by the hand. "This is a glorious day for our country!"

"It is indeed, sir," Wilkinson agreed, his smile broad.

Meeting Andrews's searching gaze, Carleton turned quickly away. The image of Rall's piercing glance locking with his, eyes widening at the shock of his mortal wound, rose to haunt him, and he found himself questioning man's definition of glory.

Chapter Five

ELIZABETH ADJUSTED THE BRIM of her hat to shade her eyes. Directly ahead, the sun's first red rays spilled over the horizon from beneath a bank of dark clouds streaming off toward the west, wind driven. Overnight the storm had given way to a steady, freezing downpour, and the clearing eastern sky promised that the lingering misty rain would soon pass as well. Already the long fingers of daylight burnished the snowy landscape to a blinding intensity.

Shortly past noon the previous day, after waiting in agonized suspense since the gunfire across the river had ceased barely an hour after it began, they had been overjoyed when Pete made it back to the inn, half frozen. With him had come the Wainwrights' younger son, Joseph, who had been stationed with Dickinson's artillery on the near side of the river, where Pete had joined him early that morning. While the battery pounded the town, the two men had followed the progress of the battle and now relayed news of the victory, brought by soldiers shepherding sizeable groups of Hessian prisoners across the river.

There had been some debate about immediately attacking Princeton, before the enemy learned of the day's action. It had been clear the army was too exhausted to face another battle so soon, however, and the decision had been made to withdraw. The first units of the army had already begun marching back to the ferry crossings, Joseph assured them, though the miserable weather made it unlikely that any would reach camp before the following morning.

Pete brought news almost as good. In passing by the Rangers' camp along the Delaware, he had spoken to the enterprising young lieutenant in charge of the support troops guarding the camp and learned that he had located a better situation for the brigade. Their new camp was much closer, spread between several farms on each side of the crossroads directly below the inn, where the lieutenant had secured shelter for both men and horses. Only one troop remained to be accommodated, and on learning of it, Wainwright offered the use of his barns and stables.

This had occasioned a studiedly casual conversation about the Rangers' commander. Having only met Andrews, the Wainwrights had assumed him to be in command of the brigade. On being informed otherwise, Wainwright insisted that both Carleton and Andrews lodge at the inn, a situation that was bound to be awkward, but could not be refused without arousing further suspicions.

Privately Tess reminded Elizabeth that she and Carleton must be more than discrete whenever they were together. But in her delight at the prospect of their being under the same roof, no matter how briefly, Elizabeth brushed her aunt's cautions aside.

That night Pete had taken it upon himself to accompany the lieutenant to the ferry to wait for the brigade's return. As the skies brightened he had hurried back to report that, although Carleton and Andrews had not yet arrived, he had left the first contingent of Rangers forming up on the Pennsylvania shore. Pete judged it would be at least an hour more before the brigade reached the new camp.

In spite of her aunt's and their hosts' protests, Elizabeth and Blue Sky had bundled up warmly and set out with Pete down the slope to the crossroads, determined to meet the Rangers on their return if they froze for it. And they had nearly done so. The relentless wind remained piercing, blowing icy rain before it, and although they were swathed to the eyes, the cold cut through the layers of clothing like a whip.

Tightening the reins to curb her restless mount, Elizabeth squinted against the sun to study a double file of horsemen just cresting the gentle rise to the northeast. For the better part of an hour the three of them had anxiously watched broken units, appearing hardly larger than black ants at that distance, straggle along the river valley from the direction of the upper ferries, heading toward the sprawling camps partly visible between breaks in the woods. With each new party that came into view, their hopes had been dashed as none had turned toward the inn. This time, however, the riders continued to move slowly westward, laboriously breaking through the ice-crusted snowdrifts that all but obscured McKonkey's Ferry Road.

Beside her, Blue Sky pointed, then clasped her hands and bounced in the saddle. "It is them!"

Elizabeth's heart lifted at sight of the Rangers' colors flying at the column's head. "I do believe you're right!" she exclaimed with relief, for a figure she was certain had to be Carleton led them.

PEERING THROUGH THE GLARE of the snow blanketing the river valley, Carleton scrubbed the rain from his face with his gloved hand. He was so fatigued that for a moment he feared the sight of the three figures riding toward him must be a hallucination. Yet they looked too solid to be a mirage.

As they drew nearer, surprise and pleasure surged through him. Pete and Blue Sky he identified at once, and on taking a closer look, he realized their companion must be Elizabeth. Garbed in men's clothing, she was swathed practically to the brim of her hat against the cold and unrecognizable to anyone but an informed observer as a woman. To him she appeared more beautiful than an angel.

Leaving his side, Andrews eagerly spurred his mount forward to join Blue Sky. She clasped his hand, her face glowing with glad welcome, while Pete urged his horse past them down the column to join his father's troop.

Conscious of the Rangers behind him with Smithson at their head, Carleton motioned the column to a halt, then rode forward, trailed by Red Fox and Spotted Pony. Emotion overcame him when he met Elizabeth's welcoming gaze, and he had to fight down a powerful impulse to throw caution aside and reach to capture her in his arms.

"You are well?" he said hoarsely, suddenly conscious of how he must look, unshaven and bedraggled as he was. His hat brim drooped, sodden, around his ears, and beneath the rain-weighted bearskin his damp buckskin hunting shirt, breeches, and boots were frozen stiff and spotted with blood and mire. His burning eyes and had to be red rimmed, his face colorless from the cold. Undoubtedly he appeared a veritable ghost.

If she noticed any deficiencies in his appearance, however, she showed no sign of it. Clearly struggling to stifle a joyful smile, she answered in a low voice, "I am now, sir, and I pray you are as well. The whole countryside has been aroused by the news that you've won a most notable victory."

"We took the garrison by complete surprise," Andrews replied, forcing a tired smile. "It was all over in little more than an hour, with only four of our men injured. The Hessians lost Colonel Rall as well as many more of their officers and the common ranks. Altogether we took almost 900 prisoners, not to mention artillery, ammunition, wagons, horses, weapons, and many other much-needed supplies."

"Don't forget the rum, Charles," Carleton broke in with a muffled laugh.

Andrew's grin broadened. "A number of the men had quite a celebration before the barrels could be staved in. They were strutting around ragged and shoeless but decked in the Hessians' brass caps, blowing their enemy's horns and shouting at the tops of their lungs."

Elizabeth laughed. "It must have been quite a sight."

Carleton couldn't turn his eyes from her, nor she from him. She bit her lip, searching his face intently.

"Mr. Wainwright begs that you and the troop that cannot be quartered at your new camp do him the honor of accepting the shelter of his barns and stables." When he started to protest, she pointed out quietly, "You're all soaked through, Jonathan. Those not already ill from exposure, soon will be. Your men need a hot fire, warm food, and a secure place to rest—and so do you and Charles. Pray accept the offer for their sake, if not for your own."

He knew she was right. It was all he could do to stay upright in the saddle. Weariness sapped his limbs of strength and slurred his speech. Glancing at Andrews and the two Shawnee, he saw they were in the same state.

The march back to the ferry and withdrawal across the icy Delaware had been worse, if possible, than the crossing Christmas night. Although the nor'easter had finally worn itself out, heavy rain had succeeded it. Then Knox had been determined to bring off all the captured artillery, which posed monumental difficulties for the gunners and further delayed the march.

To add to the misery, transporting a large body of prisoners back to the camps had turned into an ordeal for Americans and Hessians alike. By herculean effort, the army had finally reached the ferry landings, only to discover that the water had frozen well out from the river's banks. Although close to shore the ice was thick enough to bear a man's weight, farther out it gave way beneath them as they tried to cross to the boats, and many men were baptized in the freezing water before they got aboard. For men already suffering an extremity of fatigue and exposure, it had seemed an eternity in Purgatory.

"I don't know about you, Jon, but the rest of us can't take much more," Andrews intervened when Carleton hesitated. "A warm bed sounds like heaven."

Carleton frowned at Elizabeth. "If our identities become known and word reaches Howe that we were seen together—"

Keeping her expression neutral, she slanted a quick glance from him to Smithson several yards away and safely out of earshot, then back to Carleton. "The Wainwrights are also spies for the General, and their sons serve in the army. Regardless of any suspicions they may have, I'm assured they'll not betray us. At any rate, they know me as Charles's sister Jane, and Aunt Tess as our aunt Eliza Freeman. They know nothing of any other connection between us, and we'll take care to keep it so."

None of it made sense anymore. The loving light in her eyes and the seductive lure of a hot bath and a warm bed overcame Carleton's better judgment.

"I can't deny the men shelter after all they've been though," he conceded. "Very well, then. Lead on."

Elizabeth and Blue Sky rode ahead at a quick trot with Andrews and the two Shawnee warriors to announce the brigade's arrival, leaving Carleton to direct Smithson and the largest body of the Rangers to their new camp before riding to the inn at the head of Isaiah's troop. While the men headed to the stables with Wainwright, Elizabeth and Blue Sky ran into the inn, overcome with exuberance. They found Tess in the kitchen, visiting with Lydia and Chastity, who rushed to prepare a hearty breakfast.

When they entered, Tess immediately shooed them to the roaring blaze on the great hearth that took up most of the expansive room's rear wal, then helped them to quickly shed their damp outer wrappings and replace them with the clothing left folded on the settle for their return. Bustling by, Lydia eyed them with mild disapproval and clucked her tongue.

"Thou knowest the holy Scriptures forbid a woman to wear men's clothing, Jane."

"Now, Lydia," Tess protested with a smile as she secured the tapes of Elizabeth's petticoats, "the patriarchs lived in a much warmer clime. They had no acquaintance with nor'easters."

While Elizabeth shook out the folds of cloth over her breeches, Tess helped Blue Sky to slip a soft blue woolen shortgown on over her shift. "I know many women who wear breeches for traveling and also clothe their daughters so for warmth and modesty," she continued firmly. "I wear them myself when the occasion warrants, and I'm persuaded the Almighty takes no offense at his daughters' attempts to keep from freezing."

Lydia pursed her lips and shook her head. "My husband may not see it so, Eliza."

"What he doesn't see will cause him no distress," Tess returned primly.

Repressing a grin, Elizabeth donned the fine linen caraco and demure linen cap Tess had lent her. She turned her back to the door to undo her breeches beneath her petticoats, dropped them to the floor, and deftly stepped out of them. Blue Sky watched, smiling, then followed her example.

Fitted to Tess's more ample form, both garments hung loose on the younger women. Elizabeth tightened the caraco's lacings as far as they would go, then straightened her adoptive sister's shortgown and pinned it snugly down the front with straight pins. After returning the impulsive hug Blue Sky gave her, Elizabeth stepped back to survey the result.

"We're proper ladies now," she exclaimed, hands on hips. "No one shall have the least occasion to criticize our attire."

Her droll expression caused Blue Sky to giggle. Smiling, the young Shawnee matron settled on the hearthstone beside the fire and extended her chapped hands to the heat radiating from it.

Outside Elizabeth heard horsemen ride into the inn yard, Carleton calling a halt, then the muffled jingle of bridles, creak of leather, and snort of horses as the troop dismounted. It was all she could do not to run outside.

Drying her hands on her apron, Chastity went to the window and wiped clear a spot on a frosted pane. Her eyebrows rose in surprise.

"These Rangers are Negroes?"

"There's one black troop with General Carleton's brigade," Elizabeth answered, keeping her tone noncommittal, "which may be the reason they've not found accommodations elsewhere, sad to say."

Lydia joined Chastity at the window. "You may be right in that, and if so, 'tis a shame indeed. One would hope for greater hospitality for those who fight for our liberty. Hmm . . . they include Indians too, I see." She threw a guarded glance at Blue Sky.

"Oh," Chastity breathed, "the tall blond officer—he's General Carleton?"

Elizabeth bit her lip and pretended to study the leaping flames.

"That would be him," Tess said dryly.

"Bless me, he's considerably younger than I'd have expected him to be," Lydia exclaimed. "Do you know General Carleton well, my dear?" she asked Elizabeth.

Avoiding Tess's warning gaze, Elizabeth said with as much calmness as she was capable of, "We have met on occasion, but I know him only slightly."

"He's married?" Lydia persisted, her gaze growing shrewd.

Elizabeth took a deep breath. "Mmm . . . I've never heard either him or Charles refer to a Mrs. Carleton."

"He must be quite charming," Chastity murmured, her gaze fixed on the scene outside the window, her expression dreamy.

"Oh, indeed," Tess said, amusement tingeing her voice. "Charming is the perfect word."

While Chastity reluctantly retreated to the table to knead biscuit dough on the floured board, Lydia bustled about the kitchen with a satisfied air. "You never know what such connections may lead to for an unattached young lady as yourself, Jane. One should never dismiss such an excellent prospect." Smiling, she took a large meat fork from a peg on the wall. "I can't wait to meeting your charming general."

"He's not *my* general," Elizabeth objected stiffly, alarm rising in her breast. "We're barely acquainted."

"I'd make it my business to improve my acquaintance with such a handsome man were I in thy shoes," Chastity said directing her an arch look.

As the servant girl began to place pieces of dough into the cast-iron dutch oven, Lydia looked up from the sizzling ham she was tending. "Now pay attention to those biscuits, dear. I'll have nothing burnt. Everything's to be perfect for our guests, if you please. Oh, I do believe we shall have a most enjoyable visit!"

Elizabeth forced a smile and echoed weakly, "I'm sure we will."

Inwardly she cringed at the prospect. Their congenial hosts were already too interested in her and her aunt's personal affairs, and further complications were bound to arise on closer acquaintance. Perhaps Carleton had been right after all about the dangers of their lodging at the same place.

There was nothing to be done about it now, however. Glancing out the window, she saw that cooking fires already dotted paddock and barnyard. Wainwright and the men he employed were leading the horses into the stables, and she heard someone banging about in the cellar below—distributing provisions to Isaiah's troop, no doubt.

The sun was well up in the clearing sky by the time Andrews, trailed by his servant, Briggs, hastened into the parlor where the women waited. "Jane, you're looking extraordinarily well—now that I can actually see you!" he exclaimed, laughter dancing in his eyes. "You and my wife were bundled like gypsies."

He crossed the room to give Elizabeth a hearty embrace and followed it with a kiss for Tess. "And you're as fetching as usual, Aunt Eliza."

She harrumphed and pushed him toward Blue Sky. He took his beaming wife's hand and tucked it in the crook of his elbow with a warm smile before turning to greet Lydia.

Elizabeth heard the outer door open and the stamp of boots. She retreated to a seat in the farthest corner of the room and pretended extreme interest in a book she had borrowed from Wainwright the previous day.

In a moment their host ushered Carleton into the parlor and introduced him to his wife. As Carleton bowed, Elizabeth hazarded a brief glance, and her heart leaped. His presence seemed to fill the room, capturing everyone's attention like a magnet.

He had shed his hat and bearskin robe and was garbed only in a heavy, fringed buckskin hunting shirt, breeches, and knee-length boots, as was Andrews. That much was well enough, for hunting attire was common among the soldiers.

It was the shirt's exceptionally fine bead- and quillwork, the rich wampum sash that girdled Carleton's waist, the finely wrought silver necklace visible at the opening of his shirt, and the feathered tomahawk hanging from his belt that caused her stomach to clench.

Wainwright's speculations the night before the battle nagged at her. Surely these telling details, along with the fact that two imposing Shawnee warriors who bore themselves like nobility accompanied Carleton and that his subordinate officer was married to a strikingly beautiful young Shawnee woman, could not be lost on a man of Wainwright's keen intuition. All Carleton lacked was three snowy eagle feathers bound into his hair.

"I thank you for your hospitality," he was saying gruffly, his smile weary. "I'm afraid another hour out in this cold would have finished us."

"We're so pleased to have you both," Lydia returned, her tone warm, though she looked somewhat taken aback as she scrutinized him.

Wainwright turned to Elizabeth and Tess. "You've met Jonathan, I believe."

It was clear Carleton wished to avoid Elizabeth's gaze as much as she did his. Keeping her eyes on the floor, she rose and sketched a curtsey, which Tess echoed across the room, while he returned a stiff bow.

"Indeed we have. Good day, sir." It was an effort to say that much.

"I hope you are well, Miss . . . Andrews." He nodded to Tess. "Miss Freeman."

She felt unaccountably breathless and prayed their hosts noticed nothing amiss. Carleton's pause before speaking her assumed name had been barely perceptible, but Elizabeth was all too aware of the piercing glance Wainwright directed between the two of them. She detected the same reserve in Carleton as he deliberately turned his back to speak to the others.

THE MONOTONOUS TICKING of the case clock was going to drive her mad, Elizabeth decided. She curled her toes in her shoes and bit down hard on her lower lip to stifle a cry of frustration. The consciousness of Wainwright seated across the room quietly reading and Tess at the secretary writing a letter, while Lydia and Chastity bent over their sewing by the fire, grated on her nerves.

It was evident the servant girl was much taken with Carleton, though he had paid her scant attention beyond the graceful courtesy he extended to everyone. Her wide-eyed gaze fixed on him, Chastity had blushed at his casual notice and bobbed a curtsey, eliciting a frown from her mistress, who had sent her scurrying from the room, cheeks flaming, with a sharp "Enough of your airs, child. Go see to the officers' bath."

Elizabeth wanted nothing more than to be alone, but there was no place to go but upstairs, and Tess had strongly cautioned her to keep as much distance between her and Carleton as possible. That the room where he slept was down the passage just beyond theirs offered temptation difficult to resist.

Frowning, she pretended rapt interest in her borrowed book: the first volume of British historian Edward Gibbon's *History of the Decline and Fall of the Roman Empire,* published the previous year. It was soon to be followed by more volumes, and from what she had read so far, she had already determined to write to her father in London as soon as possible, requesting that he send each one the moment it was available.

The previous day, whiling away the hours until Carleton's return, she been fascinated by Gibbon's analysis of Rome's rise from a republic to an empire, and its subsequent fall due to the inevitable corruption of the civic virtues Gibbon maintained had led to its rise. Wainwright had compared Rome's history to the colonies' struggle to establish a new nation independent from England, filling her mind with both excitement and doubt. This afternoon, however, more immediate concerns blurred the words before her eyes.

After washing off the grime of battle, Carleton and Andrews had devoured the breakfast set before them, then, hardly able to stay awake a moment longer, retired upstairs to the rooms prepared for them. With eyes for no one but Andrews, Blue Sky had accompanied him, and Elizabeth had enviously watched the couple climb the stairs arm in arm.

How dearly she longed to lie at Carleton's side—to have the right to do so. Yet she had begun to doubt they would ever be so blessed.

A yawn overtook her, and she laid down her book. Rising, she stretched, ignoring Tess's glance.

"I must apologize for deserting you. I'm afraid I'm in dire need of a nap."

Lydia clucked her tongue. "I'm not surprised, as early as you rose this morning."

"I hardly slept at all last night for worrying about Charles."

Wainwright lifted his head from his book, his look penetrating, though he said nothing.

Tess blotted her letter, then folded it. "I believe I'll go with you. I had a restless night as well, and I'm about to fall off my chair." With a laugh, she rose and came to Elizabeth's side, adding firmly, "It'll do us both good to rest until dinner."

Elizabeth kept her eyes downcast to conceal her annoyance. Her aunt knew her all too well. With an inward sigh, she led the way upstairs.

THE SIBILANT HISS OF THE WIND jarred Carleton awake. Groggy, his limbs leaden, he jerked upright, oppressed by the same undefined sense of foreboding he had felt at the beginning of the march to Trenton.

Disoriented, he rubbed his eyes, then glanced warily around him. The hour following his arrival at the inn remained a blur. Drugged by exhaustion, he had taken little note of his surroundings, and it required a moment for him to remember where he was.

The sun must already have set, for the room was dark. Evidently he had slept all day.

Long unused to the softness of the white man's bed, he had pulled the covers onto the floor and collapsed onto them. Now he became aware that a chill draft seeped across the floor's planks and through the blankets that wrapped him.

Faint light filtering around the edges of the shutters provided the room's only illumination. When his eyes adjusted to it, he threw aside the blankets, rose, and padded barefoot to the window. Pushing open the shutters, he stared at the windbreak of tall pines that enclosed the inn yard, wrapped in the shadows of twilight.

During the attack on Trenton, the howl of the gale and the thunder of battle had damped all other sound. But now that both had ceased, the restless soughing of the trees and their cold, sharp scent that crept through the window's cracks pressed into his senses.

Behind him he heard the door creak open and someone enter, but found himself powerless to turn. Transfixed, he stared at the seething pines outside the glass, every sense heightened, held in thrall by the long-repressed memory that now rose stark before his mind's eye, as vivid as though he were again, as on that night, a small child lost and trembling amid the black pines of Scotland.

"Jonathan . . . what is it?"

He felt her hand on his arm and glanced down at Elizabeth, then back to the pines, only vaguely registering the distress in her eyes. The devastating sense of abandonment and worthlessness that had plagued him so often over the years paralyzed him again, blotting out, as black clouds snuff out the sun, every slender ray of hope he fought to cling to in his better moments.

The emotion must have been evident in his face for she pleaded, "Tell me." When he did not answer, she said, "If we are ever to be husband and wife, we must entrust all of ourselves to each other, good and bad."

Unable to look at her, he took a shaking breath, let it out, finally forced himself to speak. "I'd just turned three. We were at Stoughton Hall that winter—Lord Oliver, my mother . . . and Edward."

HE STARED INTO THE DARKNESS with rapidly mounting apprehension. Terror clogged his throat and constricted his lungs, squeezing the breath out of him. On all sides the spectral pines seethed, lashing the darkly clouded sky overhead, their eerie moan deepening with the rising gale.

He could not still his shaking. His thin nightshirt was drenched with the icy sleet that pelted him, burning like fire.

He pressed his small fist to his trembling lips and glanced around, fighting back tears. "Eddie," he quavered, too frightened to cry out. "Eddie, where are you? Please come—I don't want to play anymore."

For long moments he strained to hear his elder half-brother's voice, but only the rushing hiss of the pines broke the silence. The howl of wolves drawing rapidly closer crushed the last hope that his brother was still nearby, that Edward would come for him after all. With a strangled cry he turned and fled, sobbing, not knowing whether his path led back toward the Hall or deeper into the forest.

"Papa! Papa!"

Suddenly his bare foot slipped on the rocky, snow-drifted path, and he sprawled headlong across the ground, scraping his hands and knees and banging his head hard. Brilliant lights exploded in his brain. He curled up into a ball, eyes tightly closed, arms clutched over his head against the pain, cold, and fear.

"YOU DIDN'T BREAK ME," he whispered, his breath fogging the glass. "All you did was make me stronger." He didn't know whether he spoke of Edward or of the years that had followed.

He became aware that Elizabeth held him, her head pressed against his shoulder. Drawing her into a tight embrace, he laid his cheek against the crown of her head, gratitude at her nearness so intense it burned in his bones.

"I prayed the weather would keep you here until we got back."

She gave a muffled laugh. "So did I. It seems for once our plea was answered."

She slipped out from under his arm and brought a blanket to wrap around him. He drew it over his shoulders, then pulled her against him under its folds.

"You slept on the floor," she chided.

He shrugged. "I've grown unused to a soft bed."

"You and Blue Sky," she teased.

Cupping her head in his hands, he buried his fingers in her hair and lifted her face to his kiss. Her passionate response and the sweetness of her lips drove away consciousness of all else and kindled in him a fire that came far too close to breaking down his control. When at last he forced himself reluctantly to release her, he could read the pain in her eyes even in the shadowed room.

She touched his lips with her fingertips. "I don't want you to stop," she whispered, her voice breaking. "Not ever."

"Nor do I."

For some moments neither spoke. At last she gave a painful shrug and said abruptly, "How could your brother have left you out in a storm when you were so little? Was he always so beastly to you?"

With a harsh laugh, he said, "Oh, he fawned over me when Lord Oliver and my mother were around. When we were alone, it was quite a different story. I suppose he hated me from my birth—though how he conceived I was a threat to him, I can't imagine. As Lord Oliver's elder son, he stood to inherit not only his title, but also by far the greater part of our father's estate. But from my later acquaintance with him, I came to believe him capable of any evil for its own sake."

She pulled back and studied him earnestly, her face pale in the chamber's gloom. "You were the son of the young wife your father adored, while his marriage to Edward's mother had been one of convenience only. Edward must have resented that and, believing that Lord Oliver favored you, feared he would disinherit him for your sake."

Carleton made a dismissive gesture. "That's well nigh impossible under English law. And if Lord Oliver favored me, he had a curious way of showing it."

She hesitated, then asked, "What happened after you fell? Did you find your way back home or did someone come to find you?"

He stared out the window. "I thought I heard wolves, but it turned out to be the baying of Lord Oliver's hounds. I was terrified they'd tear me apart, but they only licked me. Then he gathered me in his arms and carried me back to the Hall wrapped in his coat."

"He must have discovered you gone and come right away to find you. I can't imagine what a father's heart must feel on discovering his little son missing in the night. Thank God he wasted no time and you weren't out in the storm so long you perished." When he made no response, she said, "Did he reprimand Edward?"

"I've no idea what passed between them," he said gruffly. "He took me immediately to the nursery, where I lay ill with a fever for some days. My mother had been confined to her bed for months, so she couldn't come to me, and Lord Oliver came only once that I remember. When I recovered, I saw no evidence that anything had changed . . . except that he'd hired a new nurse and arranged to send me with her to Virginia, to Sir Harry. I was taken away within a fortnight."

She pressed her hand to her breast. "He gave no explanation?"

"The day he sent me away, he held me on his lap and told me I must be Sir Harry's son now. I didn't understand what he meant."

She bit her lip. "Oh, Jonathan. He told you nothing more than that?"

Releasing her, he crossed the room and squatted to pull a glowing ember from the hearth with the tongs, then rose and went to light the small betty lamp on the washstand. A wavering flame flared, faintly illuminating the chamber.

Staring down at it, he said, "I promised I'd not be naughty anymore and kept pleading with him to not send me away. But he'd not listen. And one day he put me into a carriage with that detestable woman who took me away to a ship . . . " He clenched his teeth.

"But you'd done nothing wrong!"

He straightened and glanced over at her. "No doubt Lord Oliver blamed me for what happened—and for all the times Edward tormented me until I cried or misbehaved. So you see, he didn't favor me at all. He was a powerful man with important concerns, and the woman he loved was dying. He'd no time or inclination to deal with a troublesome little boy. I've made my peace with that."

She sank into a chair. "And so he sent you far away across the ocean to a man you'd never met." For some moments she was silent, then she said, "I wonder if there's not more—"

He came to bend over her and with a smile gently touched his finger to her lips to stop the words. "There's nothing to wonder about, dear heart. I haven't thought of it since I was very little, and I've no idea why it occurred to me now. The strain of these past weeks must have dredged it up at random. It's of no importance, I assure you."

She searched his face. "I know you loved Sir Harry. He was a good father to you, was he not?"

"I couldn't have asked for a better one," Carleton said softly. "And Black Hawk as well. I've been greatly blessed in the men who stood in the place of father to me when my sire could not—or would not."

"Had Sir Harry not adopted you, you'd have had hardly any inheritance at all. Surely that formed a large part of Lord Oliver's motive."

He regarded her steadily, keeping his expression impassive. "As I said, I've been blessed. I've no reason to feel that I was wronged in any way."

"And yet there are times when you do." She said it gently, her eyes probing his with sympathy and concern.

He grimaced and took her hand to draw her to her feet. "I'm a most tedious subject for discussion. I'd much rather talk about you."

She gave a light laugh and tiptoed to receive his kiss. "I, sir, am an open book."

The corners of is mouth tugged into a smile, and he raised an eyebrow. "You are the most mysterious of that confusing species called woman, my love. But beware. I've made up my mind to devote the rest of my life to ferreting out all the charming secrets you harbor in that lovely head of yours."

Gazing deeply into his eyes, she answered with a smile, "Then be warned that I shall devote the rest of my life to keeping you ever intrigued so you'll not grow tired of me."

Sobering, he drew her into his embrace. "That's one thing you need never worry about."

After a moment he released her and said gruffly, "I've slept longer than I intended. What time is it?"

"Almost dinnertime. Tess and I were resting in our room, and I woke when she went downstairs. Then I heard you stir and thought I'd check on you while no one else is about."

"Is Charles awake?"

"I am." Standing in the doorway, Andrews spoke in a low voice. "A messenger just arrived. The General has called a council of war for tonight. All the general officers are to meet at seven o'clock for dinner at his headquarters in Newtown—the Widow Harris's house, I'm told."

Giving him a keen look, Carleton went to fetch his boots, renewed energy flooding through him. "I'll have to leave at once, then."

"Beth, you'd better come away," Andrews warned, throwing a wary glance over his shoulder. "If the two of you are discovered—"

Carleton waved him off. "You and Tess will have to keep everyone occupied downstairs," he growled. "Beth and I have had precious little time together. I mean to take advantage of every second."

Blushing, Elizabeth shot him a grateful look. Andrews cocked his ear to the distant sound of voices that filtered up from below, then nodded, frowning.

"Keep it short." He eased the door closed behind him, and they heard his footfalls retreat down the stairs.

Rummaging through his pack to find clean clothing, Carleton said, "I suspect Washington is bent on crossing into New Jersey again. It didn't set well with him that we were unable to follow up our victory with an attack on Princeton."

Elizabeth's mouth dropped open, and she stared at him in astonishment. "How can anyone even consider another attack?" she gasped, careful to keep her voice muffled. "The men are worn out—you're worn out. You've won a great victory, and if you fail in another attempt, we'll lose everything gained and more. The news is already spreading like wildfire, and by now Howe will have been alerted. He'll not likely sit still—"

"Knowing Howe, it'll take a week for him to mount a move against us." He straightened and folded his arms across his chest, regarding her with a faint half-smile. "Personally, I wouldn't let such an opportunity go by."

She bit her lip. "The opportunity to do more killing, you mean. The horrors I saw at Breed's Hill and on Long Island fair persuaded me that war is a recourse to be resorted to only at the last extremity."

His face grim, he cut her off. "War is death and destruction, Beth. That's the purpose of it. And once a conflict is engaged, it unfolds along its individual course, no matter what's been planned. What's that old saying? No battle plan survives contact with the enemy."

He leaned toward her, the line of this body taut, his voice thick. "I'm sorry you had to see what you did. No woman should ever have to. But I'll wager the raids I led among the Shawnee were more bloody than any battles you've experienced. I believed I could command my warriors, but in spite of all my efforts there was no way I could completely control Wolfslayer. And I did try, believe me. I abhorred what he did. It tore my soul apart.

"But so it is. War, once begun, assumes a life of its own. When you unleash the Furies, they bring hell in their wake. Our Lord said that before he goes to war a wise king first counts the cost to see whether he has the resources to win or whether he'll end up suing for terms of peace. At least one side in this conflict had better have counted the cost or in the end neither side will win."

She stared at him, nonplussed. "Jonathan, I fear for all of us."

He went to gather her in his arms. "In that you're not alone."

As she turned her face up to him expectantly, he released her and stepped away. "I'd better go at once if I'm to be at the Widow Harris's in time." Seeing the disappointment come into her eyes, he added, "Can you wait for my return without the others knowing? It'll likely be late."

"Once I'm sure everyone's asleep I'll come down and wait for you in the kitchen."

He nodded, but avoided her searching gaze. "Stay in your room for a few minutes before you follow me." He spoke tersely, and without waiting for her response or glancing back, strode into the passageway and down the stairs.

Chapter Six

WASHINGTON MET THE GAZE of each of his officers in turn. "Earlier this evening I received a communication from General Cadwalader. As we supposed, he was indeed hindered from crossing the Delaware the other night because of the ice. But believing the main column still to be at Trenton, he succeeded in crossing the river early this morning with eighteen hundred men."

Carleton frowned, but said nothing as Washington raised his hand to still the murmurs that rose around the table. Taking up the letter that lay open in front of him, he put on his glasses and studied it.

"He and his men are currently in Burlington. He assures me that the enemy are in a panic, that they have fled with great precipitation as far as Amboy. He advises that we pursue them in order to keep up this panic and writes, 'If we can drive them from West Jersey, the success will raise an army by next spring and establish the credit of the continental money to support it.' "

"You propose to immediately open another campaign when the men are completely fatigued from their efforts to gain this hard-won victory through a storm the likes of which few of us have ever experienced?" demanded Sullivan.

"I am laying the matter before you, gentlemen," Washington responded, unruffled.

"They went through hell to beat the Hessians!" St. Clair objected. "How can we ask our men to endure still more suffering before they've even had a chance to recover from their efforts and bask for a moment in their glory?"

"They've tasted victory, and it has enheartened them," Carleton broke in. "When men's hearts are in a task and they have the Almighty to uphold them, they'll accomplish more than is humanly possible."

Mercer shook his head, his expression dubious. "I can't dispute that, but we also have to be practical. We outnumbered the garrison at Trenton and had the element of surprise in our favor. There's no doubt that gained us the victory. We can't count on that this time. By now Howe has heard the news. He'll undoubtedly come against us with every man at his disposal, while we have many enlistments expiring—"

"It is my opinion that orders be sent to Colonel Cadwalader at once calling him to return to camp immediately before he touches off a chain of events that will ruin us," Fermoy put in forcefully. "The army is in a very vulnerable case, and we cannot afford to take further risks."

With difficulty, Carleton bit back a caustic response.

"I agree." Eyes narrowed and fixed on Washington, Stephen growled, "We'd be fools to discount von Donop's force, which is somewhere out there—God only knows where. Then there's General Leslie at Princeton with his garrison of five thousand crack Redcoats and Hessians who'll have to be reckoned with. Either of them might be on the march to Trenton this very instant—"

"They are not," Washington snapped, his tone steely, not sparing Stephen a glance.

Greene leaned forward, his forearms braced against the table. "Who could conceive that this ragtag army of ours would attempt such a feat a second time, within days of the first? Your own arguments against it are the very arguments the British will use to justify staying snug in their beds."

"And that is where I wish to be," St. Clair grumbled, smiling ruefully at the chuckles his words elicited. "The last thing I look forward to is another campaign such as that just past. I can't conceive how my men could bear it."

Again Washington raised his hand to still the hubbub of voices raised in agreement. "You all know that, as General Mercer mentioned, the enlistments of a majority of the army's most experienced troops expire on December thirty-one, just four days from now. If they all choose to go home, only Cadwalader's militia and a few Continentals from the Virginia brigades will be left. The British will be able to crush us like an empty eggshell."

In the silence that followed, Greene said, "Following up one victory with the chance at another might not only persuade most of the men to stay, at least until the new levies can come in, but might also turn the tide of public opinion completely against the British and finally bring us the open support of France and Spain."

Certain Greene spoke for his commander, Carleton assessed the expressions of those who had voiced strong opposition to the move. Increasingly faces were softening, and he sensed a change in the room's atmosphere.

"Considering the condition of the men and the weather, I cannot advise another campaign so close on the heels of the last," Stark rumbled grudgingly, "but . . . if the decision is in favor of it, then we all ought to support it."

Washington glanced around the table. "Cadwalader holds the ground. His intelligence tells him that the British are in disarray—for the moment."

"An opportunity stands before us as it did at Trenton," Knox rasped, "and we're fools if we don't seize it. It's the bold who turn the tide of history."

"I say we roll the dice. My Rangers stand ready, sir."

Stirling had not been present at dinner, arriving just moments before the meeting. Clearly ill, his face haggard, hands shaking, he met Carleton's gaze with a firm one before turning to the others.

"You have my apologies that I shall be unable to personally participate if the decision is made in favor of this move," he said, his voice quavering. "But my brigade is at your disposal, Your Excellency. If my vote is of any consequence, I agree with General Carleton." A brief smile passed over his grey countenance. "I've not always had luck with the roll of the dice, but I like the odds for this one."

Glover thoughtfully drummed his fingers on the table. "A bold stroke might liberate much of New Jersey. It'd certainly demonstrate that our victory at Trenton wasn't a fluke."

"If we are to act, we must do so immediately, before the enlistments expire and while our enemy is still off balance." Washington glanced from Carleton to Glover. "Can your men manage another crossing?"

"They'd ship heaven to hell if they thought it worth doing, Your Excellency," Glover growled, "but most of them will be at liberty on New Year's Day. And almost to a man they're determined to return to Marblehead and take up privateering. Large fortunes are being made, and for all my cajoling, they're bent on reclaiming what they've sacrificed thus far."

Washington sighed and ran his fingers through his hair. "I cannot blame them for that. All our troops have done more than should be asked of any man. But I know not how to spare them. Can they not be persuaded to delay their departure a little longer?"

Glover hesitated. "I can't vouch for it, but I'll do everything I can to sway them."

"That's all I can ask—of all of you. For all else, we must trust in that great Providence that has so graciously overseen our efforts to this day."

All opposition now collapsed, and the decision was quickly made to cross the Delaware and invest Trenton the instant men and supplies could be readied. By the time the meeting ended shortly past midnight, Carleton had his orders. He wasted no time heading back to the inn.

The case clock in the parlor solemnly tolled once. Wrapped in a blanket, curled up on the settle in the kitchen next to the banked fire, Elizabeth roused at the flurry of approaching hoofbeats. Instead of retreating toward the stable, they slowed and stopped directly outside.

Filled with trepidation she ran to the rear door, careful to make no sound that might awaken the inn's sleeping occupants. She could hear muffled voices, then a horse being led off. This was followed by footfalls rapidly mounting the steps, and she eased the door open, wincing at its muted creak.

Carleton slipped noiselessly inside and threw a swift glance around to make sure they were alone before pushing the door shut behind him. She clutched his arm. His clothing and skin were icy from the long, swift ride through the night, and she drew him into the kitchen and to the hearth.

Dropping his cold-stiffened bearskin and hat on the hearthstone, he took her blanket and wrapped it around her shoulders. Gently, but firmly, he seated her on the settle, then removed his gloves and squatted in front of the fire. A sharp pang of disappointment cut through her. She watched him uncover the embers with the poker and lay kindling on them. When a small blaze leaped up, he stretched his hands out to its warmth.

She wanted him to hold her so desperately in that moment that she would not have cared if Wainwright or even Howe had materialized out of the darkness. But he seemed once again, as so often since she had found him among the Shawnee, inaccessibly remote.

At length he looked up, his face pale and tense in the fire's glow. Although he did not move closer, his unwavering gaze was so intense she felt his desire scorch her.

"By God, I love you, Beth," he said in a low groan. "I told myself I could do this, but every time we're together, my resolution weakens still more."

She fought back the tears that welled up. "You're stronger than I, for I have no resolution left."

He drew in a shaky breath. "It's torture having to hide my love from others or appear so cold to you when we're in company. But it's even worse when we're alone. All I can think of is snatching you up and bearing you far away where we need pretend no longer."

He returned his gaze to the flames. "In truth, it isn't strength that stays me, but weakness. If I were to touch you now, I fear I couldn't hold back."

"I thought my heart would break when you came in this morning. I was afraid to look at you for fear I'd give all away. And when you left me this evening—" Undone, she covered her face with her hands.

The silence echoed in the room. From the parlor, she heard the clock lightly chime the first quarter as though marking the precious time that inexorably fled from them with each passing moment.

"Our only recourse is to keep our distance," he said at length. "I've sworn I'll not drag you into sin and lose God's blessing on our union. And I will not."

Suddenly feeling God's protective love surround her, she smiled through tears, a deep warmth suffusing her at the certainty that her too often wayward heart could safely shelter in the steadiness of the man to whom God had entrusted her. For a moment the ache in her heart eased.

Again it was borne upon her, as it had been among the Shawnee on the night of Blue Sky and Andrews's wedding, that she had no less responsibility than Carleton. He also was human, thus vulnerable, and to tempt him beyond his power to resist would be both foolish and wrong.

"He's blessed me already in your love," she murmured. "I'm thankful, truly, just to have you near, to know that you're alive and well and that you love me."

The light in his eyes sent a thrill through her veins that very nearly left her undone once more. "Jeremiah lent me his Bible," she added hastily. "This morning after you'd gone to bed I was reading in the book of James where he writes, 'The trying of our faith worketh patience—' "

" ' . . . that we may be perfect and entire, wanting nothing,' " he quoted from memory. The corners of his mouth drew into a reluctant smile, and she saw the heave of his chest as he drew in a deep breath and let it out. "There've been many times when I clung to that promise."

"Yet how I do not wish to have patience!" she burst out, then gave a rueful laugh.

"Nor I," he admitted, his tone wry.

From the pocket inside her petticoat, she pulled out two small, thick, leather-bound volumes. "Mr. Wainwright gave these to Tess and me at dinner, saying he always keeps several Bibles on hand to give away. He wondered whether you and Charles might like to have them."

Eagerly Carleton took one of the Bibles and for some moments silently paged through it, stopping now and then to read a passage, finally looked up, smiling. She handed him the other also, and he tucked both into the pouch that hung from his belt.

"I've had to rely on memory for so long, but now I'll be able to read these words to Red Fox and the others. I know Charles will be delighted too. We'll thank Wainwright before we leave."

For long moments studied her face as though he would memorize it. "We're to occupy Trenton," he said at last. "From there we'll move against Princeton if it seems practicable, perhaps even against Brunswick to capture the British stores there if the men can bear it."

She bit her lip. "How soon?"

"The main columns are to cross Sunday. There's much to be done to prepare, and the men must have a few days' rest if we're to have any chance of success."

"But so many enlistments are up at the end of the month!"

"Washington hopes the promise of another victory may yet persuade the majority to stay, at least until the new levies come in."

"But if they don't—" She broke off, then said urgently, "Howe will come against us with every man he can muster now. We've challenged him, made him look the fool, and he'll move heaven and earth to crush us."

He gave her a grim look. "Believe me, we're under no illusions."

She clasped her hands tightly in her lap. "You're leaving right away," she guessed.

"Cadwalader's force is already in New Jersey, and I'm to establish contact with him as soon as possible. Howe will doubtless act as swiftly as the British are capable of—which is to say, we'll have time to put together a proper welcoming party. It's likely we won't return here so I'm taking my entire brigade, along with all our baggage."

He rose and glanced toward the doorway into the back passageway. "Is Charles still up?"

"He gave up waiting and went to bed a little before midnight. He asked me to have you wake him if he's needed."

"He'll have to carry orders to Smithson while Isaiah readies his troop to move out."

She stood and caught his arm. "Let me go with you this time. Please, Jonathan! I'll be careful, I promise. I cannot bear to stay behind again. Every time you ride away from me, I think the pain cannot grow worse. And each time it does."

He engulfed her in his embrace. This time his mouth found hers, and for heart-pounding moments they clung to each other, passion and fear washing over them in equal measure.

When at last he drew back, her tears spilled. He brushed them gently away and bent to look into her face, murmuring, "Don't cry, dear heart. It turns out I do need you to go with me this time. Washington is sending messages to all his field officers to summon the militias in their area. He asked me to send a messenger to Morristown with orders for General Lincoln to raise the militia of North Jersey and to harass the enemy's flanks and rear—"

"I'll do anything you ask!"

He smiled deeply into her eyes. "I know you will." Straightening, he continued briskly, "I want you to take Blue Sky with you and stay at Morristown until I send further instructions. Pete and Briggs will go along to keep you out of trouble."

"I can't vouch that they won't be persuaded to join in mischief," she teased.

He grinned. "I'll have a stern talk with them to forestall that possibility." Sobering, he directed a cautious look toward the door. "Tell the Wainwrights only that the army is going to be on the move and that the three of you women are returning to Philadelphia. In reality, you and Blue Sky will accompany my Rangers across the Delaware, then travel as fast as possible to Morristown. I've arranged for Tess to stay with the family of one of the local militia officers until we see how things develop. As soon as it's safe for her to travel to Morristown, I'll send her there as well."

"After such an inglorious defeat perhaps the British will see they can never win this fight and will simply go home," she ventured, her tone wistful.

He snorted. "Considering how often and how badly they've defeated us so far, they aren't likely to give up after one victory on our part, which they must consider merely a failure of intelligence and of this particular commander. However, it'll serve our purposes to have the enemy underestimate us—as long as we take advantage of it."

The soft creak of a floorboard from the direction of the passage brought them sharply around. Stepping apart, for a long moment each stood suspended, straining to catch any further sound.

The noise was not repeated, however, and they could discern no movement in the shadows. With his finger to his lips, Carleton motioned her to stay still and stole to the doorway. When she saw his shadowed form relax, she went to him, and he gathered her protectively against him.

"I know you to well enough not to send you off without your promise to stay in Morristown until you receive further orders from me." Although he smiled, his look was stern. "Give me your word that you and Blue Sky will not stir until I come or summon you."

"But—"

"Your word. If I don't have it, you'll stay here where you're safe."

She let out a sigh. "You have my word."

Clearly relieved, he cupped her face in his hands and bent to give her a slow, lingering kiss before drawing her with him down the passage to the narrow back stairway.

As they crept by the small room under the stairs where Chastity slept, Elizabeth's eyes were drawn to the closed door. No light showed beneath it, however, and only the muted sigh of the wind disturbed the silence. Dismissing her fears, she followed him stealthily up the stairs.

Chapter Seven

CARLETON RUBBED HIS BURNING EYES, then glared at Elizabeth. He was filthy, stained with sweat and splattered with mud and gore, some of it his own from several minor wounds that stung and throbbed.

The main column's second crossing of the Delaware had been even worse than the first. Three consecutive days of warmer weather had melted the snow, leaving the swollen Delaware and its tributaries turbulent and the roads bogged thigh high in mud. It had taken two days and the most strenuous efforts of everyone in the corps to get men, artillery, and baggage across, and then disposed in camps around Trenton.

This had been followed by two stress-filled days of anxious suspense while scouts and spies roamed abroad to determine when and where the British would attack, and then yet two additional days of a sapping, continuous running battle without rest or sleep. Carleton was ready to drop and in no mood for any opposition.

"Did I not command you to wait at Morristown until you received further orders?"

Elizabeth appeared undaunted by his scowl, while Blue Sky merely smiled. "We hear of big victory and—"

For the first time the young Shawnee matron spoke confidently in English, and in spite of his annoyance, Carleton felt a twinge of pleasure, which Andrews, at her side, clearly shared.

Refusing to soften his look or tone, Carleton growled, "It was no victory. We fought Cornwallis to a draw, nothing more."

At Blue Sky's puzzled frown, he repeated his words in Shawnee.

Settling her weather-beaten hat over her wig more securely, Elizabeth said, "A draw against the British counts as a victory for our side."

Andrews grinned his approval. "Just so."

Pete and Briggs murmured their agreement as well, while Red Fox and Spotted Pony exchanged amused glances. "When Long Knives fight . . . like Shawnee," Spotted Pony said in halting English, "they overcome British."

Quickly suppressing an unwilling smile with a scowl, Carleton returned his gaze to Elizabeth. "Nevertheless, you broke your word and disobeyed my orders. Were you a soldier, I'd demote you." Nodding toward Pete and Briggs, he added, "And did I not know you to be the ringleader, your compatriots would suffer the consequences as well."

"It was my decision, Jonathan. They weren't at fault. I waited until we received word of your success before leaving, and they merely refused to allow me to travel alone, a decision I believe you would have approved." Raising her chin to meet his challenging gaze, Elizabeth appealed, "Would you deny me the right to greet you after such a feat and confirm with my own eyes that you are well—and my sister to join her husband?"

While they were speaking, Stern materialized out of the deep shadows the buildings on either side cast across the street and came to join them. "Don't you know by now that you're wasting your breath, Jon? I've never won an argument with my niece, and it's not likely you will either."

Andrews guffawed. "I'm delighted to have my wife back with me, Jon. Nor do I credit that you'd really prefer that Beth still languished in Morristown."

Relaxing his stance, Carleton turned partially away to survey the winding streets of Somerset Court House, with its rustic houses and quaint courthouse that hugged the banks of the Millstone River. Watching Elizabeth ride away with Pete, Briggs, and Blue Sky the morning after they crossed the Delaware ahead of Washington's main force had been wrenching. Carleton had not rested easy until he received her message that they had reached Morristown safely. Relieved of concern for her, the last thing he had expected after leading his battle-weary Rangers up from the crossroads at Kingston was to encounter her and her companions riding down the street toward them.

It was now dusk, and although the sky was clear, it promised to be as dark as it had providentially been the previous night when Washington's army had stealthily crept out of their lines at Trenton and around the British flank to attack Princeton. The small village where they had sought refuge after the bitter clash that resulted was entirely overrun by Washington's tattered, spent force and the long line of prisoners and camp followers, artillery, wagonloads of supplies, and herds of livestock that encumbered it.

An hour earlier a unit of New Jersey militia had come upon the long, slow-moving baggage train of the fleeing British Fourth Brigade, but had shied from engaging its guards, to Washington's fury. Consequently, with the prisoners by necessity confined in the courthouse, the soldiers had no choice but to camp in the open, most without tents or other covering that might have been captured. The broken units that continued to straggle in simply joined those clustered around the smoky bonfires that dotted the town and its environs or simply dropped in their tracks where they stood and fell asleep on the frozen ground.

After a moment, he laughed ruefully and turned back, hands raised in a gesture of defeat. "It seems my prowess on the battlefield is greater than my ability to persuade a woman to heed me."

Stern pulled off his cocked hat. "I'll wager there are more than few men who share your sentiments," he said with a broad grin. Absently he ran his fingers through his curly hair. "My regiment is bedding down under every bush, tree, and hedgerow they can find. Have your Rangers been disposed in reasonable comfort?"

"Most of them," Andrews answered. "We're waiting for Isaiah's troop to arrive with confirmation that Cornwallis's column did indeed break off the pursuit at Kingston. We were able to secure an excellent camp on the north side of the town before anyone else got there, and while we were looking for accommodations for ourselves, we chanced across these wandering travelers." He waved his hand in the direction of Elizabeth, Blue Sky, and the two men who accompanied them.

"The only place I've been able to find with any room left at all is a house on the next street," Stern told them. "It's overflowing with officers, but I managed to commandeer the kitchen, which should have place enough for all of us. Levi's standing guard with weapons at the ready to ward off any intruders. If you don't mind sleeping on the floor, you'll at least have a roof over your head for the night."

Carleton grimaced. "Lead us to it. At this point, I'd sleep under a hedgerow if nothing else presented itself."

Hearing the slow plop of hoofs, he turned to squint at the black silhouettes of a line of horsemen approaching through the gathering darkness, the riders sagging in their saddles. Coming abreast, their leader pulled up and saluted him.

"Cornwallis's men cleared Kingston on the road to Burlington, sir," Isaiah reported, his words slurred with weariness. "We wait long enough to make sure they don't send out any detachments after us. All's quiet for now."

Thanking him, Carleton directed him down the street to the Rangers' camp. Saluting again, Isaiah motioned is troop forward, and in moments they melted into the darkness.

❋ ❋ ❋

HEAD BENT, ELIZABETH CONCENTRATED on gently sponging away the dried blood from shallow wounds on Carleton's arm and shoulder and a raw scrape on his hand. Thankfully none was deep enough to require stitches. She wrung out the cloth in the basin on the table, then spread a healing salve on the wounds, taking care to cause as little discomfort as possible.

Seated beside her on a bench at the table in front of the kitchen's immense hearth, he did not flinch. The dying fire's fitful glow burnished the hard-muscled contours of his arms and chest as he leaned against the table's board, head drooping, eyes closed, seeming hardly aware of her ministrations.

The fire flared suddenly, casting flickering bars of light and shadow across the finely modeled planes of his face. She studied him earnestly, her heart contracting at the strain and exhaustion that etched his features more deeply even than at the army's first return from Trenton.

Impulsively she reached to brush back the golden strands fallen loose from the ribbon that held his hair at the nape of his neck. Starting, he opened his eyes, and as his gaze met hers his mouth tugged into a slow smile that sent a thrill through her veins.

"It seems I shall always be nursing your wounds."

The teasing tone she attempted fell flat. Her voice trembled.

He made no response, and against her will tears welled up. "Don't be angry with me. I know I should have waited for you to come. I didn't mean to disobey your orders, but I couldn't—"

He touched his finger to her lips. "I know. I'd have done the same."

He scrutinized her face, finally gave a short, rueful laugh. "A dozen times I came within a hair's breadth of leaving my men to follow you and bring you back. After you'd gone, I kept thinking: Where's the greatest danger after all? In battle—or carrying messages between corps and daily hazarding capture and execution as a spy?"

Relieved, she murmured, "Truly, we were in no great danger on the way to Morristown. We met many small parties of our militia roaming the roads, and they afforded us protection. And as soon as we delivered His Excellency's orders to General Lincoln, he quickly set his men in motion. He even sent a detachment to accompany us all the way here."

His face turned partially away, Carleton studied the motionless, blanket-wrapped forms scattered across the stone-walled kitchen's brick floor. The only sound was the soft breathing and snores of the sleepers and the occasional pop of the fire's seething embers.

"I know I must trust you to God's care, as you must do for me. I try not to worry . . . " His voice trailed off.

Finished securing the bandage on his arm, she helped him draw on his shirt. He pulled her into his embrace then, and gratefully she nestled against him.

"Why is it so hard to trust? The Lord has watched over us every step of our way, and yet fear still overcomes me when I think of you in battle. It feels as though my emotions are wrenched this way and that, and my prayers reach no higher than the ceiling."

For a long moment he remained silent. At length, his voice grim, he said, "We needed your prayers these past two days."

She pulled back to look up into his face. "I wish I'd been with you."

"I'm thankful you were not. It was hard enough for a man to bear." He hesitated, then let out his breath in a sigh. "Unlike the Long Knives' campaigns, my warriors and I would strike hard and fast and be gone before our enemy could mount opposition. Days or weeks stretched between raids with ample time to rest and regain strength. I've grown used to warring so, to traveling light and fighting from ambush at a time and place of my own choosing, not this wearying grind of battle that drags out for days or even weeks while two armies attack head on like rutting bucks."

"And you've grown used to command," Elizabeth hazarded, suppressing a smile at his imagery.

He grimaced. "I fear I have. I've no objection to being under another's authority as long as my superior is worthy of it. The trouble is that, unlike Washington, too many are not. And negotiating the morass of politics that is the white man's military is not a talent I've cultivated. Or ever wanted to."

She gave him a wry look. "So I've heard."

He chuckled. "I admit I was born a rebel."

"Tell me what happened these past two days. We heard rumors only—little of substance."

Carleton sobered. "Thanks to Cadwalader and the Philadelphia Associators we had excellent intelligence for once. They provided us a perfect account of the enemy's dispositions and confirmed that Cornwallis was preparing to attack Trenton. As a result we were ready to welcome him . . . and we needed every possible advantage.

"The night of New Year's Eve Washington sent my brigade and Forrest's artillery with a strong force under Scott, Hand, and Haussegger to probe Princeton Road."

At first light, he told her, they ran into a British detachment a few miles from the town and for several hours inflicted heavy casualties while suffering few as they held the British at bay. At a council of war that night Washington had shared his latest intelligence: Cornwallis commanded about 8,000 Regulars and a large train of artillery, some of the best regiments of the British army.

"So few could never stand against so many unless God wrought a miracle!" she exclaimed.

"We didn't fight on our own," he agreed soberly. "There were times I felt chariots of fire waging war above us."

For some moments they sat silent, staring into the depths of the cherry coals on the hearth. At length Carleton said, "Washington summoned Cadwalader to come immediately to Trenton, and thank God he didn't delay. He and the militia came in yesterday morning just before the drums beat to arms to announce Cornwallis's advance. To our good fortune—though it didn't seem so at the time—it had been raining heavily, and the roads were so deep in mud they were all but impassible. That caused difficulties enough for us, but it was well nigh a disaster for Cornwallis."

She grimaced. "Sometimes it's an advantage to have a minimum of baggage to drag about."

"Then we've been blessed." He grinned, then sobered. "With Hand and the others, we again advanced along Princeton Road as far as Five Mile Run, under Fermoy's command—curse the blackguard! He abandoned us, but we held Cornwallis back and only gave up ground under the strongest pressure, while Washington's column finished entrenching on the Assunpink's south bank. Toward sunset the British finally drove us back into the town by sheer weight of numbers, pressing hard on our heels as we withdrew over the bridge. I can't say enough for Washington. He rode up beside the bridge and stayed there until the entire detachment had crossed, exposed all the while to the fiercest enemy fire."

Elizabeth studied him intently. "It cannot be coincidence that he escapes unscathed time and again, while men all about him are falling."

Carleton nodded. "I've come to believe that nothing happens at random. The men are learning to respect and love him, too, for the example he sets."

Leaning on the table, he propped his head in his hands. Speaking in a low voice as though to himself, he went on.

"He ordered the bridge to be held to the last extremity. And Cornwallis foolishly threw assault after assault against us. We beat them back until bodies lay piled like cordwood on the bridge and its approaches and the creek ran red with British blood."

He lifted his head, his gaze haunted. "I'll never understand such insanity—to waste your men as though their lives held no more value than a musket ball to be expended, and then discarded. I'll never use my men so."

Sensing how deeply the battle had affected him, she tenderly enfolded him in her arms. When he did not respond, she murmured, "There's more that troubles you. What is it?"

With an effort, he said gruffly, "I knew it must happen eventually, but . . . I sensed someone watching me, someone with ill intent. I looked around and saw Cornwallis seated on his horse on the rise just above the creek. His spyglass was quite clearly fixed on me."

Elizabeth's breath caught. "He knows you?"

"We were only casually acquainted in England, but he knows me well enough. While we were holding back his advance earlier in the day, I caught a glimpse of him looking in my direction and hoped he'd not recognized me. But it was certain by his expression that evening that he did. I had a strong feeling that he searched me out, in fact."

"Well, if the British didn't already know of your return, they do now," she said in despair. "The price for your capture has steadily risen in your absence, and it'll be even higher now."

His visage grim, Carleton raised his head and fixed his gaze on the far side of the dim kitchen, but she had the impression he looked beyond the structure's thick stone walls. Her throat was suddenly parched, and she longed for a drink of cool water to relieve it.

"You caution me to take every care, but you're in as much danger as I, if not more—"

"I don't go among the enemy, into the very lion's den, as you do."

"No, you fight them as a soldier of the enemy when you once held a commission in His Majesty's light dragoons and served as Gage's aide, your loyalty pledged to the king! They consider you worse than a traitor,

Jonathan. If they succeed in capturing you . . . " Her voice broke. "I can't think of your fate."

Letting out a sigh, he again leaned his head on his hands as though he were too weary to hold it up. "When it was almost full dark and we could see the gouts of flame from the musket and cannon barrels, Cornwallis gave up the attempt," he went on dully. "Their losses were too great for them to continue. By then it was apparent that we were all but surrounded, that morning would bring an assault we'd not be able to withstand. The Delaware on our left was impassable. The full might of the British Army lay before us. On our right, the lower fords of the river could be taken by a determined force, and one already lay at Philips Ford, prepared to cross at daybreak. As Knox said at the council of war last night, we were cooped up like a flock of chickens."

She drew a shaky breath. "But you are here, so the Lord obviously provided a way for the chickens to fly the coop."

"I suspect He's guided us more than we'll ever know." Straightening, he said, "You told me how Washington arranged for the army to slip across the East River to York Island after the defeat at Brooklyn. Well, this time St. Clair strongly urged that we steal a march on the enemy by slipping off along country lanes to reach Princeton, thus turning the enemy's flank. Cadwalader had provided a highly accurate map of the area, and we had men well familiar with the region to guide us, so there was complete consensus.

"I've never more clearly felt a hand of protection over us than last night. None of us had gotten any sleep for two days, but we were given strength for the task. And the night turned so cold so swiftly that the roads froze hard as iron. Although the men suffered, it was a stroke of fortune that sped our march."

She clasped her hands tightly in her lap. "Not fortune."

"No." He smiled deeply at her. "Another odd thing was that although the sky was entirely clear, the night was unusually dark, just as it is tonight. Although that also occasioned difficulties for us, it effectively concealed our movements from the enemy."

She started erect. "Did I not tell you that when we withdrew from Brooklyn across the East River a heavy fog suddenly enveloped the last of our men just as day was breaking? We were most vulnerable then, and if the British had gotten any hint that we were slipping away—" Breaking off, she shuddered.

"Yes. I thought about it a great deal last night as we made our way down those dark country lanes." He rubbed his eyes and, suppressing a yawn, went doggedly on. "At daybreak we were still more than two miles from Princeton. A heavy hoarfrost lay on every surface, and in the strengthening sunlight the trees and bushes glittered, standing out with brilliant clarity against a dusky blue sky. All was hushed and at peace. For that instant it seemed as though the whole world held its breath."

Watching him, Elizabeth unconsciously pressed her hand to her bosom.

"We'd not gone far, however, when we observed a sizeable force about a mile from us on the road to Trenton. Evidently Cornwallis had called for his reserves. I was with Sullivan's division, and the enemy saw us at the same time we saw them. Although we considerably outnumbered them, after observing us for some minutes they advanced toward us."

Greene's division had been closer to the enemy, he related, but marching through a ravine toward Princeton Road, they were unaware of the danger. Taking a detachment, Carleton had gone instantly to alert them, and along with Greene's force had converged with the enemy on high ground at a fenced orchard.

When he fell silent, she took his hand and held it to her cheek. "It was so bad, then?"

He gave a weary shrug. "I well know their worth as soldiers and expected a hot fight. Even against a far superior force and a blazing fire that tore their ranks apart, they held their ground and returned fire, volley for volley. And our men began to fall." His voice dropped. "In the orchard and the fields beyond, their mingled blood ran along the frozen ground like a hellish river before turning to ice."

Elizabeth bent her head, unable to speak. *Thank you, Lord God, for keeping him safe, and the others too.*

"More of their units came on the field. They charged with bayonets and drove our men back in disarray. I saw General Mercer surrounded, and when he refused to surrender, they repeatedly ran him through with bayonets, then left him for dead. Colonel Haslet took a bullet to the brain. We lost many such good officers, and our men fled. Had not Washington rallied them with a hail of musket balls sailing all around him, that small force would have beaten us. Instead we broke their line and drove them back. Princeton was ours by noon."

"Was not Cornwallis alerted by then and on his way?"

He smiled grimly. "He was. And considering the speed at which his army covered the distance from Trenton, he must have been in a rage at being so outwitted. But our rear guard held his column off at Stony Brook long enough that our army was well on its way to Kingston before he gained the town."

Overcome, she buried her face against his chest. "Let me stay with you! Let me fight with you! Here is where I belong. When you're gone, how I feel your absence—how I fear for your safety!"

His arms tightened around her. "You know it's not possible—"

"I can pass as a man. You can take me as your aide." The words choked in her throat.

For a long moment he said nothing. At last she felt his breast rise and fall, then reluctantly he shook his head.

"Washington was right," he admitted, his voice breaking. "We need your bravery everywhere, but most of all next to Howe. Do you remember what you said to me when Washington asked you to take on that assignment? That you could not place me above obedience to God, that there's a reason why God placed both of us in the position he has. None of that has changed."

She clung to him, weeping. He bent his head to rest his cheek against the top of hers.

"If we turn our backs now on this great cause we've pledged our lives to, then we'll deservedly lose our honor. It may well be all we're left in the end, but the freedom God endowed every human being with and the honor of His name and ours is all that's worth fighting for." Straightening to cradle her face in his hands, he lifted her chin, forced her to meet his anguished gaze. "You must follow your calling, Beth. And I must follow mine. No turning back."

She forced herself to nod, her throat so tight she could hardly speak. Fighting back tears, she whispered, "No turning back."

ROLLED UP IN HIS BLANKET on the floor, he roused long enough to draw her into his arms. She bent over him and kissed him lightly, deeply grateful that he had been given back to her once more, if only for these short hours, as a promise for their future. She saw then that he was already asleep, and smiling, she nestled against his chest, breathing in the scent of him: of ice and wind, horses and leather, sweat, gunpowder, wool, and linen . . . and blood.

They had found a place on one side of the great hearth between Andrews and Blue Sky, and Levi. Crosswise below their feet sprawled her uncle. Several other officers had commandeered space until only a narrow lane remained between the rows of slumbering bodies.

Angling her head to look up into Carleton's face, she studied the long lashes that lay against his cheeks, reddened from the cold, and his noble, regular features, softened by repose but etched still by the intense strain of the past hours. She had never seen him asleep this deeply except when he lay near death of the wound suffered while on the march from Concord back to Boston with the British. Thinking back to their journey from Grey Cloud's Town, it struck her that he had been ever alert to danger, even while sleeping. Always his rest had seemed shallow, quickly broken at the least sound or movement.

How worn he must be now to neglect both nature and training and let down his guard so completely. A pang went through her at thought of the extremity he and all the soldiers must have endured during the past days that all the inhabitants of this mighty land, both loyalist and patriot might be free. Even the indifferent. To ensure that they and their children and their children's children would never again suffer the oppression of a foreign government, but could take charge of their own destinies, elect their own government, and make their own decisions without interference.

Even as the spectre of the losses they had suffered and would yet suffer haunted her, she was grateful beyond measure. And loving him with her whole heart, she at last fell asleep in his arms.

Chapter Eight

"OH, THE LUXURY OF HOT WATER and a merry fire!" Elizabeth exulted. "I've never been so frozen and filthy in all my life as these past weeks, and I hope never to be so again." Stretching luxuriously, she sank to her chin in the steaming water that filled the brass tub almost to the brim.

It was Wednesday, January 15, 1777. Exhausted, worn, and hungry, Washington's corps had arrived at Morristown on the sixth to make a cold camp in the barren, windswept fields and valleys surrounding the village. By the time Tess arrived on the tenth, however, the army had been greatly buoyed by the arrival of Captain John Stryker and his small party of cavalry, who drove in a line of wagons loaded with winter clothing they had captured from Cornwallis's fleeing rear guard. Accounts began to trickle in of militia skirmishes at a string of towns between Princeton and New York that set the enemy to flight and captured more desperately needed supplies as well as additional prisoners.

Early on the cloudy, raw morning of the twelfth, Elizabeth and Tess had started out on the journey to New York, escorted by Pete and Briggs. At Carleton's suggestion they played the part of vagabonds, unwashed and dressed in ragged clothing with uncombed hair. The few travelers they encountered gave them a wide berth.

After crossing the Hudson River at Dobbs Ferry, on the village's outskirts along the Saw Mill River, they found the home of the trusted Son of Liberty, Jehu Martin, to whom they had been directed. Grateful the middle-aged man and his wife accepted what little information they offered without comment and asked no questions, they had spent the first comfortable night since leaving Morristown. The next morning, bathed and refreshed, with the women resuming female dress, they accepted the loan of Martin's coach.

It was late in the day before they reached King's Bridge, hampered by the drifted roads and a harsh wind. With only a cursory glance at Tess and Elizabeth's passes, the guards waved them through the checkpoint, and they had finally reached Montcoeur late the previous evening, thoroughly exhausted from the journey.

Resolutely Elizabeth warded off the memory of her parting from Carleton, the tears that threatened to accompany it, the nagging anxiety about his adjustment to the wrenching changes his life had undergone over the course of a few short weeks. Andrews and Blue Sky, Red Fox and Spotted Pony loved him, too, and were there to encourage him in her absence, she reminded herself. And God would continue to be his anchor.

Both of them had pledged to follow where their Lord led without fear or regret. To continually repine would only make the task that lay before them that much harder. If she were to succeed in her charge, she had to keep her treacherous emotions at bay and trust that Carleton would do the same.

Seated at the dressing table on the other side of Elizabeth's dressing room, head bent while her slight, middle-aged maid, Mariah, brushed out her hair, Tess threw a sidelong glance at her. Judging from her aunt's expression, Elizabeth concluded her thoughts followed a similar course, though when she spoke her tone was cheerful.

"I've had enough of wandering the world to last me a good long while. No matter what trials we face, our future and those we love are in the Lord's hand. And that is the safest place for them to be."

Elizabeth gave her a grateful smile. To direct her thoughts into safer channels, she turned her attention to Jemma, Isaiah and their housekeeper, Sarah's, fifteen-year-old daughter, who was sorting through the gowns hanging in the armoire. In only the four months they had been away, the young woman had grown tall and statuesque. Her ebony face with its delicate features had lost much of its childish contours, already hinting at the mature beauty she would one day possess.

"Jemma, you've grown as tall and beautiful as your mother. I fear in your father's absence the young men will flock around you like bees to a flower—if they don't already. Promise me you won't run away with one of the scoundrels. I don't know how we'd get along without you."

At Elizabeth's teasing the color rose into Jemma's dusky cheeks, but she was unable to suppress a smile. "Now Miss Elizabeth, don't you be saying such," she answered primly. "If I were to even think of running off with any boy, Ma would beat me within an inch of my life."

As she spoke a tall, striking black woman wearing a blue gown and snowy apron and kerchief, strode into the room carrying an armload of folded linens. "I don't need to, child," she said, sternly nodding her turban-wrapped head. "Your Pa do it for me. Good mornin' Miz Teresa, Miz 'Lizabeth. You sleep well last night?"

"Like the dead," Tess responded with a groan. "I'm not certain I've yet revived."

"Bring me a towel, Jemma, please. The water's getting cold."

Jemma wrapped a towel around Elizabeth as she rose, shivering, from the water, then wrapped her dripping hair with another. Gratefully Elizabeth huddled on a stool drawn close to the glowing five-plate iron stove, while Jemma gently worked the tangles out of her hair.

After helping Elizabeth to don shift, stockings, and stays, the young woman went to the armoire and pulled out a heavy brocade gown of rich amber satin and a matching striped petticoat. "How about this one? It looks so pretty with your coloring, and you haven't worn it since last winter."

Toasting in the fire's warmth, Elizabeth yawned. "As cold and tired as I am, just bring me the maroon bed gown and the flowered petticoat. Put that one aside for later this week. It'll be more suitable for making or receiving calls—that is, if we recover enough before the end of winter to do either."

Tess chuckled, then returned to her moody contemplation of the wintery scene visible between the window's heavy draperies. "Any social obligations can wait at least until the weather improves. Besides, we don't know how many of our acquaintances stayed after the fire last October. What have you heard of our circle, Mariah? When I left, Howe was instituting heavy-handed measures, and the Hessian soldiers—not to mention their wives—were plundering everything that could be carried off."

The slender, brown-haired maid tucked a stray curl into Tess's chignon and surveyed the result of her efforts with a sharp eye. "The city's in great distress, Ma'am. Misery and want have been the watchwords during your absence. There are many homeless, and food and many other necessaries are still in very short supply if they can be gotten at all."

Tess turned to Sarah. "How was your foray to market this morning? I can't vouch for Elizabeth, but I'm ravenous. All we had to eat on the way from Morristown was a handful of dried beef apiece each day and parched corn cooked with maple sugar."

"There be little enough to be found since the British move in, but I manage to secure enough we don't starve," Sarah said, tightlipped. "Breakfast cookin' now and be ready by the time you come downstairs."

Elizabeth threw Tess a mischievous glance. "Aunt Tess exaggerates our want of provisions on the way here . . . but only a little. I do hope you're cooking an ample supply."

Sarah chuckled. "There be enough. You goin' to need your strength to entertain all the callers you get this week. I tole' everybody who listen that my ladies just return from Boston. Said them rebels give you a real bad time and all your family there be sufferin' terribly for their loyalty to the king. They'll already be spreadin' the news far an' wide."

Tess exchanged a glance with Elizabeth. "Well done! Thank you, Sarah." Turning to her maid, she said, "That'll do for now, Mariah."

The maid quietly left the room.

"All the talk at market be that Howe's a'goin' to hold a grand celebration of the queen's birthday this Saturday," Sarah told them, while Jemma helped Elizabeth into her quilted, calf-length bedgown.

"They say he's going to be made a Knight of the Bath, whatever that is," Jemma added as she finished pinning the bedgown neatly down the front. "There's going to be fireworks, a supper party, a fancy ball, and all kinds of doings."

"Oho!" Tess said, eyebrows raised. "A Knight of the Bath, is it? I wonder if the king's enthusiasm for Lord Howe's performance will survive the news of Trenton and Princeton. "

Elizabeth laughed. "I'm sure Howe and his coterie will make every explanation of why the battles were victories instead of defeats. Hearing their excuses will be just too delicious. We must make our calls after all to put ourselves in the way of an invitation."

Tess's expression turned thoughtful. "We must indeed. There's too much to be learned at dinners and balls for us to miss such a grand event. I'll wager tongues will be loosed."

"I kept the letters that come while you be gone," Sarah broke in as she laid wood into the stove and closed the iron door. "They be on your escritoire, Miz 'Lizabeth. There be one from your pa that come a month back. And there be a number from Dr. Vander Groot and Miz Isobel."

Delight that her father had written was tempered by the reminder that Elizabeth would soon have to address the situation with Vander Groot. But as she frowned at her reflection in the mirror, she hoped fervently that she could put off dealing with the latter for a little while longer.

"THEY'RE COMING! Papa, Mama, and Abby are coming home!"

Tess caught her breath and hurried to Elizabeth's side to snatch the letter out of her hand. "How soon do they sail?" she demanded, rapidly scanning the page as she sat on the loveseat beside her. "Are they already on the way?"

Elizabeth leaned on her shoulder. "Alas, no. Papa writes that he has much business to conclude in London before they can leave."

"They plan to sail in September in time to reach Boston before the winter storms." Tess looked up, her face brightening. "That means they should arrive by the end of October as long as the weather cooperates."

Elizabeth jumped up and twirled around in the center of the room, laughing. "Only ten months! I feared I'd not see them again until the war ends—if ever."

"This is the best news!" Tess returned her attention to the letter. "Samuel wants to rebuild Stony Hill. He says he's already contacted a manager to clear the site. I'll write my caretaker right away and have him begin making arrangements for them to stay at my house until the new one is habitable."

For some minutes, they indulged in happy plans for Samuel and Anne Howard's return from London with Elizabeth's sister Abby. Then Elizabeth's shoulders slumped.

"How can I possibly continue to conceal my involvements from them? You know how angry Papa was when he heard of Jonathan's treason. Papa suspects my loyalties, but he has no idea I'm as deeply involved in what he'll consider treasonous activities as Jonathan."

Tess stared at her, stricken. "As am I. Oh, dear. He'll expect us to return to Boston. And stay."

Chewing her lip, Tess read more slowly through the letter again. When she reached the end, her expression cleared.

"Listen: 'Although I have expressed opinions in the past that I know have grieved you, our time in England has brought me to a different way of thinking. I pray that on our return you and I may share our whole hearts with confidence and love, dear Daughter. Your mother and I, and Abby too, have talked about all these things, and they send their heartiest agreement.' "

Tears brimming, Elizabeth returned to her seat beside her aunt, who hugged her with a tremulous smile. "Never underestimate God's ability to move hearts."

They clung together for several moments, then Tess straightened and indicated the rest of the letters stacked neatly on the escritoire. "Now we must do something about Pieter and Isobel."

"We'll read their letters once we're fully rested and can think how to respond. For now I'm too full of joy at Mama and Papa's return to think of anything else. And I'll hardly know Abby anymore."

"Surely the Vander Groots wonder what's become of us," Tess protested. "The longer we neglect to offer a plausible reason for our disappearance, the more questions arise and the more awkward any explanation becomes."

"I know," Elizabeth groaned. "What did you write to them before you left for Fort Pitt?"

Tess thought for a moment before offering a litany. "Well, I had no idea how long it might be before you returned, so I wrote that you'd been delayed in Boston taking care of urgent business for your parents, which was being endlessly complicated by the rebels' policies against loyalists. Because of the disruptions caused by the British overrunning York Island and the great fire, I was going to join you there before the weather turned worse, and that we'd likely not return until at least the first of the year as I had affairs relating to my estate to manage as well."

"Then they'd not expect us to return before now anyway. And considering the inclement weather—"

"How do we explain our lack of response to their letters? They'd assume the servants forwarded them and may take our silence as indifference—or worse, infer that we wish to cut off what's been a close and warm relationship."

Elizabeth buried her face in her hands. "The last thing I want is to make a breach between us," she exclaimed, looking up. "Isobel as dear to me as Abby, and Pieter—"

"Whatever Pieter has been to you in the past can be no more," Tess said firmly.

Elizabeth retreated to the window seat and pulled back the heavy draperies to stare out into the garden, where a blanket of snow glittered beneath the sun high in the clear sky. "Nor do I wish for him to be. You know Jonathan has all my heart. But I'll always love and respect Pieter as a dear friend, a colleague, a brother, and a fellow believer. His esteem means a great deal to me, and I'd not lose it. How am I to disappoint his hopes without destroying our friendship?"

"I don't know, but considering how close his family's ties are to the Howes, he must never suspect your true involvements, no matter what private opinions he may express. One word in the wrong ear, one careless comment, and not only would our mission be irretrievably compromised, but also both of us could hang."

Elizabeth got up to pace the room. "Then to allay any suspicions I must continue as I have been." She rounded on her aunt. "Oh, how I despise the shifts and dodges we must practice! When Pieter learns that my heart belongs to another, that I've deceived him—as he must in time—then he'll surely despise me. And if Jonathan should learn about my relationship with Pieter, will he not doubt my love?"

Tess regarded her with a stern look. "Neither must ever know about the other."

"How long will it be possible to keep sufficient distance between Pieter and me to avoid another declaration? It'll not be long before he'll wonder—"

"All you can do is to try to put off that moment as long as possible. In the meantime, we must answer these letters."

Her heart sinking, Elizabeth crossed to the escritoire, collected the letters, then took a seat on the footstool at Tess's feet. Starting with the earliest, dated at the beginning of November, she broke each seal and read the contents to her aunt.

His home and that of his parents had been destroyed in the great fire, Vander Groot wrote, but thankfully his great-aunt Euphemia's house had escaped the flames. As if they had not suffered woe enough for one family, they had also lost his brother's newborn daughter not long after his wife's death. Yet they praised God to hear that Montcoeur escaped the fire. Since they had heard nothing from Tess since the battle, he assumed she had already left the city to join Elizabeth in Boston. He hoped that his letter would be forwarded to them and asked that they respond with the assurance that they were both safe and well.

The next letter, sent a couple of weeks later, was from Isobel. Each subsequent missive reflected the writer's personality: Isobel's full of heartfelt prayers for their welfare and breathless details of balls, teas, and romantic encounters, her brother's more sober, but filled with a gentle warmth and sincere concern that pierced Elizabeth to the core.

In their earliest communications both wrote of their brother's heartache at losing first his wife, then his little daughter, and his deepening grief and growing dependence on having his family close by. As time passed without a response, the letters reflected increasing anxiety for Elizabeth and Tess's welfare and pleas for them to write soon. The weather had been so bad and the conditions between Philadelphia and New York so uncertain because of Howe's pursuit of Washington's force across New Jersey and the rising of the militias, Vander Groot wrote, that his family remained adamantly opposed to his undertaking a trip north to personally assure himself of their safety.

The last letter, to Elizabeth from Isobel, was dated a week before Christmas. Her brother was heartsick at receiving no news of her, the young woman wrote. She prayed that her letter would find its way to Elizabeth and that she would end their unhappy suspense by writing them at her earliest opportunity.

Her hands shaking, a hard lump in her throat, Elizabeth refolded the letters and laid them aside.

"We have to write at once and let them know of our return," Tess urged. "And we must invent a believable reason for our lack of response."

"Pieter mentioned the reasons himself," Elizabeth offered. "Considering the great disruption the war has caused, to say nothing of the almost continual rain, and then snow, since October, travel has been all but impossible. With the uncertainty that letters would reach us if they were forwarded, the servants simply held all correspondence for our return."

"Why did we not at least attempt to write from Boston to assure them of our welfare and inquire about theirs?"

Elizabeth threw up her hands, but before she could venture a response, both women started to their feet at the hollow echo of the outer door's knocker resounding through the entryway below. Hearing footfalls, followed by the creak of the door opening, Elizabeth glanced at the mantel clock.

"It's barely past eleven. Who'd call so early?"

"Surely no one for us," Tess responded, frowning.

In moments Caleb appeared in the doorway. Colonel Stern's thirty-year-old nephew and a staunch Son of Liberty, he served ostensibly as their butler. But in reality his most important role had become to assist Elizabeth, along with Pete, in planning and carrying out her clandestine activities.

Bowing, he said, "Dr. Vander Groot wishes to speak with you if it's convenient."

"Pieter?" Elizabeth gasped. She turned to Tess, whose expression reflected her own astonishment. "I thought he was still in Philadelphia."

"Obviously not," Tess returned dryly.

"I can't see him this way! I'll have to dress." Elizabeth swung to Caleb. "Send Jemma right away—"

She broke off as Jemma brushed past him. Beckoning distractedly to her, Elizabeth rushed into the dressing room.

Behind her she heard Tess say, "Bring Dr. Vander Groot up to the sitting room, Caleb. Tell him we'll wait upon him shortly."

Chapter Nine

"PIETER! How good it is to see you!"

Standing just inside the cozy sitting room's threshold, Elizabeth curtsied, while beside her Tess did the same. His expression grave, Dr. Pieter Vander Groot straightened from a deep bow and crossed the room to kiss first Tess's hand, then Elizabeth's.

Guilt stabbed through Elizabeth at her impulsive words. Yet she found herself delighted to see him again. Praying he would read nothing in her response except friendship, she gave him a smile she hoped communicated chaste warmth rather than romantic attachment.

To her dismay, he captured her other hand as well and took her in with an intensity that caused her cheeks to heat and her breath to shorten. To bolster her courage she had donned a moss-green gown of the finest wool that flattered her slender figure and looked exceptionally well on her, with her dark auburn hair neatly curled and pinned up beneath a small round cap of delicate lace. Now she regretted the choice, for the effect was clearly not lost on the doctor.

"We were overjoyed to hear you'd come, Pieter," Tess cut in hastily. "The last we heard you were still in Philadelphia. We just got home last night, and—"

"So my servant told me," Vander Groot broke in gruffly, his searching gaze never leaving Elizabeth's face.

She had forgotten how handsome he was. His hair was a darker blond and his eyes a lighter blue than Carleton's, nor was he as tall, but she found the intelligence and kindness reflected in his countenance highly attractive.

A sense of disquiet settled in her breast, and she found it hard to meet his eyes. "We were just reading your letters when Caleb announced you. Have your parents and Isobel come too? Are they well? How is your dear aunt? Are you staying at her house?" Inundating him with questions, she prayed to forestall his.

As she had hoped, his eyes warmed and he conceded a faint smile. "My parents and Isobel are still in Philadelphia and are doing well, although they are most anxious to hear any news of you. Yes, I'm staying at Aunt Euphemia's home for now." He chuckled. "She insists on returning as soon as the weather clears enough for her to travel. You know Aunt Euphemia."

"Indeed we do," Tess said with a laugh. "And we're most eager to see her."

"We were all quite concerned for your safety, you know," he chided gently. "As soon as I learned that Beth had returned to Boston and that you planned to join her there, I sent a letter by express rider asking at what address I could write to you. But evidently you'd gone by the time it arrived."

"It was here when we returned," Tess said apologetically. "I was forced to leave in a great hurry when Howe took over the city, and I foolishly neglected to bring along my address book so we could write to you in Philadelphia. Of course, everything was in such upheaval."

Vander Groot squeezed Elizabeth's hands before releasing them. "We received greatly alarming reports. Had they not been so dire nor the weather so treacherous, I'd have ridden all the way to Boston to personally assure myself of your safety. But the situation in Philadelphia was exceptionally chaotic as well, as you may imagine. Everyone was convinced Howe was on the verge of taking the city, and many people fled."

Forcing back the vivid images of the panic they had encountered while skirting Philadelphia on their return from Ohio Territory, Elizabeth drew him to the fire, and the three of them found seats before it.

"We do beg your pardon for being so long incommunicado," Elizabeth said. "Our affairs in Boston were in a great tangle, with so much damage to our property that it required all our efforts to set things as right as they can be. And then, with the battles raging around New York and rumors abounding, we all but despaired of ever returning."

How easily lies come to us now. Oh, Lord, forgive us! How much longer can we go on so? Help us to find a better way . . .

Vander Groot's calm voice drew her back from her agonizing reflections. "You were undoubtedly wise to wait until now to return. But we've all missed you more than I can say, and knowing you're back and safe will put my family's hearts at ease."

Tess reached to pat his hand. "I'll write immediately to let your parents know that all is well."

Elizabeth hesitated, then blurted out, "I'm heartsick that you and your family were subjected to such worry for us on top of your poor brother's grief."

Vander Groot sobered. Bending his head, he rubbed his brow.

"These past months have been the saddest we've ever endured. Please pray for Christiaan. His mind is much disordered, and I'm deeply concerned for his recovery. He harbors an irrational fear that his entire family will be taken from him. I'm afraid it'll be some time before he can be left unattended—if ever."

He looked quickly away, but not before Elizabeth caught the sheen of moisture in his eyes. "You know he has our prayers, as do you and the rest of your family," she murmured.

"Thank you. That means a great deal."

In spite of her concern for Vander Groot's unfortunate brother, Elizabeth could not help thinking that should Christiaan remain so disconsolate, the doctor might be forced to remain at Philadelphia indefinitely. If she could only forestall a declaration, time and distance might provide the resolution to their relationship.

As Elizabeth met Vander Groot's painful gaze, realization of the extent of his and his family's loss stabbed through her. "I was entirely shocked to hear of the great fire and that yours and your parents' home burned. I do hope not everything was destroyed."

"My parents had taken many of their personal possessions with them, but unfortunately I only brought my medical supplies, some clothing, and a few sundries. I arrived here Saturday and stopped by what had been my home to see if anything could be recovered. All is gone."

Tears welled into Elizabeth's eyes. "I'm so sorry."

"It seems there's woe upon woe," Tess echoed sadly.

"It's in God's hands." Clearing his throat, Vander Groot forced a cheerful tone. "I trust you accomplished everything in Boston that was needed."

"Yes, in spite of the rebels' best attempts to hinder us," Tess answered. "And we greatly enjoyed visiting family and friends we haven't seen for months. That alone was worth the inconveniences of the trip."

"Papa wrote that they're planning to return by the end of this year," Elizabeth added. "We'll have much to do to prepare for their coming since the British burned our home during the siege—at least what remained of it after the bombardment."

He reached to capture her hand. "I forgot that. We've both lost homes then."

Emotion clogged Elizabeth's throat. "So we have."

"I look forward to meeting your parents and sister. But you will stay here at least for now?"

"We plan to, though we've talked of removing to Philadelphia for the summer." Elizabeth chose her words carefully. "Even if Howe takes over the city, things surely won't be so desolate as they are here."

A look of surprise passed over Vander Groot's features. "I thought you shared my concerns about Howe ruling over New York with an iron hand and the Hessians' unexcelled looting—and worse. If the British do take Philadelphia, I've no confidence the situation there will be any better. In fact I've advised my family to leave the city immediately if Howe moves against it."

Focusing on the long, slender fingers that held her own captive, she impulsively put her hand over his. "Believe me, we do share your concerns—"

"But we're uncertain that claiming independence, particularly at the cost of war, is the best, or only, response," Tess intervened quickly. "The rebels have also instituted policies that seem exceptionally harsh. Where they're in control, one dare not express any loyalty to the king. Thus we face a dilemma."

"Our hope is that Howe would spare Philadelphia most of what New York has suffered so far, and we'd be able to live in peace there," Elizabeth finished for her.

Vander Groot's mouth tightened. "Between the three of us, it'll not take much closer acquaintance with British rule for me to change my allegiance."

Avoiding Elizabeth's meaningful gaze, Tess shook her head. "Now, my dear Pieter, horrors do happen on both sides in times of war. One must count the cost before embarking on such a desperate course as casting off the reins of established authority."

Vander Groot held Elizabeth's gaze. "You sound like my mother," he said with a crooked smile. But in the depths of his eyes, she saw anger and disillusionment.

Elizabeth leaned toward him. "We're as uncertain of the wisest course as you. It'll take much thought and prayer to discern God's will in this matter."

He relaxed. "Certainly there's much to consider. I look forward to talking with both of you further on the matter."

Elizabeth returned a dazzling smile. But dread twisted in her breast at the realization that her dilemma would only grow more difficult in the coming weeks.

Hoping to change the subject, she asked, "What of your parents? Will they return to New York?"

"They've moved into my brother's home and will likely settle there permanently."

"Do you plan to stay here or return to Philadelphia?" Tess asked.

Vander Groot hesitated. "That's a decision I've yet to make. Many of my former patients who are loyal to the king have returned here to seek protection from the patriots' wrath under Howe's wing. So have some others who foreswore their patriotic sympathies at promise of the king's pardon. But all is far from well in the city."

Tess cocked her head. "What do you mean?"

He sighed and shook his head. "Discontent and resentment are growing. His Majesty's officials clearly regard Americans as beneath contempt and resist attempts to return to anything resembling a normal state. Lodgings are in short supply, materials and labor to rebuild are lacking, and the weather compounds the misery."

"Then you're inclined to return to Philadelphia?"

He turned a keen gaze on Elizabeth. "I've made a number of promising contacts, and it appears that I could expect quite a comfortable living if I chose to maintain a practice there. Thus far, at least, we're spared British rule, although I realize it's likely to become a reality before year's end. I hope to make a decision within the next few months, but of course, much depends on the decisions of . . . others."

He said no more, and fearful of his meaning, Elizabeth did not pursue the subject. Learning that he would attend the celebration of the queen's birthday and General Howe's investiture into the Order of the Bath, she and Tess exclaimed over his good fortune. He assured them he would secure an invitation for them before the day was out.

A surge of excitement at the thought that the coming event would doubtless yield a wealth of intelligence was succeeded by the realization that Vander Groot's presence would greatly complicate matters. Having confided his sympathy with the patriots, what would he think of the apparent loyalty she must feign in order to gain her enemy's trust? Her aunt's forbidding countenance, however, forestalled temptation to confess her secret role.

"But one thing," she murmured. "I feel it unwise to share our private reservations with those loyal to the crown. Until we decide otherwise, it would be better for our opinions to seem unchanged."

His smile rueful, he nodded. "A wise policy. Discretion shall be our watchword."

The doctor soon took his leave, and when he had gone, the two women sat before the fire for some moments without speaking. At last Tess ventured, "It's reassuring to see Pieter looking so well in spite of all he and his family have suffered."

"What am I to do if he asks me to marry him and return with him to Philadelphia?" Elizabeth burst out.

"You can't be certain he will," Tess returned fiercely. "And in any case there's much a woman can do to either hasten or prevent a declaration. We cannot give in to weakness now. We've come too far to turn back. God will provide wisdom the moment it's needed. Let Him guide you and all will be well."

But Elizabeth couldn't help wondering whether God had led her into her present predicament to serve His own purposes. But if it was her own doing, would He rescue her from it . . . or allow her to learn obedience by suffering the unhappy consequences.

SHORTLY AFTER SUPPER that evening Elizabeth sought refuge in her bedchamber, but found no solace there. Curled up before a dancing fire, wrapped in a warm blanket and wearing muffatees to keep her hands warm, she gave up trying to compose a letter to her parents and set aside her lap desk. As she looked unhappily around her, the stark contrast between the comfort of her surroundings and the Continental Army's barren winter camp pierced her heart.

Before, she had rejoiced in the elaborate appointments of the mansion they'd been blessed to lease. The halcyon days of spring and summer had illumined the mansion's delicately tinted walls with a warm blush and shimmered across the surfaces of the elaborate furnishings, lending the interior a feeling of airiness and ease. But with snow blanketing the winter-blighted gardens and frosty night descending early, all appeared dull and unwelcoming.

Every door, window, and bed was swathed in heavy draperies to ward off cold drafts. Even the fires that blazed on the hearths and the glow of the tall tapers in the wall sconces and candelabra could not relieve the sense of gloom pervading a space that now seemed cavernous, impersonal, and cold.

She bit her lip hard, fighting back the rush of anguish. The morning she and her party had left Morristown, Blue Sky had clung to her, and her grief at their parting had wrenched Elizabeth's heart. Yet the forced cheerfulness with which Carleton had waved her off had been the hardest to bear. Unable to entirely conceal his pain at her leaving, he had stood with Charles and Blue Sky beside the large wigewa they and the two Shawnee warriors were building amid the rude huts being hastily thrown up on the bleak, snowy hills outside the small village. That she could not hold back her tears had surely only made it worse for him.

He had pressed a scrap of paper into her hand before she turned her mount onto the rutted road. The penciled note was neither dated nor signed, and she had taken care to conceal it from her companions. But with one glance at the familiar, graceful scrawl she had memorized its contents and on the journey back to New York had silently rehearsed his sweet words more times than she could count.

Giving in to temptation, she rose and crossed to the highboy, eased one of the drawers open, and lifted the scrap from beneath her silk stockings. Catching a flash of color, she laid the letter aside and drew out the delicately tinted miniature Andrews had brought her from Carleton's estate, Thornlea, on his return from Virginia the previous September, along with the news that Carleton was almost certainly White Eagle.

Her lips curving into a smile, she held it up to the light. Masterfully painted, it portrayed Carleton in his late teens, a tall, lean young man strikingly handsome and vital, full of hope and promise, with the light of laughter dancing in his deep blue-grey eyes.

Longing for the shelter of his arms, she glanced guiltily toward the door before pressing the small portrait to her lips, then hastily returned it to its hiding place. After a brief hesitation, she drew out an exquisitely hand-wrought silver Caughnawaga necklace, a matching brooch, and several fine rings, gifts Carleton had sent her from Fort Ticonderoga not long before he was captured by the Seneca and disappeared into the wilderness for more than a year.

With a sigh, she laid the jewelry back into the drawer next to the miniature, piled her silk stockings back over them, and took up the letter. Unfolding it, she scanned the message hungrily.

My Own,

I'll come to you as soon as possible. Don't be anxious—I'm well aware of the dangers, and our enemies will not find me.

God go with you! Pray for me as I do for you with every breath. Until you're in my arms again, you have

All my heart and soul,

J—

The creak of the door's opening brought her around. In the same movement she slipped the paper behind her back, but she was not quick enough. Tess had her mouth open to speak, but abruptly closed it and hurried to her side.

"What's that? A letter?"

Feeling the hot blood climb into her cheeks, Elizabeth raised her chin. "Just a note."

Tess's mouth tightened. "From Jon?"

Elizabeth nodded reluctantly.

"Signed?"

"His initial only," Elizabeth temporized.

Tess's eyes widened. "You know you cannot keep it! It's far too dangerous—"

"There's nothing to identify him, and no one will ever see it."

"Did you learn nothing from Jon's arrest? Lord Percy's soldiers tore your parents' town house apart searching for any evidence of his treason. Thank God he was wise, and they found nothing—"

"And it mattered not for they sentenced him to hang anyway."

Tess planted her hands on her hips. "Because the letter they intercepted from Washington provided more than sufficient evidence of the charge. That could not be foreseen."

"If the British become suspicious, they'll find more than enough to convict me without Jonathan's letters—" Breaking off abruptly, Elizabeth bit her lip.

Tess's voice scaled upward. "Letters?" Pressing her hand to her forehead, she muttered, "Of course you'd have letters. How could I not have thought of it?" She looked up, her expression pained. "How many?"

"Only . . . a few." Elizabeth could not meet her aunt's gaze.

Tess took a steadying breath and held out her hand. Reluctantly Elizabeth surrendered the scrap of paper she held. Scanning it, Tess gasped.

"He cannot possibly consider coming here!" she hissed. "Surely he's not so foolhardy as to walk straight into the lion's den. He'd not only endanger himself, but us as well."

Elizabeth caught back the letter and pressed it to her bosom. "I know, and yet . . . oh, how I pray he may come! If anyone can pass back and forth undetected, he can."

"I'd not be so confident if I were you. Howe has spies planted everywhere, even in our army. Why, for all we know Pieter—"

"How can you think that after this morning?"

"That may be exactly what he wants us to think."

"No, I'll never believe it! And God will protect Jonathan—and us too."

Tess glared at her. "It's unwise to tempt the Almighty, as you know well enough from past experience." Softening, she indicated the note Elizabeth clutched. "If anyone understands how it feels to love a man desperately and to be torn away from him, I do. I know how deeply this cuts. But we can never allow emotion to overrule good sense. Even this much could betray us. And him. You must destroy every letter along with anything he's ever given you that could be linked to him."

Tears stung Elizabeth's eyes. Although every fiber protested, she could not deny the wisdom of her aunt's counsel. At last she nodded, her heart aching.

At thought of the delicate miniature and the intricate silver jewelry as well as the broaches Blue Sky and the other Shawnee women had given her, however, she quickly decided that to give up the precious mementos was too great a sacrifice. Only the small portrait could be linked to Carleton, and at the first opportunity she would conceal it and the other items where no one would ever find them.

The letters were another matter. Her heart heavy, she took the small stack of ribbon-wrapped letters from the drawer.

"These are all I have . . . " *of his letters,* she added silently.

"The longer you wait, the harder it'll be. Do it now before it becomes impossible."

Her steps lagging, Elizabeth carried the letters to the fireplace. For some moments she stood paralyzed, finally allowed the letters to drop from her fingers into the flames, feeling as though she laid her own heart upon the pyre.

The paper was instantly engulfed. As Elizabeth's tears gave way to sobs, Tess came to gather her into her arms.

Brokenhearted, Elizabeth watched the paper turn brown, char, then dissolve to ash, wondering bleakly whether her and Carleton's dearest hopes and dreams were also destined to be burned away, like the letters, by the flames of war.

"I HEAR YOU'VE JUST RETURNED from a long stay in . . . Boston . . . of all places." From beneath hooded eyelids, General William Howe's gaze captured Elizabeth's.

"It was too long. And for the most part unendurably tedious, I assure you."

She was all too aware of Cornwallis, relegated to a seat to General Howe's left, beyond Admiral Richard Lord Howe and Governor Tryon. On the other side of Cornwallis, generals Von Heister, Clinton, Leslie, and Grant bobbed their heads—like ducks in a row, Elizabeth thought, biting her lip to suppress a giggle.

Admiral Howe had inaugurated the day's celebrations before noon by officially installing his younger brother as Knight Commander of the Bath, a high honor bestowed by King George III for the general's stellar performance at New York. Cornwallis had arrived from Brunswick only shortly before the ceremony, and Elizabeth was devoured by curiosity as to whether he had yet personally conferred with the brothers Howe on the action at Trenton and Princeton.

Seated between Vander Groot and General Howe, Mrs. Betsey Loring leaned on the her lover's arm. "And you went voluntarily?"

Elizabeth drew her cloak more tightly around her shoulders against the night's chill. She cast a quick glance toward Whitehall Slip a short distance away, where a detail of Royal Engineers was preparing to set off a large bank of fireworks. Clustered on the lawn and in the darkened windows of the surrounding buildings, a multitude of eager onlookers waited for the opening of the night's festivities in celebration of the queen's birthday.

"Alas, Aunt Tess had to settle some matters regarding her estate, and I had urgent business to manage for my parents, who plan to return from London in the fall." Her eyes wide with innocence, she added plaintively, "As our home was all but destroyed in the bombardment last March, and then was put to the torch by your troops, Your Excellency—understandably, of course—it'll be necessary for Papa to rebuild."

Howe shrugged. "Thus are the fortunes of war. I'm surprised your good parents have chosen to return to that hotbed of rebellion."

Elizabeth gave a tinkling laugh. "Oh, dear sir, you must not think that everyone in Boston is a raving Whig."

Howe tipped back his head and studied the distant star-points of light glimmering in the frosty air above them. "You could have fooled me."

Smiling, Tess bent toward him from Elizabeth's right. "I assure you, we have many friends and relatives in the area who are as loyal to the king as you, Your Excellency. Samuel feels they need reinforcement."

"Your parents are braver than I," Betsey chirped. "I'm sure any Tories left in that beastly town are suffering horribly at the hands of those dreadful Liberty Boys."

Pouting, she gave a shake of her head that caused the towering confection atop it, a wig constructed of powdered curls liberally studded with small British flags and men of war, to totter dangerously beneath her voluminous calash. Alarmed, the maid seated strategically behind her sprang to her feet and righted the structure.

Elizabeth exchanged a glance with Vander Groot, grateful that he served as a buffer between her and Betsey. The doctor seemed less so, however; his mouth tightened and the muscles of his jaw tensed. Elizabeth reached to squeeze his hand.

"Alas, they are indeed, Betsey. We encountered many of the trials they suffer daily, which is much of the reason why we were hindered so long from returning. Of course, with all the battles, and the rebel militias ranging freely between here and there, not to mention this abominable weather, you can understand we were reluctant to hazard the journey back even with escort until we were fully assured we could safely make it through."

Just then multiplied explosions rocked the air. Far above their heads brilliantly colored fountains of light bloomed across the black, star-studded sky. Amid the delighted exclamations of the onlookers, Vander Groot's fingers tightened over Elizabeth's.

"The more I'm exposed to this," he said in an undertone, jerking his head toward Howe and his mistress, "the less tolerance I have for it. But as we agreed . . . discretion."

Although he spoke mildly, it was evident that the contrast between their private discussions and her public behavior discomfited him. What would he think, she worried, once it became apparent she was determined to make Betsey Loring her bosom friend?

THE DINNER AND BALL that followed the day's entertainments were even more glittering affairs than Elizabeth and Tess had anticipated. In attendance at the expansive mansion on York Island's southeast side were a number of the leading Tories of the town. Their numbers had noticeably dwindled and the elegance of their clothing faded since Elizabeth had last been in the city, however. Now officers and their ladies made up the majority of the company. Brilliant British and Hessian uniforms and the elegant gowns and jewels of their ladies filled the mansion's great hall. All the allurements of food and drink, music, dance, and gambling that could be conceived were offered in such profusion that Elizabeth's senses swam.

She had chosen to wear a robe à la polonaise of luxurious amber silk brocade over a coordinating flowered stomacher and petticoat. Judging from the heated glances of the officers who swarmed to fill her dance card, the gown was having the intended effect. She had been hard pressed to save several dances for Vander Groot, and his smiling admonition not to worry about him only intensified her feelings of guilt.

The opulence displayed on every hand, coupled with the vacuous conversations that swirled around her, sickened her, especially compared to the misery and want she and Tess had witnessed earlier that week while calling on their acquaintances. Both of them had found deeply disquieting the sight of a great swath of the city lying in charred ruins crusted with layers of ice and snow, and the makeshift shelters housing the poorest of the dirty, ragged inhabitants that dotted uncleared lots all along New York's west side, where once grand mansions, businesses, and counting houses had shouldered one another.

Of the surviving houses, fine mansions abandoned by their patriot owners had been divided up among British officers, while many common troops and their dependents were forcibly quartered in private residences. Under martial law, with civil courts shut down, civilians had no recourse against the abuses that inevitably took place.

Elizabeth could not help thinking of Vander Groot's comments about the growing discontent in the ranks and even among Howe's officers. Soldiers stationed in the city appeared threadbare and sullen. Reports continued to filter in of the hardships the New Jersey garrisons suffered, constricted to crowded camps along the Raritan River between Amboy and Brunswick and subject to unremitting and increasingly successful rebel raids. Surely such a lavish celebration would only intensify it.

Painfully did she long for the earnest, unconstrained discourse she had enjoyed with Blue Sky, for Carleton's tender glances and endearments that captured her heart, and his insights and ideas that intrigued and challenged her mind. She felt herself deeply changed by their renewed relationship and her stay among the Shawnee, and she was hard pressed to pretend she was the same as before.

When the three of them were seated at a table with a number of junior officers and their women, Elizabeth scanned their dinner companions, then bent her head close to Tess's. "How I miss Lord Percy!" she whispered, careful to make sure no one around them could hear. "Despite his lamentable loyalties, he was ever so kind and charming I could almost forgive him for sentencing Jonathan to hang." She gave an elaborate shrug. "Especially since, in the end, he failed."

"To your credit." Tess bit her lip, struggling to suppress a laugh. "Indeed, it's a shame Hugh finds Howe's command so unbearable he'd rather languish in Newport than join the festivities here."

With forced gaiety, Elizabeth turned to engage Vander Groot in lighthearted conversation. Halfway through the courses, with wine flowing freely, a lieutenant of the infantry already deep in his cups began to recount the plundering he had observed by the Hessians.

"They're masters o' the art o' pillage," he drawled with obvious satisfaction, his words slurred. "Why, convoys of wag'ns and carr'ges follows them from town to town, filled to the brim with loot. And their women's the most form'dable at the task."

Many of the others at their table appeared to relish the detailed description that followed. An older captain, however, heard the lieutenant out, scowling, then pointed out that Howe had explicitly forbidden the plundering of civilians and even gone so far as order the Provost to hang offenders on the spot.

"The rebels deserve what they get," a major at the far end of the table countered.

"Such actions are not only shameful for civilized men, but it's also a fine way to turn every man, woman, and child against us," the captain pointed out. "How many in New Jersey who renewed their pledge of loyalty to the king have now turned their backs on us because they've been ground under the Hessian boot? If we wish to arouse this country to fight us to the last drop of blood, then plundering innocent civilians is guaranteed to accomplish that goal."

His protest was hooted down. Sickened, Elizabeth found it difficult to conceal her emotions, and Tess and Vander Groot clearly shared them.

To Elizabeth's relief, the meal finally gave way to the ball. For the next hours she was too occupied with Vander Groot and her other dance partners to think of anything but using every feminine wile she possessed to gain intelligence Washington could make good use of, while Tess did the same in her own circle.

It was past eleven o'clock when a servant rushed up to Vander Groot as they stood by the refreshment table in the anteroom outside the ballroom. Bowing deeply, he handed a message to the doctor. Vander Groot quickly scanned it, then looked up.

"It seems one of our fellow celebrants has either drunk too much or suffered an attack of apoplexy. I'm wanted urgently."

Elizabeth laid her hand on his arm. "Do you need me to help?"

"If I do, I'll send someone to find you. You have dance partners enough, I know, to keep you well occupied in the meantime," he added with a smile. "I hope I won't be gone long." Excusing himself with perceptible reluctance, he hurried after the servant.

When he had gone, Elizabeth glanced around, suddenly aware that the Howes were nowhere in evidence. Returning to the ballroom, she scanned the dancers, noting that not only were Lord and General Howe absent, a number of the ranking officers were also missing.

Before she could escape, she was quickly engulfed by a company of her admirers. She greeted them gaily, exchanging a witty banter that gave no evidence of her preoccupation. But every nerve focused on extracting herself as speedily as possible so she could investigate the whereabouts of the missing officers.

After several moments, to her immense relief, Betsey Loring rushed to her side. "Oh, excuse us, gentlemen," she cried, waving Elizabeth's companions peremptorily off. "I fear I must deprive you of Miss Howard's company. I require her attendance."

As the scowling officers drifted away, Elizabeth leaned on Betsey's arm, delighted at the interruption. "My dear Betsey, I've been hoping we'd have time to visit tonight, but I'd just decided it was going to be impossible to waylay you."

"We've gotten up a party for faro—but I'm sure that comes as no surprise." Betsey laughed gaily. "You know how addicted the general and I are to the game. Won't you come keep me company while we play? I know you don't enjoy it at all, but the officers refuse to talk of anything but war, war, war. Trenton and Princeton and the rebels' raids and plans for this year's campaign. I'm bored out of my wits, and I need you to keep me from screaming and making a spectacle of myself."

Elizabeth joined in her giggles, more than eager to join Howe and his officers. "Well, we can't have that. I think together we can offer sufficient diversion from such gloomy talk."

"My thoughts exactly. I hoped to persuade your dear doctor to join us," Betsey added, with a conspiratorial wink, "but apparently he's been carried off to attend some unfortunate victim of overindulgence. The two of you make such a handsome couple. Are you lovers yet?"

Although she felt the heat rise to her cheeks, Elizabeth managed to keep her jaw from dropping. "I assure you we're friends and colleague, nothing more."

Betsey gave her a knowing look. "I'll wager that won't last much longer. I can tell by the way he looks at you that he's completely smitten. You mustn't put him off, dear. Passion denied soon grows cold."

Across the room Aunt Tess was engaged amid a cluster of older officers and prominent Tories and did not see Elizabeth's hasty wave. Betsey whisked her downstairs to the library, where Lord and General Howe had gathered to play cards with a number of their officers.

Elizabeth was quickly ensconced at the faro table next to Betsey, who claimed the vacant chair at General Howe's side, across from Lord Howe, who served as the game's banker. The general gave Elizabeth a cool look, then returned his attention to the cards laid out on the table.

Without seeming to do so, she focused her attention on the two brothers. Both large, imposing men, they were very similar in appearance. Neither could be described as handsome, with swarthy complexions, heavy black eyebrows, and prominent nose and mouth, doubtless inherited from King George I through their mother, the king's illegitimate daughter.

Both tended toward melancholy, though, of the two, Lord Howe was the more charming and forceful. In contrast, General Howe seemed often ungracious and sullen and was fast gaining a reputation for indulging in the pleasures of life to the detriment of business.

Brigadier General Alexander Leslie occupied another seat at the table. A small man with a protruding lower jaw, his truculent look reflected his aggressive nature.

Next to him sat Charles, Earl Cornwallis. A tall, bluff man, well connected at court and an accomplished soldier who had married for love rather than position, he had won honors for gallantry in battle on the Continent, Elizabeth knew. Like the Howes, he considered the Americans to hold the rights of freeborn Englishmen, although he vigorously opposed the American rebellion.

Blind in one eye, he acknowledged Elizabeth with a nod, then cocked his head to look at Howe. "It still rankles that our victory was incomplete. The worst of it is that the rebels' temerity kept me from spending the winter with my dear Jemima."

General Howe tossed off the amber contents of his glass. "I'm sorry to rescind your leave to return to London, but those infernal scoundrels took the decision out of my hands. There's no one I trust more to give them a spanking, a task you accomplished with your usual aplomb."

Cornwallis's smile broadened, and he lifted his glass to his commander. "I can't say enough for the valor of my men, though the Americans proved more pesky than I'd anticipated."

"You gave excellent account of yourselves, unlike that slacker Rall," Leslie growled. "These rebels won't be so eager to challenge the might of His Majesty's army again, I'll wager."

"If you'd managed to capture that old fox Washington instead of allowing him to slip away," short, rotund General Henry Clinton interjected with asperity from across the room, "you might have put a terminus to the rebellion." Stalking to a wing chair by the fire, he threw himself into it and added maliciously, "Reports are that after he flanked you at Princeton, only to vanish into Watchungs before you even got there, you drove your troops so hard to Brunswick that they arrived completely fatigued and demoralized."

Cornwallis reddened. Pursing her lips, Elizabeth wondered whether Clinton's rancor was due to a loss at the game.

Laying down the next coup, Lord Howe broke in stiffly, "From what I've heard, both sides fought exceptionally well and suffered the corresponding casualties."

Cornwallis's guarded expression assured Elizabeth that Carleton had shared only a small part of the truth that night at Somerset Court House. "I'm confident that the men who gave their lives in service of their king would be the first to agree that what we accomplished was worth the cost," the general blustered.

"But it'll all cost us a pretty penny, don't you see?" Howe huffed, his visage assuming its usual morose cast as he studied the cards.

His ungainly body sprawled in a chair at the end of the table, General Grant pursed his protruding lips and shook his head peevishly so his jowls flapped like those of a pig. It was all Elizabeth could do to suppress a laugh.

"If your troops had been properly disciplined, General von Heister," the porcine officer squealed to the man hunched in the room's far corner, "the disaster at Trenton would have been prevented."

For a moment Elizabeth feared the Hessian commander would come up out of his chair. His hands clenched over its arms, von Heister snarled, "How I am to blame ven I haf no say in ver my men go and vat dey do in dees campaign—"

"Indeed, they are *your* men," General Howe cut him off, his tone freezing. "As their general, you are responsible for their performance. How your colonel can have let the rebels steal such a march on him is beyond me."

Rolling her eyes, Betsey leaned on his arm and indicated the cards. "Make your bet, my love. I swear, if there's any more talk of this war, I shall shriek!"

His swarthy face growing even darker, Howe shrugged off her hand. He threw down his chips as though he threw down a gauntlet.

"So far this Washington fellow has refused to be drawn into a general action where we can overthrow him in a stroke, and without that this war may well grind on for years. But, by God, I intend to put every pressure on him, and we'll see how long he can hold to his tactics."

"These rebels are a monstrous poor rabble incapable of maintaining any order on a battlefield, and their commander is the sorriest of the lot," Leslie cut in, his upper lip curled. "If Rall had properly fortified the town as he was ordered, this debacle wouldn't have happened."

The Hessian commander ground his teeth but held his tongue. A discreet glance at the players told Elizabeth that the game had been forgotten.

"I'd hardly call it a debacle," Howe snapped. "But the Ministry isn't going to be at all charmed when it receives my requisition for the troops and supplies we're going to need for a protracted war. I'm certainly not inclined to ask for money to parole the captives. Let them suffer the consequences of their incompetence."

Elizabeth let out a sigh and turned to Betsey. "Personally, I no longer think we can consider the rebels wholly contemptible, Betsey," she murmured loudly enough for those around her to hear. "It seems to me we've badly underestimated them."

"You're as bad as the rest!" Betsey cried merrily. "Is there no longer any hope of carrying on civilized discourse?"

Picking up on Elizabeth's cue, Clinton drowned the others out. "I warned everyone time and again that these ruffians were well capable of turning on us, and that we needed to be on our guard against this very kind of underhanded attack," he cried, his tone bitter. "But as usual, you refused to listen to sound advice, Your Excellency. If you'd had the sense to put me in command in the Jerseys instead of banishing me to Newport, I'd never have allowed this to happen."

The line of General Howe's jaw hardened. But although he exchanged a heated glance with his brother, he remained glacially silent.

The room fairly pulsed with hostility. The generals' incessant bickering reminded Elizabeth of nothing so much as a roiling pit of vipers. Had she not disliked the Howes so much, she would have been tempted to feel sorry for them. Still, she couldn't help admiring General Howe's ability to brush off his subordinate's unrelenting criticism as though he were of no more consequence than a fly.

It was clear Admiral Howe had had enough of Clinton's incessant buzzing, however. "You were given command of a substantial force to restore Rhode Island to the crown, sir, which you accomplished without a fight. Good God, man, what more plum assignment could one ask for than to support His Majesty's Navy unopposed in a place with a mild climate and an ice-free harbor instead of this frozen wasteland?" he added, indicating his surroundings with a vague wave of his hand.

When Clinton flushed and opened his mouth to respond, General Leslie cut in smoothly, "It's well that you've removed to Newport to keep the fleet from being iced in, Admiral. I also hear that Marblehead, Salem, and Boston are growing fat with the profits from all our ships the rebel privateers have captured." As though becoming aware of what his unguarded words implied, he added hastily, "I dread to think what havoc they'd wreak without your fleet to keep them in check."

Admiral Howe transferred his brooding gaze from Leslie to Elizabeth. "Since you were of late in Boston, perhaps you can shed some light on the activities of these rebel privateers. There must have been considerable talk amongst the inhabitants there."

Elizabeth's stomach clenched, but she allowed no evidence of discomfiture to show. "We did hear that great fortunes are being made from piracy," she responded with wide-eyed distress. "Since our acquaintances are all loyal to the king, we had no occasion to learn any specific details, but what talk we did hear was most disturbing."

Betsey pushed aside her chips with a loud sigh, her mouth contracted in a pout.

Frowning, Cornwallis drew himself up and glanced around the circle as though to make sure he had his audience's undivided attention. Elizabeth's heart constricted in sudden painful foreboding.

Returning his gaze to his commander, the earl said, "That reminds me of something I found most disturbing on our march into Trenton, Your Excellency. I meant to tell you about it tonight, but thought it best conveyed in private."

Howe motioned for the hovering servant to refill his glass. "Now's as good a time as any."

Cornwallis gave him a piercing look, perhaps thinking, as she did, Elizabeth reflected, that the general had indulged more freely in drink than was wise. "As you will, then. You remember that traitor Jonathan Carleton you thought either dead or safely stowed as a slave among the Seneca? Well . . . he's back."

A collective gasp rose from the circle around Elizabeth. It was the first time she had seen Howe shed his languid exterior. He bolted upright and fixed Cornwallis in an astonished stare.

"Damnation. Next you'll tell me that our little gadfly from Boston, the spy Oriole, has risen from the grave."

Cornwallis snorted. "I know nothing of your charming friend Oriole, but Carleton is most definitely alive. I spied him twice on the battlefield—"

Howe swung toward his brother. "What became of that . . . that Mohawk chieftain you sent to reclaim him from among the Shawnee?"

Her breath gone, feeling sick, Elizabeth noted that eyebrows rose all around the room. Clearly no one else had been privy to that information.

"The Shawnee?" Cornwallis demanded, startled. "I thought you told me he was with the Seneca."

Admiral Howe waved his hand in a dismissive gesture. "Seneca, Shawnee—whichever. This Mohawk Great Owl claimed the Shawnee war chief White Eagle who's set our western borders aflame is, in fact, Carleton, if you can credit it. And he boasted he'd bring him back to us—at an exorbitant price, of course. I was doubtful, but thought it worth pursuing on the off chance he might be right. Kill two birds with one stone, you see."

Now jaws were hanging open, all except for Betsey, who had subsided into sulky silence. Elizabeth prayed fervently that no one noted her turmoil.

Stunned, she thought numbly, *The admiral was behind this, not the general, as we assumed. I should have known. General Howe is too deficient in imagination and action to pursue such intrigue.* It was all she could do to maintain an appearance of calm instead of giving in to an overwhelming impulse to quit the room.

"What became of Great Owl?" General Howe said to his brother. "Obviously he never brought Carleton—or White Eagle—back."

Admiral Howe shrugged. "Haven't heard from him or the delegation he took with him since they left in late September. I was beginning to wonder what became of them, but I believe we can surmise the answer."

Howe stared blankly at him, then returned his attention to Cornwallis. "You couldn't have been mistaken?"

The general deliberately shook his head. "I met Carleton several times in London. As you know, his reputation was infamous after the Randolph affair, but I thought him extraordinary. He's a very hard man to forget." Stroking his chin thoughtfully, he added, "I wondered about the two Indians with him at Trenton—notable warriors, judging from their get-up and manner. Now it makes perfect sense."

"You're saying he's with Washington now?" Lord Howe demanded as though still disbelieving.

Cornwallis nodded and leaned forward. "I learned he commands a brigade of Rangers, and I can personally testify he's a most effective foe. He was in the van of the action all during the battle, and from all accounts evidently also at Princeton. I sent a detachment to take him, but he and his men fought like the very devil. No one could get anywhere close, and he seemed impervious to bullets."

Howe slouched back in his chair. "What a prize he'd make," he muttered as though to himself.

"Indeed he would, and that traitor Charles Andrews too," Cornwallis agreed. "He was there as well and stuck to Carleton's side like a burr. According to my officers, the two of them were involved in several sharp skirmishes with our foraging parties these past weeks.

They almost captured Carleton once, but in the end he fought free—with the loss of several of my best men, curse him, not to mention all the provisions the rascal robbed us of."

Feeling the color drain from her face, Elizabeth became aware that her hand was pressed hard to her breast. With an effort, she returned it to her lap and composed her features.

But not before Howe's eyes met hers. He drew deeply on his pipe and let out a ring of smoke, his gaze calculating.

The moment seemed briefly frozen in time. So rapidly did the general's attention shift back to his officers and the subtle impression of danger dissipate that she shook it off, however.

Staring at Howe in sick fascination, she thought absently that he was on the verge of a stroke. The muscles in his jaw worked and his hands clenched the arms of his chair so hard the knuckles whitened.

"I don't care what you have to do to get him—alive or dead. Move heaven and earth if you have to. Double the reward for his capture, and for Andrews as well. I've heard they're thick as thieves, and if we can get to him, we can get to Carleton."

Abruptly Betsey sat upright in her chair and clapped her hands. The sound of her laughter sent chills down Elizabeth's spine.

"Oh, my dear, don't you think the scalp of a notorious traitor would earn even greater favors from our sovereign than a knighthood?"

The corners of Howe's thick, protruding lips lifted hungrily. "Demme me, but I think you're onto something, love. Leave it to a little baggage like you to come up with such inspiration.

"What do you think, Miss Howard?" he drawled, transferring his gaze to Elizabeth.

Meeting his probing glance with a calm one very far from reflecting her true emotions, she laughed lightly. "It would seem a highly fitting end for the villain—not to mention a most effective admonishment for anyone tempted to follow his scurrilous example."

His pause almost imperceptible, Howe inclined his head, his dark eyes lingering on her. "You heard the lady then. A rich reward to the one who brings me Carleton's scalp."

Which I shall do everything in my power to deny you, she thought in grim determination. *Little do you know that in reality Oriole is still alive. And you'll not succeed in your goal. Be certain of it.*

Deliberately she toyed with the tiny rosebuds tucked into the décolletage of her bodice to draw attention to the swell of her bosom. Taking a deep breath and letting it out in a soft sigh, she met Howe's glance as it lifted from her fingers.

As their gaze met, she felt the heat in his and returned a languid smile before dropping her eyes, the familiar thrill of danger and challenge racing through her veins.

Chapter Eleven

IN THE ABSENCE OF ANY UNUSUAL NOISE or sense of danger, consciousness returned a degree at a time: first the awareness of numbing cold seeping through the layers of wool blanket, buffalo hide, and bearskin that wrapped him. Then the sound of his companions' slow, regular breaths. The faint seethe of hot coals in the fire circle, banked beneath a thick layer of ash. The familiar, oppressive scent of stale wood smoke and stink of rancid grease mingled with sour sweat that hung heavy in the confined space.

He shifted his position, felt the give of the sleeping platform's pliant weave beneath his body. The barely perceptible brightening of early dawn filtered through his eyelids. Stretching, he opened his eyes and rolled onto his back, reluctant to surrender the sweet bonds of slumber.

He had dreamed of Elizabeth. They were back with his people in Grey Cloud's town, and all anger and sorrow had gone. Every face reflected only gladness and welcome, for that day he and Elizabeth were to take one another as husband and wife.

But she was not there, and the bitter realities of the cheerless camp where he found himself now bore upon him in a flood, for a moment paralyzing him. He could feel again the sweet sensation of her nestled in his arms when he awoke that first morning at Somerset Court House. When she had turned over, opening her eyes sleepily and smiling up at him, his heart had constricted with such desire and pain that he could hardly breathe.

If only they had been alone instead of crowded together with more than a dozen others in that cramped kitchen!

He wanted her with him. Always. With every breath he took. Tantalizingly close now, only a day's ride from the camp, she seemed farther out of his reach than before in the depths of that relentless winter.

On the other side of the snug wigewa, Red Fox sat slowly up. Still wound in his bearskin, he swung his legs over the edge of the sleeping platform. Carleton suppressed a smile as the warrior eyed him with characteristic calculation.

Carlton pushed off his wrappings and rose to put on breechcloth and moccasins. Indifferent to the frigid air, he went outside to relieve himself in the vault a short distance down the slope behind the wigewa. Retracing his steps, he stopped at the crest of the rise and for some moments stood staring across the silent camp that sprawled over the hushed, snowy hills around him.

He drew in a deep breath of the cold air. A hint of breeze carried the fresh, clean scents of pine and spruce and snow, underlaid by a faint trace of wood smoke.

The light was just coming into the sky, and dusky indigo shades of night still pooled in and around the snow-frosted pines. To the east and overhead, the brilliant starpoints had begun to fade into the encroaching dawn. As he stood suspended, the rising sun's first rays suddenly flamed across the leafless treetops in a vivid band of molten red-gold above the shadowed greyish-brown trunks lower down and outlined the undulating contours of the beautiful, deceptively serene Loantaka Valley that stretched out before him.

Moving between the rude log cabins that thickly dotted the area he could see the shadowed figures of the day pickets heading out to their posts to relieve the night sentries. Many of the cabins had been inexpertly built and already sagged under the weight of snow drifted high by repeated storms.

In the shallow swale below him, where his Rangers camped at the edge of the forest, a number of compact, snug wigewas interspersed the huts, modeled on those the Shawnee had quickly thrown up on their arrival. Most of them belonged to Isaiah's black troop and to the Indian scouts the brigade continued to attract, but some of the white troops were beginning to see the wisdom of the design.

He glanced toward the northwest, where a mile and a half away the peaceful village of Morristown hugged the foot of Thimble Mountain. Twenty-six miles west of New York, the village could be reached only by passing through narrow gorges formed by the long parallel ridges of the Watchung Mountains. The range stretched southwest to northeast from the Raritan River to New Jersey's northern boundary, effectively protecting the town's approaches as well as the army's lines of communication with New England and Pennsylvania. From this stronghold Washington could monitor British movements and move rapidly in any direction to counter them.

The force of little more than 2,500 Continentals spread throughout a much wider region than the vicinity of Morristown, however. Detachments were strung from Princeton to the highlands along the Hudson River, and both officers and common soldiers had taken shelter in any habitable structure that could be leased or commandeered.

Exceptionally harsh weather had held sway throughout January and into this first week of February. The surrounding forests provided abundant wood for shelter and fire.

But supplying the army with food, clothing, weapons, and other equipment was a continuing burden relieved only irregularly and temporarily when detachments of Continentals or the militia bands roving through the region brought in goods captured from enemy supply trains. Indeed, the rebels had attacked British patrols and foraging parties so relentlessly that Howe had been forced to withdraw his troops from almost all of New Jersey.

The previous month American General George Clinton had taken possession of Hackensack, with the British precipitously fleeing before him. Units of the rebel force even camped directly across the Hudson from Staten Island. Only a narrow strip along both sides of the Raritan from Brunswick to Amboy now remained under British control, leaving Loyalists outside it exposed to their enraged neighbors bent on wreaking vengeance for the outrages they had suffered at the hands of his majesty's soldiers.

Accounts of the battles at Trenton and Princeton had spread throughout the colonies like wildfire, reigniting patriotic fervor and armed resistance to Britain. Widely viewed as vindication of the glorious cause, the victories had garnered lavish public praise for Washington, with the Continental Army repeatedly cited as the instrument of God's redeeming providence.

As a result, increasing numbers of those who had pledged loyalty to the king in November and December were tossing aside their oaths and joining the rebellion, while the timid who had previously hesitated to join the fray grew bold. In spite of the winter storms, new recruits continued to filter into the camps, the majority signed up for three years instead of one, in accordance with Washington's demands.

The General had also insisted that every unit and soldier of the Continental Army now be designated as simply American rather than by State, as had been the custom before. "It is the greater name," he had told his officers, and Carleton had seen the wisdom of it.

Shaking off his reverie, he strode the rest of the way to his wigewa. Smoke twined upward from its smoke hole and also from that of the smaller wigewa beside it that belonged to Andrews and Blue Sky. A trail of footprints led from the smaller structure toward the sturdy log cabin at the base of the rise that served as his headquarters.

Hearing the crunch of approaching footsteps, he turned to see Captain Mark Jeffreys approaching, bundled in a thick greatcoat, woolen scarf, and gloves. Carleton's handsome twenty-year-old aide came to a halt and touched his fingers to the brim of his cocked hat, grinning.

"Mornin', sir," Jeffreys greeted him in an easy drawl. "Fine day for walkin' out 'thout clothes."

Carleton lifted an eyebrow. "You ought to try it, Jeffreys. Good for the soul."

Considering him dubiously, Jeffreys wiped his dripping nose with a handkerchief. "The body too, I'd say. You're the only one of us that hasn't gotten sick so far."

Chuckling, Carleton motioned him to follow, then ducked inside through the wigewa's hide door flap and stamped the snow off his moccasins. Jeffreys greeted the two warriors with a nod and eagerly joined them at the blaze they were nursing in the fire circle, hands extended to its heat.

Spotted Pony took in Carleton's bare chest with a grimace. "I wish I were as you and did not feel the cold."

Carleton shrugged. "Heat or cold, it is all the same. One gives way to the other." He put on leggings and drew a hunting shirt over his head before squatting beside them, grateful for the fire's warmth in spite of himself.

Red Fox coughed. "We have camped here only a single moon," he rasped, his voice hoarse. "If we live until *Shkipiye kwiitha,* the Sap Moon, we will do well."

Carleton directed a concerned look at his cousin, then reassured, countered, "Have you not said the same every winter we've spent together? But Blue Sky's medicine appears to have had a good effect. You look much improved today."

Red Fox grunted, his expression registering skepticism. Just then Andrews pushed his way inside, cheeks and nose red, breath pluming in the still air. Close behind him followed Briggs, burdened with an armload of firewood. Jeffreys sprang to his feet to help the servant stack the wood tidily by the fire circle.

Rubbing his chapped hands together vigorously, Andrews greeted the others. "I'm glad to see you're on the mend, Red Fox," he added with satisfaction, ignoring the warrior's scowl. "I told you Blue Sky knows how to break a fever."

"She did me some good too," Jeffreys agreed. He glanced at Carleton as he rewound his scarf around his neck and pulled on his gloves. "I'll ride in to headquarters, turn in our returns, and get the orders for the day, if that'll suit, sir. And I'll draw the brigade's rations while I'm there."

"You mean to say we actually have rations this week?" Carleton drawled.

Jeffreys conceded a wry smile. "We do, and our boots will be spared a while longer."

"Excellent. Hopefully by the time you return breakfast will be ready."

"Save some for me."

Carleton returned his aide's salute, congratulating himself again for singling out the young Marylander, who had joined his brigade a couple of weeks earlier. Jeffreys had quickly taken over the burden of paperwork and correspondence that consumed so much of Carleton's time and even managed the Rangers' irascible quartermaster with ease. A born horseman, he had proven to be intelligent, disciplined, and trustworthy as well as a natural leader who grasped assignments quickly and carried them out with efficiency, anticipating what was needed before being asked.

"Our raids are the cause of our present lack," Andrews grumbled. "Howe's minions have become shy about shipping supplies to their garrisons. Their soldiers are consequently becoming as much tatterdemalions as ourselves, while their commander whiles away the winter in balls and banquets at New York."

"We'll pray our French and Spanish friends speed their wares our way," Carleton returned. "Then maybe we can give Howe less to celebrate."

Andrews turned to his servant. "Blue Sky's fetching our portion of the rations, Briggs. Head on over and help her."

The servant saluted and followed Jeffreys outside.

"What of our horses?" Carleton said. "Have we lost any more?"

"Another dead this morning. Unfortunately they're not in as good case as we are. The poor beasts have dug through the snow and eaten to the ground what little grass was left."

Carleton laid another branch on the fire. "At least the General's strategy of denying the British forage for their animals is ensuring they suffer more than we do in that regard."

"No horses means no supply wagons, no artillery for battle, and no cavalry," Andrews agreed with satisfaction. "By the way, I'm sending Smithson out with a detachment to range farther west in hopes of finding better forage for our own. If the other units beat us to it, we'll find ourselves in the same state."

"Smithson seems markedly less peevish of late."

Andrews reclined on the sleeping platform. "He's entirely too cheerful. I'm convinced he plans to leave us at the first opportunity and take the other malcontents with him."

"Good riddance, as far as I'm concerned. They fight each other more than the enemy."

"They'll leave us in even greater need of recruits than we are now," Andrews pointed out.

"If Spotted Pony and I return to our people at Pooshkwiitha, the Half Moon, we can report to the council and bring back those willing to fight with us."

Eyes narrowed, Carleton glanced from Red Fox to his brother. "I've been thinking the same thing. We can use as many seasoned warriors as you can persuade to come. And it will be well for us to reassure the council—and learn whether Raging Bull and his party still seek to turn our people against us."

"I agree," Andrews said. "But be warned that many more of the men will leave if the numbers of Blacks and our people increase. A substantial number are already discontent."

"More than large numbers of warriors, we need canny ones. I seem to remember that God commanded Gideon to thin the ranks of his army until only those who wouldn't shrink from the battle were left."

At the warriors' questioning looks, Carleton briefly recounted the story. "If we try to stand toe to toe with Howe on his terms, he'll grind us to dust," he concluded. "The British army is composed of hardened, well trained, professional soldiers. Ours is not. These last battles are a perfect example of what's to be accomplished when we use tactics they're not trained for."

"All well and good," Andrews said, "but we need food, clothing, and weapons if we're to continue to fight. Continental dollars are worthless. No merchant will take them, so we can't buy what we need, and the British goose is offering fewer golden eggs for us to gather."

Carleton's grin turned into a scowl. "What the deuce has become of Stowe? He's had long enough to ride to Thornlea and back twice by now."

Yawning, Andrews stretched. "Considering that he had to not only free all your slaves, but also arrange for the management of the estate—to say nothing of this weather—I'll be surprised if he returns within the month."

"He'd better hurry. I hope he thinks to bring clothing along with the food and other supplies." Carleton flicked the fringe of his hunting shirt. "Every shirt we have is threadbare, and our leggings and moccasins are wearing through."

"Stowe always thinks of everything," Andrews noted smugly.

Carleton chuckled. "So he does. How's the rest of the army faring?"

"Gaunt as scarecrows, most of them. A few look suspiciously well fed, which makes me wonder whether those two good horses that disappeared last week merely strayed off after all," Andrews said darkly.

Cumbered with bundles and wrapped to the eyes, Blue Sky slipped into the wigewa with a similarly burdened Briggs at her heels. Giving the men a cheerful nod, she pushed back the blanket hooded over her head and settled cross-legged on the opposite side of the fire circle from Carleton.

He watched her fill a small black iron kettle with water from an earthenware jar and hang it from a tripod over the fire. When the water boiled, she stirred in parched corn and bits of dried venison, then add maple sugar to the mixture.

In spite of the privations that had become commonplace, a happy glow enveloped the young matron. She appeared even more beautiful in the reflection of the flames. Marriage clearly agreed with her.

And with Andrews too, Carleton thought. Smiling, he threw a sidelong glance at his friend, who watched his wife's every move with pleased satisfaction.

Carleton had never seen a couple more joyful in each other. A pang of envy stole through him, but resolutely he cast it off. That way lay only despair.

They were just finishing breakfast when one of Washington's aides, Captain Tench Tilghman, ducked into the wigewa. Straightening as much as the tall officer could without hitting his head on the roof, he saluted.

"Pardon the interruption, General."

Carleton got quickly to his feet. "His Excellency's quinsy has not grown worse, I hope."

"No, sir, nor better, unfortunately. But he asks that you attend upon him immediately."

Carleton raised his eyebrows. "It must be an important matter if he sent you, Captain Tilghman. I met with him just yesterday. Did he say what is so urgent?"

"Only that you're to come without delay." Nodding to Andrews, Tilghman added, "The colonel too."

"YOU'RE INVOLVED in whatever this is, I take it. What's going on? It must be important for the General to summon us from his sickbed."

With Andrews behind him, Carleton stood halfway up the broad, curving stairway of Jacob Arnold's expansive three-story tavern on Morristown Green, where they had met Stern coming down. The stocky colonel squeezed Carleton's arm, but avoided his gaze.

"He'll fill you in. I'll wait for you below." He disappeared down the stairway.

When Carleton threw him a questioning glance, Andrews shrugged. "Obviously he doesn't want to talk to us."

Carleton mounted the rest of the stairs, tension tightening his gut. Tilghman had ridden ahead and before they could knock admitted them to the front room, which Washington used as both bedchamber and office. Although the room was spacious, it was crammed with a four-poster bed, a highboy, a washstand, a large table and chairs, and a good deal of the General's camp equipment, much of which overflowed into the adjoining dressing room. A large ballroom and more bedchambers, home to Washington's aides and a few of the higher ranking officers, occupied the rest of the second floor, with more officers finding accommodations on the floor above.

Carleton transferred his gaze from Tilghman's noncommittal countenance to a younger, brown-haired man he did not recognize to Washington's pale, tight-lipped visage. What he saw was not reassuring.

After dismissing his aide, the General motioned the rest of them to sit at the table. They complied without speaking.

"This is Caleb Stern, Colonel Stern's nephew," Washington said without ceremony, his voice raspy from the severe sore throat he had been nursing for several weeks. "He serves as butler to the Miss Howards in New York and has brought intelligence gained from General Howe's mistress."

Eyes narrowing, Carleton said, "My understanding was that Miss Howard would report directly to me." He tried to keep the stiffness out of his tone and failed.

"That was our agreement. However, this time—"

Carleton's chest constricted. "They're not in some trouble?"

"Not at the moment." Washington pulled out a handkerchief and covered his mouth as he coughed, then cleared his throat. "It is you who are in danger."

Carleton exchanged glances with Andrews, then gave a short laugh. "I've been called here urgently to learn that? I'm fully aware there's a price on my head, and—"

"I recommend that you give careful attention to what Mr. Stern has to say, General Carleton."

Although Washington spoke softly, he might as well have shouted. His expression as freezing as his tone, he indicated to Stern's nephew that he was to speak.

Without ceremony Caleb gave a terse account of the conversation between Howe and Cornwallis at the ball a little more than two weeks earlier, concluding with Mrs. Loring's comment about making a gift to the king of Carleton's scalp. "Miss Howard has been near frantic to warn you ever since, but with the weather so harsh and security so tight, I wasn't able to slip out of New York until last night. She thought it best General Washington be alerted first," he added delicately.

Carleton heard him out in stony silence, all too conscious of his commander's narrowed scrutiny. Dismissed, the younger Stern left the room along with Tilghman.

Washington fixed Carleton in a piercing gaze. "You are aware that Cornwallis saw you during the battle. That he recognized you. That attempts have been made to capture you during the raids you have led." His tone was flat, but there was anger behind it.

Carleton returned a smoldering glance. "I am."

"But you told me nothing of it, sir."

"You knew as well as I that it was inevitable the British would learn of my return. I didn't think such minor incidents noteworthy—"

Beside him Andrews jumped as Washington slammed his hand on the table. "Not noteworthy? One of my top officers foolishly placed himself at the forefront in battle, within easy reach of the enemy, on repeated occasions. General Cornwallis said they almost took you!"

"They didn't succeed."

"Plans are afoot to complete the job as soon as possible."

Carleton gritted his teeth. "They'll kill me before they capture me."

"Then they will have succeeded in their aims," Washington said testily. "And if they do manage to capture you alive, they will parade you publicly to your execution as a lesson for all who have the temerity to oppose them. But you, sir, do not deem the matter of any importance."

Carleton sprang to his feet. "You're a fine one to chastise me for taking the van in battle, Your Excellency," he burst out, witnesses be cursed, knowing he took his career—and his life—in his hands. "Your life is much more important to our cause than mine, yet in every battle you risk it without a second thought."

To his surprise, Washington answered mildly, "Sit down."

Carleton obeyed, his jaw set.

"No reward has been offered for my capture or death," Washington pointed out. "And my Life Guard is always with me."

With an effort Carleton matched his tone to his commander's. "In the heat of battle you're often in advance of your guard and thus exposed to a determined assault—as at Princeton, when you made yourself a fine target for the enemy. It's God's grace alone that spared you. Were you taken or killed, the rebellion would be at an end, and Howe knows it full well. There's no one else who can hold this army together or who has any hope of leading it to victory."

Washington waved his words away. "No man is indispensible."

Although the General again spoke quietly, Carleton sensed that he had scored his point. Satisfaction was short lived, however.

His face clouding, Washington continued, "Be that as it may, I am unaware of any extraordinary danger to me, whereas you are now once more in the enemy's sights. Mr. Stern tells me that General Howe has doubled the reward for your capture. Or for your dead body. He is not particular, as long as he can make a gift of your scalp to George the Third. The British will never forgive or forget what they consider your treason—"

"Treason *you* recruited me for," Carleton broke in, his voice thick.

For a tense moment the two men faced each other silently, at checkmate. At length Washington said, "Yes. I recruited you, and when you justified my confidence beyond my expectations, how did I reward you? By separating you from your betrothed and sending you to negotiate with the Indians, a decision that tore your life apart. So you see, you have become my burden. Do you think the consequences you endure as a result of my orders do not haunt me?"

Taken off guard, Carleton stared into the air before him, only dimly registering that Andrews's hand closed over his arm.

"Your Excellency, with your permission I'll assign General Carleton a personal guard."

"Thank you, Colonel Andrews. Assign a guard to attend you as well. The reward for your capture has also been doubled, and I wish you to take every precaution to avoid that fate." He nodded toward the door. "Leave us for now."

Andrews rose and saluted. "Yes sir." Turning to Carleton, he met his blank stare with sympathy, then withdrew from the room.

"Capital!" Carleton burst out as soon as the door closed. "Then I'm to be a prisoner in my own camp."

Washington's gaze turned flinty. "Continue this insubordination, and by God, in spite of our long friendship, I will be most happy to oblige you. Just so there is no misunderstanding, you will not leave camp unless you have my express permission. If you disregard my orders, sir, I will have you arrested and court-martialed."

Stunned, Carleton again sprang to his feet. "You wouldn't—"

Rising, Washington drew himself up to his full height. "Flout my authority, and you will suffer the consequences."

It took a moment for Carleton to find his voice, then he said more quietly, "Sir, you've given all your generals free rein to attack enemy detachments at their discretion as long as they don't allow themselves to be drawn into a general action. Your policy has been most effective, and I think I've justified your confidence over these past few weeks."

"You have more than justified it. You have acted with vigor and effectiveness, and you have kept casualties low—"

"As a result, you propose to set me aside—"

"Prove to me that you are capable of prudence when it is warranted and that you will be bound by my authority—in this, at least," Washington concluded dryly.

In Carlton's mind arose the vivid memory of standing at the edge of a dark clearing, his warriors surrounding him, stripped and painted for battle and waiting for his command to unleash their battle cry. He forced back the cold anger that rose in his breast . . . and saw the comprehension in his commander's eyes.

For a tense moment Washington regarded him without speaking. At last he said softly, "I am your friend, Jon. Not your enemy. Regardless of what happened out there on the frontier."

Livid and shaking, Carleton said hoarsely, "Am I dismissed, sir?"

"For now. You will report to me at nine o'clock tomorrow morning and every morning thereafter."

Sketching a perfunctory salute, Carleton stalked to the door.

"Let it go."

He turned slowly to meet Washington's pained gaze. "I know it is not as easy as all that, but—"

"You're right," Carleton said through gritted teeth. "It isn't."

Washington spread his hands. "In the end, it's a matter of the will. And courage. Let it go and come back to us, Jon."

Carleton gave a harsh laugh. "You're much mistaken. The problem, you see, is that it won't let *me* go."

Without giving Washington time to respond, he turned on his heel, threw open the door, and stalked from the room, feeling as though the Furies pursued him.

DOWNSTAIRS IN THE TAVERN'S wide central hall, he found Andrews waiting with Stern and his nephew, their expressions reflecting varying degrees of concern and trepidation. For a moment Carleton was equally tempted to laugh or to curse.

He glanced quickly around. Through open doors on either side he could see into the front and back parlors and the formal dining room. In each, officers clustered at tables piled with maps and papers. The buzz of their voices mingled with the muted tones of the customers nursing their pints in the barroom off to one side and the clatter of dishes in the kitchen at the back of the building.

He drew Caleb with him outside, ignoring Andrews and Stern, who followed but kept their distance. "Miss Howard is well?"

Caleb nodded. "As well as can be, sir, considering her concern for you."

"Tell her I am well and not to worry. And assure her of my love."

"She sent the same to you, sir."

"Tell her also that, thanks to her, I am confined to camp for the foreseeable future." Carleton allowed a faint smile to play over his features. "And warn her I'll not soon forget that she went over my head in this matter. The next time we meet, which I devoutly pray will be soon, I intend to impose suitable consequences for her perfidy."

Caleb grinned. "I'll forewarn her, General Carleton. But as you know her, I doubt she'll be much daunted."

Carleton snorted. "There's not much that daunts my lady. In truth, I love her for it, but don't tell her so, else she'll be much emboldened, and I'll hold you accountable."

"Your secret is safe with me, sir," Caleb said with a laugh.

Chapter Twelve

"I KNOW YOU'RE ANGRY, JON, but please listen to reason."

"I'm so far beyond anger," Carleton returned, seething, "that there's no word for what I feel."

Andrews sighed, at his wit's end. "Listen to me! Washington is right. This is very serious. You came within a hair's breadth of the hangman's noose back at Boston not two years ago. Remember? I was there. As desperate as your situation was then—and I also had a taste of it in that cursed gaol—if Howe manages to capture you again, he'll ensure that even Oriole won't be able to rescue you. And you know he's going to make every possible attempt now."

He watched Carleton prowl up and down the wigewa's constricted length, shoulders hunched to keep from hitting his head against the bent willow saplings that supported the roof. "So I'm to be locked up in this cage for how long? The rest of the war—which promises to drag on for years?"

Andrews waved his arms. "Not likely, and you know it. You're too effective, and Washington needs you too much to have you sit idle for long. My guess is he's trying to get through that thick skull of yours the necessity of taking reasonable precautions."

"When you begin to take what most men term 'reasonable precautions,' you become so bound in speculation and fear that you might as well be chained in irons!"

Andrews let out an exasperated breath.

Carleton rounded on him. "And what of you? Do you mean to cower behind your personal guard when it comes to battle?"

For a moment Andrews stood still, then he turned away, shoulders slumping. "What's the use? Neither of us can do it. Nor can Washington."

"My point exactly," Carleton said smugly, glancing at Red Fox and Spotted Pony, who lounged by the fire, watching them with unconcealed amusement. "Nor can Beth. Or Blue Sky, for that matter."

Andrews let out a groan. "Tell me about it. I try to impress upon her that I only want to keep her safe, and she looks at me with fond amusement as if I'm a wee bit daft. Are all Shawnee women so stubborn?"

Carleton chuckled. "It's common to the female sex."

"The thought that she might come to harm well nigh drives me insane."

"Now you understand my dilemma."

Andrews gave his friend a wry look. "What do you suggest?"

Carleton folded his arms across his chest. "We could turn our backs on all of it and return to our people."

The two warriors exchanged looks, and Spotted Pony said eagerly, "They will welcome us home with much joy."

"We'd have to find a way to get Beth out of New York," Andrews pointed out.

Carleton looked quickly away, hands clenching. "That's easily enough done."

Andrews regarded him with sympathy, wrestling mightily with his own emotions. Before he could speak, Red Fox said, "If you abandon the Long Knives, White Eagle, there can no longer be any question that you are one of us. And Golden Elk too."

Andrews expelled a breath. "More and more I long to return to our people. They—my wife—have captured my heart, and each day the truth bears upon me more strongly that when this war ends, I'll not walk among the Long Knives again."

Carleton arrested and fixed him in a piercing look. "You are so determined?"

Suddenly Andrews knew the truth of it. "I am."

"When this war ends . . . "

"Moneto has called us here—all of us." Andrews looked from one to the other. "You know it as well as I. We've no choice but to stay until his purpose is accomplished."

As though he spoke to himself, Carleton muttered, "For now. But it's yet to be determined what that purpose is."

LYING ON THE SLEEPING PLATFORM wrapped in blanket and bearskin, Andrews propped himself up on one elbow, his head supported in his hand. "I wish I knew what he's thinking. He doesn't tell me the half of it."

"It is wise to think more than you say," Blue Sky responded lazily, snuggling into the curve of his body.

He glanced down and brushed the hair back from her cheek. "I don't dispute that, but neither should one keep secrets from one's closest friends and allies. I'm just worried about what he's likely to do. You didn't see him when he was raging."

She gave a sleepy smile. "White Eagle always does what is right."

"Hmpf."

He lay down and drew her against him, nuzzling the back of her neck. Giggling, she turned her head to accept his kiss. As always, his heart melted.

"You grow more beautiful every day," he whispered against her satin skin. "And I love you more every day."

She rolled over and took his face between her hands. "Truly Moneto blesses me. Did not White Eagle say he would?"

"He did." He smiled, gazing deep into her eyes, then sobered. "And it's my duty as a man, as your husband, to keep you safe. As a boy I was taught I have no honor if I don't protect my wife."

"But this is not our custom, my husband," she insisted patiently as she had each time he brought up the subject. "You are no longer Long Knife. A Shawnee man understands that his woman is his equal and helps him in everything he does."

He released a sigh, silently acknowledging the futility of his arguments. "I will do my best to learn our people's customs." Changing the subject, he said, "I was afraid you'd be lonely when Healer Woman and her aunt went away."

"I miss my sister, and auntie too. I hope I will see them again soon."

"At least you've made a new friend. How is Mary doing since her husband died?"

"I think it helps her when we sit and talk about him. I tell her about Pathfinder and that I have no one then too. And that Moneto will care for her as he does for me."

"Your English is growing better." He touched her lips lightly with his. "Doesn't she have family to go home to?"

She shook her head. "She will stay and wash the soldiers' clothes for money." She hesitated before saying with a smile, "Today she tells me she will have a baby in Sha'teepakanootha, the Wilted Moon. I tell her we have our babies together."

It took a moment for him to absorb her words. He lay unmoving, finally propped himself back up on his elbow to study her, eyebrows raised.

"What do you mean, you'll have your babies together?"

"In the *Sha'teepakanootha* I will give you a son," she whispered, her eyes filling with tears.

He stared at her, stunned. "Blue Sky—"

Radiant, she touched her fingers to his lips. "You are not pleased?"

He kissed her fingertips. "I'm beyond pleased. A baby . . . it's the last thing I expected right now, but I'm delighted! How long have you known?"

"I think so since soon after we come to this place, but I wait until I am certain."

He let out a whoop and captured her in his arms. "A baby! A son—" He drew back. "But how do you know it'll be a son and not a daughter? If it's a girl, I'll be equally pleased."

She looked up at him with adoration in her eyes. "I will give you a daughter, yes, but first a son. We will have many sons and daughters."

Holding her close, he slipped his hand down to her abdomen, feeling the slightest swell beneath skin and muscle. She pressed her hand over his.

"When *Hotehimini kiishthwa,* the Strawberry Moon, comes, we will feel him move," she murmured, smiling.

After she finally fell asleep, he lay for a long time watching her, deeply stirred by gratitude—and by fear. He had given little thought to the possibility that she would become pregnant at some point, had not anticipated that it would happen so soon. Not now. Now he saw that he had been foolish to ignore the complications that must arise when the inevitable happened.

The birth of children was certainly not usual. It was an event as ancient as Creation. But it seemed to him a wholly new thing, the first conception since the dawn of time.

For it was his child this time. And hers. Their first. A mysterious melding of their two bodies and minds and lives to bring forth another human being. Of them, but unique. Unlike any other.

They would truly become a family now. Forever bound together in the circle of life.

Or would they? How was he to keep her and their child safe in the midst of war, while not seeming to do so in order to please her? Always his mind returned to this worry.

He released her and rolled over onto his back. Staring into the darkness unseeing, joy and terror washing over him in equal measure, he reflected ruefully that becoming a proper Shawnee husband and father was going to be considerably harder than he had anticipated.

HEARING THE RUMBLE of approaching hoofbeats, Carleton pushed back the stack of papers Jeffreys had placed before him on the camp table for his signature. When the horsemen came to a halt in front of the sturdy log hut that served as his headquarters, he accompanied his aide outside. The guards posted on either side of the door hastily stepped out of their path, carbines shouldered.

It was the end of February, and over the past few days a brief thaw had turned the packed snow on the camp's roads into a quagmire, refreezing it at night, then melting it again when the sun rose. The horses of the company that drew to a halt in front of the building were liberally spattered with mud, as were their riders. Beneath heavy coats, the latter were garbed in new hunting shirts, breeches, and boots that matched the Rangers,' and they were similarly equipped with carbines, pistols, and sabres.

They were also mostly black, with only a handful of white men among them. At the rear of the party several black women and older children rode in heavily loaded wagons ahead of what looked to be a substantial herd of horses, driven along by more mounted black men. The entire party looked strangely familiar.

Noting from the corner of his eye that Andrews, Briggs, and Isaiah were hurrying from the far side of the camp to join them, Carleton turned his gaze on Stowe. He swung down from the saddle of a fine bay gelding unperturbed, came to attention, and gave a brisk salute before turning to order the troop to dismount, which they did in fine style.

After briefly introducing Stowe to his aide, Carleton surveyed the line of horsemen with a frown. "It's high time you got here."

"My apologies, sir," Stowe returned, the livid scar that ran from his left eye to his jaw puckering his face even more. "I been a mite busy carryin' out your orders."

"I can see that. I take it these are volunteers."

"They be indeed, sir."

Carleton nodded to the men in the front ranks. "Moses, Billy, Justice. You're doing well, I trust."

The men touched their fingers to the brim of their hats. "Yes, sir," Moses returned in a bass rumble. "We thank you, sir—"

"No need for that," Carleton cut him off.

"After I freed 'em as ye directed, I got to thinkin'," Stowe explained. "So I told 'em if they joined up to fight, ye'd promise 'em a horse, weapons, clothing, and food for the duration . . . and twenty dollars and ten acres o' prime farmland at the end o' the war too, just to sweeten the deal. O' course, ye'd naturally maintain their elderly and the women and children at Thornlea if they'd carry on there meanwhilest. Thought that'd make things easier all around."

Carleton's eyebrows rose. He took in the white men at the far end of the line, recognizing them as small landholders from the neighborhood surrounding Thornlea, the vast estate along the Blue Ridge in Virginia that he had inherited from his uncle and adoptive father, Sir Harrison Carleton.

After greeting each by name, Carleton took in Stowe's tall bay gelding, then nodded toward the men's mounts. "Those are my horses."

Stowe considered the animals thoughtfully. "So they be. Didn't touch yer breedin' stock, though, sir."

"I appreciate that," Carleton said, his tone dry. "And their weapons . . . ?"

"Tapped yer account to supply 'em."

Carleton folded his arms and regarded him with a frown. "You exceeded your authority, Stowe."

His servant ruminated for a moment, rubbing his chin as he studied Carleton with his good eye. "That I did, sir. Seemed to me as they'd be good fighters."

Carleton paused for a deliberate moment before clapping his hand on the older man's shoulder. "Well done, good and faithful servant," he said with a laugh.

"Thank'ee, sir," Stowe returned, his mouth twisting into a satisfied smile.

"Now you'll have to promote Captain Moghrab to major, which will grind Smithson no end," Andrews broke in with a wink at Isaiah. "And if Red Fox and Spotted Pony bring along a contingent of warriors when they return from reporting to the council, he'll positively caper with delight."

Stowe's face brightened. "If ye don't need me here for the time bein', I'll go back and help 'em." At Carleton's questioning look, he shrugged and frowned down at the ground. "This likely lookin' widow was makin' eyes at me a'fore we left. Been thinkin' 'bout her, and I just might see if she's agreeable."

Carleton threw up his hands, but couldn't suppress a grin. "Red Fox and Spotted Pony have been agitating to bring back their wives, so you might as well bring one along too. They'll keep Blue Sky company and relieve Colonel Andrews's mind—especially now that she's with child," he added, directing a pointed glance at the beaming colonel.

When the others had congratulated Andrews, Carleton told Stowe, "I fear few of our people will join us, but you should find a sympathetic audience among the other tribes. Just don't be overly zealous in giving away my money," he cautioned. "I'm not a rich man, after all."

Andrews rolled his eyes and exchanged an amused glance with Stowe. "Doubtless you're still on the verge of bankruptcy, as you've been ever since I've known you."

Carleton gave him a sober look. "I will be in short order if I'm not careful, and all of us will suffer for it. As you well know, Congress has no power to levy taxes, and little inclination to do so, considering that a prime cause of this war is Parliament's attempts to tax us without our consent."

Andrews gave a rueful laugh. "Ironic, isn't it? Our high ideals have caught us in their toils."

Isaiah pulled off his hat and scratched his head. "We few sacrifice everythin' so the rest sleep peaceful in their beds."

"That's how it's always been," Carleton said. "The result is that resources are stretched to the breaking point, and provisioning the army becomes the responsibility of the officers. We make whatever shifts we must to feed, clothe, and equip our men so they can fight."

Clamping his hat back on his head, Isaiah growled, "We wastin' time talking 'bout what can't be changed. Accordin' to the Gen'l's orders, we need to get these men inoculated if they ain't had the pox yet. Their women an' children too."

Stowe threw a dubious glance at the new recruits. Many of the faces reflected alarm.

"Half the camp is down sick from it," Andrews noted, "but the men are recovering. When the new campaign opens, we'll be thankful we took the precaution."

After ordering Isaiah to see to the men's accommodations and arrange for their inoculation without delay, Carleton watched them march off leading their horses, with their supply wagons and families following. It occurred to him that his brigade was beginning to resemble the outlaw force David had gathered in the Stronghold when pursued by King Saul. Considering that the British were equally determined to capture and execute him, he reflected with grim humor, perhaps that was exactly what was called for.

Turning abruptly, he found Jeffreys studying him intently. "If you've any reservations about serving with Blacks and Indians, now's the time to speak up."

Jeffreys scratched his head and studied his boots before looking up to meet Carleton's challenging gaze. "I wasn't raised that way, sir," he conceded. "But seems to me that if a man is willin' and able to fight for our cause, he ought to be given the chance."

"Fair enough," Carleton returned. "It's not always the case in the army, Jeffreys, but I'm determined that in my brigade, at least, each man will rise or fall on his own merit."

He waited until Jeffreys went back into the cabin before turning to Stowe, who lingered. "You sent *Destiny* and the others back to Marseilles as I directed?" he asked, referring to the merchantmen he had ordered sent to France to be refitted as men of war.

Stowe spit reflectively into the snow. "Ye'll have a nice little fleet by the time yer uncle finishes with 'em. I wrote 'im ye'd be needin' 'em by end o' July at the latest."

"Excellent. I'll respond to le comte's latest letter and let him know my plans. I intend to apply to Congress for letters of marque and reprisal as soon as I can get away so we'll be ready by the time the ships return. I want to put them to good use as soon as possible."

As Stowe turned away, Carleton stopped him with a hand on his shoulder. "Say nothing of this to Jeffreys, at least for now." At his servant's questioning look, he said, "He's a good man and doubtless trustworthy, but he's only been with us a short time. The fewer people who know about this, the better."

Chapter Thirteen

"JUST A SIP OF BROTH," Elizabeth coaxed, bending over her patient. "It will strengthen you."

She cradled the emaciated, middle-aged woman's head to steady her and pressed the cup to her lips. The woman swallowed barely a mouthful before sagging back onto the pillow.

"Thank'e," she whispered. "I thought 'twas all over for me. Ye've been a godsend. My babe—?"

"We've found a satisfactory wet nurse, and he's thriving," Vander Groot said kindly. "Please don't trouble yourself, Mrs. Weldon. I'm confident both of you are on the mend."

The woman took a shaky breath, tears springing to her eyes. Elizabeth set the cup on the bedside table and clasped one of her patient's worn hands in hers. Laying her other hand gently on Mrs. Weldon's brow, Elizabeth studied her sallow complexion and hollow eyes, feeling the familiar, subtle healing force flow from her. In moments the woman's eyes drifted shut.

Elizabeth rose from her chair and glanced around the spacious, sunny room lined with cots. A sickly woman or child occupied each, and coughs, sniffles, and occasional low groans rose from all sides. At the other end of the house, nurses tended several women suffering from the pox.

"You have a rare gift of healing, Beth," Vander Groot said in a low tone, gathering her hand between both of his. "It's God given, and you must never neglect it."

The thought of the young doctor's gentle, expert ministrations to their patients brought memories of father flooding over her. She was suddenly overwhelmed by a deep loneliness for him, and for her mother and sister. How long it seemed until their return in the fall!

Blinking back tears, she forced a smile. "Your gift is greater than my poor skills," she objected, "and I'm more than grateful for all your help and guidance. I couldn't have undertaken this work without you."

The passion and longing that warmed his eyes drew a blush into her cheeks. She bit her lip, regretting her impulsive words.

"We work well together," he murmured, his voice dangerously tender, "and we're much suited to one another. I thought so long before Howe took over the city if you remember. I'm more convinced of it now than ever."

A knot formed in her breast. Hastily she disengaged her hand from his and returned her gaze to the sleeping woman.

"They nurse their men and children until they're so sick they can't stand any longer. But no one takes care of them."

For a painful, awkward moment he made no response, and she was afraid to meet the probing gaze she sensed on her. She knew he felt the subtle change in their relationship, the invisible walls she had erected to keep him at arm's length not only because of Carleton's return, but also due to Tess's cautions against exposing their clandestine roles. A change all the more evident for the occasional instances, as now, when she inadvertently dropped her guard, only to hastily retreat when he broached a tender declaration.

"It's unconscionable that the military hospitals refuse to treat the soldiers' women and children. I admire you greatly for taking on such a ministry." His tone was stiff.

She led the way out into the passage. "How could I do any less? You work as hard as I—harder even. And you've lent your home for this work."

She stopped, feeling she was babbling. Glancing up, she saw that his face had gone blank.

"Aunt Euphemia's, you mean," he said with a shrug. "She was more than happy to offer its use for a women's hospital since . . . " He broke off.

"How's she doing?" She felt herself on safer ground now.

"According to Isobel's letter, she's made some improvement since my visit last week. But she's still bedridden, and I doubt she'll improve any further. I'm afraid we won't have her with us much longer."

"I'm so sorry to hear it. But it's a great relief to hear that Christiaan's grief is gradually moderating."

She was pleased to see that his face brightened. "I'd almost given up hope my brother would recover from the double blow of losing his wife and child. But now I'm confident he will."

"Aunt Tess and I pray for him and your aunt daily. For all your family, in fact . . . and you, of course."

His glance remained veiled. "That means a great deal to me."

Dropping her eyes, she sought a different subject. "Both Isobel and your parents continue to urge Aunt Tess and me to come for a visit as soon as possible."

"I'll add my voice to theirs. No one is safe here to walk unattended outside their homes, and the air is too unwholesome at any rate."

Wrinkling her nose, Elizabeth glanced toward the windows closed and locked against the heavy miasma that fouled the air now that temperatures had warmed. The stench rose from the brackish water in the harbor and the refuse of the poor, sick inhabitants crowding ruined buildings, an encampment for the destitute called Canvass-town, and the abandoned fortifications remaining from General Lee's failed attempt to secure the city against British attack the previous year, and was rapidly becoming intolerable. She could hardly imagine the stench the hot days of summer would arouse.

"We've missed your family terribly and are much tempted to accept their offer," she said, careful to keep a deliberate space between them. "Philadelphia would be a welcome change, but . . . " Hesitating, she glanced through the open door of the makeshift ward.

Vander Groot followed her anxious gaze to the patients visible inside. "The new doctor and the nurses I'm training will be quite able to take over by month's end. I assure you, the work will continue as long as needed even if we're absent for a while."

"Then perhaps we'll take your suggestion," she said.

The previous week the Continental Congress had returned to Philadelphia from Baltimore, where they had fled in December when the British appeared poised to capture the city. The thought of meeting some of Congress's more famous members stirred a thrill of excitement, and she decided to have a serious talk with her aunt about the possibilities a move there might open.

FROM THE CORNER OF HER EYE, Elizabeth noted that the distinguished-looking man whose ardent attentions had occupied her aunt since their arrival at the soiree had finally given up his attempts at seduction and gone in search of more pliant prey. As tactfully as possible she extricated herself from her own cluster of hopeful suitors and hurried to join Tess on the chairs across the room before someone else could appropriate the single empty seat. A favorite gathering spot for officers and loyalists, the opulent Inclenberg mansion owned by wealthy businessman Robert Murray was, as usual, crowded with scarlet coats and the brilliant dress of wealthy civilians seeking diversion from the harsh realities of British occupation.

"I thought he'd never take the hint," Elizabeth hissed under her breath. "I was on the point of coming to box his ears in order to rescue you."

Tess rolled her eyes. "It's a shame his appearance doesn't reflect his character so one would be warned not to get near the bore."

Elizabeth laughed. "Hopefully your prospects will be brighter in Philadelphia."

They were interrupted by a commotion across the room. Howe had just entered with his paramour on his arm. With a grand wave of his hand, the general crowed, *"Toujours de la gaieté,"* as they glided toward the card room.

Elizabeth took in Betsey's elaborate gown and the satisfied simper on her face before rolling her eyes at her aunt. Giving a slight shake of her head, she stared down at her clenched hands.

"I hate the thought of putting so much distance between me and Jonathan when we're at last fairly close," she murmured, glancing around to make sure no one was within hearing. "Not that it matters since he's been forbidden to leave camp and can only send messages through Caleb and Pete."

"You knew what would likely happen once you sent your warning to General Washington instead of directly to Jon," Tess reminded her in a whisper.

"I was afraid he'd ignore the danger if I didn't. You know how he is." Elizabeth's shoulders slumped. "I'm relieved that he's safe for the time, but that doesn't make the separation any easier. How I long to see him!"

Just then Vander Groot strode into the drawing room and paused to scan the assembly. Elizabeth had not expected him to attend the dinner party since over the past weeks he had expressed an increasing dislike of Howe, his mistress, and his most senior officers, all of whom were currently playing cards in the adjoining room.

Overcome by longing for Carleton, she felt herself unequal to another warm encounter with the doctor. She laid her hand on Tess's arm, but before she could propose a quiet retreat from the room, Vander Groot glanced in their direction and immediately began to weave through the crowd, only pausing here and there to briefly greet an acquaintance. When he reached them, his face relaxed into a smile that softened his handsome features and caused Elizabeth's heart to quicken its beat.

With the approach of several close acquaintances, they were drawn into an exchange of pleasantries. Then dinner was announced, and they were ushered into the mansion's expansive, ornately furnished dining room.

Vander Groot was seated at the opposite end of the table from Elizabeth and her aunt, between two of Howe's aides. Elizabeth noted with a strange unease that during much of the meal they and the doctor appeared to be engrossed in conversation. From time to time Vander Groot's brooding glance sought hers.

When they finally arose from the table, the men heading to the library and the women to the drawing room, he intercepted Elizabeth before she could escape. "May I speak with you privately?" He indicated the open door of an unoccupied sitting room a short distance down the passage.

At the door of the drawing room, Tess glanced back at her questioningly. Motioning her go on, Elizabeth faltered, "Of course. Has something happened?"

Without answering, he drew her into the small room and to the warm fire crackling on the hearth, there to study her intently, his gaze troubled, his countenance unnaturally pale.

"What is it, Pieter?" she asked, forcing a light laugh. "You almost frighten me."

For a moment longer he hesitated, before blurting out, "I hardly know how to convey my . . . concerns. At dinner there was much talk about an officer in Washington's army, one with whom you're apparently acquainted . . . " The words trailed off, and he bit his lip.

A wave of sick dismay swept over Elizabeth. Ever since the night of the queen's birthday celebration, she had prayed that idle talk would not reach Vander Groot's ears, that Howe's orders to suppress news of Carleton's return and of his connection to White Eagle would be obeyed. She might have known such discretion was not possible in the British army, but at least it had taken some while for the information to become a matter of public gossip.

There was nothing for it now but to be as forthright as safely possible to be. She tilted her head and forced a smile.

"I assume you refer to General Jonathan Carleton. Yes, I was acquainted with him until he was exposed as a spy for the patriots. I'm aware it's commonly rumored that he and I were romantically involved." She dismissed the subject with an expressive shrug.

"Were you?" he demanded, his voice choked.

She held his gaze without allowing hers to waver. "I could hardly avoid him. My parents frequently invited him to our home, and he was very much engaged in our social circle. But a romance—hardly. When we were together our habit was to argue about any and every subject that arose. He's intolerably arrogant, conceited, and insufferable." She threw a hasty glance toward the doorway to make sure no one was in the vicinity, then leaned closer to the doctor. "I have many sympathies with the patriots, as you do, but be assured I was not charmed in the least to discover that he had joined them."

Vander Groot perceptibly relaxed. "After the conversation I was party to tonight, I'd begun to think him the object that stands between us."

She bent her head, pierced to the heart. It required all her resolve to force the lie from her lips.

"Certainly not."

For some moments, Vander Groot remained silent. "According to my dinner companions' account, after defecting to the rebels Carleton was long absent. No one knew what had become of him. Rumors are that he joined with the Shawnee—became, in fact, the war chief White Eagle, whose savage raids have devastated the border settlements."

She waved his words away. "I can hardly credit it . . . but on the other hand, I wouldn't put it past the scoundrel."

Again he gave her a searching look. He began to reach for her hand, then abruptly pulled back.

On impulse she laid her hand on his arm. "Pieter . . . you know how very highly I think of you. I hold you as a most dear brother and colleague, and I value our friendship beyond measure. I pray that will be enough for you, for it would break my heart utterly to lose the sweet companionship we've been blessed with."

"I can be nothing more to you than that?" he said, his voice breaking.

On the verge of tears, she gazed deep into his clear blue eyes, now darkened with pain and longing. "That is much, is it not?" she pleaded softly. "What can be more precious than the communion of heart to heart that God has bestowed? If this is His best for our lives, then we must cherish it and let go hopes for . . . something else."

He took her hands and raised them to his lips. "I shall always love you, Beth," he said with a groan. "Nothing can ever change that. If you're confident it's God's will for us to remain friends only, then I accept it and wish you joy."

Not waiting for her response, he released her, turned on his heel, and strode from the room, his shoulders slumped.

Chapter Fourteen

Carleton studied the short, plump woman who poured steaming amber liquid into a china teacup and set it on the table in front of him. Attired in becoming elegance and fashion, with a pleasant face that belied her determined air, she hovered over her husband, clearly as devoted to him as Carleton knew Washington to be to her.

"I can't tell you how delighted I am to see you again, dear madam," he said with genuine pleasure, accepting the lump of sugar she offered. "It's been far too long since I last visited you at Mount Vernon. You're looking exceptionally well."

As she graciously returned his compliments, he took in the well-appointed, comfortable chamber where they sat, then glanced across the table at his superior. Washington leaned contentedly back in his chair, a coil of smoke twining upward from his pipe.

He lifted his cup in the General's direction. "And you're looking much better, Your Excellency. I see Mrs. Washington has improved not only your living arrangements, but also your health."

The General's eyes twinkled. "My wife is always the best medicine for me."

With an affectionate glance in his direction, Mrs. Washington excused herself and bustled out of the room.

After she had gone, the two officers spent some time discussing the enlistments expiring at the end of the month, lagging recruitments, and the highly successful *petite guerre* the militias, along with some Continental units, had been waging. Washington bemoaned the bewildering intelligence Elizabeth and his other spies transmitted. The reports seemed to indicate Howe would open the new campaign with a move up the Hudson instead of the offensive against Philadelphia that had previously seemed to be his intent. Should a strong British force strike south from Canada, the ability of the American force stationed at Fort Ticonderoga to hold, even if bolstered by New England militia, would be in question. And if Ticonderoga fell, then the string of forts below it along the Hudson would be open to attack from north and south.

"The country seems to entertain the idea that we are superior to our enemy and that the British are afraid of us." Washington concluded. "No matter what course Howe settles on, we must avoid a general engagement that could result in defeat and change that opinion."

"We'll endeavor to maintain it at all costs," Carleton said, smiling.

Washington's eyes narrowed. "To do so we must be the driver of events. If we allow ourselves to be drove, the tables will be turned and the country dispirited. To relapse into our former discredit will be ruinous to our cause."

Carleton eyed his commander warily. Over the past weeks, sober reflection had impressed on him the necessity of discretion if he was to regain his former freedom. Thus he had voiced no further complaints against the strictures imposed on him and made every effort to appear in compliance with Washington's orders, while patiently biding his time.

Instead of the buckskins he much preferred for comfort and convenience, he carried out his duties impeccably arrayed in the Rangers' new French-dragoon-style uniform of short dun-brown coat with forest green facings, buckskin breeches, and dark green leather helmet trimmed with gold chains and a flowing blond horsehair crest, all designed to his specifications. And he obediently appeared at every social affair Mrs. Washington and the other officers' wives devised and went out of his way to charm both his colleagues and the ladies. So much so, in fact, that he had made himself the object of considerable speculation regarding his attentions to several eligible young women from the area in addition to a couple of officers' daughters.

And in spite of the occasional snide remarks directed at him by some of the other officers, his assigned guard surrounded him everywhere he went. They had already gained him favor, and currently waited below in the street in full sight of the building's second-story windows.

When Carleton had been ushered into the room, Washington was just turning from the window. His commander's look of approval, which Carleton had enjoyed often of late, raised his spirits—and hopes—even more.

He felt incredibly virtuous. At the same time, he knew that he must continue to keep a tight curb on his tongue if he was not to undo the progress he had made toward his goal.

"Your strategy is working, sir," he said now, careful to keep the irony out of his tone. "My experience among the Shawnee taught me that a hard, unexpected strike followed by a swift withdrawal denies the enemy time to react and spreads fear and confusion. Our raids have not only persuaded the British that our army is twice the force it is in reality, but they're driving up Howe's costs in money, men, and supplies. Eventually the price must become too great for the British to sustain."

Washington laid his pipe on the saucer of his teacup. "General Braddock's expedition back in '55 demonstrated much the same, as I am sure you remember. But it is imperative that the army be well drilled in traditional formations. We will not be able to avoid a general engagement forever, and if it comes before we are well prepared, I am afraid our defeat will be more disastrous than that at Brooklyn Heights." He leaned forward in his chair. "You sent Colonel Andrews with a troop to support General Maxwell's militia, as I directed?"

Carleton nodded. "He just returned this morning, in fact. I asked to meet with you to report on their action. According to Colonel Andrews, they held their own in quite a sharp engagement with a British patrol and, in spite of being heavily outnumbered, drove them down toward Elizabethtown. He was quite impressed with Maxwell, by the way."

Washington chuckled. "Scotch Willie is an extraordinary character, to be sure. He fights as hard as he drinks. I just hope his excesses will not render him useless."

"I didn't see any indication of that," Carleton acknowledged with a smile at thought of the intense, personable Scotch-Irish general. "Andrews seemed to feel that even Howe would have a hard time gaining the upper hand against him."

Washington rubbed his chin. "The British are changing their tactics, and his brigade is suffering greater casualties as a result."

"He came up to meet with me yesterday," Carleton said, keeping his expression guileless and his tone neutral. "Maxwell was very pleased at how our troop performed and proposed that I seek leave to move our camp down near him at Westfield so we can work in concert. It would help him and also allow my Rangers to gain experience and confidence for the upcoming campaign." As an afterthought, he said, "I'm sure you're aware of the difficulties in finding forage for our horses with the army concentrated here. Maxwell assures me there's abundant forage down on the plain."

The General regarded him with suspicion. "Not to mention that a move to the other side of the Watchungs will also place you within an hour's ride of New York."

Less if I have my way, Carleton countered silently, but he squelched the thought.

"That's where the enemy is, sir." Deciding to take the bull by the horns, he added, "And with Miss Howard closer, we could secure intelligence from her more quickly."

Washington harrumphed, regarding Carleton with skepticism. To Carleton's encouragement, he hesitated before growling, "I am sure you are aware that there is considerable criticism of your Blacks and Indians, especially on the part of our Southern officers. You know my concerns about a slave uprising if we accept Blacks into the army."

Carleton bit his tongue. As much as he opposed it, he understood the concern.

Patiently he pointed out, "It's becoming a practical necessity, Your Excellency. The campaign season is almost upon us. As their enlistments expire, most of the men leave, and not enough of the new levies have come in to fill our ranks."

Washington drummed his fingers on the table in frustration. "I must still deal with the dissention and consequent decline of discipline that results. Major Smithson's return to Virginia is a perfect example."

"Smithson left with my blessing, and only one troop went with him. I'd expected more." Carleton gave Washington a hard look. "Do you want us to fight with you . . . or leave? There are enough people in this country who are willing to sit back and hope that someone will hand their freedom to them without their making sacrifices. The Blacks and Indians in my brigade are fighters—I take none others. They're Americans too, and they've proven themselves in action. They believe in freedom for themselves, their families, and their land. Are you willing to send such a body of men home and lose their passion, their service, and their allegiance when you could make good use of them?"

His mouth tightening, Washington inclined his head with obvious reluctance. "If we do not enlist them, the British will. I cannot deny that your Rangers have proven their worth nor can we afford to lose anyone who will fight."

"I also want to fight, and I've proven my worth on the battlefield, I think," Carleton said forcefully. "I've sat idle too long. Will you release me to join General Maxwell? I swear you'll not regret it."

Washington got to his feet, Carleton following his lead. "We do need you in action, General Carleton," he said formally. "Move your encampment down near Maxwell's. Continue to keep me apprised of all British movements—and any intelligence Miss Howard uncovers."

DISMOUNTING NEXT TO HIS MARQUEE, Carleton pulled off his helmet and gloves and wiped a streak of mingled dirt and sweat from his brow with the back of his hand. With a smile of grim satisfaction he surveyed the train of heavily loaded British supply wagons and glum prisoners that filed past under guard, netted by the day's raid.

It felt unutterably good to be back at the head of his command, Carleton reflected. Even before his brigade had been completely settled on the lowlands northeast of Westfield, they had joined Maxwell's force for a series of bitterly fought raids that had, for the most part, been highly successful. As Washington had warned, they now encountered stiffer resistance than they had the first weeks after Trenton.

A thaw had set in these last days of March, and across the wooded hills and plains below the Watchung range, rutted roads and lanes were streaming with ice-melt and deep in mud. All around them on the greening fields, new recruits and veterans alike were being drilled with increased intensity. For once all things felt not only possible, but certain of accomplishment.

When Andrews rode up, he called out, "We've done a good day's work, Charles."

"I should have known you'd manage to arrange everything to your satisfaction," Andrews responded, smirking as he pulled his mud-spattered mount to a halt.

"One day you'll also learn the value of submission to proper authority," Carleton returned with expansive benevolence.

Andrews gave a short laugh and dismounted. "Or at least the appearance of it."

"I'm merely following orders."

Andrews regarded him in amused affection, arms folded over his chest. "Now that we're so much closer to New York, what are your plans? I'm sure you have some."

Carleton's smile turned smug. "With Howe doubtless emerging from hibernation in just a few weeks, our most urgent need is for solid intelligence as quickly as we can get it."

"And I wonder where we'll obtain that. Did the General also order you to go directly to the source?"

"Well, Beth did just alert us that Howe's looking for river pilots who are familiar with the Delaware," Carleton returned. "He has details out cutting timber and building transports and a pontoon bridge, all of which lends credence to an attack on Philadelphia. I'd say it's highly advisable for us to keep in close contact with our agents."

Just then Carleton's aide approached, his uniform as fouled as theirs, whistling cheerfully in apparent good humor. Directing Andrews a warning look, Carleton beckoned Jeffreys to join them, and they spent some minutes discussing the disposition of the prisoners and captured goods.

A fortnight earlier, before their move to the Jersey lowlands, Red Fox and Spotted Pony had left for Ohio Territory, taking Stowe with them. Their first-hand report of Washington's success at Trenton and Princeton would do much to persuade at least some warriors to join them, might possibly even convince the tribe as a whole to change their allegiance, though Carleton had little confidence they would abandon their long-held support for the British.

He missed his two cousins and his servant more intensely than he'd expected, and he longed for the warm fellowship of his people ever more deeply. The hours spent around the fire in the council house during the winter months or beneath the stars on summer evenings trading stories and laughter, playing games and observing rituals, debating issues that affected the tribe, and sharing the wisdom gained from personal experience or handed down from ancient times by the elders had knit his soul to clan and tribe.

Red Fox and Spotted Pony had filled much of the void, as had Stowe, who, along with Andrews, had been a constant presence in his life since his years in England. At first after they had gone, he'd felt lost, especially since Andrews was becoming more preoccupied with Blue Sky as her pregnancy progressed, which was understandable and right.

In their absence, Carleton found himself increasingly relying on Jeffreys, not only for the move to their new camp and the ordinary daily routines, but for friendship as well. Personable, efficient, and unassuming in his manner, over the past weeks Jeffreys had naturally stepped into the roles of confidante and friend, quickly gaining Carleton's respect and a good measure of his trust. He recognized much of his own younger self in his young aide, in fact. At the same time, just as he had with his privateers, he made a point of never speaking of Elizabeth in Jeffreys' hearing nor referring to his role in gathering intelligence for Washington. And he forewarned the others to do the same.

By nature and experience Carleton did not easily trust anyone with his whole heart. Although appearing open and forthright when it suited his purposes, he erected subtle boundaries with a natural charm and grace that deflected personal questions without seeming to, even at times with those the closest to him. Where Elizabeth was concerned he was doubly cautious, always on guard to protect her safety.

He had hoped dearly to see her on her birthday, but that had passed two days earlier with no possibility of his getting away. Although either

Caleb or Pete regularly brought reports from her, along with brief, verbal messages for him alone, the constant yearning of his heart was not eased.

No one could fill the void her absence left in his heart, more painful even than the loss of his people. It seemed a lifetime since they had been together, and the longer the time stretched out, the more it felt as though part of him were missing, an essential part he didn't know how to live without.

As Jeffreys left to carry out his orders, he passed Isaiah coming toward the marquee. Carleton waited until his aide was out of sight before motioning him and Andrews inside for a private conference.

Andrews had been right, as usual, he reflected. He did have plans.

Chapter Fifteen

WAITING AT THE EAST RIVER DOCKS in Vander Groot's coach, Elizabeth trained the doctor's spyglass on the derelict sloop anchored a distance out in the harbor, where it was buffeted by gusts of a cold early April rain. Her hands shook, but when the lens finally came into focus, she could make out a detail of sailors heaving something over the side: wrapped forms whose shape clearly defined them as human bodies.

Determined to stand as witness, she counted five, six, seven . . . eleven in all. One by one they slid down the gangplank and dropped into the bay, sinking with hardly a splash. When the detail moved out of view, she lowered the spyglass to her lap with a muffled sob.

A week earlier, on the twenty-sixth of March, she had listened in disbelief while Miss Cameron, a slender, colorless young woman surely no older than she, described her younger brother's plight aboard one of the prison ships in New York harbor. It had been Elizabeth's twenty-second birthday, but after Miss Cameron's recital, she had been unable to enjoy the party Tess had arranged for that evening.

Vander Groot had heard rumors about the conditions American prisoners endured on these rotting hulks—hellholes, he called them—and several times had been solicited by someone whose son or husband or father was imprisoned to discover their relative's fate and petition

Lord Howe for their release. But every effort to gain information or permission to minister to the prisoners had been rebuffed. So when a messenger had arrived at the hospital earlier that day to summon the doctor to attend upon the ship's captain, who had fallen ill and refused to allow one of the notoriously incompetent navy surgeons to treat him, Elizabeth insisted on accompanying him. He had warned that she would not be allowed aboard, but she was determined to know immediately everything he learned.

She had waited more than an hour already, shrinking back into the shadows of the closed coach whenever someone passed by. A few minutes more, and to her relief—and dread—she saw a figure descend the ship's ladder. Soon the boat waiting below cast off to bob across the rain-swept waves toward the line of wharves along the East River.

At length Vander Groot came up the steps from below the dock and hurried to the coach. He climbed in, shaking the rain from his drenched coat and hat, and dropped heavily into the seat opposite her.

"The ship's surgeon is a drunkard totally incapable of his task," he said with contempt. "I don't blame the captain for refusing to allow the man to touch him."

Searching his face, which was drained of color, she covered his hand with hers. "Did you learn anything? Were you able to see any of . . . the men?" She caught herself before saying our men.

His glance seared her. "Thank God Miss Cameron has only heard reports. Had she been able to visit her brother, she'd be beyond distraught."

Elizabeth bit her lip. "It's that bad, then?"

His jaw hardened. "Worse. Much."

He rapped his knuckles sharply on the side of the coach. They heard the driver's gruff acknowledgement, then the jingle of harness, and the coach lurched forward.

"After calling on the captain and doing what I could for him, I lucked upon a midshipman whose mate was down with a fever and no more eager to suffer the surgeon's ministrations than the captain," Vander Groot continued. "The midshipman was grateful enough that he showed me about the ship and eventually conducted me to the hold where the prisoners are kept."

His face haunted, he choked out the words. "You'd not believe the conditions they live under—and die under, dozens at a time. It's worse than the Provost's gaol or the one at the North Dutch Church—no sanitation, little food in evidence, and that rotted, with not even fuel to cook it or to warm themselves that I could see. There was much evidence of typhus, dysentery, scurvy, infections of all sorts, and some of the men had obviously been beaten. But I'll spare you further description. It was hard enough for me to bear the sight; you couldn't. Such suffering should be enough to wrench the hardest heart, yet evidently it is not."

Elizabeth felt ill. Horrified. Astounded that anyone could treat another human being so, even an enemy.

"They were . . . dropping bodies over the side while you were aboard." She groaned and pressed her hand to her mouth. "Mr. Loring is responsible for this. His position as commissary of prisoners is payment for providing his wife for Howe's bed."

"I heard Loring sells most of their rations, charges for provisions for those who've died, and keeps the profits. Cunningham, the provost marshall, stops their rations outright so they starve. It's known he even goes so far as to poison or hang them to reduce the numbers of his prisoners more rapidly."

Vander Groot stared out the window, but she had the impression he did not see the grey, wet landscape they passed. "I can no longer justify the cruelties of British military rule wherever they hold sway. To say nothing of General Howe's character—and his brother's."

Abruptly turning to her, he burst out, "I despise the way Howe looks at you when he thinks his lover does not see—as though he'd devour you. Do you not feel it?"

She bent her head, bile rising in her throat. "It nauseates me," she said truthfully. "Unfortunately, as long as we remain in New York, we're under his power. To deny his invitations would arouse suspicion of our loyalty. I'm confident, however, that as long as Betsey entertains him, he'll not touch me. He's too besotted with her to endanger their relationship. That hasn't changed since Boston."

He nodded and let out his breath. "I've come to believe that he's not half the man General Washington is. By all accounts, he is a man of integrity, one who seeks to do what is right."

Elizabeth fought to keep her jubilant emotions from reflecting in her face and voice. "From what our patients tell me, there's great anger among the common soldiers at Howe's indulgence in balls and parties while his army is reduced to salt rations. And a growing number of the lower-ranking officers share it. Even some who were once Howe's staunchest supporters are resentful. I've heard more than one question whether their loyalty to the king is reflected in their sovereign's toward them. Oh, Pieter, what's to be done?"

His gaze focused on her and sharpened. "I've never believed a people ought to throw off the legitimate rulers God instituted to govern them. But if what the British are doing doesn't justify the most desperate course of opposition, nothing will. It's intolerable, Beth. If we don't take up arms to stop them, we voluntarily cast off all rights guaranteed us under British law.

"It's common knowledge that many who counted themselves Tories are exchanging their green and red uniforms for blue and buff," he added. "Many who swore oaths of loyalty to the Crown last fall are swearing allegiance to Congress this spring and using their writs of protection to make cartridges."

Torn, Elizabeth hesitated on the brink of confessing her true allegiance and role. Guiltily remembering Tess's warnings, she said slowly, "Regardless of the odious actions of his ministers, it seems such a drastic a course to foreswear allegiance to the king altogether."

Giving her a dark look, he leaned toward her, his body tense with anger. "Who gives the Ministry the authority to institute unjust policies, and then approves them? The king is the root of these ills. The patriots are right—George the Third has forfeited all right to rule over us."

"What will you do?"

He clenched and unclenched his hands. "First I'll try once more to gain access to the men aboard the prison ships and do what I can to help them. But if Lord Howe again refuses to allow it . . . then I'll join the army and fight them to the last drop of blood."

The coach rattled to a stop, and Elizabeth saw they had arrived back at the hospital. As Vander Groot helped her down she said, "What will your parents think? Have you written to them about this?"

"They've taken such a hard stance against the rebellion," he said as he ushered her into the house. "I fear they'll simply counter that those who have the temerity to fight against our divinely ordained king must suffer the consequences."

He followed as she crossed the parlor and sat down hard in a chair by the fire, her head bent and supported in her hand. It was a struggle to keep from weeping.

"Surely they cannot turn a blind eye to such brutality."

"I pray they will not. Perhaps my example will cause them to rethink their loyalties as well."

She gazed intently into his eyes and found only earnest resolve there. And yet caution warned her to suppress the words poised on her lips.

"When . . . how soon will you speak to Lord Howe?'

"Tomorrow, if he'll see me. Then, unless he gives me leave to care for the prisoners—which I don't expect—I'll leave for Morristown as soon as possible on the pretext of returning to Philadelphia."

"No doubt the army needs physicians—"

"I mean to fight!"

She took a shaky breath. "You're the most admirable of men for following your conscience, Pieter. I know Aunt Tess will agree with me. If you're so determined, then . . . you have our prayers. If there's anything we can ever do—"

"You and Tess will go to my parents? Promise me that."

She rose to take his hand. "You have my word."

His fingers tightened over hers. "May I call on you before I leave?"

"Of course. Will you come for dinner tomorrow night?"

He agreed eagerly.

Returning home, Elizabeth confided their conversation to Tess. They spent the evening pondering the possibilities Vander Groot's decision had opened and committing their concerns to prayer.

THE NEXT AFTERNOON Pete drove Elizabeth and Tess into town to call on several of their acquaintances. They were determined to learn as much as they could about the prison ships and the soldiers being held aboard them.

She and Tess returned to Montcoeur toward nightfall, having learned little in response to their casual, indirect comments and enquiries. As tempted as Elizabeth was to go straight to the provost and demand information about Miss Cameron's brother, she knew her interference would do more harm than good.

If Lord Howe cannot be persuaded to treat the prisoners humanely or at least to allow their relatives to visit them and provide basic necessities, she reflected anxiously, *then we must find some way of freeing them. But how?*

Compressing her lips, she considered how she had smuggled intelligence and munitions out of Boston for more than a year without getting caught, had even smuggled Carleton out of a heavily guarded gaol with little more than boldfaced courage. Surely she could find a way to bring succor to the men suffering aboard the prison ships.

Yet here she did not have a secret band of conspirators and other essential connections as she'd had in Boston. A large number of the city's residents had fled, and those remaining were either staunchly loyal, in desperate straits and dependent on the British for security and the means to live, or already under suspicion.

If only she had access to a detailed chart of the harbor showing where every British ship lay, with Vander Groot's help she might be able to devise a plan. But he was set on joining the army, and there was no one else she could trust to work with her.

When the carriage pulled to a halt at the front steps, she concluded, heart dropping, that there was no way to reach the prisoners. Even if Washington could be persuaded to devote the fledgling Continental Navy to the task, they had neither the ships nor the firepower to overcome the entire British fleet. And even if they did, the British might well simply kill the men rather than surrender them.

Overwhelmed by an unaccustomed and deeply distressing sense of hopelessness and the painful longing for the strength and comfort of Carleton's arms that followed on its heels, she followed her aunt up the steps to where Caleb held open the mansion's front door.

THE DUSKY SHADES OF TWILIGHT wrapped the greening garden in misty light. Warning his companions to silence with a finger to his lips, Carleton unlatched the kitchen door, taking pains to make no sound. Swinging it open, he stepped quickly inside, Andrews and Isaiah crowding on his heels.

Jemma was the first to look up from a large, oaken table, where she transferred biscuits from a pan to a plate. Catching sight of her father, she ran to him with a squeal.

"Papa!"

Sarah rose from the pot she was stirring over the fire, a broad smile spreading across her face. "Well, I do declare! Gen'l Carleton, Colonel Andrews," she said with a nod to each, "You be most welcome." When her eyes found her husband's, a tender light warmed her gaze.

TESS HANDED CALEB HER CLOAK. "We're both exhausted and won't bother to dress tonight. Please have Sarah serve dinner as soon as possible."

"Yes, ma'am."

He helped Elizabeth out of her cloak, and then retreated down the passageway to the kitchen.

"Don't forget Pieter is joining us for dinner," Elizabeth warned.

Tess sighed and moved to follow Caleb down the passage. "I'd forgotten. I'll go alert Sarah."

"I'll be in the drawing room," Elizabeth called after her aunt.

On the room's threshold, she stopped abruptly, realizing she had left her reticule and gloves in the carriage. Pete was driving around the far end of the house toward the stables when she came back outside. Waving and calling his name, she ran to stop him.

While she retrieved the items, the sound of approaching hoofbeats drew her attention. Glancing toward the road, she saw Vander Groot rein his horse through the gate onto the carriageway, and her hopes for a few minutes of solitude fled.

With apprehension she noted that he was dressed for traveling and that bulging packs hung behind his saddle. His interview with the admiral had gone ill then, she concluded. Hastily she dismissed Pete and went to meet the doctor.

"We had the devil of a time getting here," Carleton growled.

Jemma tilted her head, amazement furrowing her face. "Only a ghost could make it through the lines without getting caught."

"Who said we aren't ghosts?" Andrews returned with a muffled laugh. "You think we're flesh and blood and not a mere figment of your imagination?"

"We run into patrols twice, and you hide just like me," Isaiah pointed out. "If we be a figment, then why you worry about the British capturing us?"

Carleton rolled his eyes. "Isaiah, you worry far too much. Didn't I tell you we'd make it unmolested?"

"We still got to get back," Isaiah noted grimly.

"Have some confidence in me," Carleton protested. Grinning, he turned to Sarah. "The Miss Howards are at home, I devoutly hope."

"They be gone in town—" Sarah began.

She was interrupted by Caleb, who just then stepped through the door. His eyebrows rising at sight of their unexpected guests, he said, "The ladies just arrived. They asked that dinner be served right away."

The words were hardly out of his mouth when Tess followed him into the room. Looking from one to the other, her eyes widened.

"Bless you for coming—but you must be mad to beard the lion, dear boys!" she exclaimed as she hurried to embrace Carleton and Andrews in turn.

Vander Groot dismounted and looped the reins over the hitching post, then came to take the hand Elizabeth held out to him and tucked it into the crook of his arm. "I apologize for arriving early, but I hoped we might have a moment to talk privately before dinner if it isn't inconvenient."

Returning his smile, she accompanied him into the house. "Not at all. I'm glad you've come."

Indeed she was. Especially was she eager to hear about his meeting with Lord Howe. At the same time she feared the intimate interview his leaving was likely to occasion, and a part of her wished he were anywhere but there.

Leading him into the drawing room, she settled on a chair, deliberately foregoing the sofa. After a brief hesitation, Vander Groot took a seat across from her.

"You met with the admiral?" she asked.

"I was coldly told he was inaccessible all day," he answered, every line of his body taut with tension. "It's as I feared. He refuses to talk to me about the prisoners. But even if I could have met with him—" He made a dismissive gesture.

She bit her lip. "You'll not wait another day?"

He shook his head. "No reason to. Nothing will change, and I'm resolved. I've let it be known among our acquaintances and at the hospital that Aunt Euphemia's condition grows worse—which it does—and that I'm going to my family in Philadelphia for an indefinite period. And I will go to them as soon as I may, but after I first stop at Morristown to volunteer my services."

She stared down at her clenched hands. "I . . . Aunt Tess and I will miss you very much."

He sprang to his feet and came to kneel before her, captured her hands in his. Head bent, she squeezed her eyes shut, willing him not to say what she knew he would.

"Beth," he entreated softly, "will you not look at me?"

She forced her eyes to meet his, tears already blurring her sight.

With gentle passion, his fingers caressed hers. "It's unlikely we'll see each other again for some time," he said, his voice husky. "Only tell me I may hope that one day you'll change your mind, that—"

"I cannot encourage your hopes, Pieter," she said on a ragged sob, her tears dropping onto the tender hands that held hers. "Please . . . to speak of this again only makes it more painful for both of us."

A HUBBUB OF HAPPY CONVERSATION filled the room.

"Where's Beth?" Carleton broke in.

"In the drawing room, I believe. You're fortuitously arrived. You can join us for dinner . . . oh, but—" Tess caught her breath and pressed her fingers to her lips.

Just then Pete strode in through the back door. "Pa!"

Grinning, Carleton moved to the door leading into the passage. "I'll go surprise her while you visit."

The delight that had brightened Pete's face at sight of his father changed to sudden alarm. "Wait!" he blurted out.

Already crossing the room's threshold, Carleton hardly heard him. Buoyed by a flood of joyful anticipation, he strode down the passage.

SILENCE HUNG SUSPENDED between them. Fearing to look at Vander Groot and read the torment her words had wrought, Elizabeth blinked back her tears, her throat so tight she could not speak.

"Who is he," he asked at last, his tone laced with pain, "the one you love? Despite your protestations, I feel someone between us."

"There's no one! Please believe me. I . . . it's only that . . . " She let the words trail away.

He released her and rose abruptly. She lifted her eyes to his, then, seeing the pain there, impulsively sprang to her feet and tiptoed to kiss his cheek.

"There are things I cannot tell you. Please don't think ill of me."

Tenderly he enfolded her in his arms, bent his head until his forehead touched hers. "I could never—"

Behind them the door was flung open. Both started, and Elizabeth pulled out of Vander Groot's arms, whirling round and stepping away from him in the same movement. Immediately she gasped and pressed her hand to her bosom, her heart pounding so hard she felt lightheaded.

In the doorway stood Carleton.

Chapter Sixteen

"JONATHAN!"

Joyful surprise gave way to alarm. Elizabeth directed a dismayed glance at Vander Groot, then, guiltily, back to Carleton.

He regarded Vander Groot coldly, the joy and expectancy that had illuminated his face a moment before extinguished. For a suspended moment, none of them moved. Then Carleton drew himself stiffly to his full height, his eyes shading to the hard, wintry grey she most dreaded.

Her breath catching, she turned to see that the color had drained from the doctor's face. He returned Carleton's stare, tight lipped, his gaze taking in his rival's buckskin garb and moccasins, the tomahawk dangling from his belt.

By swift degrees, comprehension dawned. An ironic smile twisted Vander Groot's lips.

"I take it," he said, "that this is the infamous White Eagle who's the subject of everyone's gossip. All that's wanting is the feathers."

"You're mistaken," Carleton drawled, his tone deliberately insolent. "For the full effect you need war paint. I apologize for the lack."

Behind him, Andrews appeared in the doorway. He took in the scene with a single, swift glance.

"Jon," he said, his tone heavy with resignation, "Pete was trying to warn you—"

Not turning, Carleton raised his hand to cut him off. "I fear the warning has come too late."

"Do you need me?"

"Not for the moment." Carleton fixed his gaze on Elizabeth. His voice brittle as glass, he added, "Stay nearby. I'll call for you."

Feeling sick, Elizabeth met Andrews's level, emotionless gaze. Without a word or sign, he stepped out of the doorway and quietly closed the door behind him.

His face an unreadable mask, movements lithe as a cat's, Carleton stalked to the center of the room, his moccasins making no sound on the rug.

He held out his hand, relieved that Elizabeth flew immediately to his arms. Protectively he caught her to his side, while he studied her companion with icy calculation. Comprehension, devastation, and loss were etched clearly on his rival's features.

"Jonathan, this is Dr. Pieter Vander Groot," she said, lifting her face to his, her voice quavering. "I mentioned him to you—that I assisted in his practice last summer . . . " Her voice trailed off.

He made no response, too aware of the tension in her body when she glanced back at Vander Groot. "Pieter," she faltered, "this is—"

"General Jonathan Carleton," Vander Groot cut her off. "The descriptions I've heard were most apt." He took a quick, shallow breath. "Despite your denials, you are most obviously in love." His voice broke.

"I can imagine what you must be thinking—"

"I doubt that you can."

Carleton saw that the doctor's words cut her deeply, and the pain that leaped to her eyes cleft his own heart. He stared at Vander Groot, pierced by the doubts and fears of the past months.

How could he have believed he could simply come back and take up the life he had left behind? He had been gone too long after all. The obstacles he and Elizabeth faced were too great.

Whatever she felt for him, in his absence she had come to love this man. And he, her.

At that moment, she looked up at him, and he saw in her eyes that she read his thoughts. Gently she reached up to caress his cheek, tenderness suffusing her features.

"No, my love," she murmured. "You must not think it. Not ever. It's not possible for me to stop loving you."

He released her, pulling away from her touch as though it burned him. "Then you only use him to gain intelligence," he said coldly.

"Intelligence!" Vander Groot glanced from one to the other, clearly stunned.

"Pieter is my dear friend and colleague," she objected. "I'd never use him unkindly or betray his confidence any more than I would yours."

"Would you not?" Vander Groot broke in, his voice trembling. "Is it mere coincidence that my family has been close to the Howes?"

"Ah, just so," Carleton rasped. "Washington spoke truly. It's hard enough to think of what you must do. To see it is intolerable."

ALMOST STAGGERING, Vander Groot clasped the back of the chair beside him, but Elizabeth hardly noted it. Mouth open, she stared at Carleton in disbelief, anger following hard on pain.

"I've done nothing to compromise my virtue, sir," she snapped, drawing herself up. "Nor your honor."

Carleton drew in a quick, sharp breath. "Beth, that's not what—"

"You're a spy . . . for Washington?"

Ashen, wanting nothing more than to flee, she pressed her hand to her breast and swung around to face Vander Groot. "Pieter, I—"

"Tell him nothing!" Carleton said sharply, his face hard as stone.

Vander Groot gave them a stiff bow. "Pardon me. I'll leave you to your private discussions."

When he moved toward the door, Carleton stepped into his path. "Alas, I fear I cannot allow you to leave. You understand."

Vander Groot regarded him with disdain. "I understand no such thing, sir. Step out of my way. You cannot mean to keep me here."

"Not here, indeed. But your admitted connections to the brothers Howe pose grave danger to Miss Howard and her aunt. No doubt you're off to report to them—"

"I'm off to Morristown to enlist in the army if it's any concern of yours."

"Pieter's in sympathy with us, Jonathan," Elizabeth broke in urgently.

Carleton folded his arms and gave her a searching look. "And you know this for a fact?"

"I know him to be trustworthy," she answered, not flinching from his scrutiny.

"Then he'll have no objection to accompanying us since his stated design is to join the army."

Livid, Vander Groot threw back his head and met Carleton's gaze with a challenging one. "I've no intention of accompanying you or anyone else under compulsion."

"I care not one whit what your intentions are. Go with us you shall, nevertheless."

The blood rushed to Vander Groot's face at Carleton's mocking tone.

"Surely that isn't necessary," Elizabeth pleaded.

"Your safety's at stake, not to mention that of everyone in this household—and mine. Were he to betray us, my party wouldn't make it halfway back to camp before a British detachment howled on our heels."

"I'm no traitor! You have my word, sir. I'll betray neither Miss Howard nor . . . anyone else."

Carleton regarded Vander Groot with eyes of steel. "Your word means nothing to me," he said thickly. Glancing behind him, he called, "Charles, I need you."

Andrews threw open the door and stepped inside so quickly it was clear he had been standing right outside. "Sir?"

"Take him back to the kitchen and keep him under close guard until I come."

Without a word, Andrews motioned for Vander Groot to precede him. His jaw clenched, the doctor looked from the two men to Elizabeth.

She bent her head. "I'm so sorry. Truly, I never meant—"

He lifted his hand to cut off her apology. "I'm the one who's been betrayed," he said, his voice shaking. "And don't think I'll ever forget it."

Giving her a wide berth, he strode out of the room. His footfalls and the click of the door closing punctuated his exit.

At a loss what to say, Elizabeth groped blindly across the room and sank into a chair, so unsteady she feared her legs would not bear her up. Feeling Carleton's gaze on her, she stared at her clenched hands and waited.

After a tense moment he came to kneel before her on one knee and gathered her hands in his. Forcing them to unclench, he wove his fingers between hers. When she lifted her eyes to his, she found only love and concern in his steady gaze.

"Forgive me for lashing out at you. I admit I feel the sting of jealousy when I see you with another man, but it's my worthiness of your love I doubt. Not you. Never you."

Pulling one hand free, she reached quickly to forestall his words. "Oh, Jonathan, of course I forgive you. You're more than worthy of my love, and you have it all. Don't doubt that for one instant."

He recaptured her hand, his face softening. "Indeed, you've given every evidence to persuade me of it. You're not to blame if there are times when I question everything, and I was wrong to chastise you for it."

She bent her head close to his. "I know some of what you've suffered and how difficult it is for you to trust."

He released a sigh. "Both of us must always remain on guard, and that affects our relationship as well. Please believe I never meant to imply that your actions are dishonorable in any way or to reproach you for what you must do in service of our cause. It's the danger you place yourself in that concerns me."

"You're a fine one to talk," she chided with a smile, "considering that you're behind enemy lines as we speak."

He allowed a wry smile, then sobered. "I think you don't know the full extent of the power you hold over men's hearts or how painful it is for me to see you wield it." When she began to protest, he added quickly, "I know full well the realities of being a spy and the perils you face beyond the physical dangers. I've experienced how it tears at you, body, mind, and soul. When I lay in Gage's bosom, I did things I abhorred, things that will weigh heavily on my heart all my life, though they were necessary for the safety of our people and country. Would it have been easy for you to watch me do them had you known?"

Stricken, she looked down, tears gathering in her lashes, finally shook her head. "I couldn't have rested one moment in peace. And now, with every battle, every engagement with the enemy, no matter how small, I live in dread that you'll not return." Her voice trembled.

Regarding her earnestly, he said, "I watch you rush fearlessly ahead, Beth, and I wonder whether you take into account what this role you play does to your heart . . . and to us."

Her shoulders slumped. "General Washington was wise to forbid us to wed. I thought him wrong then, but the separations and fear for each other we must endure are more painful than I imagined possible, and it would only be worse were we married. But now I wonder if the course we've chosen will end up tearing us apart anyway."

"It will only if we let it." He hesitated before adding, "If you ever want to stop—"

"No! We've both gone too far." She added with despair, "I couldn't even if I wanted to. I so long to go back to Boston, but I've no home left there. Even when Papa and Mama rebuild Stony Hill, that will be their home, not mine. So you see, I understand how you feel, torn between two worlds."

"As once you told me, where you are, that is my home."

Smiling, she brushed away her tears. "Where you are. Where God blesses us."

He studied her as though he would memorize every detail of her, reached to push back a strand of hair that trailed onto her neck, then cupped her cheek in his hand. "I wish dearly you'd lay aside this assignment, but neither of us can make that decision for the other. Know that I trust you always to do what is necessary, and what is right. Lives have been saved because of your courage. Including mine. I'm most grateful for it—for you."

She turned her head to kiss his hand. "I trust you as well, dearest . . . and God to keep you safe. No matter what comes."

She could feel the tension drain out of him. With a faint smile he murmured, "Before I forget, Blue Sky made me promise to tell you she's with child."

Elizabeth clasped her hands, unable to suppress a squeal. "Oh, how blessed she is! And Charles will make such a good father."

He returned her smile with a slow one, but after a moment she saw the longing come into his eyes. Her heart contracting, she slipped from the chair to kneel in front of him. He touched his lips lightly to hers and bent to kiss the tender skin beneath her ear.

"Someday we'll be equally blessed in home and children," she murmured, her voice husky.

He let out a sigh and, drawing her to him, rested his cheek against the crown of her head. "I grow tired of living on hope, Beth. I want us to be together now, not someday."

"Oh, so do I! But God has a good future for us, my love. He'll bring His promises to pass, just as He brought you back to me."

Capturing her gaze to smile deep into her eyes, he brought her hand up to kiss each fingertip, her palm, the inside of her wrist, slipped up the sleeve of her shirt to trail kisses to the crook of her elbow. Fire ignited in her veins, and at her soft gasp, he buried his fingers in her hair and pulled it loose of its bonds to tumble over her shoulders, then tipped back her head to kiss the curve of her neck, the hollow of her throat, the silken valley partially revealed at her shirt's opening. All strength drained out of her, leaving her lightheaded and panting with desire.

"You are God's gift to me," he murmured. "I want to spend my life loving you. I want to cherish you with my whole body."

"Oh, Jonathan, never let me go!"

For long moments she gave herself up to his embrace and the passion of his hard, hungry kisses and caresses that blotted out all consciousness of time and any other urgency. At length he pulled reluctantly back, took a shaking breath, finally rose and drew her gently to her feet. She swayed against him and laid her head on his breast, certain there could be no sweeter shelter than his arms.

When he released her, he pulled a small package from the leather pouch at his belt. "I hoped to come on your birthday, but I was unable to get away in time. I hope this will serve as a small token of that future."

In happy anticipation she tore open the package, then gasped. Inside nestled an exquisite pair of delicately ruched elbow-length silk gloves. Eagerly she pulled them on.

"They fit perfectly. Oh, and they match my new spring gown as though they'd been made for it!" She stopped and studied him through narrowed eyes. "In fact, they're too perfect to be a coincidence."

He grinned. "I have my own spies."

"Jemma and Sarah, no doubt. But thank you—I love them!"

She carefully pulled off the gloves and set them aside before throwing her arms around his neck. Heat coursed through her at the touch of his lips against hers, but at last she drew back, a troubled frown creasing her brow. He searched her face with concern.

"Don't worry. They can't be traced back to me. I made sure of that."

She looked down to keep him from seeing the tears that insisted on welling up. "Last winter Aunt Tess discovered I'd saved your letters. She made me burn them all."

He regarded her silently, at last conceded, "That's undoubtedly wise. We can't be too careful." Frowning, he added, "And that includes whom we trust."

"But Pieter is trustworthy," she protested. "Is it really necessary to drag him back to camp so ignominiously?"

"I've no choice. He has power to do you harm."

"Love, I know him well. He'd not betray me any more than I would him."

"He seemed to imply otherwise," he reminded her, his voice hard.

"He spoke in anger only, as did you. Can you not trust him for my sake?"

"You cannot know the depths of his soul any more than he knew yours. You give your heart too freely."

"I gave my heart to you. Was I not right in trusting you? In loving you?"

"And I love you," he said huskily. "By God, I'd take Satan himself prisoner did he threaten you."

Biting her lip, she faltered, "What . . . will you do with Pieter then?"

"He'll remain with my brigade, where I can personally keep him under watch. We're in great need of skilled physicians, so he'll have employment enough."

"But as a prisoner!"

"He must prove his loyalty. He has but to betray my trust once, and he'll spend the rest of this war in gaol."

She sighed, finally pleaded, "Promise me you'll treat him fairly."

His jaw tensed. "That's up to him. I'll treat him as justly as he deserves."

"May I speak with him for a moment in private? Please." At his probing gaze, she added, "You've nothing to fear in our relationship. I love him as the brother I never had."

He eyes narrowed. "His love for you is not brotherly."

"He and I have had this discussion more than once, Jonathan. I've not deceived him about my affections, I assure you. But Pieter is so like Papa. When we work together, it's like having him back again."

Carleton's expression eased. "I know how much you miss your family."

Brightening, she briefly related her parents' change of heart. "When they come home, you'll have to speak to Papa about us," she teased.

He raised an eyebrow. "You think I did not? That I'd have asked you to marry me without your father's permission."

Her jaw dropped. "You spoke to him? When?"

Chuckling, he drew her back into his arms. "The day he told me they were leaving for London. He brought up the subject, and I was glad he did."

She buried her face against his chest to hide her smile. "I should have known. His opinions are so much changed now that I think he'll approve our marriage as he did at the first."

Gently he lifted her chin until her eyes met his warm gaze. "I hope so. I very much value his esteem, and your mother's." He hesitated, then asked, "Are you and Tess still resolved to go to Philadelphia, as Pete told me the last time he came over?"

"We are. The situation here grows worse and worse. It'll be impossible for us to stay much longer."

She explained that their plan was to find a suitable establishment in Philadelphia, then return to New York long enough to oversee a more permanent move. They hoped to be settled in Philadelphia within a couple of months and, depending on Howe's plans, remain for at least the summer.

Carleton released her to prowl around the room. "We've gotten so much conflicting intelligence about Howe's designs that it's impossible to determine whether he'll move against Philadelphia or north up the Hudson to support Burgoyne's strike south."

"My impression is that Howe's very much fixed on Philadelphia," she told him, "if he ever opens the campaign, that is. I assumed he'd move as soon as the weather allowed, but the weeks are wearing away, while he gives little evidence of interest in anything other than gambling, drinking, and dallying with his mistress."

Carleton gave a short laugh. "I wouldn't be the least surprised if he abandoned Burgoyne to his own devices. But no matter. We're making good use of the time to train new recruits and build up supplies. The longer Howe delays, the more difficult he'll find his task."

She let out a frustrated groan. "Of course, you would move your camp so much closer to New York just when we're planning to leave!"

"It seems to be our fate that our paths always lead us away from each other," he agreed, his tone rueful. "But Philadelphia is not so far away, and if you're right, we'll be joining you there soon. You can keep us informed of Congress's doings. Not everyone is trustworthy even in that worthy body, and it'd be well for us to know what intrigues go on behind the scenes. Washington has some inkling that

General Gates has been agitating to overthrow him, and he'd know the truth of it."

"I'll make contact with the Massachusetts delegation as soon as we're settled. John Adams was acquainted with my father some years ago and I'm eager to meet him again, even if in disguise."

"You'll need a plausible identity and a reason to contact Adams." He rubbed his chin thoughtfully. "I'll invent that for you while you're gone. Your plan was to leave by the end of the week?"

"Yes. We've arranged to visit Pieter's family . . . " She let the words trail off.

"No need to change your plans. Before we leave I'll dictate a letter for the good doctor to write to his parents, informing them of his decision to join the army. You can deliver it personally and allay any concerns they may have. Then as soon as you return here, send Caleb or Pete to me. I'll have everything prepared for you by then."

When he had secured her promise to tread carefully while in Philadelphia, he engulfed her again in an embrace. His kisses left her breathless, her cheeks rosy.

While she hurriedly repinned her hair, he cautioned, "Keep your interview with Vander Groot short and confide in him no more than absolutely necessary. He may be trustworthy, as you say, but the more people who know even a little of our business, the more likely sooner or later someone will drop an unguarded word that'll leave us exposed. Unwitting or malicious, the damage will be the same."

ANDREWS USHERED VANDER GROOT into the room. "I'll be just outside," he told them. Leaving the door open, he took a post where he could see them, but far enough away that he could not easily overhear their conversation.

When Vander Groot made no move to take a seat, Elizabeth asked, "Will you not sit down, Pieter?"

"Thank you," he returned stiffly, "but I'd rather stand."

She regarded him with sorrow. "For weeks now, I've been trying to find a way to confide in you without hurting you. I hate that you had to learn the truth this way. Can you ever forgive me?"

"You didn't go to Boston, did you?" he demanded coldly.

"No. Colonel Andrews and I went to find Jonathan."

"To Ohio Territory?" Disbelief tinged his tone.

She nodded.

"Among the Indians."

"Yes." She barely managed a whisper.

"According to rumor he didn't return willingly."

She sighed. "He'd go back if he didn't feel under compulsion to stay until this conflict is ended. His greatest concern is for his people's future after the war."

He gave her a brooding look. "He's so much changed, then, that he considers himself one of them?"

She looked down, her throat too clogged with emotion to speak.

"And this is the man you've chosen to spend your life with," he exclaimed, "one who treats you as coldly as any Shawnee warrior, who accuses you of unspeakable things—"

"That isn't what he meant!"

"And you believe his . . . explanations?" he demanded, incredulous.

She fought to stifle an exasperated laugh at the futility of trying to explain to each other these two men she loved. "I know him, Pieter. You've met him one time. How can you judge him any more than he can judge you?"

When he stiffened and drew back, she stopped. Silence stretched between them.

At length he said quietly, "You've been working with him from the first?"

His steady, piercing gaze brought the color into her cheeks. Mindful of Carleton's warning, she said carefully, "Not . . . until we returned."

It was clear he noted her hesitation. "For General Washington, then." When she did not answer, he rushed on, his voice breaking, "You insisted there was no one else, even denied to my face that you were involved with him! I flattered myself that you cared for me—as you made it seem—and hoped in time you might grow to love me after all if only you could put aside what I conceived to be understandable fears. Now I find you loved him all along. How am I to believe you when you deny that your purpose from the first was only to use me and my family to get close to the Howes?"

The memory of her and her aunt's first meetings with Mrs. Van Cortland and the Vander Groots rose up to convict her, while the memory of Carleton's earnest warning rang in her ears. To face hanging would have been easier than to hear the devastation in Vander Groot's voice. It was not possible for her to meet his anguished gaze.

"I never meant to . . . cause you pain, Pieter. You must believe that."

"Was anything you told me the truth? Or was it all a lie?"

She caught her breath at his caustic tone and forced herself to look up. "I've always told you as much of the truth as I dared," she protested, forcing the words past the tight lump in her throat. Tears trickled down her cheeks.

"You could have trusted me!"

She choked down a sob. "It wasn't my own safety alone I had to consider. The lives of many others depended on my discretion."

"Including your aunt and servants, judging from what General Carleton said."

Drawing herself up with quiet dignity, she said, "We serve a great cause that you now acknowledge to be just and have pledged to join. Everything we've done has been to end the injustices you, by your own word, abhor, and to stop a tyrant you say you despise. Does that count for nothing?"

He looked quickly away, but not before she saw that his face softened almost imperceptibly.

"You came into my life at a time when I didn't know whether Jonathan was alive or . . . dead. He'd been missing for almost a year, and all our efforts to find him failed. I finally came to believe him lost to me, and I desperately needed someone I could feel safe with, someone who was kind and good and to whom I could entrust my heart. But that was unfair to you, and I beg you to forgive my weakness.

"Truly, if it were not for Jonathan, I'd have given my love to you. I care deeply for you as a most dear and beloved brother, and I'm heartsick that I've hurt you so. But Jonathan is the man God created for me, and I'm confident the Almighty has a true love for you as well."

"That's cold comfort."

Noting that the resentment in his tone had eased, she said humbly, "I know it is, but time will bring healing if we let it. I believe God brought us together for a reason. Please don't allow any fault on my part to blind you to His purpose or hinder you from obedience."

He made a quick, dismissive gesture and answered stiffly, "I hope I'm more mature than that."

She studied her clenched hands before looking up. "You accused me of betraying you and said you'd never forget. Did you truly mean that?"

He stared into the air before returning his gaze to her. "I spoke in anger. I hope you know me well enough to believe me incapable of harming you or anyone you love. But whether even time can heal this wound . . . " He shook his head and turned away.

Tears sprang to her eyes, but before she could speak, he abruptly swung back and burst out, "Beth, tell them you won't do this anymore! Please stop before it's too late to turn back. I fear for you if you go on!"

"I can't," she said, feeling numb. "This is the charge I've been given. I won't abandon it."

She became aware of movement in the passage outside. When Andrews stepped into the room and beckoned to Vander Groot, she rose.

"It appears I must go," he said gruffly.

"You're wrong about him, Pieter," she burst out, "and he's wrong about you. Some day both of you will know it."

As he followed Andrews out of the room, she said sadly to his rigid back, "God go with you and keep you safe."

He did not look back at her, however. Fighting back tears, she trailed behind the two men to join Tess and the servants in bidding Carleton's party godspeed, wondering how it was possible to feel at the same time such joy and such sorrow.

Chapter Seventeen

HER FACE CREASED WITH ASTONISHMENT and dismay, Verbena Vander Groot lowered the letter she had been reading to her lap and met Elizabeth's sympathetic gaze. "I can hardly credit this!" she burst out. "I believed our son as loyal to the king as we've always been, and now he's joined the rebel army." Turning to her husband, she demanded, "How could this happen without our knowledge? Andreas, did you ever detect any hint of this change in him?"

Every line of his body reflecting distress, Mr. Vander Groot sprang to his feet and took a turn around the smaller of the stately brick mansion's two parlors, where they sat. "Thinking back on it now, I wonder that I didn't suspect it. Over the past year Pieter and I had a number of discussions about British policies and how even those loyal to the crown have been abused in too many instances."

"But to foreswear allegiance to our rightful king—"

"Oh, Mama!" nineteen-year-old Isobel cried. "Pieter spoke of his doubts and questions—and anger—often enough, if you'd only listened, but you never took his concerns seriously." Glancing at the slender, wan young man seated near a window, she bit her lip. "Of course. . . we've been so distracted ever since last fall . . . "

Elizabeth transferred her gaze to the Vander Groots' younger son, Christiaan. Only twenty-three, he had suffered more grief than common for one so young, she reflected, her heart contracting. She judged his form to have once been as robust as his older brother's, but she could see that the flesh had fallen from him over the course of the past months, leaving him with a fragile, unhealthy appearance that his naturally pale coloring did not enhance.

Since their arrival at Christiaan's expansive city house early that afternoon, he had made every effort to join in his family's obvious delight at their reunion, but it was clear his thoughts were often far away. Now, drawing in a breath with an effort, he turned from the window through which he had been staring vacantly as though he registered little of the lushly greening garden visible through the wavy glass panes.

"I'm not surprised, Father," he said in a voice that gratified her with its steadiness. "Before Margrit . . . while she was on childbed, we talked to pass the time. Pieter shared much of what he'd seen and heard, and I thought then he couldn't in conscience support the British much longer when their policies are so unjust and are having such ill effect on the country. To be frank, I sympathize with his views."

"So do I," Isobel murmured, frowning down at her clenched hands.

Her mouth falling open, Mrs. Vander Groot regarded her children with astonishment. "But such things are common in times of war," she protested. "Those who defy their legitimate sovereign must expect that he'll impose harsh measures to put down their rebellion."

Elizabeth threw a cautious glance at her aunt. "We heard many disturbing accounts of the depredations of the Hessians—and the British as well—from many soldiers and even officers. But we had no idea of the extent of the devastation until we passed through the countryside on our way here."

Her expression stern, Tess gave an unsparing account of the wasteland the British had made of New Jersey and the horrors they had visited upon private citizens without regard for their loyalties. When she finished, Mr. Vander Groot stood with slumped shoulders, his face chalky, while his wife pressed her hands to her bent head, tears dropping into her lap.

Isobel sat rigidly erect, high color in her cheeks. "I care not what you think," she flung at her parents, trembling. "I'm proud of Pieter, and I agree with him wholeheartedly."

"So must I," Mr. Vander Groot said forcefully. "We've heard similar reports and discounted them or, to our shame, closed our ears. But judging from what you describe, no person of sensibility can possibly remain loyal to such a despot as George the Third." Turning on his heel he stalked to the window behind Christiaan and glared at the scene outside. "Blast the scoundrel!"

"Andreas!" Mrs. Vander Groot exclaimed.

Frowning, Elizabeth pretended intense interest in the flowered pattern of her petticoat to keep from jumping up and running to hug him. She knew she dared not glance at her aunt lest her delight betray her.

Gazing unhappily at her husband, Mrs. Vander Groot wrung her hands, but at last admitted with reluctance, "I cannot disagree entirely with your sentiments. And yours, my dear," she added with a warm look at her daughter. "Indeed, knowing our Pieter, he would take a stand against such a great wrong."

Christiaan returned Isobel's smile. Watching them with affection, Elizabeth wavered between joy at their friends' change of heart and guilty shame at all she and her aunt were forced to conceal from them. She longed to pour out all her heart, but Carleton's undisputable warnings less than a week earlier about the dangers of betrayal twisted like a knife in her breast.

"But what of Lord and Admiral Howe?" Mrs. Vander Groot exclaimed, her face reflecting a new concern. "We've long been friends, and all our acquaintances support the crown. How are we to turn our backs on them? The thought of losing everyone's esteem—"

"If that happens, so be it, Mama," Christiaan said firmly. "We cannot allow others to determine our actions. Even friends can be wrong, and if they reject us for following our consciences, their acquaintance is not worth having. By closing our eyes to this outrage, we make ourselves complicit in it."

"An excellent point, Christiaan," Tess approved. "Changing our allegiance was difficult for us too, but we felt we were left no choice."

Christiaan smiled. "Be assured you've made it an easier decision for us." Including Elizabeth in his gaze, he added, "My parents and sister have shared a great deal about you both, as has Pieter. Now I feel I know you as well as they do and consider you my friends as well."

Elizabeth leaned toward him. "Pieter also told us much about you, Christiaan. We've prayed all these months for your comfort and strengthening."

"We're so pleased to see you doing better," Tess said. "I'll write Pieter this very night to ease his concerns. You had him very worried, you know."

Christiaan inclined his head. "Thank you," he said gravely. "I'll not deny that I'd given up hope of life during those dark months. But I felt your prayers and believe they've had much healing effect. Little by little I'm coming to accept God's design for my life and find peace again."

Dabbing at her tears, his mother reached her other hand to clasp Tess's. Leaning over the back of Christiaan's chair, Mr. Vander Groot laid his hands on his son's shoulders, while Isobel rose and flew to embrace and kiss her brother, then returned to her seat on the sofa beside Elizabeth.

When Elizabeth drew her into her arms, Isobel laid her head on Elizabeth's shoulder. "I've missed you so! How hard it's been to be parted from you all these months! We've needed you here, and all that kept us from going to New York to drag you back by main force was knowing that Pieter needed you more."

Her giggle warmed Elizabeth with its sweet earnestness, but tears quickly welled into the younger woman's expressive eyes. "You cannot know how happy we are now you've finally come!" she exclaimed, blinking them back.

"I know how happy we are to be here," Elizabeth returned, placing an affectionate kiss on her friend's brow.

Raising her face to Elizabeth's, Isobel clung to her. "Don't leave us again! Promise you'll stay with us forever!"

Gathering her close, Elizabeth looked over her head to meet Tess's pain-filled gaze, her own heart aching. "We'll stay as long as we may, sweet sister, but I cannot promise that God will not direct us to other paths. You know we must all follow where He leads and trust that He'll comfort us if ever we must be parted again. And you've happy news that will bring great changes to your life before year's end."

Isobel gave a squeal and directed a reproachful glance at her mother, though her radiant smile belied it. "Mama, you promised! You know I wanted to tell them myself."

"How could I keep such good news from our dear friends?" Mrs. Vander Groot objected, her smile almost as radiant as her daughter's.

Tess laughed. "Your mama's joy was so apparent when we arrived that we pried the glad tidings out of her. Now tell us all about this young Mr. Martin Lamb you're so fond of."

For the next quarter hour, Isobel entertained them with raptures about the handsome, wealthy young merchant she was engaged to marry. His surname must certainly be most appropriate to his character, Elizabeth concluded as the family shared plans for a December wedding. At length, however, the realities of the Vander Groots' situation bore in on them.

Pieter's defection could not help but raise inconvenient questions if it became known. And should the British capture Philadelphia, they might well face reprisals, even be forced to abandon the city. Returning to occupied New York was no longer an option, and Washington's success in preventing the British from capturing the city now seemed to the Vander Groots their best hope.

Tess suggested that for their safety and Pieter's his service with the rebels simply not be shared. All anyone outside the family needed to know was that his practice had taken him elsewhere and he was unable to visit. With obvious relief, their friends agreed.

On asking about Mrs. Vander Groot's aunt, Euphemia Van Cortland, Elizabeth and Tess were grieved to learn she was not expected to live out the week. Mrs. Vander Groot and Isobel ushered them to a comfortable, well-appointed chamber at the back of the house, overlooking the rear gardens. Taking the chair at the elderly woman's bedside, Mrs. Vander Groot gently chafed her aunt's hands and called her name, but received no response.

Looking down at the frail, bent old woman under the coverlet, Elizabeth noted how shrunken she seemed since they had last visited with her the previous summer, and how deeply the wrinkles etched her finely boned face. Mrs. Van Cortland was scarcely more than a skeleton now, her grey hair thin, her closed eyes sunk into her head. A tide of bitter emotion flooded over Elizabeth at the memory of her tireless enthusiasm for life and how she had welcomed her and Tess on their arrival in New York. She had gathered them under her wing without reserve, introducing them to her grand-nephew and his family and, unwittingly, into the social circles that had provided the intelligence they had been sent to gather.

As she glanced at her friends' sorrowful faces, a deeper grief oppressed Elizabeth, as did the memory of Pieter's angry accusations days earlier. But gathering what remained of her resolution, she pushed the painful reflections away for the moment, knowing it was impossible to dispel them for long.

"She's been a mother to me since my own died when I was a young girl," Mrs. Vander Groot murmured, tears falling. "Without her I'd not have found so much happiness."

"She made us so welcome when we first came to New York," Tess said, for Elizabeth could not speak, "and now she goes before us and will welcome us to the arms of our Savior when our time comes to go home."

"Aunt Euphemia never awoke, and she passed gently into her eternal home," Elizabeth wrote in a letter to Vander Groot four days later. "She had insisted that no one mourn her, and though there were many tears, her funeral today was truly a celebration of her long and blessed life. Our only regret was that you could not be here in body, though we felt your presence with us, as our prayers are with you."

She finished the letter with a detailed account of his parent's change of heart toward the patriots, and Isobel and Christiaan's support, then sprinkled sand over it. Setting it aside to dry, she wiped her pen and laid it down. With a sigh she released her sorrow at Mrs. Van Cortland's passing and breathed a prayer for the Vander Groots' grief to find comfort and for wisdom, guidance, and steadfastness in their change of allegiance.

Dreamily she gazed through the half-open window to the mansion's grounds below. Her third-floor bedchamber faced onto the orchard at the rear of the mansion's long, narrow city lot, now washed in the shades of twilight. Weeks of warming temperatures and alternating sunny skies and gentle rains had begun to coax the trees into luxuriant bloom. The lush, manicured gardens of Philadelphia reminded her of those that had characterized New York before the great fire. Following the dreary, seemingly endless months of winter and the privations that now gripped that city, the sight fed her soul.

After a moment, she transferred her attention to her serene surroundings. The chamber she occupied next to Tess's equally spacious one offered every elegance and comfort. She had immediately felt at home on settling into it, and over the past days the sharp consciousness of the secrets she and her aunt harbored had given way to a quiet determination to cherish the Vander Groots' friendship and trust God to work all things for good even in this matter.

The prospect of settling in Philadelphia for the summer, where they could enjoy their friends' society on a daily basis as well as temporary respite from the most stressful demands of their clandestine roles raised Elizabeth's spirits. Especially did she and Tess rejoice in returning to regular church attendance, a precious habit that had been denied them in New York, where almost all the congregations' buildings had either been destroyed in the fire or were being used by the British as arsenals, prisons, barracks, and stables.

She found herself praying that Howe would change his mind about attacking the city. To think of such a pleasant community being destroyed by war and the resulting casualties filled her with dread. At the same time the knowledge that she and her aunt would be forced to find a pretext to follow Howe if he turned his attention elsewhere only darkened the unease that hung in the back of her mind like a gathering storm. That, too, she could only entrust to the Lord's provision.

She greatly enjoyed the walks and carriage rides they took along the broad, tree shaded thoroughfares. Isobel's handsome, affable fiancé, Martin Lamb, often accompanied them, and she and Tess were quickly coming to regard him with as great an affection as the Vander Groots clearly did.

Elizabeth already had some familiarity with Philadelphia as she had traveled there with her parents as a child and at fourteen had accompanied her aunt on an extended visit. Situated between two major navigable rivers, the broad Delaware on the east and the narrower Schuylkill on the west, it had been one of the foremost ports of the British Empire and now held the same position in the fledgling United States. Pennsylvania's founder William Penn's pledge of religious tolerance for all had attracted not only Quakers, but also Mennonites, Pietists, Anglicans, Catholics, and Jews. A continual stream of new settlers passed through the city, some establishing residence there, while others sought better opportunities along the frontier.

Offering an expansive harbor that accommodated ships of the deepest draft, the only direct road south to the Shenandoah Valley, and the Forbes Road leading west to Pittsburgh and Ohio Territory, it boasted as well several newspapers, regular mail routes, a college and library, and the continent's first hospital, an institution Elizabeth was eager to visit.

Within the city's environs lay four pleasant Commons that drew residents outside into the warm, sunny weather for picnics and strolls. A ten-acre wooded central square accommodated a market house and schoolhouse as well as the imposing bulk of the Pennsylvania State House, where the Second Continental Congress held its meetings. Classically Georgian in design and surmounted by a square bell tower and steeple, it had a smaller wing attached to either side of the central building by a gracefully arched arcade.

The massive red brick structure dominated the downtown area. Each time their coach rattled past, Elizabeth pressed her nose to the glass to take in the scene and hastily search the passers-by for recognizable faces. Once she caught a fleeting glimpse of John Adams and John Hancock conferring with evident passion on the building's steps. Heart pounding, she clasped her hands in the effort to suppress an excited bounce.

In the days that followed Mrs. Van Cortland's funeral, the Vander Groots kindly offered every assistance in finding suitable summer lodgings. In spite of their intentions to spend only a fortnight before returning to New York, it was the very end of the month before Elizabeth and Tess found a home for lease that was both acceptable and affordable. Located in a neighborhood only a few blocks from Christiaan's home, the gracious three-story town house offered easy access to the Delaware and other routes by which she and Tess might steal out of the city if escape became necessary.

Pressed by the Vander Groots to delay their departure, they did not get away for another week. They finally reached Montcoeur on May 7 to distressing news of a British raid on Danbury, Connecticut, the previous week. A great quantity of much-needed miltary stores had been destroyed before the local militia, led by General Benedict Arnold, drove the British off.

"If it weren't for bad news we'd have no news at all!" Elizabeth burst out in frustration.

While the two women had been gone, at Elizabeth's direction Caleb had slipped across the river and traveled to Peekskill to determine the situation in the army's Northern Department. He brought news of Colonel Stern's regiment, which had been transferred to General Putnam's command in February.

Assuring them that Elizabeth's uncle and her cousin, Levi, were well, he relayed rumors that had been rife among the corps stationed in the Hudson Highlands. Credible sources confirmed that the British planned to make another strike from Canada in the attempt to sever the New England states from the rest of the country and that Governor Carleton was to be replaced as the commander by General John Burgoyne, who was expected to arrive from England at any time.

"Governor Carleton tried that last fall and was checked by General Arnold," Tess pointed out. "What does he think is to be gained by another attempt?"

Shaking his head, Caleb said, "Apparently Burgoyne thinks it'll give him a chance at glory no other opportunity presently affords."

"Vintage Burgoyne," Elizabeth snickered.

After Caleb left them, she followed Tess into the library. Breaking the wax seal on the first of the letters waiting for them, Tess scanned it, then handed it to Elizabeth.

"Here's a diversion from the bad news—or possibly more of it, depending on your perspective."

Eyebrows raised, Elizabeth read the summons from Betsey Loring to call on her aboard Admiral Howe's flagship, the *HMS Eagle*, the instant she arrived back in town. It was the very last thing she wished to do.

"Can't we just grab what we can't live without and leave for Philadelphia in the morning?" she pleaded, more than half in earnest.

Tess grimaced. "She specifically asks for you, so you'd better call on her tomorrow and find out what's so urgent. Perhaps Howe is ready to open the campaign, and she'll spill some details of what he's planning."

The next morning Elizabeth reluctantly made the required call on Betsey Loring. Crossing the bay in the *Eagle's* boat, she cast carefully guarded, resentful glances toward the moldering prison ships. They swung sluggishly at anchor some distance away, no doubt to spare the delicate senses of the exalted British commanders the despairing moans and nauseating odors that emanated from their victims.

Once aboard the *Eagle,* she was ushered into the admiral's quarters, a constricted space that was nevertheless spacious for a man-of-war. She was not surprised to find her hostess ensconced at a card table playing faro with the Howes and several aides. With the ship's gentle rocking, undulating bars of sunlight reflected from the waves through the rear bank of windows, illuminating the stale tobacco smoke that hung heavy in the air and shimmering through the varying colors and levels of liquor in the glasses at each place.

Drawing Elizabeth into their circle, Betsey exclaimed brightly, "Here you are at last, dearest Elizabeth! It's about time you returned! We've been monstrously dull ever since you and your aunt left. How was your visit with the Vander Groots?"

Elizabeth returned her smile, doing her best to squelch the amusing image of the present company languishing at the faro table ever since her departure. "Most pleasant indeed. One could not ask for more delightful society—"

"I'm sure you fairly basked in the charming company of your dear doctor!" Betsey motioned for the servant to bring Elizabeth a drink.

"Oh . . . yes, he's always most charming indeed," Elizabeth temporized.

Betsey gave her a knowing look. "Ah, then he doesn't make your heart thrill, I take it. He's clearly besotted with you, however, and time does march on. Not that you're so old yet, love, but keep in mind that one has many more eligible suitors while one's bloom is still fresh. A young lady of your station can't afford to turn up her nose at the prospect of such an advantageous alliance." She gave a coarse laugh. "If it doesn't provide all one might wish as far as romance is concerned . . . well, one can always indulge in pleasant dalliances to supply what's wanting." She slid a meaningful glance toward Howe, who appeared completely engrossed in the cards in front of him.

Elizabeth could not help reflecting on the advantages of Mrs. Loring's marriage to the brutish commissary of prisoners responsible for her countrymen's deplorable situation, a man who evidently valued his wife's virtue and reputation far less than the preferment he gained by providing her as the British commander's paramour. "Aunt Tess and I plan to return to Philadelphia for the summer," she said coolly. "We found a lovely house that will serve perfectly—"

"Now you're abandoning us . . . for Philadelphia?" General Howe said in a languid drawl, raising his dark gaze from the cards to fix on her.

"Only temporarily, Your Excellency," Elizabeth responded, relieved at the change of subject. "The season is rapidly progressing, and no doubt you'll open the campaign soon. When it comes to battle, we'd prefer to be well out of musket shot."

The general exchanged glances with his brother. "Ah . . . but what if I decide on Philadelphia as my goal? Will you not be in the middle of the action then?"

She tipped her head to cast an alluring glance at both men. "I'd think it more likely you'll head north up the Hudson and support General Burgoyne's venture to split New England from the rest of these rebellious States." She gave a light laugh. "But then what does a mere woman know of military matters?"

"You know about Gentleman Johnny's campaign," Admiral Howe observed, eyebrows arched.

Elizabeth tasted her drink, then set it aside with an elaborate shrug. "It's common gossip, Your Lordship. I'm only repeating what can be heard on every street corner."

"Demme if we can keep even our closest councils secret from those perfidious revolutionaries," the admiral growled.

Not if you continue to be so careless about security, Elizabeth thought as she directed him a glance of feigned sympathy.

General Howe selected a card and scrutinized it before again lifting his gaze to Elizabeth. "I suspect, my dear Miss Howard, that you know more about . . . military matters . . . than half the officers in the rebel army."

A chill fell over Elizabeth. When the others laughed, however, she joined in their mirth.

"You may be right in that," she conceded wryly, "in which case the success of your arms is assured."

"It may not be as easy as all that." Lord Howe stretched back in his chair. "France sends fair words to us but to you Americans, materiel and officers."

"Pray do not include me among the rebels," Elizabeth objected with a smile. "However . . . while my aunt and I were in Boston, we did hear talk of France secretly providing aid to our misguided countrymen."

Lord Howe snorted. "If France believes their support for the rebels is secret, they're sadly mistaken. However, should we administer another spanking to the rebels on the battlefield as we did last fall, mayhap they'll rethink their misbegotten course."

Elizabeth turned to General Howe, expectantly. "Then surely there'd be little advantage in taking Philadelphia, Your Excellency, when Washington's army is so close at hand right here."

General Howe tossed back the contents of his glass and motioned to the servant for a refill. "That old fox has been resistant to meeting us head to head. Of course, he knows he can't win in pitched battle, so every time we make the slightest show against him, he runs away."

"To fight another day." Elizabeth twined around her finger the lock of hair that trailed onto her bosom, noting with mingled triumph and revulsion that General Howe's gaze followed the movement.

What concerns me most is the perils you face beyond the physical dangers.

Her heart contracted as Carleton's warning rang in her mind. Again a deep loathing of the deceptions she practiced pierced her.

Lord Howe threw down his cards and folded his arms. "Unfortunately so. If we threaten the rebels' capital, however—"

"Then he'll have no choice but to crawl out of his lair," General Howe concluded, his words slurred. "He can't allow us to take Philadelphia or the rebels'll lose what little popular support they have, and the treaties they're attempting to negotiate with France and Spain will be forfeit as well."

"So they will," Lord Howe said thoughtfully, his lips pursed. "It's something to consider, isn't it, Billy?"

Chapter Eighteen

"I OFFER TO YOU MY CREDENTIALS, Monsieur Adams." Speaking in a cultured French accent, Elizabeth accompanied her introduction with a deep bow, hat in hand.

"Yet another Frenchman with designs on a commission!" the balding, forty-one-year-old congressman exclaimed in exasperation, throwing up his hands. "We're overrun with 'em."

"Monsieur, you are most mistaken," Elizabeth protested, returning her hat to her head. "As agent to Admiral le Comte de Caledonne, I have been sent to seek of you letters of marque and reprisal for le comte's nephew, your Brigadier General Jonathan Carleton. Le comte is outfitting a number of the general's merchant ships for war, for he desires the honor of attacking your enemy—and soon, it is devoutly to be hoped, ours as well. General Carleton would have presented himself to you, but he is understandably engaged elsewhere, thus he requested me to beg your attention to this matter."

Eyebrows rising, the stocky man she had intercepted just outside the spacious tower stair hall of the State House stepped back to take her in from her plumed cocked hat and the elaborately dressed white tie wig beneath it to her elegantly tailored amber silk coat with embroidered lapels, set off by matching smallclothes and embroidered waistcoat, down to her sheer white hose and high-heeled, silk-bowed shoes. Pretending complete indifference to his scrutiny, she pulled a lace-trimmed handkerchief from her coat pocket and raised her chin to delicately dab her nose.

During the fortnight she and Tess had spent in New York, Carleton had arranged to have a wardrobe tailored for her disguise, every garment cut in the latest French fashion and of the very finest materials. Fully confident that no one would ever guess she was other than a young French nobleman, she reflected that Carleton knew what he was about when it came to style.

Frowning, Adams took the papers she extended to him, and with a sharp glance at John Hancock, the president of the Congress, unfolded and scanned them, while his elder cousin Samuel peered over his shoulder. Elizabeth waited with expectancy, certain that even the Howes would have taken the documents to be authentic. Which they were, though Carleton had, by necessity, signed them in lieu of his uncle in Marseilles. Finally looking up, Adams handed the papers to Hancock.

"Everything appears to be in order." Adams' expression nevertheless remained unconvinced.

He was echoed with considerably greater enthusiasm by his companions. Samuel rubbed his palsied hands together, smiling broadly beneath the wreath of wispy white hair that encircled his balding pate.

"General Carleton!" he chortled. "We've heard much of this man." With relish he repeated the rumors of Carleton's exploits as a Shawnee war chief.

She bowed again. "I believe it is so."

"Then he would seem to be our enemy, not our friend, Monsieur Tesseré," Adams noted, scowling.

"Ah, but he has rejoined General Washington, John—"

"Not necessarily a recommendation as far as I'm concerned," Adams cut Hancock off, nostrils flaring.

"It should be, considering that you supported our commander for his post," Samuel pointed out dryly.

"I've had time to repent."

So Adams does indeed oppose the General, Elizabeth thought. *Contentious New Englanders.* She choked down a laugh.

"By all accounts Carleton's Rangers have been highly effective in the *petit guerre* Washington's been waging since the affair at Trenton," Hancock said.

"The *militias* have been waging," Adams corrected him with asperity. "In any event, I have to question where Carleton's allegiance truly lies. I've heard he's become more Shawnee than American, and they're notable allies of the British."

"Now, John," Samuel chided, "set aside your suspicions for once and consider that we've just been handed a great coup. The fact is that General Carleton has been highly successful in battle, regardless of whom he's attacking. That would undoubtedly carry over to the naval war, especially as he has excellent reasons to despise our enemy."

He slanted a quick glance at Elizabeth. "When we first heard about him, I did some investigating. He was adopted by his father's elder brother, Sir Harrison Carleton, who turns out to have been a staunch Son of Liberty—and listen to this: He was murdered by Lord Dunmore's soldiers in a squabble over import duties. A prime motivation for revenge, I'd say. On his uncle's death Carleton inherited a merchant fleet that circumnavigates the globe, and he's reputed to be even richer than you, John," he concluded with smirk at Hancock, "which certainly can't do us any harm."

Hancock's eyes narrowed. "Don't forget that while serving as General Gage's aide-de-camp, he transmitted intelligence to the Massachusetts Committee of Safety as Washington's agent. Had he not managed to escape, the British would have hanged him for it. You can imagine the price they've put on his head."

"It is my understanding, sirs," Elizabeth interjected, "that George the Third wishes his scalp to decorate his private chambers, a desire General Howe has dedicated himself to fulfill."

Samuel Adams fixed his gaze on her with shrewd interest. She had been in disguise when she and Paul Revere met with him and Hancock in Lexington two years earlier to warn that the Regulars were headed their way, but for a moment she was afraid he recognized her from that night. To her relief, after a moment he turned his mild gaze back to his cousin.

"If General Carleton has hatched a plan to dedicate part of his fleet to wreaking havoc on the British Navy, who are we to stand in his way when we'll be the beneficiaries?"

"Our navy's too small to prevail against the greatest naval power in the world all alone," Hancock agreed, his narrow face eager. "We have much to gain if a French admiral of Caledonne's stature is willing to get involved."

"Caledonne's reputation speaks for itself," Adams conceded grudgingly. He pulled out his watch and scrutinized it. "In fact, you're fortuitously arrived, Monsieur Tesseré. The Navy Committee meets in five minutes, and I was just on my way there. If you'd be so kind as to accompany me—" With a bow and the sweep of his hand, he indicated she was to precede him through the archway that led to the stairs.

"Most gladly, Monsieur Adams," she drawled, smiling. "If you allow, I will do my best to persuade your committee of the merits of General Carleton's petition."

IN FACT, THE MEMBERS of the Navy Committee received warmly the details she presented of the ships, their armaments and crews, and Carleton's strategy for their deployment, as guided by Caladonne's advice. It was a coup indeed, she decided smugly.

Even Adams and Stephen Hopkins, a delegate from Rhode Island and brother of Esek Hopkins, commodore of the small American navy, appeared suitably impressed. The committee wanted to meet with Carleton before issuing the letters of marque, Adams told her, but he saw no obstacle to approval. She assured him she would immediately pass the committee's request on, both pleased at the prospect of Carleton's coming to the city and alarmed by the dangers such a visit might hold.

Held in the Committee of Assembly Chamber on the second floor, the meeting ended shortly after noon. When she returned downstairs with the members, she eagerly accepted Hancock's invitation to sit in on a congressional meeting before they adjourned for lunch.

He escorted her into the Assembly Room, crowded with rows of tables swathed in green cloths. The Declaration of Independence had been passed in that very chamber less than a year earlier, and as she looked around her, she choked back a thrill of exultation.

Facing the equally spacious Supreme Court Room across the broad central hall that bisected the building front to back, the chamber easily accommodated the small number of delegates in attendance that spring, though she guessed it to be cramped when the full membership was present. She was disappointed that so many of the members were absent, including a number she had hoped to meet. Thomas Jefferson had resigned his seat in favor of a seat in the Virginia Assembly, and Benjamin Franklin was with the other American commissioners in Paris negotiating for a French alliance. Others had taken a leave of absence or were temporarily away on personal business.

Samuel Adams insisted on introducing her around, and they were soon joined by stately Elbridge Gerry, another member of the Massachusetts delegation, whose reputation as a bold, visionary leader was well deserved. She soon occupied the center of attention not only for her supposed connection to Caledonne, but also to Carleton, whose story appeared to be widely known and the subject of considerably more speculation than she wished.

Of those she met, Virginian Richard Henry Lee especially impressed her. Strikingly ascetic in appearance with his flowing white hair, Lee was one of the prime movers of Congress and a close friend of Patrick Henry, whose eloquence in debate he was reputed to rival. The previous year he had introduced the resolution that called for Congress to declare the colonies' independence from Britain.

Also present was New York delegate General Philip Schuyler, commander of the Northern Department. When they were introduced, Elizabeth noted that the general seemed distant and preoccupied—not surprising as he was fast becoming a lightning rod for criticism from the New England delegations because of what they considered high-handed patrician ways. While making her way across the room, she caught snatches of conversation among several delegates confirming that Schuyler had lost the militias' support, and that during the past months General Horatio Gates had met several times with Congress, pressing a suit to supplant him—if not Washington as commander in chief.

With Schuyler at a table across the room from where Elizabeth was seated with Adams and Gerry was handsome forty-year-old Major General Arthur St. Clair. A chestnut-haired, blue-eyed Scot and veteran of the British 60th Foot, he had fought with distinction in the Seven Years War and afterward settled on a large estate in Pennsylvania. Like Schuyler and Gates, both former British officers, he had cast his lot with the patriots.

Elizabeth was brooding on the significance of St. Clair's visit to Congress and wondering what he and Schuyler discussed with their heads so close together, when Hancock caught her attention as he took his seat behind the president's table on the low dais at the head of the room. The delegates who lingered at the back moved hastily to take their seats, and when Hancock struck the gavel, the hubbub of voices stilled.

The two hours that followed seemed far too short. Fascinated, Elizabeth listened intently to Samuel Adams' report on revisions to the draft of the proposed Articles of Confederation for the States. Several amendments were proposed and after acrimonious debate, voted down. The draft was sent back to committee for further revision.

During the discussion, Elizabeth took great interest in Adams's whispered explanations of various points. John Dickinson, who had written the original draft, had proposed a strong central government in which the States would be equally represented and which would, among other powers, be able to levy taxes. Wary of a strong central government due to their experience with Britain, however, the Congress was in the process of altering the draft to establish a loose confederation of sovereign states with a federal government whose powers were carefully limited.

"Each State will retain the power to collect its own taxes, issue currency, and provide for its own militia," Adams told her. "One thing we don't need is a standing army in time of peace, which opens the door to entirely too much mischief, to say nothing of the expense."

This was succeeded by considerable discussion of the state of the spring campaign—or lack thereof since May was almost gone and there were as yet no signs of movement on either side. Adams rose to speak several times, complaining at Washington's foot dragging and suggesting that Congress send a resolution advising their commander to attack his adversary at the earliest opportunity. This sparked hot words between those who supported Washington and noted that Congress had provided no budget for military action, and those who advocated replacing him with Gates. Others argued for giving command of the Northern Department to Gates, replacing Schuyler.

While Schuyler bitterly defended himself, Adams leaned toward Gerry, his resentful gaze fixed on the general. "Our officers worry one another like mastiffs, scrambling for rank and pay like apes for nuts," he growled in an undertone. "There is surely no principle that predominates in human nature so much in every age of life, from the cradle to the grave, in males and females, old and young, black and white, rich and poor, high and low, as this passion for superiority!"

Gerry shot him an amused look. Struggling to suppress a laugh, Elizabeth pretended to be absorbed in the ongoing debate while reflecting that Washington would surely approve Adams' sentiments since he was constantly being lobbied for promotion by this officer or that.

Sobering, she focused on the matter at hand, memorizing each argument and its advocate for her report. She was so absorbed that when the tower clock overhead tolled twice and the body adjourned for lunch, she found it hard to believe the session had lasted so long. Pleading a previous engagement, she declined invitations to join several of the members, then stopped in the central hall to take her leave of the two Adamses, Gerry, and Hancock. Before she could excuse herself they were interrupted by St. Clair, who drew Hancock to one side.

"I leave for Albany this afternoon, and from thence I'm bound to Champlain to take command of Fort Ticonderoga," he said in a low tone. "I'm greatly concerned that Governor Carleton will attempt another strike down the Hudson. Reports have reached Schuyler that reinforcements are on their way to him from England."

To Elizabeth's amazement, Hancock shrugged off the general's concerns. "You've nothing to worry about. By all accounts, despite any deficiencies the fort is impregnable. And it's certain that most, if not all, the Canadian forces will sail to New York to support Howe. There's no probability of an active campaign in that quarter this year."

St. Clair appeared taken aback. "How can you be certain?"

"General Gates himself assured us of it. I believe we can trust his judgment—if anyone knows the situation, he does."

Too stunned to speak, Elizabeth listened in dismay while St. Clair, his concerns obviously set at rest, made his goodbyes, then left. When

Hancock rejoined them, she burst out, "Monsieur, I could not help but overhear your discussion, and I fear you have been greatly misled."

Her companions regarded her as though she had sprouted a third eye. Her mind racing, she considered what a man of Monsieur Tesseré's station would be expected to know.

Adams folded his arms and pursed his lips. "Apparently you're unaware that last fall General Arnold turned Governor Carleton back on Lake Champlain with considerable losses. I don't imagine he's eager to try it again."

When the others agreed, Elizabeth assumed a pose of indifference. "According to our . . . ah . . . contacts at the British court—and I assure you they are numerous and well connected—General Burgoyne is on his way to take the command from Governor Carleton as we speak. He is bringing reinforcements and supplies for a campaign down Lake Champlain to the Hudson. I have been assured his goal includes the taking of Fort Ticonderoga."

By now a number of the other delegates had gathered round, including Lee, and a debate ensued about the probability of the British resuming their goal of separating the New England States from the rest by a strike down the Hudson, with Lee at the forefront of those who believed they would. All agreed that Ticonderoga was impregnable and that the British could not succeed in taking it. Satisfied that a warning had at least been delivered, Elizabeth excused herself and left.

She hurried to Bradford's London Coffee House, a popular three-story establishment on High Street, where Caleb had secured a private chamber for the exclusive use of Monsieur André Tesseré whenever "he" was in town. A loyal patriot, the proprietor had sworn to ask no questions and turn a blind eye to the Frenchman's comings and goings.

Jemma was waiting when she slipped into the room. While Caleb nursed a pint in the taproom, the young maid helped Elizabeth change into an afternoon gown and dressed her hair with expert speed.

They had just finished securing her disguise in the chest that held the rest of Monsieur Tesseré's wardrobe, when they heard three soft raps at the door. Joining Caleb in the passage and locking the door behind them, they slipped away unnoticed with him through the building's rear exit.

With Caleb and Jemma following several steps behind, Elizabeth returned to the town house where Tess waited eagerly for her report, congratulating herself on the morning's success.

Chapter Nineteen

THE CANVAS SIDE WALLS of the Rangers' hospital tent were rolled up to keep the temperature inside tolerable against the hot early July sun that already beat down relentlessly that morning. As Carleton ducked inside, the men who lay or sat on the cots straightened to salute him, and he greeted each by name, pleased to see that only a handful remained.

Standing by the camp table at the back of the tent, uniform coat hanging on the back of his chair and shirt sleeves rolled up, Vander Groot conferred with one of his assistants. He looked up at Carleton's entrance and came to meet him.

"No new cases of dysentery, I take it?"

"Fresh rations and proper sanitation make all the difference," Vander Groot answered. "And thankfully the few casualties from Cornwallis's attack at Westfield were relatively minor. Most of the men are already back on duty."

Carleton gave him a keen look. "If the British continue to drive toward the Delaware, we'll need every troop at full strength."

"Miss Howard seemed fully convinced Philadelphia is Howe's object."

Carleton grimaced. "He's as fickle as the wind."

Vander Groot moved to the outer perimeter of the tent and thoughtfully considered the bustling camp around them. "With my family in the city, I pray this is only a feint." When Carleton remained silent, the doctor threw him a glance over his shoulder. "I've . . . heard nothing from Miss Howard since her letter informing me of my great-aunt's death," he said with an effort. "I assume both she and her aunt are settled near my parents by now."

Carleton gave a curt nod, continuing to study the doctor through narrowed eyes. Although Vander Groot's manner toward him was no longer stiff with suppressed anger and resentment as when he'd first been brought into camp, tension still hung between them, more noticeable in what they did not say than in what they did. Yet during the three months Vander Groot had been a prisoner, he had been a model one, performing his duties with such faithfulness, expertise, and evident concern for his patients that he had earned Carleton's commendation if not yet his entire trust.

Even when his brigade had rejoined Washington's corps at Middlebrook on the edge of the highlands toward the end of May, and during the skirmishes with the columns Howe had flung out from New York into the New Jersey interior, the doctor had made no move to desert his post. As a result Carleton had reduced the guard that always attended him, giving him a greater measure of freedom. Freedom that had defined limits, however.

"Considering how close your family has been to the Howes—" he began abruptly.

"You've read their letters as well as Miss Howard's," Vander Groot cut him off. "You know my parents' change of heart on that score."

Carleton inclined his head. "A change due in large part to your sudden allegiance to your country. I'm curious as to why you discovered it—if indeed you do not have . . . other motives."

"You think that all along my purpose has been to spy for the British?"

Carleton shrugged. "You tell me. After three months I still don't know what to make of you. For all I know your intent might have been simply to impress Miss Howard—"

"I was never aware of her true allegiance," Vander Groot snapped. "By her own admission, to which you were witness, she and her aunt led me—led my entire family—to believe them loyal to the crown. If I'd wished to impress her, I'd hardly have confided my change of feelings." He hesitated, then added coldly, "And I assure you I'd never have pursued her had I any inkling that her affections were engaged elsewhere."

Ignoring the latter, Carleton drawled, "What are your feelings? And why the change?"

Vander Groot's jaw hardened. "Why are you a patriot?"

Carleton gave a harsh laugh. "I hardly know whether I am anymore." He waved his words away. "Forgive me. That's unworthy and untrue. I count myself very much a patriot—for the Shawnee first, but also for the Long Knives. I could never rejoice in their destruction. I admit there are times when my patience gives way at their ignorance and I speak hastily, times when I feel I've no allegiance left to them . . . and yet in my heart I know I do."

He nodded toward the scene visible through the tent's open flap. "My people's future is tied to my white kindred in great measure, thus I wish them well, nor do I forget the heritage they bequeathed to me. Believe me, to fight them gave me no satisfaction. Nor did I have any choice."

Vander Groot regarded him with a brooding look. Realizing he had revealed far more than he had intended, Carleton clenched his teeth and turned away.

"You may not believe me, but I do have some sense of how you must feel—and I respect you for it," Vander Groot said quietly. "Truly, watching you these past months, I've come to admire your leadership and the obvious care you have for all your men—whether Black, Indian, or White. It's clear you hold dear what was stated in our Declaration of Independence, and I want you to know that I also believe that God created all people equal, and that they deserve to be free."

Clearing his throat, Carleton glanced at the doctor, then quickly away so he would not see the effect of his words. It was some moments before he again met Vander Groot's steady gaze.

"This is a new revelation?"

Ignoring the edge of sarcasm in Carleton's voice, Vander Groot said earnestly, "My parents reared their children to believe so from an early age. And the Scriptures confirm it. During the course of the past year, I began to see the hypocrisy of king and Parliament claiming to have our best interests at heart, while pursuing a course of destruction and pillage. To be fair, General Howe made some effort to put a stop to the worst of it, though with little effect. The thought of families left destitute, children orphaned, women raped, and homes plundered is horrifying enough, but what ended it for me finally was the prison ships."

When Carleton gave him a questioning look, he said bitterly, "I'm not surprised you've heard nothing of the horrors our unfortunate men suffer imprisoned on a collection of rotting hulks in New York harbor. Few people know of it. In spite of Admiral Howe's refusal to grant permission, I managed to get aboard one of them, and what I saw would make the devil himself blanch."

With barely controlled passion Vander Groot sketched the situation of the prisoners and their unhappy families. When he finished, Carleton expressed his outrage in blunt language.

"I'll make sure His Excellency is aware of this," he said at last. "Strong protests to Lord Howe and public condemnation may have an effect."

Vander Groot's mouth compressed to a hard line. "I cannot support a regime that would either treat men so—even an enemy—or simply turn a blind eye to it."

"There are abuses on our part too," Carleton pointed out soberly. "In time of war when passions are enflamed, men do what they'd otherwise not—and later regret."

"I'm not so naïve as to believe our side blameless," Vander Groot protested, "but from all I've heard and read, our leaders, General Washington first among them, are trying to stop such outrages and establish a more just society and government."

Carleton sighed. "Yet many of them are slaveholders." He shook his head. "It'll take constant vigilance if we're not to lose what we've only begun to catch hold of, and that imperfectly. I've no great confidence in human nature, though I'm hopeful that by God's grace we may in time alter the dismal record of history.

"I admit I was apprehensive about bringing you here," he added, changing the subject abruptly, "but you've done well, Dr. Vander Groot. We were in sore need of someone with greater expertise in medicine than the usual run of army surgeons, and you've more than proven your worth. I believe God had a hand in bringing you to us, even though it was against your will. I hope in time you may feel the same."

"I'll not deny that I'd have preferred to enlist voluntarily," Vander Groot admitted, a faint smile shadowing his features, "yet I'm glad I can be of service to my country, no matter the circumstances. My intent, however, was to fight, not sit on the sidelines."

"Miss Howard commended your medical skill, and I'd be remiss if I didn't make the best use of your abilities. But fight you will as occasion warrants it. And if Howe has indeed ceased dithering and made up his mind to open the campaign, your opportunity may arise sooner rather than later."

Vander Groot hesitated before saying, "I appreciate the greater freedom you've given me these past weeks, general. It's made my service here less . . . objectionable."

Carleton gave him a piercing look. "We may have our differences, but your actions have earned you greater latitude. You've done more than you had to in not only making improvements to the brigade's hospital on your own initiative, but also voluntarily assisting in the army's main hospital as your duties allow."

"I remain a prisoner, however," Vander Groot pointed out.

"So you will until you fully prove your loyalty to our cause. That'll take time."

The doctor folded his arms and regarded Carleton with a frown. "And when I do so?"

"Then you'll receive a commission as major."

"Nevertheless, I'll not be free to leave."

"Like the rest of us, you'll be at liberty when this war is over," Carleton said. "If we're victorious, then all of us may claim to be free."

IT WAS MID AFTERNOON when Carleton hurried back to the Rangers' camp following a lengthy meeting of the general officers. According to the latest intelligence, Howe had pulled all his forces back to Amboy. More foreign troops had arrived, and detachments from Rhode Island were pouring into the town. A portable bridge was under construction, and British agents were recruiting pilots familiar with the Delaware River.

Clearly a move was afoot. Washington's mind was finally settled that Howe's sights were indeed on Philadelphia and that his force would likely travel there by sea.

It was long past time for Howe to open the campaign and whatever decision he made, Carleton hoped he would make it quickly. The need for action nagged at him like the ache of a sore tooth, and he knew he wasn't alone in the sentiment. With his corps grown to over 8,000 men, fully equipped, well drilled, in high spirits and spoiling for a fight, Washington was eagerly anticipating finally grappling with Howe in full-scale battle to test his own mettle and that of his troops.

To Carleton's gratification, the General had assigned him to support General Benedict Arnold's advance force, currently posted along the Delaware at Chester, six miles southwest of Philadelphia. Intercepting Jeffreys at the edge of the camp, Carleton sent his aide to begin making arrangements for the move.

On impulse, he dismounted and turned his stallion over to Stowe, then strode between the tidy rows of tents to the creek that wound along the edge of the woods at the camp's perimeter. His brooding look sent those who approached scuttling away, and with relief he ducked beneath low-hanging branches into the cool, dense green shade and crossed the stream. Stopping at the top of a gentle rise on the far side, he leaned back against a mossy tree trunk and drew in a deep breath of the moist air.

Pierced by a deep longing to hold Elizabeth in his arms again, he allowed joyful visions of her to fill his head. His need of her was more than the solace her love provided. She anchored his soul, and even the thought of her could keep him from plunging into the dark abyss that had plagued him since childhood. When she was not with him an essential part of his being was missing, and he felt restless, at loose ends.

His earlier conversation with Vander Groot continued to nag at him, and for some moments he pondered the night when their paths had intersected. It occurred to him to wonder whether God might have brought this worthy doctor into Elizabeth's life to comfort her and keep her heart safe until Carleton's return, whether He had delivered Vander Groot to him now to provide much-needed medical care for his men. Or could there be some other reason, as yet unseen?

Had their wholly unexpected meeting been, in fact, a divine appointment? Vander Groot's service during the past weeks almost persuaded Carleton to think so. Almost. For the future was as yet unknown, and so, he told himself, he must always remain on guard as he did with Jeffreys.

There was a difference between the two men, however. For the doctor was a believer. The genuineness of his faith was evident in all he did. Most telling was that Elizabeth, who knew his heart best, trusted him without reservation. And despite his harsh denial to her, Carleton trusted her instincts more than any other's.

Day by day he felt a growing sense deep down that his and Vander Groot's association was no mere coincidence, that in the coming months he would need the doctor beside him as surely as he needed Andrews and Stowe, Red Fox and Spotted Pony. And while he contemplated the coming whirlwind, over him fell a fearful foreboding that in a day of desperate trial he and those he loved best would depend greatly upon Vander Groot's courage and faithfulness, and that the doctor would not fail them.

Red Fox and Spotted Pony were waiting for Carleton when he returned to his marquee. The sun had lowered in the western sky, providing welcome relief from the incessant heat and humidity. For a while they sat together in comfortable silence, cross-legged on the long grass beneath the tent's awning, smoking pipes filled with fragrant killegenico.

His cousins had returned at the beginning of June after a swift, unsparing journey back from Ohio Territory. A small number of women accompanied them, including the two warriors' wives, Laughing Otter and Rain Woman, who brought along their older children. Stowe also had his new native wife in tow, a plump, pleasant-faced matron named Sweetgrass who was clearly as devoted to him as he was to her.

Andrews and Blue Sky had soon shifted their tent to the edge of the camp among the new arrivals. By now the settlement reminded Carleton of Grey Cloud's town, and he took sweet comfort in the nearness of his people. All that was lacking to make it a home was Elizabeth.

That a sizeable contingent of warriors had joined them greatly encouraged Carleton, even though most were Miami, Kickapoo, Mingo, or Wyandot, with a few Delaware among them. Of the Shawnee, most were members of the small Christian fellowship he had gathered.

He was disappointed but not surprised that in spite of Red Fox and Spotted Pony's strongest arguments, the majority of the Shawnee either refused to abandon their allegiance to the British or remained determined to stay aloof from the conflict. In long, private discussions since their return, they had related that in spite of the efforts of the Shawnees' principal sachem, Cornstalk, to keep their people neutral, the younger warriors of the tribe increasingly flocked to Blue Jacket, a sachem of the Piqua sept who insisted that the British would help the tribe reclaim the lands lost to the settlers. Under his leadership, the limited war White Eagle had led was rapidly widening and had become notably bloodier in his absence.

"The respect and good will of our people toward you remains strong, White Eagle," Red Fox had assured Carleton. "Only Raging Bull and those closest to him still bear resentment for Wolfslayer's death."

"Your medicine is too powerful for them to speak against you in the council," Spotted Pony said. "But you are still only one man, and they do not believe the Long Knives can prevail against the British king."

"Cornstalk was right," Carleton told them. "No matter which side we fight on, the Long Knives and the British will be like two great stones that will grind us to dust."

"This is not all," Red Fox had warned before continuing. The principal sachem of the Iroquois, the Mohawk Thayendanegea who was closely allied with General Sir William Johnson, the British superintendent for Indian affairs in the north, had gathered a large war party from among the settlements of the upper Susquehanna and Delaware, with more loyalists than Mohawks joining him. They had begun ferocious attacks against the patriot militias in the area, who had been harassing those loyal to the crown.

"They are more loyal to Thayendanegea than to the British king, and they are fearless in battle," Spotted Pony had concluded.

Becoming aware that Andrews and Blue Sky strode toward them, Carleton set aside his troubling reflections to welcome them into the circle. Blue Sky was radiant in a loose shirt and petticoat that gave room for her expanding girth. Bending over her solicitously, Andrews steadied her as she lowered awkwardly to the grass, then took a seat beside her. Watching them, Carleton suppressed a smile.

Before long, Laughing Otter, Rain Woman, and their children, along with Blue Sky's friend Mary, then Stowe and Sweetgrass came to join in their discussion of the move to Chester, news that had Blue Sky almost bouncing with excitement to see Elizabeth again. Then Isaiah and several of his officers expanded the group further, along with some of their women and children.

At Red Fox's urging, Carleton retrieved from his marquee the volume of Gibbon's history of the Roman Empire Elizabeth had sent him. Finding it intensely interesting, he had begun reading it in the evenings to whoever wanted to listen, explaining various points as he went along.

Looking up from time to time while he read, Carleton was amused to see that as usual Andrews and Isaiah were deep in a discussion of theology with Captain James McLeod, the passionate young Scottish chaplain who had joined the brigade on their move to Middlebrook. Sewing in hand, the women talked quietly among themselves. Spotted Pony and Stowe stretched lazily across the grass, eyes closed.

The children had scampered off to play, and their high-pitched cries and laughter echoed in the still, humid air as they raced through the long bars of light and shadow the westering sun cast across the grass. Nearby a mixed team of troops surged up and down a long, grassy space, playing stickball with furious intensity against a large party of warriors.

His marquee seemed to have become a magnet, he reflected. In the late afternoons whenever they were in camp, once the drills and duties of the day were done, it had become customary for members of the brigade and their women to gather to visit and play games. Often after sunset dances of their various cultures spontaneously sprang up and became friendly competitions that lasted long into the night.

Suppressing a smile, he returned his attention to his reading.

Red Fox showed his usual keen interest in Gibbon's history, leaning forward to listen raptly. His dark eyes intense, he noted, "Are not the British fathers following the path of these Romans? Have they not become equally corrupt?"

Carleton absently stroked his jaw. "It occurred to me that might be Gibbon's point."

The warrior's eyes narrowed. "Then will the Long Knives not also do the same in their own councils?"

Carleton considered him thoughtfully. The insights the warrior frequently offered impressed him. Red Fox was rapidly becoming fluent in English, and Carleton decided he would teach his cousin to read and write and make him officially his aide as he already was in practice.

"If history is any indication, this seems to be the white man's tendency," he agreed.

"The Shawnee are not so, nor our brothers."

"Our people are subject to our own temptations and failures," Carleton pointed out. "Unless we guard our hearts, I fear we may in time take on much of the white traditions and enter upon the same path. We must pray for wisdom, my brother."

As he spoke, a profound sense of assurance and peace warmed him. Elizabeth might be absent for the time, but little by little much that was precious was being given back to him, and for that he was deeply grateful. All his desires and hers would surely be given them in God's time as well. Anxiety and impatience were nothing more than lack of faith.

While he pondered the matter, Vander Groot strode by, headed toward his tent. He always kept aloof from the evening gatherings, and on impulse Carleton beckoned to him.

"Come join us, Pieter."

Vander Groot hesitated, clearly noting Carleton's deliberate use of his first name. When Carleton shifted to make room for him at his side, the doctor came slowly to take the offered place.

They lingered until Jeffreys returned to report on progress being made for the impending move. Soon the women hurried away to prepare the evening mess, and the men drifted off for their turn at guard or to finish the day's duties. When Vander Groot moved to follow the others, Carleton motioned him into the marquee.

After an awkward hesitation, the doctor said, "Since we're moving so close to Philadelphia, gen—"

"My friends call me Jon," Carleton cut him off. "And yes, I believe you'll be able to safely call on your family as long as you're careful not to draw undue attention to yourself."

Vander Groot studied him for a moment, then said tentatively, "I assume you plan to call on Beth . . . Jon."

"I have business to discuss with her," Carleton said curtly. Relenting, he added, "Even did I not, you know I'll go to her whenever I can. Merely transmitting intelligence back and forth is less than satisfying."

Vander Groot conceded a faint smile, then sobered. "But if you're seen together, will it not put you both in grave danger?"

"That's what I want to talk to you about, Pieter." Carleton placed his hand on the doctor's shoulder. "I think we can work out arrangements to avoid unnecessary complications for all of us."

Chapter Twenty

AFTER ANOTHER DAY'S ROUND of social engagements, Elizabeth sought solitude in the garden, while Tess busied herself upstairs writing letters in her chamber. A brilliant sunset cast bars of golden light through the surrounding trees, blazing in vivid colors among the profusion of flowers and bushes.

The day's heat and humidity had finally begun to relent with descending night. Grateful for the tinge of coolness in the air, she found a seat on a weathered garden bench and drew her shawl around her shoulders. For some moments she drank in the fresh breeze suffused by the rich scent of roses, the muted twitter of birds settling into their nests, and the rustle of wind in the treetops.

The previous week, on the fourth of July, the new nation had celebrated the first anniversary of the signing of the Declaration of Independence with the firing of cannon, jubilant parades, and evening fireworks, to the discomfiture of the city's loyalist residents. A little less than a month earlier, Congress had adopted an official flag for the fledgling United States: a circle of thirteen stars on a blue field against thirteen alternating stripes of crisp white and blood red some had begun to call the Stars and Stripes. While watching this symbol of the new republic furl in the breeze against the sky, Elizabeth had been overcome by a powerful surge of pride and joy.

This evening, however, a restless longing she could not quite define pierced her heart. Returning from his last circuit to Middlebrook, Caleb had brought news that the Rangers were preparing for a move to Chester to complete Arnold's defensive line around the city. In the guise of André Tesseré, she had immediately met again with Adams and a delegation from the Naval Committee to assure them that Carleton would wait upon them at his earliest convenience and to beg that they keep news of his movements in the greatest confidence. She had heard nothing since, and daily it was becoming more difficult to ward off the anxious anticipation that consumed her.

The opening of a door and murmur of voices drew her from her reverie. Squinting through the gathering shadows, she gazed toward the house, thinking her eyes surely deceived her.

Caleb ushered two men outside onto the terrace, one shorter and younger than the other. From what she could make out in the dimming light, both were elegantly clad, though the younger man's sky blue garb overshadowed the amber brown of his companion's. It was the former's familiar figure that immediately caught her attention, and she sprang to her feet in delight.

"Pieter!"

He strode to her across the lawn, followed more slowly by the taller man, who came to a halt discreet yards away. After returning her curtsey with a bow, Vander Groot straightened and took the hands she extended to him.

Answering her flood of questions with a smile, he explained, "I've gotten leave to visit my family, though I've not seen them yet. My friend wanted to take care of other business first. Yes, all is well, and I've found my service quite gratifying. I've just been commissioned as major, and I'll have the chance to fight, which is what I wanted."

Delighted, she said, "Then you've gained Jonathan's trust as I knew you would—and he, yours, I most dearly hope."

"I won't deny I was determined to despise him," he admitted. "We made a very poor beginning, but then a couple of weeks ago something changed between us." At her questioning look, he conceded a faint smile. "Since then he's drawn me into his confidence and made every effort to charm me. And he's succeeded. I'm finding him . . . admirable. He demonstrates a rare talent for leadership and for inspiring the loyalty of those who serve under him."

"I'm so glad you're getting on well. And I pray your confidence in me will one day be restored as well," she added wistfully.

His fingers tightened over hers, and he studied her earnestly. "I understand much now I didn't then, and find it hard to blame you, though I wish you'd confided in me much sooner. I assure you, I'd have been worthy of your trust."

At the gentle reproach in his tone, she hung her head. "Truly, I believed so at the time." Looking up in appeal, she added earnestly, "I had to take many things into account, but I prayed much and sought the Lord's wisdom every day. Please believe how sorry I am that I hurt you and that I never intended it."

For a long moment he stared into the darkness, at length said hoarsely, "I do."

He bent to kiss her hand, then straightened and released her to motion his companion forward. He made no move to introduce the stranger, and Elizabeth noted something in his expression that put her on guard.

Moving with a pronounced halt in his step, the man came to join them. Elizabeth acknowledged him with a curt nod, her heart too filled with happiness to pay him much heed.

By now in the fading light it was difficult to make out his features clearly, but she noted that he wore an elaborately curled white tie wig beneath a feathered cocked hat; an elegantly cut coat, waistcoat, and breeches of the finest satin; spotless ruffled linen; and buckled shoes, all in the latest French style. On a cursory inspection he appeared some years older than Vander Groot, with a more expansive girth, though judging from his height, he must once have cut a fine figure.

Sweeping her a graceful bow, in a cultured French accent he said, "François de Villemont at your service, mademoiselle"

She gave a deep curtsey. *"C'est un plaisir, monsieur."*

Glancing up as both of them straightened, she found herself looking directly into his smoky blue-grey eyes. The light in them and the finely modeled planes of his face caused her breath to catch and her jaw to drop.

"Jonathan." The word came out in a husky whisper.

Closing his eyes for a moment as though overcome by emotion, he clasped her hands tightly. *"Toujours vous ne me laissez sans souffle,"* he murmured, recapturing her gaze. *"Chaque fois que je vous vois, je suis étonné tout recommencer."* Always you leave me breathless. Each time I see you, I am amazed all over again.

Vander Groot cleared his throat. "If you'll excuse me, I'll wait inside."

Elizabeth hardly heard him, was only vaguely aware that, turning abruptly, the doctor strode to the terrace door and let himself into the house. The moment he disappeared from sight, Carleton cupped her face in his hands and buried his fingers in her hair.

She tip-toed to slip her arms around his neck and eagerly gave herself up to his kisses, the strength going out of her as his lips found hers. Pressing into his embrace, she gave way to the passion that kindled in her veins, heating her to the core of her being.

It was some moments before she could draw back to catch her breath, trembling. "When—?"

"Yesterday," he said with a smile that stole her breath all over again. "I wanted to surprise you. We're camped a short distance beyond Chester, and I came as soon as I could get away."

Stepping out of his arms, she motioned to him to turn around while she considered him with admiration. "How elegant you look in civilian dress—though you've gained weight," she teased, patting his generous waistline.

"Army food. They feed us so well." His eyes danced with laughter.

She pressed her fingers to her lips to suppress a giggle. "I'd never have recognized you were it not for your eyes."

"A high compliment coming from the mistress of disguise." He drew a wry face. "I'm pleased to see I've accomplished my goal of saving my scalp for a little while longer."

She bit her lip. "I know it's vain to protest the risks you take—and I have to admit I'm overjoyed that you've come. I only wish you'd never have to leave again."

He took a deep breath and released it. "I'm grateful for whatever time we're given," he said gruffly.

"How does Blue Sky? And Charles? And Red Fox and Spotted Pony and their wives?"

He smiled at the barrage of questions. "Blue Sky is blooming, and Charles is a most devoted father-to-be. The others are all well, though they miss their homes and kindred mightily, as do I. How I wish we could go back there and leave all this behind!"

Even in the darkness she could see his breast rise and fall in a deep sigh and the sadness that passed over his features. She felt an equal pang and laid her head on his shoulder while he engulfed her again in his embrace.

"I was not made to sit idly by the fireside, I'm afraid," she admitted with resignation. "Could you do nothing as long as it was in your power to make a difference?"

He shook his head and smiled deep into her eyes. "You and I are too much alike." Enfolding her hand in his, he said, "Let's go inside and join the others. Caleb was going to let Tess know we're here."

Eagerly Elizabeth led him into the house, where they found her aunt in the parlor, visiting with Vander Groot. At Carleton's appearance, she sprang up and came to embrace him, first exclaiming over his disguise, then protesting the danger he placed himself in.

"Philadelphia is overrun by loyalists and spies," she remonstrated. "You can't be too careful."

"That's why I came in disguise, though I'd have had to come in any case to meet with the Naval Committee." Carleton cast aside cocked hat and wig in relief. "A plague on these instruments of torture," he added with a laugh, rumpling his hair.

"It's startling what a difference one can make by changing one's hair and dress and adding a limp, not to mention a few pounds," Vander Groot observed with a smirk.

Carleton struck a pose. "The deuce, sir, I must protest," he said with a languid drawl that left them all engulfed in mirth. "I think my expanded . . . ah . . . profile lends a certain imposing aspect to my figure. Think you not?"

It was by now full dark, and anxious to see his family, Vander Groot soon took his leave. They found seats, with Carleton joining Elizabeth on the sofa.

"How soon can you arrange a meeting with the committee?"

"Within a couple of days, I'm sure," Elizabeth answered. "They're most eager to meet you. Will you stay the night or must you go back to camp?"

Andrews and Jeffreys had everything under control, he explained, and he planned to stay overnight. Early on the morrow, however, he would slip away to join his guard outside the town, and then ride in openly with them to take rooms at Bradford's London Coffee House until he concluded his business with Congress.

Disappointed that he could not be persuaded to stay longer with them, she was forced to concede that the decision was a prudent one.

She took comfort that her own room at Bradford's would provide opportunities for them to meet while he stayed in the city even though she would have to maintain her pose as a man.

After Caleb served wine and withdrew with instructions to have Sarah prepare a chamber for Carleton, Tess raised her glass in his direction. "So, not content with being merely a war chief and a commander of cavalry, you're taking on privateering as well."

Carleton grimaced. "Not personally, I assure you. Although I do have a little experience, I'm an indifferent sailor. Thankfully my merchant fleet includes a number of excellent French and Spanish captains, who, I have every confidence, are not only motivated but can also be counted on to acquit themselves as well as any officer in the British navy."

Elizabeth studied him over the rim of her wineglass with a faint smile. "Why is it that I doubt your disclaimers? Every time a crisis arises, you manage to meet the challenge in your usual inimitable fashion."

"You much overstate the case, my dear," Carleton protested. "As I keep telling you, I'm a man of simple means and abilities."

"You'd like everyone to think you unexceptional, Jon," Tess interjected, smiling, "but your strategy to deflect attention isn't working. Be warned that we, at least, have learned that modesty is merely one defensive weapon in your very formidable arsenal."

"Judging from the talk I heard at Congress, your reputation has spread much farther than you've any idea of," Elizabeth noted soberly, "and perhaps farther than is entirely safe."

Frowning, Carleton shrugged off their comments. "Since my uncle is well connected at court, I thought I might as well make good use of the opportunities that affords me," he explained. "France has opened her ports to our ships, but the government is still dragging its feet over signing a treaty with us. The advantage I hold is that when Sir Harry first established his import business years ago, le comte negotiated the right for him to trade freely and to maintain offices and warehouses in France even in time of war. That right was transferred to me on Sir Harry's death. My ships come and go as I please, regardless of the cargo they carry."

"What about the rest of your merchant fleet?" Tess asked. "I assume you're not converting every ship to privateers."

"Certainly not!" Carleton exclaimed. "War is ruinously expensive at best and this one particularly so. It's unlikely it'll soon be over, and if I'm not to be bankrupt, I need an income—especially to support a wife and, hopefully, children in time," he added with a warm glance at Elizabeth. "All my ships are already well armed and manned by very capable crews, with marines aboard to guard against attack, so those that aren't converted should be able to continue plying their trade without hindrance by the British."

"How many of your ships are you devoting to privateering, if I may ask?" Tess prodded. "Elizabeth has most annoyingly refused to reveal any details."

"I thought it better to heed your warning against sharing information with those who don't need to know," Elizabeth teased.

"In this case, I think we can relax our caution." He gave her an affectionate look before turning back to Tess. "There are a dozen in all, and they'll have considerable firepower among them. Fully equipped, *Destiny* alone is equal to any British first rater, and they have no warships that can match her for speed and maneuverability. I received notice before we left Middlebrook that she and three others are already on their way back to Salem, equipped to meet any British ship of the line they might encounter. The last should be ready to sail by the end of August."

"With such a fleet at your command, Jonathan, why not petition Congress to make it part of the Continental Navy?"

Carleton regarded Elizabeth with a pained expression. "My dear, I've no ambition or expertise to become an admiral, and I'd settle for no lesser rank. Besides, a privateer enjoys considerably wider latitude to act and is subject to much less oversight."

"Aha!" Tess cried. "The truth will out. Washington only thinks he has you under his thumb."

Making an airily dismissive gesture, Carleton chuckled. Just then Caleb entered to announce dinner. And as they adjourned to the dining room, Elizabeth's heart soared at the prospect of having him with her for the next few days.

OUTSIDE THE COMMITTEE of Assembly Chamber, members of the Naval Committee clustered around Carleton, some reaching to clasp his hand, others pressing questions or offering their opinions. Following as they descended the stairs, Elizabeth smiled with satisfaction. The meeting had gone even better than she had hoped, and the requested letters of marque nestled safely in her pocket. Even Adams, whom Carleton had won over with an astute quote from Thucydides, had been suitably impressed.

She couldn't help admiring the graceful, dashing figure Carleton cut. His blond hair was smoothly combed and tied back with black ribbon. Clad in a perfectly tailored dun colored short uniform coat with forest green facings, buckskin breeches that hugged his muscular thighs like a second skin, and polished knee-length boots, and holding his crested leather helmet under one arm, he towered over most of the delegates.

From the moment he entered the State House, he had charmed everyone he met with unstudied ease, as much in his element, she thought, as he was as a war chief among the Shawnee. Expecting a savage warrior, rustic backwoodsman, or they knew not what, the delegates had been taken off guard to encounter a cultured, articulate gentleman-officer educated in the classics and equally conversant with the hard issues of government and war they daily wrestled with.

As though sensing her scrutiny, Carleton threw a wry glance at her and winked before returning his attention to fellow Virginian Richard Henry Lee, with whom he had immediately established a warm rapport. Flooded by fierce pride, she struggled to maintain the haughty expression suitable to her role as Le Comte de Caledonne's agent.

To Lee's urging that he sit in on the general session of Congress about to begin, Carleton hesitated. "Unfortunately, I must get back to camp as quickly as possible. I received a message from General Arnold early this morning. His Excellency has ordered him and General Lincoln to Albany to support Schuyler's forces. That leaves my Rangers to man the defenses here until the main corps arrives."

Standing in front of him, hands on his waist, posture so erect he appeared about to tip backward, Adams broke in querulously, "You've my admiration, general. I've nothing so grand in my composition, I'm afraid. The pride and pomp of war have no charms for me. Laurel wreaths belong to men of your quality—" he nodded toward his fellow delegates, "while we labor away in obscurity in these halls. I doubt future generations will remember our contributions, such as they are."

Carleton accorded him a graceful half bow. "You're far too modest, Mr. Adams," he said with quiet sincerity. "Your reputation and accomplishments are widely known, as are those of your fellow delegates. Your contributions in guiding our country's course are immeasurable. I assure you, the world takes note of them and they'll not be forgotten."

Adams inclined his head, his expression reflecting surprised gratification. "You do us honor, sir."

GIVING IN TO LEE'S PERSISTENCE, Carleton finally agreed to delay his departure a little longer. With Elizabeth, he accompanied the Virginian to his table in the Assembly Room. Although it was only eleven o'clock, the heat was already stifling as the windows were tightly closed and shuttered to keep the delegates' deliberations private. All around the room the members were soon vigorously plying fans.

It took considerable effort for Carleton to pretend no more interest in Elizabeth than her role warranted. Distracted by thoughts of how charming she looked in her elegant clothing and fashionably styled wig, he had difficulty keeping his eyes off her.

Had he not memorized every detail of her face and form, he would have been hard put to identify her. She spoke in a lower voice and lengthened her stride, making her movements less constrained than a women's. None of the delegates demonstrated the least suspicion that she was other than a highly placed young Frenchman—a somewhat effeminate one to American eyes, to be sure, but from Carleton's acquaintance with French courtiers, he judged that only enhanced the authenticity of her appearance and manner.

He wrenched his gaze to Hancock, who struck the gavel to open the session. Sixty-one-year-old New York delegate Philip Livingston rose to verify the spreading rumor that, with Burgoyne preparing to lay siege to Fort Ticonderoga, General St. Clair had deemed it prudent to withdraw his outmatched force from the post with hardly a shot fired.

Arnold had included the report in the confidential message Carleton's guard delivered that morning, and he had warned Elizabeth of it while they rode to the State House. Neither of them was fully prepared, however, for the onslaught of fury the stunned delegates directed at Schuyler and St. Clair for what they deemed gross incompetence, if not outright treachery. The New England members were the most vocal, with John and Samuel Adams in the forefront of demands to immediately remove Schuyler from command, cashier St. Clair, and subject both to court-martial.

Livid, Carleton exchanged glances with Elizabeth, swearing under his breath. His satisfaction at the morning's success entirely evaporated, and it was all he could do to contain his temper and keep an outburst in check.

After listening for some time in tight-lipped silence, Lee turned to him. "What's your opinion of St. Clair's actions, general?" he said in an undertone.

"Forgive me, Mr. Lee, but what they're saying is utter nonsense. They haven't the faintest idea of what St. Clair faced."

Giving him a calculating look, Lee rose and asked for the floor. Acknowledged, he said, "I believe General Carleton is the most qualified man in the room to speak to the issue. I yield the floor to him."

"The chair recognizes General Carleton." Hancock noted.

For a moment taken aback, Carleton hesitated, then rose amid eager murmurs. He looked around at the expectant faces upturned to him, carefully considering the most politic assessment of the fort's loss . . . and discarded it.

"I understand your consternation, gentlemen," he said with blunt vehemence, "but I do not share it. The loss of any particular place, even one as renowned as Ticonderoga, will have little negative effect on the campaign. It may, in fact, have a positive one by tying up men and provisions to hold it that the enemy can't afford to spare.

"The army, on the other hand, is indispensible to the defense of our country. Without an armed force we, our homes, and our families lie at the enemy's mercy. As long as it exists, the enemy has to reckon with it—"

"If you ask me," New Hampshire's Matthew Thornton broke in, "it's monstrous cowardice to fly cravenly from such a formidable citadel when it might so easily have been held."

Carleton turned to the rest of the assembly, fighting exasperation. "Sirs, this is equivalent to censuring General Washington for having withdrawn from Long Island last summer, when he saved the army by doing so and made possible the victories at Trenton and Princeton. I assure you, Ticonderoga could not be held against a force as superior as Burgoyne's—"

"Balderdash," Adams growled. "Everyone, including Schuyler himself, assured us that Ticonderoga was impregnable."

Ignoring the covert pressure of Elizabeth's foot against his, Carleton rounded on Adams, eyes narrowing. "Then they were mistaken. Have you ever visited the fort, Mr. Adams?"

His round face flushing, Adams drew himself stiffly up. "Not personally, but—"

"I spent some time there, and the fort is untenable without considerable improvements in its defenses and a much larger garrison than St. Clair had at his disposal. His choice was to lose Ticonderoga, along with his entire force, artillery, and supplies, or to save his men and confront Burgoyne on defensible ground at a more advantageous time and place. He made the right decision, sir. If there was any fault, it was that he waited too long to withdraw and consequently suffered losses during the retreat that might have been spared."

Throwing caution entirely to the wolves, he rasped, "I'd have handed the fort to Burgoyne with my best wishes a month ago. Let *him* waste men and materiel in the attempt to defend it."

An angry hubbub of voices immediately filled the room. "And to think we just issued such a man as this letters of marque!" one of the committee members cried.

As long as he had stirred up controversy, Carleton decided, he might as well stir it to a boil. He swept his opponent a deep bow.

"You did, sir, and if my ships do not escort a dozen fat prizes into port within a month of sailing, I'll happily return them."

This time he felt a decided tug on his coat. Conceding that he was making no headway against the inevitable, he offered his kindest respects to the delegates, thanked them for hearing him out, and sat down, studiously avoiding Elizabeth's exasperated gaze—and Lee's slyly approving one.

The acrimonious discussion continued, and it quickly became clear that his arguments had gained some adherents, although, in the end, not enough. The majority voted to relieve St. Clair of his command, replace Schuyler with General Gates, and call for an investigation of both officers' actions.

As the delegates broke for lunch, Carleton reflected bitterly that Washington's rival, who had never held command in a major battle, would now command the entire Northern Army against a formidable foe. Outside, before mounting to ride back to camp with his guard, he fumed, "When will these deuced politicians stop trying to make military decisions for which they're supremely unqualified?"

"I'm so proud of you for charming everyone," Elizabeth replied placatingly, "and for not losing your temper when sorely provoked."

He regarded her with suspicion. Her eyes were alive with mirth and her mouth twitched. He couldn't repress a rueful laugh.

"You have the letters?"

"I do." She pulled the papers out of her pocket and handed them over.

"I suppose it's no matter, then. We achieved our purpose." He slipped the papers into his pocket and began to mount, then stopped and turned back. "I can't help feeling for Schuyler and St. Clair. They're good man and experienced officers whose talents we can't afford to waste. But St. Clair's career is destroyed because he took the most prudent course at Ticonderoga, and Schuyler's because he didn't please the New England delegates. The same could happen to any of us for simply making the best judgment we can under circumstances Congress is ignorant of."

"Washington's also received his share of criticism and condemnation."

"Especially from those vying to replace him." Sighing, he shook his head. "Officers who prove incompetent, negligent, or cowardly ought to be removed, but in too many cases they're promoted because they've made the right connections, while those who lack them but deserve commendation are passed over. Schuyler may be arrogant at times, but he's effectively hindering Burgoyne's advance despite limited resources. I wonder if Gates will do half as well."

He could tell she was biting back a response to his tirade. "You New Englanders are an intractable, opinionated lot," he growled.

She gave him an arch look. "We are."

"Proud of it, too, aren't you?"

"As proud as you Virginians are of your vast superiority."

He chuckled in spite of himself. "We can't help it. It's in our blood." He grimaced. "And I was getting on so famously with your prickly Mr. Adams. Now I've doubtless made an enemy of him. I seem to have an unconquerable penchant, when faced with fire, to throw fuel on it."

She smiled sweetly at him. "Woe betide anyone who runs afoul of the two of us if we're ever in a humor to rave at the same time."

Returning a lazy smile, he drawled softly, "That's why I love you. We're so much alike. I'd kiss you if no one were about."

She threw a sidelong glance at his guards, who waited astride their horses just out of earshot, before sweeping him a deep bow. "And I'd return it in double measure." Straightening, she said regretfully, "Alas, Monsieur, I must leave for France immediately to assure your uncle, le comte, of our success."

"I'll make sure he's aware of it," he returned dryly, "while you, my love, return to your feminine arts."

Mounting, he looked down at her, his gaze lingering deliberately on her lips. "Fly away home, little oriole," he murmured. "You'll come to me at camp as soon as you can?"

"I will, beloved," she promised, her eyes brimming with emotion.

With a last, lingering glance, he reined his horse around, joined his guard, and led them at a trot down the street, not allowing himself to look back, while visions of tender rendezvous to come overflowed his mind.

Chapter Twenty-one

It was early Sunday morning, August 24, overcast after a night of storms that had done little to cool temperatures. Church bells were just beginning to peal when the long line of Continentals approached at a brisk march down Chestnut Street with flags fluttering, on their way to Middle Ferry on the Schuylkill.

Reports that far to the north generals Stark and Lincoln had defeated a sizeable British detachment at Bennington in the newly formed state of Vermont, and that in New York near Oriskany, St. Leger had abandoned Fort Stanwix at General Arnold's approach, had given the patriots cause for celebration. This heartening news had been countered by alarming rumors that Howe's fleet had finally appeared in Chesapeake Bay after vanishing at sea for weeks. Just as he had the previous summer before the Battle of Long Island, the British general held everyone in suspense as to his intentions.

The previous evening Elizabeth and Tess had learned that Washington's army would parade through Philadelphia that morning on their way south to meet the coming threat. An hour earlier they had hurried downtown with the Vander Groots to find a large crowd already gathering along the army's route. Most onlookers wore a festive air, and when the first ranks came into view, marching to the brisk rattle of drums and shrill pipe of fifes, a cheer rose from the crowd. Only a few of the bravest loyalists gathered on the fringes, casting dark looks in the soldiers' direction.

At the army's head rode Washington, resplendent in his dark blue and buff dress uniform, with the awkwardly tall, thin young French major general Carleton had told Elizabeth about, the Marquis de Lafayette, at his side. Flanked by Greene and Knox, they were followed closely by Washington's bodyguard, Captain George Lewis's troop of Continental Light Dragoons in white uniforms faced with blue.

As Elizabeth watched them pass by, her heart swelling with pride, Isobel clutched her arm in a painful grip. "There he is! Oh, does he not look handsome? Pieter! Over here!"

Bouncing on tip-toe, she waved vigorously at her brother, who rode at the head of Carleton's guard, impeccably uniformed and equipped, the blond horsehair crest of his helmet flowing jauntily in the breeze. Vander Groot glanced toward them, then quickly forward again, his mouth twitching as though he suppressed a smile.

Before Elizabeth could agree with her friend that he looked very handsome indeed, Mrs. Vander Groot ordered sternly, "Isobel, such behavior is unseemly!"

"Soldiers on parade are not to attend to the onlookers, Daughter," Mr. Vander Groot pointed out gently. "We won't serve Pieter well by distracting him from his business."

Isobel blushed prettily and directed an embarrassed look up at her fiancé. With an affectionate smile, Lamb bent to assure her that she had not transgressed propriety too severely.

Pretending not to see Tess's warning look, Elizabeth edged closer to the street, eagerly seeking Carleton in the phalanx of Rangers that followed Vander Groot, their green and gold battle flag snapping in the wind. At sight of him, she caught her breath, then bit her lip hard in the effort to maintain proper decorum.

Astride his gleaming bay stallion, he rode with Andrews and Red Fox on one side and a young captain she guessed to be his aide and Spotted Pony on the other. She couldn't help noting how the finely tailored style and cut of the Rangers' new uniform enhanced Carleton's sun-bleached blond hair and emphasized the tanned, lean, muscular length of him.

His gaze briefly crossed hers, but he gave no sign of recognition. Urging his mount forward, he was quickly past.

She clasped her hands, disappointed that the summery azure gown she had chosen with such careful forethought, with its crisp white ribbons and fetchingly tilted, flower-bedecked straw hat, had not drawn at least a raised eyebrow or an approving nod. He so rarely saw her in feminine dress, and although she well knew his apparent indifference was calculated, for an instant she was tempted to stamp her foot in annoyance.

The impulse was quickly squelched by the murmurs that rose from the crowd. She swung around to watch the large band of imposing, brilliantly painted and clad native warriors that had captured the crowd's attention pass by. They were succeeded by the rest of the Rangers, with the dismounted troops bringing up the rear.

A long column of infantry twelve ranks wide followed them, tramping smartly in step to fife and drum, and behind them rumbled the artillery. All the soldiers wore green sprigs in their hats, and the line seemed to stretch on and on.

More than a month had flown by since Carleton had met with Congress. In the intervening weeks he had ridden into the city a handful of times, twice in disguise to secretly visit her and Tess, the other times openly on official business, attended by his guard. Vander Groot's family had insisted on meeting his commander, and Carleton had obligingly called on them—and charmed them exceedingly according to Isobel's breathless report, which drew knowing glances from Elizabeth and her aunt. She and Tess had pleaded another engagement during his visit to forestall any complications as he had become far too recognizable for them to safely be seen together.

Under cover of nightfall and in disguise, Elizabeth made regular, stealthy trips back and forth to the Rangers' camp, which lay on a pleasant, tree-dotted meadow just south of the small town of Chester at the confluence of Chester Creek and the Delaware. Caleb, Pete, or both always accompanied her, and her appearance with the two known and trusted couriers soon became routine and aroused no undue interest.

The opportunity to renew her relationships with Blue Sky and the other Shawnee women had been a delight. To see her adoptive sister great with child and witness the love and devotion she and Andrews shared had given Elizabeth great pleasure.

Sweetest of all were the hours she spent with Carleton alone in his marquee in thoughtful, intimate discussion or laughing repartee laced with sweet kisses and caresses that knit their hearts ever more closely. Although fleeting, the time they shared seemed to her a foretaste of heaven.

In the press of the crowd Pete jostled against her, dispelling her happy reflections. As he muttered an apology, she noted his glum expression.

Following his glance to the troops that marched by, she said sympathetically in an undertone, "I know how much you'd like to be marching with them."

Slanting her a sideways glance, the tall, lean youth shook his head, longing in the set of his features. "Wouldn't mind it for a while, but it's the navy I'm aimin' for. Someday . . . " Breaking off, he shrugged.

Elizabeth glanced around to make sure the noise of the throng masked their conversation. "You know how much I want to keep you with me . . . but it's not fair to you. You've wanted this for so long. Why don't you talk to General Carleton about signing on with his privateers when the campaign ends this fall? They'll undoubtedly be in need of experienced sailors."

His features brightened, and he met her gaze with a cautious one. "I'll still have Caleb," she reminded him around the lump forming in her throat.

Grinning, he gave a short nod. "Next time we ride out to camp," he agreed eagerly.

For almost two hours they watched, until the army's ranks began to dwindle away. When the crowd began to disperse, John Adams with several other delegates to Congress brushed by, and Elizabeth quickly turned away, tipping her head down so the brim of her hat shaded her features.

"I must admit they make an impressive sight," Adams was saying, "though they have not yet quite the air of soldiers one would prefer. They don't step quite in time or hold up their heads entirely erect, nor do they turn out their toes so exactly as they ought. And think you not they all ought to cock their hats the same way?"

As the men strode off, debating the issue, Elizabeth met her aunt's amused glance. "Jon's right about us New Englanders," Tess said with a laugh.

"Just don't tell him so or he'll be impossible to live with," Elizabeth protested.

When Tess turned to follow the Vander Groots, Elizabeth glanced back at the last of the soldiers tramping by. Across the street, a flash of color drew her eye to a rough-looking man in a green uniform with a young woman on his arm. Although they received hostile glares, the soldier strutted along as though daring anyone to stand in his way.

Astonished that a member of the loyalist militia would boldly hazard the predominantly patriot crowd, she looked more closely and, as the crowd around them parted, caught a glimpse of his companion. The girl threw an arch glance across the street, and Elizabeth turned hastily away, her heart suddenly pounding.

It was Chastity, the young Quaker servant from the inn at Newtown. That she was Quaker no longer was evident both from her garish gown and the shameless boldness of her manner. Although she had changed exceedingly in the months since Elizabeth and Tess had stayed at the inn, there was no mistaking her identity.

Hemmed in by the crowd, Elizabeth glanced around anxiously for her aunt, finally glimpsed the bobbing feathers atop Tess's hat. Hurriedly Elizabeth pushed her way through the press to catch up with her and the Vander Groots, praying the girl had not seen her—or at least had not recognized her.

What's she doing in Philadelphia? Elizabeth wondered, appalled. *How greatly she has changed! And the soldier she's with—from the King's American Regiment, judging by his uniform.*

Could Chastity have taken up with this man while still at Newtown? Arguing against it was that Lydia was a stern taskmaster who allowed no slacking in her servant girl's attention to her duties. And as her dress and manner had proclaimed her a Quaker at the time, it seemed unlikely.

But now? How had she met him, and where? How closely were they involved, and what might she have confided to him?

Elizabeth's mind whirled with questions—and the resolution to make every effort to avoid a closer encounter with the girl.

Since the hour for worship services had passed, they returned with the Vander Groots to their town house. Over a late breakfast their discussion revolved around what would likely happen in the coming days or weeks.

One thing was certain: An all-out battle for Philadelphia loomed. Although Congress and many of the city's patriots expressed firm conviction that Washington's army would be the victors, the Vander Groots agreed with Elizabeth and Tess that the outcome, and thus the safety of the city's residents, remained very much in doubt.

Already many of their neighbors were hastily packing to remove from the city. Daily, increasing numbers fled from the coming storm, taking everything they could pack in wagons, carriages, or any available conveyance, strapped to horses or carried in arms. As it had the previous December, panic flowed outward like a tidal wave.

At length Lamb forcefully recommended his country estate near Lancaster as a sanctuary until the city's safety was assured. The Vander Groots accepted his offer with relief, and they all pleaded with Elizabeth and Tess to join them.

When the two women pointed out that they would soon have to return to New York to close up Montcoeur before traveling to Boston to meet Elizabeth's family on their arrival from London, the others argued they could just as easily leave from Lancaster. Both Tess and Elizabeth remained firm, however, that they would stay in Philadelphia until they judged it too dangerous to remain. At last the Vander Groots and Lamb returned home to finalize their own plans.

"The army's need for intelligence will be greater now than ever before, and I mean to stay as long as possible," Elizabeth told her aunt when they had gone.

Reluctantly Tess agreed. "If the last routes of exit from the city are in danger of being cut off, we must get away immediately," she cautioned. "You know Jonathan won't want us to jeopardize our safety in any event."

Knowing she was right, Elizabeth suggested, "Then let's pack as much as possible now so we're ready in case we're forced to leave at a moment's notice."

With an approving nod, Tess rose from the table and hurried away to confer with the servants, while Elizabeth went upstairs to begin packing, vainly attempting to ward off the memory of Chastity hanging boldly on a loyalist soldier's arm.

Chapter Twenty-two

HIS UNIFORM SOAKED THROUGH, Carleton squinted into the impenetrable shadows beyond the dilapidated porch where he squatted. He was grateful the heavy rain had cooled the wilting August heat, but repeated growls of thunder and the downpour's incessant drubbing made it impossible either to hear any unusual sounds or to make out details more than a foot away, and he remained tensely alert.

The previous day, Tuesday, August 26, at the head of their guards and a small contingent of warriors, he and Andrews had ridden out of the army's camp near Wilmington with Washington, his Life Guard and aides, Greene, and the Marquis de Lafayette. Keeping a careful eye out for enemy patrols, they had spent hours in the saddle riding up hill and down dale, through field and forest, seeking information from local residents about the British force that had landed at the head of the Elk River on Monday.

At Washington's insistence, they had ventured within two miles of the British force encamped outside the picturesque village of Head of Elk before turning back at nightfall. They had not gone far when heavy rains forced them to seek shelter uncomfortably close to the enemy lines in a farm house whose owners, they soon discovered, were Tories.

While Carleton pondered their situation, Andrews and Red Fox materialized out of the early morning blackness almost before he sensed their presence and knelt at his side, as drenched as he. "I'll feel a lot more easy when we quit this place," Andrews grumbled, keeping his voice low.

"So far no one has come along, and our hosts, unwilling as they may be, have behaved themselves," Carleton pointed out.

"That may be due to the fact that we're holding them under close guard," Andrews returned dryly. At Carleton's chuckle, he frowned. "All that's needed is for an enemy patrol to blunder into the vicinity. We'd have a hard time hiding such a large party."

Carleton made a dismissive gesture. "I doubt we've anything to worry about on that score. The weeks Howe's men spent aboard ship in this heat and humidity have sapped them, and they've also lost a large number of horses. They'll need to rest and commandeer more mounts and draft animals before they can advance. Besides, who'd be out on a night like this?"

"We are."

"We're soldiers."

"So are the British, in case you hadn't noticed!" Andrews hissed. "We're half an hour's ride from Howe's lines—at least we were the last time we reconnoitered. Fatigued or not, they could still steal a march on us. Daybreak's no more than half an hour away, and they may be on the move by the time we ride out."

"Come now, Charles, that just adds to the excitement of the moment. Where's your sense of adventure?"

Andrews regarded Carleton through narrowed eyes. "I've as keen a sense of adventure as you, but you see things differently when you've an infant on the way." At Carleton's sympathetic look, he added, "The General could have made better use of the weeks he spent marching and countermarching, trying to figure out what Howe meant to do—if you want my opinion."

Red Fox grunted. "Our Father Washington must learn to take advantage of the enemy's indecision and attack first."

"Action is on the way now," Carleton countered, adding, "It's a good thing we took the trouble of scouting the area before the army got here."

Andrews snorted. "Now if the General and the rest of his party would only listen to us—"

"You know His Excellency doesn't like to take anyone else's word for things, Charles." Abruptly Carleton stopped and raised his hand for silence.

While they were speaking, the rain had tapered off, and the black forms of the trees and hedgerows were gradually emerging through the first, misty light of the coming dawn. Carleton rose, his companions following his example. For tense minutes they watched and listened.

At last Carleton relaxed. "Must have been my imagination. Let's reconnoiter the area before Washington decides to move out. Where's Jeffreys?"

Andrews frowned. "I haven't seen him for a couple of hours. I assumed you sent him to rouse the men."

"I didn't, but he's always anticipating my orders, and that's undoubtedly what he's about. He's a good man."

"He is," Andrews agreed.

Carleton noted that Red Fox gave him a sharp look, but before the warrior could speak, Jeffreys strode around the corner of the decaying farmhouse. Coming to a halt at the base of the broken steps, he saluted.

"Good morning, sir. The men have had breakfast and are ready to move out any time. I assumed you'd want to scout the area before the General heads back to camp."

Carleton threw Andrews a smug look before returning his gaze to his aide. "Thank you, captain. I do indeed. Form the men up. We'll probe the enemy's lines to determine whether they're getting ready to march." He turned to Red Fox. "Bring your men too, just in case we run into trouble."

"I doubt they'll be needed," Jeffreys said. "I took a turn around the farm, and everything's quiet."

Carleton raised an eyebrow. "You took a turn around the entire farm . . . in a downpour?"

Jeffreys grinned and indicated his drenched uniform and muddy boots with a wave of his hand. "There was no sign of anything out of order, sir. The more men we bring, the more likely we'll be spotted."

"Let me be the judge of that."

"Very good, sir," Jeffreys returned amiably, saluting. "It never hurts to have reinforcements on hand."

THE LAND THEY RODE THROUGH was serene and fertile with few hills, divided by picturesque hedgerows, woods, and tree-fringed streams. It promised to be an oppressively hot, humid, airless day equal to the previous ones, and their wet clothing dried slowly, keeping them cool for at least a little while.

The detachment had not ridden far, however, before Carleton could feel the sweat running down his face and chest. By the time the leading edge of the sun showed above the horizon, all of them were drenched with sweat. Red Fox alone appeared relatively comfortable in breechcloth, leggings, and moccasins, and Carleton wished mightily he had donned similar garb.

Near Gray's Hill, still a little distance from the outer British lines, Red Fox first noted the faint chop of axes cutting into wood. Within seconds they could all make out hoarse shouts and the crash of falling trees.

For some minutes, screened by the trees that lined the stream's banks, Carleton cautiously led the detachment along a tributary of the

Little Elk River whose course meandered toward the sound. Judging from the strengthening noise ahead of them that the enemy was not far off, he left Andrews with the Rangers concealed in a dense grove and posted Red Fox's warriors a quarter mile farther along.

Leading their horses, Carleton, Red Fox, and Jeffreys continued to a bend in the stream. There its course veered sharply to reveal no more than three quarters of a mile ahead of them a large body of scarlet-clad soldiers.

Motioning his companions to a halt, Carleton focused his spyglass on the enemy. "British engineers," he said quietly after a moment. "They appear to be busily engaged in repairing a bridge. There's a strong detachment of cavalry . . . and several officers on the far side, though I can't make out who they are."

He watched a while longer, then turned to the others. "It looks as if they're almost finished. Their camp isn't far down the road, and I'd like to make certain the main column isn't getting ready to move out. We don't want to run into them when we escort His Excellency back to Wilmington."

Jeffreys pointed out Gray's Hill off to their right. "We'd have a perfect view of the camp from that height. There's only a short distance to cross in the open to get to those woods below it. If we're careful, we shouldn't attract notice."

Frowning, Carleton assessed the distance to the woods. "Good. Tell Andrews to bring his detachment up this far on the double. And bring your warriors too, Red Fox. If we run into any trouble, we can signal them from the top of the hill." He swung into the saddle. "I'm going forward, so don't delay. Both of you meet me at the woods as quickly as you can."

Saluting, Jeffreys eased back through the trees and out of sight around the stream's bend. Red Fox, however, lingered.

"Maybe you better go on foot."

"I can ride across that open ground more quickly. See, the officers and cavalry are off beyond those trees now, and the engineers are fully occupied shoring up the bridge." Carleton pulled off his helmet and secured it on the saddle's pommel in front of him. "From this distance, if anyone spots me, they'll assume I'm just a local farmer on my way to market," he added with a grin.

Red Fox scowled, but giving Carleton a curt nod, he melted into the underbrush. Keeping a close eye on the distant party of engineers, Carleton eased Devil out of the trees and onto the narrow plain at a deliberate walk.

NO SOONER HAD HE REACHED THE WOODS at the base of the hill than an enemy detachment materialized out of the underbrush—spirits, surely, rather than men of flesh and blood, so suddenly did they surround him. His first, shocked comprehension was that he had ridden into a trap.

Squealing, Devil reared, hooves flailing, sending Carleton's helmet tumbling free. Cursing, he tore his sabre from the scabbard.

Two soldiers on his right dodged the razor-sharp edge to drag down his arm, while another on his left ripped the reins out of his hand. Unbalanced, swearing violently, he caught Devil's mane with his free hand, while gripping the animal's sides with his legs to keep from falling, somehow managed to jerk his arm free and bring his sabre down in a brutal blow that cut through the helmets of the men who bore upon him and drew blood. They fell away, but by now five more had come up on his left, ducking past his mount's bared teeth and flailing hooves.

In desperate resolve, Carleton warded off his attackers on the right with his sabre while grasping for the saddle holster on his left. Before he could wrench the pistol free, the soldier at his stirrup dashed it from his numbed fingers with a savage blow that sent it spinning into the air.

Swarming to the front, a body of soldiers wrestled Devil's head down, while those on either side manhandled Carleton out of the saddle by main force. He struck the ground with a stunning impact that knocked the breath out of him, and his hair, pulled loose of its constraining ribbon, fell across his face, almost blinding him. Sabre lost, he fought to roll free, gasping to drag air into his lungs under the weight of the men who crushed him to earth beneath their bodies, shouting while they delivered vicious blows to his face and gut.

"We got 'im! Kill 'im—kill the bastard!"

"Take 'is scalp!"

"No—the Gen'l wants the privilege!"

"Whatever ye do, don't let 'im go!"

He was pinned at all points, ground into the dirt by hands and knees and elbows, hardly able to move no matter how furiously he wrenched against his captors' hold. Shards of memory fled through his brain: the relentless beatings administered by the British when he'd been arrested for treason, the months of brutal abuse by the Seneca, their vicious reprisals when he'd sought to flee—and an incoherent plea: *Charles . . . Red Fox . . . my God, where are you?*

Then all devolved on one telling conclusion: *Jeffreys.*

Dragged to his feet, he groaned as his captors twisted his arms viciously behind him, saw that one held ropes and, teeth clenched, writhed to break their hold, tried to kick them away. Every effort at resistance met with savage blows that doubled him over.

They'll kill me before they capture me.

His boast to Washington mocked him now. The sharp, metallic taste of blood filled his mouth, and ignoring the pain he fought them with every ounce of his considerable strength. It took ten of them to wrestle him to his knees and hold him while they began to bind his hands.

He had all but given himself up for lost when the sudden, chilling ululation of the Shawnee war cry raised the hairs on the back of his neck. On the sweating, contorted faces bending over him, feral, gloating looks of triumph gave way by swift degrees to shock, dismay, then terror.

Rough hands shoved him to the ground as his captors sprang up and away to meet the attack that burst upon them with the force of a thunderclap. Ignoring the multiple protests of wrenched joints, throbbing bruises, and stinging scrapes, Carleton rolled over and sprang to his feet, swept his tangled hair back with one hand while hastily retrieving his weapons and helmet.

Devil muscled his way through the melee to his side, and he clawed into the saddle. Ripping loose each pistol from its holster in turn, he fired point blank at the soldiers who sprang for him and dropped them to the ground.

By now Red Fox had reached his side, his eyes alight with a fierce fire, while behind him Andrews's shouted commands sounded over the thunder of hooves. As his detachment swept into the fray, Carleton joined them at a gallop, and they scattered the enemy, driving them pell-mell back toward the British light cavalry that now ate up the ground between them, closing at a rush to within a quarter of a mile. Wasting no time, Carleton sent the warriors off with several terrified prisoners in their charge and orders to ride hard for the farmhouse, alert the General's party, and escort them back to the Wilmington camp at all speed.

Ignoring Andrews's shout, he wheeled his mount around in a swirl of dust to face the swiftly oncoming detachment. Deliberately he waited until he recognized the officers at their head: Cornwallis, and with him Howe. A mad recklessness exploded in his breast then, and he began to laugh. Jerking his sabre from its sheath, he swung it over his head, at the same instant drew on the reins to bring Devil up into a rear.

"Catch me if you can!" he taunted.

The instant the stallion's hooves touched the ground, Carleton thrust his sabre into its sheath, reined Devil around, and laid on the spurs, shouting to the rest of the detachment to follow. Calculating that their pursuers' mounts were in poor condition after long weeks confined in the hold of transport ships, he slanted well off to the northwest at furious speed, leading the enemy on a chase that took them far from Washington's temporary quarters.

By the time they splashed into a densely wooded swampland they had scouted the previous day, the British lagged far behind. For some time, as silent as ghosts, they wove a stealthy, circuitous route through the dense, marshy growth.

When they reached the far edge of the swamp, Howe's detachment was nowhere in sight. But as Carleton began to urge Devil toward the road, Andrews blocked his path, face flushed, teeth gritted.

"You might as well have waved a red flag in front of a bull," he accused in a low voice. "Howe will spare nothing to capture you now."

Carleton gave a harsh laugh. "Let him try his worst."

"Oh, he will," Andrews countered soberly. "What did you think you were about, Jon? Jeffreys told us your orders were for us to pull a half mile farther back and wait for your return. I couldn't fathom why you'd want us to fall back when we were in no danger of discovery where we were, and when I questioned him, he couldn't give me a coherent answer."

"That's because he lied." Briefly Carleton related the orders he had given his aide.

Andrews stared back the way they had come, the muscles in his jaw tensing. "He said nothing about your advancing. Thank God I noticed that Red Fox and his warriors had disappeared, and Jeffreys had no explanation for that either. By then I knew something was seriously amiss and thought I'd better talk to you directly."

"Where's Jeffreys now?"

"In the rear under guard."

Carleton let out his breath. "Thank you."

Andrews met Carleton's gaze with a hard one. "You took a great risk going forward alone. At the very least, you should have waited until our warriors reached you."

Gingerly fingering a throbbing bruise on his jaw, then the bloody corner of his mouth, Carleton grimaced. "I should have. I'll not make that mistake again."

Andrews expression softened. "They made a right mess of you. You'll need some cleaning up before you report to the General."

"Let's head back to camp and have a talk with Jeffreys. I'm devoured with curiosity to hear the story he comes up with. Then Vander Groot can patch me up, and I'll go report to Washington. He'll learn what happened one way or the other, and I'd better be the one to tell him first."

"THERE MUST BE SOME MISTAKE," Jeffreys protested. Sweating in the afternoon's scorching heat, he twisted on the camp chair to relieve the pressure on the ropes that bound his hands behind him.

Carleton's jaw hardened. "The mistake was yours, captain. You deliberately disobeyed my orders."

"I told the colonel to hold his men in reserve, as you said."

"That's not what Colonel Andrews told me. What are you playing at? You were to advise the colonel to immediately bring his detachment forward."

Jeffreys appeared entirely crestfallen. "Obviously I misunderstood—"

"Misunderstood?" Carleton snapped, livid. "I couldn't have been more clear. As a result of your 'mistake' I was very nearly captured by an enemy detachment lying in ambush in the very place you urged me to go."

"My apologies, sir. I'm horrified at what happened. I assure you, I had no knowledge of—"

"Oh, I very much doubt that."

Jeffreys stiffened at Carleton's caustic tone. "Why, sir. . . you can't imagine I—"

"Do you think me stupid? They were lying in wait for *me*. No one else. How could they have known where to find me if you'd not alerted them during your little stroll around the farm this morning?"

"That's—how could I have known exactly where we'd go?"

For a long, tense moment, Carleton stared him down. "You knew very well we'd scout the enemy lines again before withdrawing from the area, so there was nowhere else to go," he said, his voice dangerously soft. "You yourself pointed out that hill to me as a fine place to get a view of Howe's camp."

Just then Andrews ducked into Carleton's marquee. Sketching a salute, he said, "Pardon the interruption, general, but it's urgent I speak to you in private."

His face stony, Carleton led the way outside.

"Jeffreys is not who he claims to be," Andrews told him, suppressed anger in his tone. "One of our prisoners is the captain of the detachment that ambushed you. Red Fox took it upon himself to question him—and the man was most cooperative once he learned what our warriors would do if he didn't spill his guts. Turns out Jeffreys is really Lesley Harding, a lieutenant in the King's American Regiment."

Carleton swore. "Loyalist militia. I should have known."

"That traitor's been in constant communication with Cornwallis, and through him Howe. His assignment was to get close to you and deliver you into their hands. But there's more. The captain said that as soon as you were secured, Harding was going to lead them to the farmhouse to capture Washington."

Regarding Andrews with a hard look, Carleton gave a short laugh. "Ironic, isn't it, how your sins have a way of coming back to haunt you."

Taken aback, Andrews protested, "Your spying, you mean? This is different!"

"No it isn't. That's what I hated from the beginning. Harding was simply following orders as I was when I betrayed General Gage."

"He certainly played his part with aplomb," Andrews noted, his tone acid.

"So, I've been told, did I."

"He obviously relished it, whereas you despised that role," Andrews objected hotly.

"What difference does that make in the end?" Carleton cut him off. "The results are the same. How easily we reduce the line between good and evil until it's only a matter of interpretation."

Andrews's eyes narrowed. "The law's clear. A soldier caught out of uniform behind enemy lines in time of war is to be hanged. You would have been, if not for Oriole."

Arms crossed, Carleton threw back his head and for long moments stared into the air. At last he turned abruptly and strode back into the marquee, Andrews on his heels. His entire body felt stiff and sore, but that was nothing to the bitterness of his soul as he bent over Harding.

"I trust you're aware of the penalty a soldier faces when captured behind enemy lines . . . . Lieutenant Harding," he said, his tone mocking.

The color drained out of the younger officer's face, but he did not drop his gaze from Carleton's steely one. "Perhaps now you know how it feels to be betrayed by one close to you, one you trusted completely," he flung back.

"Touché." Carleton smiled coldly. "But I never trusted you completely. I trust *no one* completely. And alas, you chose the losing side in this contest."

"That's yet to be determined," Harding countered, his look and tone defiant.

"England cannot afford to sustain this war forever, and we'll never give up." Carleton shrugged. "Be that as it may, it's your fate that concerns me at the moment."

Harding drew in a shallow breath. "You were spared the noose."

"I was rescued. By God, I'll make certain you'll not be."

"You were in my shoes and you know what it's like," Harding returned, his mouth tightening. "I'd think you'd have no stomach to hang another man for doing his duty."

Straightening, Carleton considered this for a moment. "You're right. I don't. Neither did you leave me a choice. There's a high price on my head, as I'm sure you well know. If I don't make an example of you, others will be emboldened to seek the prize, and I've no intention of exposing myself to betrayal again—or of enabling General Howe to make a gift of my scalp to that tyrant who sits on England's throne."

For tense moments, the two men stared at each other. Finally Harding swallowed and slumped back in the chair.

"Then you'll hang me?"

"That's the penalty for spying. Perhaps you'd rather I turned you over to the tender ministrations of my warriors. Your choice."

As he spoke, Harding blanched.

"I thought not." Carleton motioned to Andrews to take the prisoner away.

"If it's any consolation," he said as Andrews jerked Harding to his feet, "I did come very near to trusting you with information that would have caused immeasurable harm and relieved me of the regret I feel in imposing this sentence. As it is, I'm truly sorry for its necessity, and I commend you to God."

⊛ ⊛ ⊛

"I apologize for the delay in reporting, but I first wanted to make sure my suspicions were warranted." When Washington made no response, Carleton met his commander's probing gaze with a rueful one. "Sir, I believed my warriors and guard were right behind me, but I should have waited for them to come up before advancing. I assure you I'll not make that mistake again."

"We all make mistakes. The wise man learns from them . . . if he survives." Washington mopped his brow with a handkerchief and squinted through the late afternoon sunshine at the gleaming white tents sprawled across the gentle hills and hollows of the Wilmington camp. "Thankfully you did. Were it not for your quick thinking and action, we would all be in Howe's clutches now, and I commend you for preventing that."

Carleton kept his expression neutral, judging it prudent to say nothing of Howe and Cornwallis's approaching close enough to identify him—and that he'd flung a challenge at them.

"The man who betrayed you, this Harding fellow—"

A sick feeling twisted in Carleton's gut. "Executed, Your Excellency."

"You had no choice. Not to impose the due penalty of a traitor's actions is a grave mistake, and a great injustice."

"That doesn't make it any easier."

"No. It doesn't." Abruptly Washington changed the subject. "Shortly after we got back this morning I received orders from Congress to immediately dispatch you to Gates at Albany."

Carleton straightened, frowning. "You sent Colonel Morgan's riflemen to him just last week."

Washington let out an exasperated sigh. "And we could ill afford to spare them. Nor can we spare your Rangers; however, orders are orders. You are to follow on Morgan's heels."

"After the victory at Bennington, I'd think Congress would consider the Northern Department well supplied with troops."

"They are undoubtedly eager to follow up that victory with a more decisive one. According to reports Schuyler sent back before Gates succeeded him, Burgoyne has advanced so far that he has lost contact with his supply base, which leaves him dependent on what he can forage locally. The militias are doing everything in their power to deny him every necessity, and his army is consequently on short rations."

"That's all to the good," Carleton approved.

"It gets better. After Bennington the majority of Burgoyne's Indians deserted him. Without native scouts in the backcountry, an army is blind, as you well know." Washington paused before adding, "I admit I was opposed to your bringing so many Indians and Blacks into your brigade, but they have been effective. Your tactics are particularly suited to the northern campaign, and evidently the members of Congress were considerably impressed with you—"

"I'm sure they were," Carleton drawled.

"They asked for your opinions, and you were honest. That always makes an impression."

Carleton gave a short laugh. "Usually a bad one."

Washington chuckled, then sobered. "This transfer will remove you from Howe's grasp for a while. Having come this close to capturing you may well harden his resolve to accomplish it."

Leaning back against the tree under which they stood, Carleton folded his arms and studied his commander. Although Washington was aware that Burgoyne had been involved in determined efforts by the British to find him after his escape from a British gaol and subsequent disappearance into the wilderness, Carleton knew his commander was ignorant of the long-standing rancor between them.

Or that Burgoyne had been the one to openly accuse him of treason before Gage and Howe at Boston. And that he had personally set the trap to capture Carleton, with Oriole as the bait. In reality this transfer was akin to leaping off the spit into the hot coals.

A slow smile crept over his face as he gingerly rubbed his bruised jaw. The more he thought about it, the more the opportunity he'd unexpectedly been handed appealed to him.

Washington noted it too. "I see the prospect of facing Burgoyne on a battlefield pleases you," he said.

"Indeed it does," Carleton answered, adding mentally, *Much more than you know.*

Chapter Twenty-three

THE EVENING WAS OPPRESSIVELY HOT and sultry, and the unmoving air hung heavy over the sprawling camp. Lazy streamers of mist rose from the Chester and Delaware rivers, and underfoot the meadow's trampled grass soaked their boots with the falling dew.

After the swift ride from Philadelphia with Vander Groot, her aunt, Pete, and Caleb, sweat trickled profusely beneath Elizabeth's loose smock and breeches. Her cocked hat and wig caused her scalp to itch, and she was sorely tempted to cast them off. The majority of the soldiers who rushed past had assumed more comfortable Indian dress for the journey before them, she noted, wishing she could do the same.

"Native societies seem to think nothing of their women going topless in hot weather," Tess muttered, gesturing toward a Kickapoo matron who shepherded her children past. "At the moment I'm well nigh willing to hazard the scandal."

"You might start a new style," Vander Groot returned, his tone dry, eliciting snickers from Pete and Caleb.

Elizabeth suppressed a giggle. "In weather like this it seems a most sensible one."

The five of them had entered the camp stealthily through the warriors' section, pausing only long enough to greet Blue Sky and the other Shawnee women before Spotted Pony and the two warriors who met them at the edge of the woods hurried them toward the camp's center. On all sides Elizabeth saw evidence of a hasty departure. Most of the tents and their contents were already packed in wagons hitched to draft horses and oxen. The rest were rapidly being pulled down, while the mounted Rangers saddled their horses and loaded them with weapons and equipment and the dismounted troops packed knapsacks and gathered rations.

At last, across the camp, Elizabeth caught a glimpse of Carleton with Andrews and several other officers, and her heart contracted. Even in the twilight and despite the distance between them, his tall, lean figure was unmistakable. Clad in breechcloth and moccasins, he wore his blond hair loose, and she caught the ghostly gleam of three white eagle feathers woven among the strands. The rapidly failing light of sunset burnished the contours of his hard-muscled shoulders, arms, and thighs with a golden glow, lending him a hauntingly wild, untamable mien that sent a thrill through her.

Yet the knowledge that he was once more bound for battle, this time at a great distance, tore at her heart. It would be weeks before news of the northern campaign trickled back, perhaps winter before they saw each other again.

If they both survived the coming whirlwind. And if they did, she wondered how many more separations still lay in store.

As they drew nearer, the evidence of his near capture that marked his face, torso, and limbs became apparent. Biting her lip, she threw a worried glance at Vander Groot.

"I examined him carefully," he assured her. "As I said, he suffered no serious injuries, only scrapes, cuts, some bad bruises—all of which I attended to. He'll be stiff and sore for a few days, that's all."

She let out her breath and touched his arm. "It comforts me greatly knowing you're with him, Pieter. There's no one I trust more than you, dear friend."

His gaze unreadable, he nodded toward Carleton, who had caught sight of them and, with Andrews, now strode in their direction, his movements noticeably stiff.

❋ ❋ ❋

CARLETON ACKNOWLEDGED the others with a brief nod before turning an intense gaze on Elizabeth. Letting out a low groan, she gently touched his bruised cheek and swollen lip.

"Oh, your poor face!"

With a crooked smile, he captured her hand. "It'll heal soon enough. Don't worry, dear heart—I'm fine."

"Pieter told us about Captain Jeffreys," she murmured. "I'm so sorry, Jonathan. I can't imagine how horrible it feels—not only to be betrayed, but then to be forced to carry out such a harsh punishment."

Teeth gritted, for a long moment he stared out across the twilit camp. The hour he had spent with his chaplain, Captain James McLeod, had brought a measure of peace, but each time his thoughts returned to the morning, a bitter tide of anger and regret bore over him. Taking a shaking breath, he at last turned his gaze back to those who surrounded him and read the same sympathy and concern on each face that etched Elizabeth's.

"What's done is done," he said gruffly. Becoming aware of the bustle that flowed around them, his expression hardened and he reluctantly released Elizabeth's hand. "My marquee's still standing. We'd better meet there, where we'll not be observed. I'd not take the chance there are more traitors among us."

Motioning the others to follow, he led the way and ushered them inside the marquee's concealing walls. "Thank you for bringing them here safely, Pieter," he said to Vander Groot. "You've taken leave of your family?"

"I have. They plan to leave for Lancaster within the next couple of weeks."

"A wise course," Carleton approved.

"So your brigade's being transferred to Gates's command," Tess said. "I have to wonder what political machinations were behind that decision, but at least it'll take you out of Howe's reach for now."

"And put you into Burgoyne's." Worry furrowed Elizabeth's brow.

"I prefer to think it'll put Burgoyne in my sights," Carleton countered, eliciting a laugh from the others.

"Judging from the latest intelligence, it sounds as if he's already gotten himself in some trouble," Andrews said with relish. "We just may be able to put a crimp in his tail."

"How soon are you leaving?" Elizabeth asked.

Briefly Carleton explained that he and the mounted troops would depart by midnight and push hard to join Gates as quickly as possible. The dismounted troops, wagons, and camp followers would leave at daybreak, following more slowly to spare the women, children, and draft animals.

Tess shook her head. "Regardless of what happens on either front, we'll be forced to remove from the city within a month, if not sooner. It's not only the danger or that we'll be needed at Boston, but that food and every other necessity have become dear beyond measure. And with battle looming and so many of the residents fleeing, the situation is only bound to become worse."

"It's not safe for you to stay!" Vander Groot burst out. "I dearly wish you'd reconsider removing to Lancaster with my family."

Carleton rested his hand reassuringly on the doctor's shoulder. "I see little danger for the time being, as long as Howe remains true to form. He's a gambler at cards, not on the battlefield. I'll wager he'll push forward slowly and wait until his corps is back to full strength and well supplied before initiating battle."

"That'll give Washington time to finish entrenching at Red Clay Creek," Andrews put in. "And our skirmishers will slow the British down even more."

"Well, Sir Willy's obviously not been in a hurry so far," Tess noted acidly. "Beth and I agreed we'd stay until the last routes out of the city are threatened, but for now the greater problem is securing provisions so we can live. Our resources are dwindling."

Carleton went to several buckskin packs stacked at one side of the marquee. From one he retrieved a small bag, which he brought to Tess.

Giving him a doubtful look, she opened it. Her jaw dropped at the sight of the Spanish coins that filled it, and she thrust it back at him.

"I can't take this, Jon! I've enough money for now—"

He took her hand in his and firmly closed her fingers over the bag. "Keep it. Your safety and comfort are my first concerns. I've found that cold coin will overcome a multitude of obstacles."

"But you'll need supplies for your journey north," Elizabeth protested.

He made a dismissive gesture. "Believe me, love, I'm well supplied. There's plenty where that came from, and I can always send for more."

"I'll make sure the ladies have everything they need and get out safely when the time comes, general," Caleb put in. "You have my word."

As Carleton thanked him, Pete shifted from one foot to the other. "Miss Elizabeth said I might speak to you about joining your privateers—"

Raising his hand, Carleton cut him off. "She sent the request yesterday, and I have your orders." Going to his camp table, he retrieved a sealed letter and brought it to the youth. "You're to report to Captain Boudin of my ship *Destiny* at Salem—but only after you escort Miss Howard to Boston," he added firmly, indicating Tess with a nod.

Pete accepted the letter with a broad grin. "Yes, sir!"

Just then Isaiah stuck his head inside the marquee's opening. He glanced from his son to Carleton, his look sober.

"General, we're 'bout ready to move out, and we still need to take down this marquee."

Seeing that Elizabeth bit her lip and bent her head, Carleton said, "Put the men at ease, major. I'll be there in a few minutes," then asked the others to wait outside.

DETERMINED NOT TO GIVE WAY to grief for Carleton's sake, Elizabeth clung to him, her face pressed against his chest, her arms encircling his waist. He felt like a rock to her as he held her tightly, silent and unmoving.

"Don't be sad. We've been farther separated."

She raised her face to his. "Your birthday's in three days," she mourned. "We've never celebrated it together, and now I'll miss it again! How miserable it was last year, not knowing where you were or even if you were alive."

His face softened. "But I am, dearest, and God gave us back to each other. This time, it'll not be so long—"

"How can you know that?" she demanded, her voice choked, vainly blinking back tears. "What if Gates can't stop Burgoyne? He took Ticonderoga with hardly any effort."

"You know St. Clair wisely let him have it. Before Gates took over, Schuyler laid every obstacle in Burgoyne's path and wiped the area clean of the provisions his army needs. They'll soon find it impossible to either go forward or back. By the time we get there, the battle may already be won."

She pulled away to wipe her nose and tears on her shirt sleeve and forced a wavering smile. "I'll pray it's so."

"Perhaps you can do more than pray. Once Philadelphia's fate becomes apparent, I'll need someone to report to me. With Clinton confined to New York, there should be no danger between here and the Hudson, and I've every confidence Caleb can bring you safely to me."

She tiptoed to throw her arms around his neck. "Oh, yes! You know I'll do it!"

His shoulders slumping, he released her reluctantly. "This may not a good idea after all, Beth. I want you with me more than anything in the world, but I know how much you've missed your parents and Abby. Depending on how the two campaigns develop and when you're able to get away, it's possible they might arrive at Boston before you do. I can't ask you to forego the joy of being there to greet them."

For a long moment she hesitated between the deep ache to embrace her family the instant they came home and the turmoil that raged in her breast each time she and Carleton were separated, even if only for a little while. The fear that he would be snatched from her again, this time forever, haunted every waking hour when he was absent, and even the months since his return had not eased it.

At the same time, although the prospect of her parents' return home caused her great joy, a part of her dreaded the inevitable confrontation that must accompany it. How would they perceive the dangerous role she had undertaken? How could she ever explain her service to the rebels and the consequent deceptions she had been forced to practice?

At length she said, "According to Mama's last letter, their ship won't leave until the end of September, and it'll be a month or more before they reach Boston. It's possible both campaigns will be ended by then, which will leave me free to go home. We'll simply have to trust that the Lord will work everything out for the best."

He cupped her face in his hands and returned her gaze with an earnest one. "Please consider what I asked you before. I'll understand any time you choose not to continue in this role. Do what's best for you, little Oriole, and know I'll make other arrangements as needed."

She gave a tremulous smile. "Ask me again in the spring," she whispered. "I'll see this campaign through, and then . . . " She broke off with a shrug.

He released her, his expression grave. "Be careful of the Howes, dear heart, especially Sir William. He's cold and ruthless, and from what Pieter told me, he's had his eye on you."

Stiffening, she tossed her head and gave a light laugh. "Well, Pieter is wrong. I assure you General Howe's too profligate, too debauched, too occupied with his mistress and drinking and gambling to pay any attention to a flea like me. He's the last person I need to be afraid of."

"Don't be so sure of that," he warned soberly. "After the run-in I had with him this morning, I'm beginning to think there's more going on behind that vacuous exterior than any of us suspect. Clearly he's no stranger to intrigue, and one who's adept in that art can smell it a mile away. His interest in you may well be a reflection of his suspicions."

"Be assured I'll take every care to stay out of his sights, as you do," she said with a smile. "In any case, both of us will soon be safely beyond his reach."

Her heart grown lighter, she paid no heed to his brooding look as he escorted her outside into the night.

ELIZABETH HELD BLUE SKY tightly in her arms, smiling to feel the protesting push and prod of the babe as the young matron's bulging belly pressed against her. At an especially vigorous kick, Elizabeth pulled back, and both of them burst out laughing, with Tess joining in their mirth.

"My son is already asserting his will, I see," Andrews noted, his grin broad.

"He's undoubtedly inherited his father's hard head," Elizabeth retorted, reaching for him. "May this little one be a great blessing to you both," she whispered in his ear as they embraced.

Laughing Otter, Rain Woman, and Sweetgrass crowded in, and with prayers and hugs, Elizabeth and Tess took their leave. "May God keep you safe on your journey," Elizabeth called as Caleb and Pete hurried them away. "I'll see you at Albany as soon as I can."

"Promise you'll come by *Sha'teepakanootha,* the Wilted Moon, to catch my son when he is born," Blue Sky answered, smiling and waving with one hand, the other resting on her belly.

Waving back at her, Elizabeth happily gave her promise and ran to catch up with the others already disappearing into the shadowed woods.

HIS ARM AROUND BLUE SKY'S SHOULDERS, Andrews returned Elizabeth's wave, then looked down to find his wife smiling up at him. "We must hurry or we will be left behind," she said.

He expelled a breath in exasperation. "Blue Sky, you know I can't take you with me this time," he reminded her, determined that for once he would prevail. "You must go with the rest of the women in the morning."

"But I—"

Her protest was cut off by Sweetgrass, who stepped between them, hands on hips as she glared at the younger woman. "Do not argue with your husband!" she admonished. "You will hurt your baby by riding fast with the men, and slow them down too. Fighting is a matter for warriors, and we women must tend to our own affairs."

Blue Sky's mouth dropped open, but before she could speak, Laughing Otter took her firmly by the arm, while Rain Woman shook her finger in her face. "Sweetgrass is right and so is Golden Elk. Respect your husband. Bid him goodbye now and come with us."

Chastened, Blue Sky looked up, starlight glittering in the tears that pooled in her dark eyes. "Forgive my disrespect, my husband," she whispered.

Fighting to hold back a laugh, he threw the women a grateful glance. This separation would be longer than any they had endured since he had taken her as wife, but as much as it cut his heart to leave her behind, he knew the unsparing journey that lay before the mounted troops would test their endurance. In her advanced pregnancy, she could never bear it.

He took her in his arms and kissed the top of her head, then lifted her chin until she met his eyes, determined to press the advantage while he held it—which he suspected would not be long. "Promise me that you'll ride in one of the wagons when you tire," he said sternly. "It's best for you and our son."

With uncharacteristic meekness she gave her assent. Relieved, he let out a sigh, knowing she would keep her promise.

Savoring the sweet kisses and caresses of their parting, he at last released her to the women's care and ran across the shadowy meadow to join the troops already mounted and waiting for him. A deep ache possessed his heart at the thought of the days that lay between them until he again held her in his arms, but resolutely he banished the painful longing from his consciousness and sprang into the saddle.

Chapter Twenty-four

"I'D BETTER RUN STRAIGHT HOME before Mama sends Sophie to fetch me." Sighing, Isobel stopped on the town house's graveled walkway, her parasol tipped to shade her pretty face from the sun. "I've still so much to pack, and Martin is coming this evening."

It was Tuesday, September 9. The Rangers had been gone more than week, and the British had resumed their deliberate march toward Philadelphia. The Vander Groots were the latest of Elizabeth and Tess's acquaintances to join the steady exodus from the city.

"I can't believe you're actually leaving for Lancaster tomorrow," Elizabeth mourned. "It'll be horribly lonely without you. I'll miss our walks terribly."

"Oh, so will I!" Isobel exclaimed. "But the reports this morning that the army has pulled back to Brandywine Creek and the British are moving toward Kennett Square has Mama in a panic. She insists we leave now while the road to Lancaster is still open."

"We're resolved to stay a while longer," Elizabeth said, closing her parasol and twirling it over her shoulder. "Unless the British take the city, there's no rush for us to leave as long as we reach Boston before the beginning of October."

Impulsively they embraced, then Isobel pulled back to study Elizabeth with a sad look.

"Ever since we first met I've prayed and hoped that you and Pieter—" When Elizabeth began to protest, she cried, "Oh, Beth, there's someone else, isn't there? You're in love. Does Pieter know?"

Elizabeth could hardly speak for the lump in her throat. "He knows."

"Who is he? And why have you kept your feelings a secret all this time?"

Her throat gone dry, Elizabeth chewed her lip. She had known questions would inevitably arise but had prayed the Vander Groots' departure for Lancaster would forestall them.

"It's General Carleton, isn't it?"

Her friend's gentle question brought the color flooding into Elizabeth's cheeks. "Why . . . what makes you think that?"

Isobel gave her an arch look. "He's so handsome and charming, and when he called on us several times I caught a look in Pieter's eyes that made me think they were rivals. Clearly Pieter loves you, so . . . " Her words trailed off then, clasping her hands, she exclaimed, "I so wish you loved him too, but—a general and a Shawnee war chief—"

"Isobel, please—"

"Don't worry! I promise I won't tell anyone. Pieter warned us how dangerous it is for him, and—"

"Why, Miss Andrews! Fancy meeting you here."

Elizabeth froze, certain her heart would stop. Although the young woman who addressed her spoke with a coarseness that had not characterized her speech at Newtown, Elizabeth could not mistake her voice.

Isobel regarded Elizabeth with curiosity. "There's no Miss Andrews here," she said, transferring her gaze to the girl behind Elizabeth. "Who are looking for?"

Stifling a groan, Elizabeth swung to face Chastity. The young woman wore the same gown she had two weeks earlier when the Continental Army marched through the city. It was ragged and none too clean. Seeing her more closely now, Elizabeth noted with both apprehension and pity the hollows in her cheeks, the dark circles beneath her eyes, and the bulge of her belly beneath her loosely laced bodice.

"She's the one, all right," Chastity was saying, triumph in her eyes as she stepped closer. "I'd never seen no one as pretty as th—you, Miss Andrews."

All too aware of Isobel's raised eyebrows, Elizabeth gave Chastity an imperious look. "I'm afraid you mistake me for someone else. I'm not familiar with you or with any Miss Andrews."

The girl's eyes widened. "Oh, I'm sure I'm not mistaken. Remember—you and thy aunt stayed at the Wainwrights' inn at Newtown back in December with—"

"I most certainly did not!"

"That Indian girl was with you, and—"

Elizabeth had just opened her mouth to cut off Chastity's profusions when Isobel said innocently, "Indeed you must be mistaken. This is Miss Howard—Miss Elizabeth Howard. She and her aunt were in Boston in December."

Nausea twisted Elizabeth's stomach. It was all she could do to conceal her horror.

"Who is this Miss Andrews you're looking for?" Isobel continued kindly. "Do you know where she lives?"

"Jane Andrews and her aunt Eliza Freeman," the girl said sullenly, throwing Elizabeth a resentful look. "I saw you in a shop the other day too, and I'm not mistaken."

"I'm afraid you are," Isobel responded with a reassuring smile. "Miss Howard and her aunt reside in New York—"

"Isobel, there's no purpose in listening to this any further," Elizabeth said sharply, keeping her voice low. "The girl is either confused or determined on mischief. Let's go inside."

She pulled Isobel after her, but they had only taken a few steps up the walk when Chastity flung after them, "I know you, no matter what you say, Miss *Howard.* I could tell you was in love with that handsome general even though you denied it. What's his name? Carleton. Yes, that's it—General Carleton."

Elizabeth felt lightheaded, and it was clear from Isobel's alarmed expression that her dismay showed too clearly on her face. Putting her arm around Elizabeth's shoulders, Isobel drew her to the front door. When Elizabeth glanced apprehensively back, Chastity had a smug look on her face.

"I heard you that night in the kitchen with him," she called after them. "Couldn't understand all you said, but I heard enough. And I know it was you. If you want to find me," she added with malice, "I'm staying down on Third Street. You might want to look me up. I got a baby on the way, and I'll be needin' some help."

In a state of shock, hardly able to breathe, Elizabeth allowed Isobel to pull her inside and into the parlor. When she glanced fearfully out the window to where Chastity had stood, the girl was gone.

She started as the clock on the mantel began to toll eleven. Completely unnerved by the shock of the unexpected encounter, she fought vainly to still her trembling.

In spite of the dangers she daily grappled with, in spite of Carleton's warnings, she had never expected to be so suddenly and so completely exposed.

"You're very pale. If you need a doctor—"

"No! No, I'm fine." Despite all effort, Elizabeth's voice quavered.

"You're not. Something's very wrong." Isobel drew her onto the sofa and sat next to her, studying her with concern. After several moments she said quietly, "Who are you really? What are you involved in?"

Elizabeth's thoughts raced, but she could find no explanation that was even vaguely plausible. Her mouth dry, she whispered, "You must swear to me before God that you'll never tell anyone what I confide to you. Not your parents, not Christiaan, not even Mr. Lamb."

Isobel considered her words. Finally she gave a firm nod as though she had come to a decision.

"It must be quite dangerous, then. Very well. You have my word."

As briefly as possible, Elizabeth outlined her role and Carleton's, then looked up in appeal to find Isobel staring at her, eyes wide and shining.

"Pieter knows all this?"

Frowning down at her clenched hands, Elizabeth said, "Since last spring when he . . . joined the Rangers. Can you ever forgive Aunt Tess and me for deceiving you and your parents about our involvements? You cannot know what anguish we've suffered because of it, but we dared trust no one."

"You're spies!" Isobel exclaimed, keeping her voice low. "For General Washington! Oh, how very romantic!"

Elizabeth covered her face with her hands, tears trickling through her fingers. "It isn't romantic! It's all deception and lies, and there are times when it threatens to come between even Jonathan and me." She broke into sobs.

Isobel enveloped her in her arms. "Don't fret! Even God's chosen people sent out spies into the land to gather information for their safety. Without the work you and others do, our cause would long ago have been lost."

Leaning her head on her friend's shoulder, Elizabeth dabbed at her tears. "Oh, Isobel, I try to go on bravely, but more often of late I fear I'll be utterly broken. A part of me thrills at the excitement and danger and rushes ahead heedlessly. Yet another part of me longs so to marry Jonathan, to have a home and children of my own, as you will, to live at peace and concern myself with small daily tasks that have no import beyond the walls of my home. How can I sort out the two?"

Smiling down at her, Isobel caressed her cheek. "You will, dear sister. When your work is done, then the day of peace will come in its time, and your heart will be ready for it. Don't doubt that!"

"I say that to Jonathan too, but I *do* doubt it." Again Elizabeth broke down, weeping. "And now what of Chastity?" she said through her sobs, "I saw her across the street the day the army marched through the city. She was with a soldier from the loyalist militia, and obviously she's carrying his child. Now she knows my name. If she tells him about me—"

"We must stop her before she can do so," Isobel said firmly. "Your aunt will know what to do. We must solicit her help at once."

At thought of Tess, relief and calmness replaced Elizabeth's distress. "You're right, of course," she agreed, drawing herself up. "Aunt Tess will be home in a little while, and she'll set everything right."

Resolutely she dried her tears. "But now you must go home and finish getting ready for your move before your mother becomes anxious."

Assuring her friend that she and Tess would take care of the matter and promising she would write as soon as everything was settled, Elizabeth bade Isobel a fond farewell. Yet after the young woman had gone, she paced the floor until Tess's return, a sickening sense of fear and dread twisting in her breast.

"YOU FOUND HER?"

Tess patted Elizabeth's hand. "It's all taken care of. Her wastrel of a lover abandoned her without so much as a farewell-thee-well when his unit moved out, and she was in a sad state. The place she's living in is little more than a hovel, and she'd been reduced to begging for food. Needless to say, she was more than happy to take the money I offered and agree to my terms."

"How much did you give her?" Elizabeth asked apprehensively.

"Twelve Spanish doubloons. The coins Jon gave us were a godsend. This should set her up for quite a while unless she's terribly profligate."

"She won't tell anyone—"

"She promised she wouldn't, and particularly that she'd not breathe a word about either of us to her former boyfriend should they ever meet again."

"Thank you," Elizabeth murmured, hanging her head. "I'll pray she keeps her word."

"I'm confident she will," Tess assured her. "She knows how to get in touch with me now, and I made it clear that as long as she keeps quiet, she can come to me anytime she's in want—at least until you're out of danger, though I didn't tell her that. Before I leave for Boston, I'll make sure she has enough to get her through the winter and the birth of her baby. I made her promise never to approach you again, but if an unexpected need arises, she can send a message to me, and I'll take care of it."

Elizabeth buried her face in her hands. "I'm so sorry this happened—"

"Don't be!" Tess said forcefully. "We couldn't have foreseen this any more than Jon could foresee Jeffreys' betrayal. It's the hazard we face in our line of work," she added with a sigh.

Elizabeth reached for her, the tears overflowing. "What would I ever do without you?"

Tess drew her into her arms. "God gave us to each other, and you've blessed me like the daughter I never had. Remember what it says in Zechariah: 'Fear not, but let your hands be strong.' Truly, we have nothing to fear as long as God is on our side."

Chapter Twenty-five

"I SAW THEM! From Birmingham Meeting House, one has a view for miles, and with my own eyes I watched the redcoats marching up the west bank of the Brandywine on their way to the ford at the forks. And no one about! They'll succeed in flanking the army if nothing's done!"

Glaring from Elizabeth to Pete and back, the sturdy middle-aged farmer emphasized his rant by tearing off his hat and slapping it across his thigh, sending dust flying. Snorting, his lathered horse rolled its eyes and sidestepped nervously, tossing its head up and down.

"Now I happen to know a narrow defile just this side of the river where the British could be held by a mere two-hundred men," the man continued. "But do you think General Washington and his staff would send anyone to investigate? Why, no! Their intelligence, I was informed with disdain, did not confirm it. Well, *I* confirm it!"

Elizabeth eyed him dubiously. That his windblown clothing appeared to have been hastily flung on, sweat plastered his thinning hair to his head, and both man and horse were covered in dust gave credence to his claims.

"Squire . . . ?"

"Cheney, young man. Thomas Cheney at your service. A staunch Son of Liberty, I'll have you know."

Squinting against the blinding sun, she rubbed the sweat from her brow with the back of her hand. From early that morning, September 11, she and Tess had heard heavy gunfire from the direction of Brandywine Creek, southwest of the city, and, anxious to gain some news of the battle, had briefly ventured out. The town was in great confusion, with crowds scurrying to and fro and rumors running rampant.

At last, against her aunt's vehement objections, Elizabeth had thrown on her disguise and shortly after noon rode out into the sapping midday heat to see what she could learn. Taking Pete with her, she insisted Caleb stay behind with Tess in case any emergency arose. Between Dilworth and Chadd's Ford they had run into Cheney on his way back from Washington's headquarters in a state of high dudgeon.

"Squire Cheney, are any Continental units posted near Birmingham Meeting House?"

"A few patrols, nothing more!" he exclaimed, his jowls quivering.

"Who's the nearest?"

He rubbed his stubbled jaw. "Sullivan, I believe. His division lies over there at Brinton's Ford on the other side of those hills," he added, pointing. "But he's two miles, at least, from Birmingham."

"We'd better warn him then, if no one else has," she decided, exchanging glances with Pete. "Can you conduct us to him?"

He agreed with alacrity, and they rode hard for the line of wooded hills that marked the creek's winding course. Judging from the angle of the sun, she guessed it to be no earlier than two-thirty when they came upon the Continentals' right wing. At sight of her pass from Washington, the pickets hurried them through the lines and directed them to Sullivan while Elizabeth contemplated the possibility of inventing orders from their commander.

The subterfuge turned out to be unnecessary. They found the handsome, aristocratic general conferring with one of Washington's aides, a confounded expression on his face.

"I warned His Excellency this morning that Howe'd attempt to flank us, but he didn't seem overly concerned. We've heard nothing since then. Now you tell me the British are at my back!"

"The reports we've received all day have been so contradictory we could make nothing of them, sir," the aide apologized. "But Colonel Bland just alerted us that they're across the creek and marching on Birmingham Meeting House. General Washington has dispatched Stirling's and Stephen's divisions. They're on the way, and you're to follow and take command."

The general swung around, consternation in every line of his body. When his gaze fell on Elizabeth and her companions, she stepped boldly forward and presented her pass.

"I just arrived, sir, but Squire Cheney here can confirm that Howe's on our flank." She turned to the stocky farmer. "Did you encounter Stirling or Stephen on your way back from Birmingham?"

With a disgusted look, Cheney shook his head. "Like I said, I only ran into a couple of patrols."

"Then we've no idea where they are." Sullivan uttered a stream of bitter invective. "But no matter," he concluded with sarcasm. "We'll doubtless find them if the British don't first."

Motioning to an aide, he sent him scurrying with orders for his subordinates to form up the brigade. By three o'clock they had pulled back from the creek and were moving north at a quick trot. Within less than five minutes they ran into Colonel Moses Hazen's regiment falling back from Jones's and Buffenton's fords, where Sullivan had posted them early in the day.

Calmly Hazen reported that a strong enemy force was on his heels. As though his words had conjured them up, British soldiers suddenly materialized at the edge of the woods in front of the column and began methodically to deploy into battle line.

Glancing over his shoulder, Hazen said, "Ah, there they are. Right on time."

To Elizabeth's astonishment, now that he was in sight of the enemy, Sullivan appeared unfazed. Calmly he swung his column around to the right, while keeping an eye on the British detachment, which showed no inclination to oppose the column's movements. Giving the enemy a wide birth, they continued on their way without interference.

A short while before four o'clock they approached Birmingham. Situated on the brow of a hill, the tidy stone building the local Quaker congregation used as a meetinghouse overlooked the road to the Brandywine's upper fords, which were just visible at a distance. According to the running commentary of the garrulous squire who rode at Elizabeth's side, the meetinghouse had been commandeered by the army for a hospital. Elizabeth reflected unhappily that they would likely need its services very soon.

Directly ahead of them a large force of Continentals came into view, extending to the right of their line of march at the base of a broad, wooded prominence Cheney identified as Plowed Hill. As Sullivan's column moved closer, her stomach clenched at sight of an enormous body of British and Hessian soldiers sprawling across the fields northeast of the village and along the top of a steep hill as barren as a skull directly behind the small community. Battle flags furling lazily in the hot breeze, weapons and blood-red uniforms glowing in the brilliance of the lowering sun, they waited in suspense, apparently resting up before they unleashed chaos on the peaceful countryside.

The messenger Sullivan sent forward soon brought back confirmation that the columns commanded by generals Stirling and Stephen indeed made up the American force. Sullivan wasted no time deploying his column to anchor the left of the existing line. While his battle line snaked outward, the general spurred his horse to the top of the hill to join a cluster of officers posted there. With a quick glance at her companions, Elizabeth jerked her head in Sullivan's direction, and they galloped forward to bring up the rear of Sullivan's party.

Dismounting, for some moments Sullivan conferred with the two generals while they assessed their extended position. Tethering their horses near the hill's brow, Elizabeth, Pete, and the squire eased into the outer fringes of the aides who clustered around them.

"The line seems strong enough," Sullivan concluded, lowering his spyglass. "The artillery looks to be effectively placed, and we've both flanks secured by woods."

Stirling shook his head. "You posted your troops about half a mile ahead of our line," he said, pointing to the gap. "That leaves an opening between us that Howe won't hesitate to exploit."

Sullivan scrutinized the line more closely, then scowling, sent one of his aides off at a gallop with orders for his division to pull back on the double and come into line with the other units. Within minutes, Pete pointed to where Sullivan's column had begun to run back toward the main battle line.

It was in the confusion of that moment that the British force suddenly congealed into three columns that of one accord began to pour forward through the fields and down the distant hill along a wide front. In the van at the far left she could make out two riders, one sitting tall and erect on his charger, an imposing figure she guessed to be Cornwallis. His swarthy companion, who slouched astride a large, bony steed that shambled like a farm horse, she made out to be Howe.

In an inexorable flood tide, the enemy force lapped around the village, and then plowed through it. Pete called her over to the left flank of the hill, and as Elizabeth looked apprehensively down, through the trees she caught a glimpse of the mixed Maryland and Delaware brigade that brought up the rear of Sullivan's wing. They were racing along a constricted lane through a thin wood to reach their new position, when suddenly the leading British detachment burst from the concealing trees, bayonets fixed.

Meeting Pete's dismayed gaze, she pressed her hands over her mouth to stifle an outcry.

The enemy collided with the flank of Sullivan's brigade in a brief, violent shock, succeeded by a savage melee impossible for Elizabeth to sort out. Then the Marylanders and Delawares were in headlong retreat, scattering pell-mell to all sides as fast as their legs could carry them, leaving behind the crumpled bodies of their comrades.

In what seemed only seconds, each successive unit of Sullivan's column splintered. With horrifying suddenness, the entire Continental left wing dissolved into random units in desperate flight.

Behind her, in profound rage, Sullivan was rehearsing at the top of his lungs every obscenity she had ever heard, and more. He sprang into the saddle, screaming for the artillery to open fire on the advancing British, then he and his aides swept by her at a gallop and descended the hill, while she stood paralyzed.

Stirling, Stephen, and their coteries had also vanished, as had Cheney, and only Pete remained with her atop the prominence. Oblivious of the musket balls and grapeshot that whirled around her, plowing up the ground and rattling in the trees to release a flurry of riven leaves and splintered branches on her head, Elizabeth watched transfixed as the red-clad soldiers fought to force their way uphill, only to be beaten back by the units Sullivan managed to rally.

"It's like Long Island all over again," Pete muttered, grabbing the reins of their skittish horses, who squealed and pranced nervously, wide eyes rolling.

Gone numb, she nodded, feeling trapped in one long, recurring nightmare. Again no one had paid heed to the danger. Again she had learned too late that the enemy moved to flank them and arrived with no time left to sound a warning.

By now billows of choking gun smoke were drifting up from the center of the Continental line that fronted Plowed Hill. Stirling's and Stephens' battalions held, and the British front staggered against them and recoiled. But in a dreadful dance that wrought wreckage on both sides, the enemy regrouped, driving valiantly forward again and again, gaining ground with each thrust.

Deafened by the hellish roar of musket and cannon fire, the screams of officers and cries of the wounded, Elizabeth coughed with every breath, a sickening dismay churning in her gut, while all across the plain below her, the carnage steadily widened.

She started as Cheney appeared at her elbow, his round face flushed and streaked with sweat and blood. Shocked into action, she grasped his arm.

"We've got to report to the General!"

"That's why I came to get you!" he shouted back. "Stay here much longer, and you'll—"

"Duck!" Pete shouted hoarsely, as a round of solid shot arced close overhead.

All three of them crouched and looked up fearfully as the missile descended to splinter the tree at their backs. Of one accord, they moved to quit the hill, passing Sullivan who raced up the slope on foot to meet Stirling coming up from the far side.

"We no sooner rally one company than another breaks," Elizabeth heard Sullivan exclaim in disgust, "but I'm resolved to hold this hill by any means to the last drop of blood!"

She threw a hasty glance over her shoulder toward Lord Stirling. The corpulent general's ruddy, open countenance was fouled with smoke and dirt, but vastly unperturbed. "We've been up for the challenge before, John," he said, smiling like a wolf. "No reason why we can't do it again."

❀ ❀ ❀

IF ANYTHING, THE CLAMOR of battle was even louder at Chadd's Ford.

"Your Excellency," she panted, breathless from the urgent ride, "Howe's reached Birmingham Meeting House, and Sullivan's heavily engaged. His left has broken."

Washington exchanged a grim glance with Lafayette, who hovered at his side like a melancholy stork, before glaring at her. "You have chosen a fine time to report to me now, when the gunfire from that quarter has made it blindingly evident that Howe has once again flanked us."

A sudden, thunderous cannonade from the heights above the ford drowned out his words. Elizabeth clapped her hands over her ears, as did her companions and several members of Washington's party.

He wheeled his white stallion to take in the blazing batteries, then rounded on his officers. "I would guess there are at least two brigades opposing Sullivan, but we had better ride over and determine the situation for ourselves. Order General Wayne's division to hold the ford at all cost, and tell Greene and Nash to head to Birmingham with dispatch to support Sullivan."

He motioned to another of his aides. "Find someone who can guide us to Sullivan by the best and shortest route," he ordered, his jaw clenched.

Both aides saluted and spurred their mounts. While they waited, Elizabeth detailed the action at the meetinghouse to Washington and those with him. She was interrupted by the second aide's return. He escorted a farmer of advanced age and halting gait to the General.

The man's bony, pinched face testified that he had come only under the harshest compulsion, and the next few minutes were spent in an effort to bully elderly Joseph Brown into guiding them to Birmingham. Elizabeth felt exceedingly sorry for the feeble old squire, who complained bitterly that he was unequal to the task and made every possible excuse to avoid compliance.

At last, in an excess of impatience, one of the officers leaped from his saddle to confront the man. "If you don't instantly get on your horse and conduct the General to the meetinghouse by the nearest and best route, I shall run you through, sir!" he said through his teeth, bringing his nose to within an inch of Brown's. "And don't think for one instant I'll not make good my threat!"

For a suspended instant, Brown stared at the officer's hand that gripped his sword hilt, then without a word swung abruptly around and clawed into the saddle. The officer was instantly astride as well, and in a swirl of dust, the entire party spurred forward, leaving the road to veer cross country.

To Elizabeth's astonishment, Brown's sturdy mount flew over fences like a bird on the wing. Directly in front of her, the head of his horse almost lying on the flank of the farmer's, Washington leaned far over his mount's neck, repeatedly shouting, "Push along, old man! Push along!"

Despite the urgency of the situation and the difficulty of catching her breath, she was hard pressed to stifle laughter that bordered on hysteria.

ALL THOUGHT OF MIRTH fled as they neared Birmingham.

They came on the battlefield at the moment Sullivan's entire line finally shattered under the relentless pressure of the enemy's overwhelming numbers. It was quickly apparent to Elizabeth that an intense fight had followed after she left to find Washington. Now she watched in horror as each brigade in turn wavered, then broke.

Within minutes a cascade of men poured onto the road to Dilworth, casting their equipment aside as they ran. Uttering an oath, Pete tore his pistols from the saddle holsters and emptied both at the red tide boiling toward them.

At numerous points during the day she had longed for Carleton's steadying presence, but never more so than now. Had he and the

Rangers reached Gates's camp safely? she wondered. Had it yet come to battle with Burgoyne? Was he safe? And what of Blue Sky and the others? It might be weeks before she learned their fate, or he hers.

Despairing, she watched Washington, with Lafayette and his aides at his side, spur his stallion into the thick of the retreating horde without apparent concern for his life, while musket balls and grapeshot whirled among them like monstrous bees. The General leaned from his mount to shout encouragement and challenge to his men, offering a pat on the shoulder or the clasp of a hand to the spent, shaken men. Breathless and trembling, her thoughts a constant plea for divine protection, Elizabeth followed in his wake, Pete and the faithful squire at her side as they took their commander's example for their own.

Somehow in the confused melee Caleb found them. "Your aunt's beyond worried for you, and I've had all of sitting and waiting I can endure," he growled as he drew his mount alongside hers and Pete's.

He shouldered a rifle, and the strap of a cartouche box crossed his chest. Unable to speak, she gave him a grateful glance. Returning it with a scowl, he sprang from the saddle and, leading his mount, swerved off to melt into the stream of battle. Pete watched him go through narrowed eyes as he reloaded his pistols but continued to stick to Elizabeth's side like a burr.

By degrees the fearful torrent began to coalesce into a form of order. Resistance steadily stiffened as increasingly the fugitives turned to direct a galling fire on the close British pursuit that threatened to sweep them away. Taking cover behind every tree, fence, hillock, and building they could find, they forced their tormentors to purchase with blood every foot of ground they conceded, while bringing off as many of their wounded as they could.

When it seemed human flesh could endure no more, a formidable force suddenly spilled from the hills and woods to the west. For a suspended moment Elizabeth feared it was yet another British column come to finish them off. Then with a flood of relief she identified Greene riding in the van.

She was near Washington when Sullivan galloped up. "General, if Greene deploys up the road there," he shouted over the din, pointing in the direction of the small village of Dilworth, just coming into view, "we can pass through his ranks while he strikes the enemy's front and flank!"

Washington threw a calculating glance in the direction Sullivan indicated, then motioned to one of his aides. Quickly the young officer spurred his mount toward the advancing brigades.

As Greene's force slanted off toward the village, Cheney shouted to Elizabeth and Pete, "We'd better head for the town! We're mad to stay here without weapons!"

For the first time since arriving on the field, Elizabeth realized she had stuck her loaded pistol into her breeches pocket before leaving the house, a precaution that seemed absurd now in light of the raging battle. Deciding it might yet come in handy, she gestured wearily to the good squire to lead the way, suddenly overcome by bone-deep exhaustion. Also sagging in the saddle, Pete made no objection.

With the sun hanging low above the treetops, they fought their way through the press to where Greene's column struggled to form a battle line against the tide of Sullivan's retreating column just outside the village boundary. A whirlwind of blazing fire and hand-to-hand combat ensued, worse than any Elizabeth had yet experienced.

Repeatedly she and those around her cringed and ducked low as bullets and cannon shot screamed by. Her shirt was pierced in several places by musket balls, but miraculously she remained otherwise unscathed. Pete bled from shallow wounds to his arm and thigh, while Cheney nursed a stinging graze across his brow, and Caleb rejoined them with a bloody strip of cloth binding his leg.

Ahead of them Weedon's Virginians had formed into line and now spread out to allow the broken American regiments to pour through to the rear, Elizabeth and her companions among them. As they passed, the brigade closed behind them to block the enemy's way.

At once a heavy American volley tore through the advancing grenadiers, in a heartbeat slicing through their ranks like a mighty scythe. British cannon fire responded, and following a fierce half hour, while the shadows lengthened and darkness gathered over the hills and hollows, Greene's force finally pulled back through the town to join the general withdrawal toward Chester, while the British, also spent, at last gave up the pursuit.

Beyond Dilworth Sullivan's and Greene's combined columns merged with a stream of Wayne's, Maxwell's, and Armstrong's battered divisions retreating from Chadd's Ford. The multiplied sound of feet and hooves tramping wearily along the dusty road filled the night.

The battle along the Brandywine had also gone badly, Elizabeth learned from some of the soldiers who straggled into Chester. After Greene's withdrawal to join Sullivan, the Hessians had forced their way across the creek, covered by a heavy artillery bombardment. For almost two hours the American force had fought stubbornly from behind any cover they could find, exacting a terrible toll before finally being pushed from the field by the larger force.

Yet almost to a man, they demonstrated a cheerfulness that greatly heartened Elizabeth. "We didn't do so badly after all," one said to another.

"We stood against the best they could throw at us," his mate agreed.

"We'll do even better next time," echoed a third.

But although their words encouraged her, she couldn't help wondering whether the day might not have turned out quite differently had Carleton's Rangers and Morgan's riflemen been there to join in the fray.

Chapter Twenty-six

HARDLY REGISTERING THE DEEP CHILL that seeped into every pore, Carleton pressed back against the rough bark of the tree where he lay concealed, squinting to make out the faint track that bisected the woods directly beneath his perch. The first tentative blush of dawn had begun to brighten the sky high overhead. Lower down, mist rose from the rugged, heavily wooded terrain in ghostly steamers, blurring the warriors crouched on the branches around him and in the underbrush below.

Approaching warily, still at some distance, he could make out the halting tramp of soldiers making their way cautiously forward, underlaid by the muffled jingle of harness and creak of caisson wheels. Satisfied that the British foraging party he and his warriors had scouted an hour earlier still blundered blindly toward them, Carleton gauged that they were no more than a quarter of a mile out.

He looked down to see Andrews, with Isaiah and a small party of his black troop, materialize out of the fog and move soundlessly into position. Glancing up, Andrews lifted his hand, thumb upturned. Carleton nodded in acknowledgement, then raised his bow overhead. In the tree next to his, Spotted Pony did the same, passing the alert on.

As the light strengthened, the fog correspondingly thickened, shrouding the forest in muted tentacles of shifting grey. From a distance sounded the soft call of a whip-poor-will, echoed several seconds later by Spotted Pony.

The detachment included only a handful of Indians scouts, and Carleton's warriors had made sure neither they nor the soldiers who pressed nervously in their wake guessed their presence. Stripped and painted black from head to toe, his war party was all but invisible in the shadows of the fog-wrapped forest.

A glimpse of red showed through the underbrush a short distance ahead of them on the track, and Carleton came alert. He raised his bow, arrow nocked, signaling to his warriors. When the first red-coated ranks emerged from the mist, bayonets advanced, he aimed, drew back hard on the string, and let fly. A swarm of arrows released instantly from all sides, announced by an eerie ululating war whoop that echoed through the forest reaches.

Screams and curses burst from the soldiers, and the red line staggered, losing half their numbers at once, while those at the rear took to their heels. With tomahawk or scalping knife in hand, Carleton and the warriors with him dropped from the branches. On all sides Andrews, Red Fox, Isaiah, and their men were already in savage motion, firing rifle or musket and reloading rapidly to fire again, cutting down those not fleet enough of foot to escape. In brief moments dead and wounded sprawled on all sides and a clutch of prisoners shrank from the triumphant howls of the warriors who surrounded them.

When a party started after the fleeing survivors, Carleton called them back. "Let them carry our warning to General Burgoyne. Take the prisoners and wounded back to camp, and don't forget those field pieces," he added, nodding toward the two nervously side-stepping horses hitched to four-pounders. "We'll put them to good use."

Knowing it impossible to prevent the warriors from plundering the living and dead of anything of value, Carleton gave stern orders that the prisoners were not to be harmed. With Andrews at his side, he led the detachment on a circuitous route back through the dense, tangled undergrowth, while behind them the warriors drove their terrified prisoners along with cries of triumph.

By degrees, as night gave way to dawn, the euphoric tension of battle drained out of Carleton. As he strode along, he drank in the beauty of the vast northern uplands' unspoiled grandeur, cloven at irregular intervals by steep ravines where pristine streams and waterfalls tumbled far below, adding their faint roar to the ceaseless sigh of the wind through the pines, the stealthy scurry of forest creatures through the underbrush, the wild chime of birdsong.

As the sun rose higher, the fog began slowly to lift. All around them the wooded ridges showed the first light blush of scarlet and gold. Since his Rangers had joined the Northern Army, warm days had increasingly given way to cold nights when moon- and starshine gilded heavy dews and frosts, then to dense fog that hovered over valley and river until the sun hung high in the sky.

Even though it had been less than a year, he had been gone from the wilderness too long, he reflected, a pang going through him. As often before, he wondered at the wild, primeval, seemingly unconquerable longing in his spirit that called out to this untamed land and the native peoples that inhabited it—a longing that would not allow him to find true peace or joy or satisfaction apart from them, and that only Elizabeth's arms could soothe.

That this Eden that drew him so powerfully was now riven by war to feed the pride, ambition, and greed of outsiders seemed to him an obscenity. Surely this had never been the Creator's intent, and yet it had always been so on the earth, allowed, at least for a season, to serve inscrutable purposes.

Against his will Carleton had been drawn into the fearful business of war. And most of all he feared the savagery that rose up in his breast when he grappled with an enemy, when any and every violence seemed possible—nay, even right.

He became aware that as he and Andrews ducked through underbrush and climbed over and around the rotting trunks of fallen trees and through tangles of vines, his friend's gaze reflected the same triumphant light Carleton saw in the eyes of his warriors each time they returned from battle. And knew to be in his own. These raids had been Andrews's first experience of Indian warfare: striking an enemy in swift, deadly stealth from ambush, then withdrawing as swiftly to disappear into the forest keeps. Clearly he was finding it a revelation.

"Be careful, Charles," Carleton cautioned, "or it'll consume you."

"No more than you," Andrews flung back. "I've never noticed you holding back when it came to a fight."

"That's what I mean. When you go to war, you make a contract with the devil. Like Lady Macbeth, I wonder whether the blood can ever be washed from our hands."

For a time they strode together in silence, then Andrews muttered, "I've never seen fighting the likes of Morgan's and Poor's men on Friday."

"And Burgoyne's. Give the devil his due, Charles. At least Burgoyne fought at the head of his troops—unlike our own fearless commander."

"To be fair, Gates excels in administration and makes sure his men are well supplied," Andrews pointed out. "He did good service as Washington's adjutant general."

"I'll give you that," Carleton conceded. "I'm not so convinced he'll ever make an effective field commander, though."

Andrews gave a short laugh. "I question whether we'd have checked Burgoyne if Granny Gates had his way. If it hadn't been for General Arnold, he'd have let Burgoyne blunder into our lines, then simply played defense. Talk about the devil, Arnold's totally mad—or possessed."

"One has to be to fight a war." Feeling Andrews's narrowed gaze on him, Carleton kept on walking.

⊛ ⊛ ⊛

RIDING FAST AND HARD, on September 5 Carleton and his mounted troops had reached the Northern Army at Van Schaick's Island at the mouth of the Mohawk River. There, a little more than two years earlier, he and his companions had left the Hudson and turned their canoes into that tributary, following the stream northwestward on the way from Ticonderoga to Oriskany to begin negotiations for the Iroquois' support against the British.

From Albany every mile north had brought to Carleton's mind haunting images of the journey that ended in his capture and enslavement by the Seneca, then finally to rescue by the Shawnee, who had carried him ever farther west.

That the memories oppressed Andrews too had been apparent from his grim silence much of the way. He had never confided his emotions on that terrible day, when a brutal ambush had torn them away from each other, or the extent of the efforts he had made to find Carleton. Only an occasional comment or look since his return had told Carleton that his friend also had suffered much.

The Rangers had arrived at the Mohawk in time to meld into newly promoted Brigadier General Joshua Stern's Massachusetts brigade at the rear of Gates's army on their move upriver, first to Stillwater, then farther north. On September 10 the army had taken possession of the highest promontory in the area, where the Rangers' dismounted troops, baggage, and camp followers had caught up with them several days later. Known as Bemis Heights for the farmer who kept a tavern below on the Hudson's west bank, this broad, wooded plateau offered a magnificent panorama of forested ranges for miles in every direction, commanding the river valley a few miles south of a nondescript village called Saratoga.

Adding to the reinforcements Washington sent north, militia units continued to flood to Gates's standard, outraged by atrocities such as the murder in July of beautiful young Jane McCrae by Burgoyne's Indian allies while she traveled to her wedding, an act that galvanized opposition to the British across much of the country. By now Gates's force included more than 9,000 effectives, and at Bemis Heights he had chosen a defensive position beyond peer.

Beneath the heights a rutted wagon track, the only road to Albany for miles, ran along a constricted, well-defended defile entirely cleared of cover. The advancing British force would either have to pass down this road or traverse the ridges above it. The first choice would leave Burgoyne's army exposed to American artillery fire. The second would force them to grapple head-on with a rebel force that outnumbered them, in primeval forest laced with steep ravines and only occasional small clearings—terrain in which their disciplined formations and massed artillery would be at the greatest disadvantage.

Burgoyne had chosen the latter course, while shipping his supplies downriver. But although his officers chafed for action, Gates seemed determined to wait patiently for the British to blunder blindly into his fortifications. On Friday, September 19, as Burgoyne approached at the head of three columns in an attempt to reconnoiter the American lines, shadowed all the way by Carleton and his warriors, General Benedict Arnold had finally goaded his reluctant commander to allow him, Colonel Daniel Morgan, and Major Henry Dearborn to oppose the British advance.

Early in the afternoon the two armies collided at a small clearing known as Freeman's Farm. Bolstered by Brigadier General Enoch Poor's New Hampshire Continentals, the Americans initially staggered the British advance, but Burgoyne's force rallied and held back their attackers with bayonets and cannon fire. After a tense standoff, the rest of Poor's brigade came on the scene, and the action turned vicious as American sharpshooters began to do terrible execution, deliberately aiming for enemy officers.

All during that seemingly endless afternoon, Carleton had chafed under Gates's order to hold his Rangers in reserve. While the battle ebbed and flowed, he could only watch from the edge of the forest along with a number of other sidelined officers. From time to time he had made out Burgoyne and his generals, exposed to American fire at the head of their troops, while his own commander was nowhere in evidence.

For hours the fighting seesawed back and forth across the clearing, with infantry and artillery firing as fast as they could load. The wooded ridges magnified to deafening proportions the reverberation of musketry and cannon fire, which could be heard for miles.

Continually bolstered by fresh militia, Poor's and Morgan's detachments relentlessly winnowed the enemy's ranks until the sun hovered at the western treetops and Burgoyne's exhausted force stood amid piles of their dead and wounded. Had Stern's and Ebenezer Learned brigades not gone astray as they groped through the forest toward the battle, and the Brunswick troops of Major General von Riedesel not arrived to rescue the faltering British columns, a large part of Burgoyne's army might well have been obliterated. As it was, the casualties they suffered were twice the losses of the Americans—a staggering total that Burgoyne, far from his supply lines and any hope of reinforcement, could never replenish.

Twilight had at last descended on the devastation, and after a prolonged, sporadic exchange of gunfire, silence reigned. The Americans melted back into the forest shadows, leaving the British to endure a freezing night on the battlefield among the thickly scattered wounded and dead before slipping back to the safety of their camp the following morning.

In the days that followed, while Burgoyne's army dug in, Carleton's brigade, joined by Gates's Indian scouts, had begun their silent, deadly raids against parties sent out to scout or forage.

Denying the British both intelligence and desperately needed supplies, they took prisoners and plunder, brought in deserters in increasing numbers, and spread terror within the enemy force. They directed the unnerving fury of their efforts most effectively against the dwindling numbers of Indians who still remained with Burgoyne, and daily more abandoned him.

Hundreds of miles from their supply lines in unfamiliar terrain difficult to traverse, the British were surrounded by a force of Continentals and militia whose ranks, as their anger, were growing rapidly, who stood between them and either advance to Albany or retreat to the distant refuge of Ticonderoga, garrisoned by troops Burgoyne could dearly have used now.

Carleton's prophecy had come true: Burgoyne's early success had become his trap.

"ANOTHER SUCCESSFUL RAID, I see," observed Captain James McLeod in a thick Scottish burr when Carleton and his men returned to camp a couple of hours later. Giving Carleton a keen look, the chaplain tipped his head, eyebrow raised, the sun sparking his curly red hair to flame.

"It's only been a few days since the battle, but Burgoyne's men seem to be getting the message, if he isn't," Andrews responded. "The detachments they send out are growing considerably more cautious, and they're bringing along artillery."

"For whatever good it'll do them," Carleton put in, his jaw hardening. "They have to see us first, and so far they haven't."

"What's Burgoyne waitin' for?" McLeod asked. "Ye'd think he'd either ha' attacked or retreated by now."

Carleton considered him thoughtfully, arms folded. "Our intelligence indicates he's hoping either Howe or Clinton will come to the rescue. But Howe has his own troubles, and I doubt Clinton will leave New York undefended long enough to come this far. Burgoyne may not know it, but he's on his own."

McLeod rubbed his chin. "Hoist with his own petar."

"Quite."

Vander Groot approached from the direction of the hospital tent. "How many wounded, Jon?"

"Only a couple of ours. A considerable number of the enemy, though. You'll be busy through the night, I'm afraid. Do what you can for them."

Nodding to McLeod, Vander Groot motioned to those carrying the wounded, and the two men led the way to the hospital. Just then Gates strode past. Without slowing his stride or offering any acknowledgement, he directed a cold glance at Carlton, which he transferred to the warriors before hurrying into the cramped cabin that served as his headquarters.

"What does he hold against you?" Andrews growled. "Ever since we arrived, he's treated you like a pariah—not to mention making clear his disdain for the rest of us."

"Perhaps it's because we're not wearing proper uniform," Carleton quipped. "You have to admit a large, armed party of naked men in war paint can be somewhat off-putting."

"We're irregular troops. We fight like Indians. Didn't Washington think Gates was behind our reassignment for that very reason."

Carleton threw a calculating look after Gates's back. "Evidently his guess was wrong." He shrugged. "My impression is that Gates considers us renegades."

Andrews rolled his eyes. "Little does he know."

Just then General Benedict Arnold joined them, his pale grey eyes more intense than usual. Coupled with his swarthy skin, high, sloping forehead, prominent nose, and black hair, they lent him a sinister look. After dismissing Andrews to supervise the disposition of their prisoners and the captured weapons, Carleton turned to the general, eyebrows raised.

Arnold threw a quick glance around as though making sure no one was close enough to overhear their conversation before asking gruffly, "Have you a moment to talk?" When Carleton nodded, the general led him toward his cabin.

As he had often over the past week, Carleton admired the impressive network of defenses Gates's Polish engineer, Tadeusz Kosciuszko, had laid out. Batteries guarded the corner and center of each wall of the extensive three-sided breastwork, while a steep ravine at the rear made an attack from that quarter a virtual impossibility. Strong breastworks and batteries situated below the promontory to sweep an enemy advancing along the road or the river's opposite bank made it clear that the cost to overrun the American fortifications would be extreme.

Colonel Daniel Morgan intercepted them at Arnold's cabin. Characterized by a fiery temper, he was a huge bear of a man who in battle signaled his riflemen with a turkey call—a strange but effective device. A veteran of Braddock's disastrous campaign during the Seven Years War, he had lost the teeth on one side during the subsequent Indian wars when a bullet tore through his neck. In spite of crippling pain in his back and joints, he was universally acknowledged as the best backwoods fighter in the country.

Ushering them into his cabin, Arnold shut the door behind them before turning to Carleton. "Don't you get cold running around in the forest like that at night?"

Carleton regarded him with a frown, puzzled. "I don't think about it."

Arnold grabbed a linen towel from his washstand and pitched it to him. Carleton caught it in midair.

"This is what you wanted to talk about?" he said, with difficulty suppressing a laugh.

"No, no," Arnold responded brusquely. "Wipe the paint off, man—at least your face."

Morgan gave a deep-throated guffaw. "Thought you'd been 'round Indians long 'nough to get used to a little war paint, Bennie."

"Don't call me that!" Arnold snapped. He frowned at Carleton. "I have, but there's something about you Shawnee that's . . . " He made an impatient gesture.

"I know. Off-putting. That's our plan." As he scrubbed the black paint from his face, Carleton added, "Apparently Gates shares your feelings."

"I noticed he treats you the same as he does me, though you've all the fame, fortune, power, and position anyone could want," Arnold returned petulantly. "Unlike you, I've had to rely on sheer pluck and genius all my life."

Carleton bit back the response that sprang to his tongue.

"Even so, when I first arrived we seemed to get on famously," Arnold continued as though oblivious of the effect of his tirade, "but ever since the battle last Friday things have gone sour. I can't fathom why. If it hadn't been for me, our forces wouldn't have stirred out of camp."

"Gates didn't," Morgan put in.

Keeping his expression impassive, Carleton handed the towel, now stained with black paint, back to its owner. "Perhaps he feels threatened by your prowess on the battlefield. The whole camp's talking about it. Even worse, you maintain close relationships with not only Washington and Schuyler, but their friends as well. All reasons for jealousy on Gates's part."

Giving Carleton a resentful look, Arnold waved him and Morgan to the camp chairs in front of his table and flung himself into the one behind it. "Well, in that regard you've similar credentials, Carleton."

When they were seated, Arnold threw the stained towel back at Carleton and motioned to him to cover his privates. It was all Carleton could do to keep from enquiring whether Arnold felt threatened. Fighting the impulse to snicker, he draped the cloth across his lap, grinning at Morgan, who made no attempt to stifle his mirth.

Arnold seemed not to mark their amusement. "Gates is so . . . unimaginative. All he can think of—if he thinks at all—is defense."

"That's certainly not the case with you," Carleton said with a smile.

He noted that Arnold instantly preened himself. "I've never believed a war could be won by lurking behind breastworks, and I wanted to talk with both of you because I'm convinced you agree with me."

Ah, so we're to have a bit of intrigue, Carleton thought in amusement.

Arnold hesitated before continuing, "You heard Gates and I had quite a row last night?" When his guests indicated they had, he burst out, "He never so much as mentioned me in his report to Congress. Then in his orders this morning he removed your regiment from my command, Morgan, and put it directly under his."

Morgan nodded, his expression grave. "I knew nothing of it in advance."

"When I demanded an explanation, he told me he was unaware that I held any command in the army!" Arnold complained, livid with fury. "He's ordered Lincoln to return as division commander, whereupon he'll have no further use for me, he said. I've requested permission to return to Washington's corps."

Carleton wrestled down the thought that Arnold sounded like a whining child. "I don't blame you," he said, meaning it. "He's making a grave mistake to push aside an officer of your energy and enterprise merely for base personal motives. You're needed here, and I hope you'll reconsider leaving before the campaign's ended."

"Can't vouch for the rest, but I'll support you," Morgan broke in.

"So will I," Carleton said. "And I'm certain the majority of the officers will back us up."

Arnold let out his breath as though relieved. "Sooner or later Burgoyne's going to have to make a move. If I'm not here to take charge and it's left up to old Granny Gates, Burgoyne will sweep us out of his way, no matter the odds in our favor."

Considering Arnold's well-deserved reputation for arrogance, Carleton let the remark go with only a sidelong glance at Morgan, who returned a smirk.

The colonel soon excused himself. After he had gone, to Carleton's surprise Arnold thrust at him a full report on the situation around Philadelphia and along the Delaware River. After poring over it, Carleton looked up, frowning.

"Washington sends reports directly to you?"

"Well . . . it comes from one of his aides," Arnold admitted, his expression smug. "I get intelligence before Gates does, though he doesn't know it. Oh, there was something for you too." He rummaged through the papers on the table and finally tossed a sealed envelope to Carleton.

He instantly recognized Elizabeth's handwriting. Although his heart increased its pace, he allowed no evidence of his emotions to show, pleased that Arnold demonstrated no interest in the letter's sender or what its contents might be.

When Carleton returned to his cabin on the camp's outskirts, Stowe had a hot bath ready. Washed and dressed, as soon as his servant left him he eagerly broke open the letter's seal.

Dearest of my heart,

The reports that accompany this include the outcome of the battle looming when you left, which you've doubtless received by now. Our men fought valiantly—nothing more could have been asked—but the enemy's greater numbers finally told. Much has happened since then, and I fear another engagement is imminent that will determine the city's fate.

We are well, and if events do not conspire to keep us here longer, we hope to leave within days of your receipt of this. How I have longed to fly to your arms! I pray you and all those with you are safe and well and that God will keep you so.

Until I come, with all my love—

Though she had left it unsigned, she was as present with him as though he held her to his bosom, taking possession of his senses and breaking down the barricades he'd erected to keep the ceaseless longing for her at bay. He breathed a silent plea for her safety on her journey. After reading her words again to secure them in his memory, he carried the letter to the fireplace, laid it on the embers, and watched it flame, then dissolve into ash.

Chapter Twenty-seven

On the heels of the battle, chaos and fear gripped Philadelphia. Along the trampled roads leading to Brandywine Creek, weapons, haversacks, and all manner of military equipment lay as thick as mown hay in the fields.

For days a flood of American troops boiled through the city, and with them came large numbers of wounded. Elizabeth chafed at the lack of medical supplies and wished mightily that Vander Groot were there to assist in giving them aid. But Tess refused to allow her to leave the house, and Caleb forcefully backed her up.

Pushed back to the Schuylkill, Washington interposed his battered army between the British and the only passable fords. Rumors soon circulated that Congress had sent express riders in all directions to the militia commanders with orders for them to immediately send reinforcements, but Elizabeth wondered anxiously what good the militias could do even if they came.

After the initial panic subsided, she roamed along the river in disguise with Caleb and Pete as her constant companions. They saw American troops cutting the ropes of the ferries and tearing down the Schuylkill bridge. On Tuesday, September 16, they were again confined to the house while rain fell in torrents, heightening the gloom that hung over Philadelphia. Elizabeth consoled herself with the assurance that such a violent storm would make action impossible for both sides.

By Saturday the twentieth, with the two armies continuing to maneuver around each other as though playing a chess match and the last of Congress's members hastily departing for Lancaster, she and Caleb watched while American details dug through the river banks to flood the plain outside the city. Early the next day the soldiers began to strip the residents of food, wagons, horses and cattle, blankets, shoes, and all manner of supplies even to metals for casting armaments, including the bells from the churches. Caleb's stubborn resistance and the sight of Elizabeth's pass signed by Washington were all that saved Tess's coach and their horses from the foraging troops.

Reports that Howe's army had reached Swedes Ford on the far bank of the Schuylkill magnified the atmosphere of terror. With few horses and conveyances remaining, large numbers of residents in sympathy with the patriots fled on foot, bringing with them as many of their possessions as could be carried or pushed along in handcarts. By now much of the neighborhood around the town house stood dark and shuttered.

Unable to learn what was going on outside the city's boundaries, Elizabeth paced the floor. Every fiber cried out to head north to find Carleton, yet at the same time she feared to leave in case she might uncover some intelligence that could aid Washington.

Meanwhile, the days continued to drag out in anxious suspense.

"I'M SORRY I HAVE TO LEAVE so suddenly just now when it appears Cornwallis is poised to march into the city," Tess complained as she took a small case from Pete and set it into the coach.

"It can't be helped," Elizabeth assured her. "If Mr. Easton is as bad a manager as it appears from Perry's letter, you'll have quite a muddle to clear up when you get home. Don't worry about me and Caleb. We'll leave the moment it becomes too dangerous to stay."

It was early in the morning of what promised to be a fine day. The larger portion of their possessions had been shipped to Boston in the aftermath of the battle, and Sarah and Jemma bustled in and out of the house, carrying the remaining boxes and parcels, which Caleb and Pete secured on the roof of the coach or tucked inside.

Distracted, Tess pressed her fingers to her temples. "Your father was certain he was the best man to oversee rebuilding Stony Hill. But if Perry's right," she said, referring to the caretaker of her estate in Roxbury, "I'll have to remove him and hire someone more trustworthy. Bother!"

"You're the right person for the job," Elizabeth teased. "If Papa arrived to find all gone awry, he'd simply shout at everyone, and nothing would get done."

Tess chuckled. "I may do the same. Thankfully your parent's ship doesn't sail until tomorrow, and they won't reach Boston for at least a month. That should give me time enough to set things back on course."

She gave Elizabeth a stern look. "There's no telling what the conclusion of this dance between Washington and Howe will be, but I'm afraid it'll end badly. Promise me you won't wait any longer to find out what happens. With everyone fleeing the city and the British rumored to march in within a few days, I'll worry every minute until you're safely away from here."

Elizabeth gave her aunt an impulsive hug. "Caleb's more than able to protect me, and I've the Vander Groots' cook and butler and Isobel's maid to look after my needs until we leave for Albany. Believe me, I'm as anxious to get away as you are."

"I'm sure you are, considering the warm welcome you'll have when you get to Gates's camp," Tess said with a smile. "You'll take a ship up the Hudson?"

"It's the fastest and easiest route. Jonathan recommended it, and we can stay with the Martins at Dobbs Ferry while we make arrangements for passage. Now don't worry!"

After they had all embraced and said their goodbyes, Caleb helped Tess, Sarah, and Jemma inside the coach. Elizabeth turned to Pete.

Studying his countenance, she murmured, "Why are you sad? You should be excited at the opportunity to finally go to sea as you've longed for."

Staring down the deserted alley behind the carriage house, he shifted from one foot to the other. "I keep thinking about Sammy," he said in a muffled voice.

She laid her hand on his arm, tears starting to her eyes. "I miss him too. And Will. We've lost so many good men."

"Sometimes it feels awful lonely," he said, his expression bleak. "He's gone, and if anything happens to me, Ma and Pa . . . " He let the words trail off.

"Don't think that. God keep you safe, Pete! I don't know what I'll do once you're gone. You, your family—you've all blessed me incredibly. I couldn't have done any of this without you."

He gave a faint smile, and she tiptoed to kiss his cheek. In the last year he'd grown rapidly, and he towered over her now.

"Thank you," she whispered, fighting tears. "For everything. Godspeed."

For a moment he embraced her, then stepping away, he climbed up to the driver's seat and gathered the reins. The coach rolled forward and turned into the lane.

"I'll see you in Boston in a few weeks!" she cried, waving at the women who leaned out of the coach's windows for a last goodbye. Standing beside Caleb and trying hard not to feel abandoned, she watched until they disappeared from sight.

❂ ❂ ❂

"OH, MY DEAR ELIZABETH, I was beginning to think I'd never see you again!" Betsey Loring exclaimed dramatically, bustling across the foyer as Elizabeth descended the stairs. "You can't imagine how appallingly dull it's been in New York since everyone went off for no reason at all that I can tell! What's been accomplished? Just more battles and the capture of this quaint city! What a to-do!"

Greatly taken aback, Elizabeth dipped in a hasty curtsey, which Betsey returned with a languid one. Thinking of the two bags in her chamber upstairs, which she had just finished packing for a hasty departure, Elizabeth stifled a sigh of frustration. Howe's mistress was the last person she had expected or wanted to see.

"I . . . was astonished when you were announced," she said truthfully. "How ever did you get through all this confusion?"

Betsey flipped open her fan and waved it languidly to cool her flushed cheeks. "One can accomplish anything when one's determined, and no one is more so than me," she said loftily. Her tone turned petulant. "The past few weeks have been so wanting for entertainment that I even began attending the Coldens' soirees. If that isn't desperation, I can't imagine what is! I finally couldn't endure it any longer and thought I might as well languish here as in New York—and then I thought of you and your aunt!"

Sensing a peculiar strain in the older woman's manner, Elizabeth decided it must be the effect of the disorder that held sway over the city. "I apologize Aunt Tess isn't here to greet you. She left for Boston yesterday. Arrangements for my parents' homecoming have all gone awry, and she was wanted immediately to straighten things out."

"One must do things oneself if they're to be done right," Betsey returned with an airy wave of her hand. "But you stayed behind!"

Thinking fast, Elizabeth did her best to appear weak. "There's been a fever going about, and I've felt ill most of the week. but I'm much better now and hope to follow Aunt Tess within a few days." Leading the way into the parlor, she led Betsey to the sofa and sat beside her.

"Do you think it safe to be here all alone? I know for a fact that Lord Cornwallis plans to march into the city tomorrow morning. Naturally our soldiers would never do anything untoward, but—"

Of course they wouldn't, Elizabeth thought. "I'm not so sure of that, Betsey. Rumors are flying that the city's to be set to the torch, and watch companies were formed last night for defense. They're setting up blockades and dragging cannon into the streets."

"Oh, that's what those men were about!" Betsey exclaimed. "They needn't go to the trouble. I promise you, no one will be hurt and the city will remain unscathed. It's the Liberty Boys I'm concerned about. One never knows what they might do."

Elizabeth gave her visitor a guarded look. "I'm quite well protected, have no fear. Our butler, Mr. Stern, is a dead shot." Smiling sweetly she added, "How long will you stay? Are you lodging with His Excellency?"

"I am, but he's not coming in for some time, and he'll not be settled enough at his new headquarters for me to join him until tomorrow."

"Oh, I assumed he'd personally take possession of the city," Elizabeth said innocently, wide-eyed. "His headquarters isn't far away, I hope."

"Oh . . . somewhere north of here," Betsey responded vaguely. She glanced brightly around. "How charming your little house is!" She tipped her head and reached to pat Elizabeth's hand. "I hoped it wouldn't be inconvenient for me and my servants to stay the night."

It was the worst Elizabeth had feared. Concealing her dismay, she forced a warm smile. "I'd be delighted to have your company, of course."

"Lovely! I've so looked forward to visiting with you, dear, and now we'll have plenty of time to catch up. But tomorrow morning we'll have to go down and watch the army march into the city. No doubt it'll be the best entertainment of the year!"

How will we ever leave now? Once Cornwallis marches in, he'll set guards at every road out of the city!

Murmuring her agreement, Elizabeth called Caleb and directed him to prepare rooms for Betsey and her party. While they were occupied settling in, he assured her quietly that he and Isobel's maid had secured their baggage in the loft of the carriage house at the rear of the property where no one would accidentally come upon it.

It was all Elizabeth could do to contain her disappointment. She had hoped that by now she and Caleb would be well on the way to Trenton and the ferries across the Delaware. The prospect of spending the rest of the day with her visitor while she crowed over Cornwallis's triumph on the morrow was almost more than Elizabeth could bear.

ELIZABETH UNCONSCIOUSLY PRESSED her hand to her bosom as three immaculately uniformed horsemen cantered up Second Street toward where she and Betsey stood at the edge of the noisy crowd. The beautifully accoutered steeds pranced as though putting on a show for the onlookers as they swept by.

Behind the horsemen trotted a large body of light horse. The rest of the army followed in a line that stretched back down the street and out of Elizabeth's sight. The blinding midday sun intensified the brilliant colors of the uniforms and glittered across polished swords, muskets, and bayonets. Every face was grave, every eye turned forward as the ranks advanced in perfect step.

By the time the first units had passed, the street was so filled with soldiers that those on its edge had to pull back as far as possible to avoid being trampled. British grenadiers succeeded the light horse and were followed by a long train of artillery.

The contrast between this professional force and the volunteer corps that had preceded them a month earlier could not have been more calculated to squelch resistance, Elizabeth thought. As she scanned the excited, cheering crowd that jostled around her and Betsey, many of them waving small British flags, while others threw flowers at the soldiers, all calling out to them as though they were saviors, her heart sank.

The shrill pipe of fifes and harsh rattle of drums drew her attention back to the street as a large, brightly uniformed band stalked by, playing "God save Great George, Our King." With Betsey bouncing on her toes beside her, Elizabeth curved her lips into a broad smile by sheer force of will and joined in waving vigorously at Lord Cornwallis and the city's prominent loyalists who followed in the band's wake.

By the time the sun had reached its zenith and begun its slow descent, she had concluded that the parade would never end. The effect was numbing—a very deliberate show of power meant to intimidate. And accomplishing its purpose.

A closer look revealed that most of the common soldiers wore faded clothes threadbare in places, and shoes scuffed and badly worn. Their uniforms were clean, however, and although some of the men were wan and weary, they appeared healthy enough.

Advancing up the street came another train of artillery followed by Hessian grenadiers and another large band. Chewing her lip, Elizabeth threw a dispirited glance across the street . . . and met Chastity's smug gaze. The breath went out of her.

What's she doing here? Aunt Tess said she promised not to bother me again, yet she acts as though she meant to find me.

Hastily Elizabeth caught Betsey's arm and suggested they return to the town house for luncheon. To her relief, the older woman eagerly agreed.

For Elizabeth, the hours that followed were a puzzle fraught with anxiety over the unexpected appearance of the two women. With her usual robust appetite Betsey devoured the luncheon the Vander Groots' cook supplied, gossiped about their mutual acquaintances in New York, and asked about the Vander Groots in detail. When they left the table for the parlor, she questioned Elizabeth about when Tess had gone, when her parents were expected home, how arrangements were faring, and the plans Elizabeth had made for the journey to Boston.

It all seemed very innocent, nothing unusual for Betsey, who, Elizabeth had long ago concluded, was an incurable gossip. But the afternoon left her strangely uneasy, and she answered Betsey's questions in the most general terms. She had to conceal her delight when the older woman finally said her goodbyes a little after four o'clock and fluttered out the door with her entourage in tow.

She felt compelled to watch from behind the parlor curtains until the elegant coach and four disappeared down the street. For a moment she pondered whether Betsey had harbored a concealed motive in her visit, but if so, she couldn't fathom what it might have been.

She became aware that there was no gunfire or any noise of disorder or alarm in the vicinity. Concluding that the brave show of the watch companies the previous day had been just that, she dismissed her concerns about both Betsey and Chastity and hastened to find Caleb.

DECIDING THEY MUST LEAVE that night while there was still a possibility of finding an unguarded exit from the city, they finished their preparations with all haste. After she had paid and dismissed the Vander Groots' servants, Elizabeth hurriedly arrayed herself in masculine dress, then ran to the carriage house. Caleb was waiting impatiently, the horses saddled and loaded with their packs.

With dusk, complete calm had settled over the town. The residents who remained had apparently taken refuge in their houses, and night descended with unbroken peace. Avoiding the common, now occupied by a sprawling camp, they led their horses as quietly as possible along the most deserted streets, where shuttered houses testified that their occupants had fled.

The previous day, while Elizabeth entertained Mrs. Loring, Caleb had carefully scouted the north end to locate all routes of escape the British might leave unguarded. Hessian grenadiers were posted at the end of the first two lanes they crept down, and they turned back, taking care to attract no attention, grateful that the waning moon had not yet risen.

Cautiously Caleb led the way to a narrow, dusty track that cut across a darkly shadowed meadow behind one of the newer neighborhoods at the city's edge. To their great relief, it lay deserted.

As soon as they were well clear of the town, they swung into the saddle and spurred their horses to a gallop, following the broad Delaware north toward the Trenton ferries. From there long miles lay before them, across New Jersey to Dobbs Ferry, by ship up the Hudson to Albany, then yet farther north to Gates's camp in the vast wilderness beyond.

Yet as her thoughts sped in happy anticipation to where Carleton was, the miles between them seemed to Elizabeth no distance at all.

Chapter Twenty-eight

SHE RETURNED HIS KISSES and caresses hungrily, the heat of his passion burning away the weariness and cold of the long, fast journey north journey like a blazing fire. Gazing deep into his eyes, she touched his face, and he kissed her fingertips, her palm, her wrist, then buried his fingers in her loosened hair, cupping her head with both hands as he found her mouth again. When he finally pulled back, she was rosy and breathless.

Her arms around his waist, she looked up at him, heart overflowing. "How I love you!" she whispered. "How I've missed you!"

"Every moment you're gone from me is the worst torture I can conceive," he groaned, caressing her cheek. "We learned yesterday that General Clinton is on his way to attack the forts on the Hudson's highlands, and I've been terrified ever since that you and Caleb would run into his fleet on your way north."

She pulled his head down to hers and kissed him deeply, finally released him with a sigh. "We didn't encounter any British force or hear any rumors of an attack, so we must have been a little ahead of him."

"I thought you'd never get here!"

"We didn't mean to stay so long, but Washington and Howe have been playing a chess match around Philadelphia ever since Brandywine, so we waited to see what developed. But after Aunt Tess was called back to Boston and Cornwallis marched into the city, we felt it too dangerous to stay longer."

Releasing her, he listened, tight-lipped, while she described the exodus from the city and Congress's removal to Lancaster, then followed with an account of Cornwallis's parade into Philadelphia and the efforts General and Lord Howe were making to break through American defenses guarding the Delaware. She began to tell him about Betsey Loring's strange visit, but thought better of it.

"Believe me, Philadelphia is no great loss," Carleton told her, pacing up and down the small one-room cabin. "Howe will find it as draining to his resources as Ticonderoga is to Burgoyne."

He came to capture her in his arms, and for some moments they were again lost in kisses and caresses that left her trembling. "It's been torture only knowing the little you could send by courier—which I'm grateful for, though you took a risk in doing it." he chided at length, giving her a stern look.

"No more risk than Washington's reports were subject to," she protested with a smile. "But how do you think I felt? I'd not even that much, though we received Gates's report about the battle on the nineteenth. How goes it now? Has there been more action?"

Capturing her hand, he drew her to a camp chair and pulled his beside it. "Only for my warriors. We've all but shut down the enemy's efforts to scout and forage. According to the prisoners and deserters we've collected, their situation is desperate. They've reduced rations by a third. Burgoyne can't dally here much longer. We keep expecting him either to make another push or withdraw toward Fort Edward, but it's already the fourth of October, and he's still holed up in his camp."

"Surely he can't mean to stay here for the winter!" she exclaimed.

"He has to know his army will starve and freeze if he does. If the reports about Clinton moving up the Hudson are true, then doubtless he's waiting for rescue, but, alas, that isn't going to happen."

They talked for a while longer, then Carleton sent for Vander Groot. While they waited, Elizabeth hastily tamed her loosened hair and again covered it securely with her brown wig and battered hat.

Captain McLeod accompanied the doctor, and they conferred for some minutes, finally agreeing that, as Dr. Robbie McLeod, the chaplain's cousin, Elizabeth would serve as Vander Groot's assistant at the hospital. It was a pose that would not only allow her to be useful, but also give her the run of the camp, while guarding her true identity from exposure. With a sly wink, McLeod volunteered to drill her in an authentic Scottish brogue, an offer she readily accepted over Carleton's and Vander Groot's teasing and laughter.

Later that evening, stretched out on the grass between Andrews's and Spotted Pony's tents, Carleton lazily watched her visiting with Blue Sky, her friend Mary, and the other Shawnee women. His heart swelled to see them all chattering with one another as naturally as though she belonged to them. As she did.

How he longed to see her in a fine gown and jewels, her glorious dark auburn curls piled high. Or, equally, in the bright dress of a young Shawnee bride.

In the midst of war and violence there was, at least for this moment, a sweet peace that brought healing to his soul. The only thing that could have made it more complete was if they were free to share one bed. But while she stayed, Elizabeth would sleep in a tent next to Mary's—undoubtedly wise since the young widow appeared to be ready to deliver her baby at any moment—and he was resolved to be content in her nearness.

He turned his attention to Caleb, who sat nearby, deep in conversation with Andrews, Red Fox, and several others. The more time Carleton spent with the younger Stern, the more he was drawn to Elizabeth's soft-spoken, intense cousin and trusted his care for her safety. If Caleb's service to her was not so essential, especially now that Pete had joined his privateers, Carleton reflected, he'd solicit him to serve as his aide along with Red Fox. The two men seemed to get along well, and Caleb had volunteered to serve with the Rangers until he and Elizabeth left for Boston. The way the brigade was developing, Carleton would need a couple more aides very soon to manage administration—a chore he chafed at.

His musings were interrupted by Louis Teissèdre, his rotund, bald-pated French agent, who came to sit beside him, pewter cup of wine in hand. *"Vous n'êtes pas toujours un homme facile à trouver, general,"* he grumbled. You are not always an easy man to find. "I expected to meet you in Philadelphia only to discover that you had exchanged civilization for this barbaric wasteland."

Grimacing, Carleton sat up, cross-legged. "That's why I employ you, Louis," he said in the same language. "You're one of the most resourceful men I know."

"Bah, you flatter me!" cried the Frenchman jovially. "But we waste time. My constitution can only endure these primitive conditions for so long, after all, and I have every intention of heading south tomorrow for friendlier climes. Therefore, to business!"

For the next half hour, Carleton listened intently to a detailed recital of his accounts and the location of each of his merchant ships and the cargoes they had delivered or were to take on. Teissèdre followed up with an equally detailed report on the ships that had been converted to privateers. *Destiny,* he told Carleton, had arrived in Salem a month earlier with a rich prize she had taken on the way from Nantes. The last he head heard, she was now patrolling off Nova Scotia.

Carleton's eyebrows rose. "Nantes? What was she doing there?"

Teissèdre gave a Gallic shrug. "Her captain found a detour necessary to bring to the prize court a fat British merchantman she captured on the way from Marseilles." He added that he had learned on arriving at Philadelphia that the *Invictus* was on her way to Marblehead with a sloop she had taken off the Azores. "Between the two," he concluded expansively, "their crews, to say nothing of you, will be much enriched."

Just then Vander Groot strode between the tents to where Elizabeth sat with the women, and bent to speak with her. After a moment she rose, and together they approached Carleton.

Getting to his feet, Carleton bid Teissèdre godspeed on his travels and dismissed him. When the Frenchman had gone, he turned to Elizabeth and Vander Groot.

"The condition of one of our prisoners has worsened," the doctor explained. "He needs immediate surgery. I know Beth—ah, that is to say, my new assistant, Dr. McLeod—has just arrived, but he's willing to assist me, if that's all right with you."

The doctor's smirk drew a chuckle from Carleton. "Certainly, if you're up to it," he said to Elizabeth.

"I am, and I might as well get started."

Vander Groot smiled down at her, then quickly directed a tentative glance at Carleton. "I'll make sure she doesn't get overtired."

"Beth makes her own decisions, in case you don't know it by now," Carleton responded, with a muffled laugh. "I hope you can do the man some good."

Vander Groot relaxed and nodded. Turning to Elizabeth, he said briskly, "We'd better hurry, then. We're dealing with an infection in addition to . . . "

Directing a glowing smile at Carleton, Elizabeth hurried off with Vander Groot.

Warmth spread through Carleton as he watched until they moved out of his sight, their heads together, conferring while they walked. It seemed to him that at last all his world was in as perfect harmony as was possible in the midst of war.

Chapter Twenty-nine

IT WAS EARLY AFTERNOON, Tuesday October 7, when Carleton stepped into the rough log cabin that served as General Gates's headquarters. His superior raised his head from the papers in front of him on the camp table long enough to give Carleton a cursory glance, then returned his attention to the requisitions he was signing.

Holding his annoyance in check with difficulty, Carleton saluted. "Sir, Red Fox and his men just came in. They've been shadowing a sizeable detachment moving in this direction. Burgoyne's personally leading them, and they're bringing along ten field pieces."

Gates threw down his pen and looked up as his twenty-year-old aide, Colonel James Wilkinson burst through the door. The supercilious glance the colonel directed Carleton heightened his dislike of the man.

He had just returned from the advance guard, Wilkinson reported. From a low rise about half a mile outside the camp's breastworks, he had watched several columns of the enemy approach, enter an uncut wheat field, and sit down, while foragers began to cut the wheat.

"Several of their officers climbed onto the roof of a small cabin carrying spyglasses, apparently attempting to reconnoiter our left, though I doubt they can make out our lines through the woods."

Gates's interest now seemed miraculously engaged. "What would you say are their intentions?"

"I think, sir, they offer you battle."

Gates's eyes narrowed. "What's the nature of the ground, and how, in your opinion, ought we to respond?"

Ignoring Wilkinson's smug look, Carleton held his tongue.

Wilkinson gave an elaborate shrug. "Their front is open, their flanks rest on woods that provide cover for an attack, and their right is skirted by a lofty height. I'd indulge them."

Gates rubbed his hands together. "Order Morgan to begin the game."

As Wilkinson saluted and turned to leave, Carleton interjected quickly, "Sir, I'll be more than happy to support Morgan if you please."

Wilkinson came to a halt and glanced back, his upper lip curled, while Gates tipped up his head to regard Carleton over his glasses. "I've no objection if you want to take a couple of your troops along, general—as long as Morgan can use you. I'll leave the decision to him."

Throttling the thought that he outranked Morgan, Carleton gave Gates a crisp salute, turned on his heel, and brushed past Wilkinson without an acknowledgement. He preceded the colonel out the door, not bothering to determine whether he followed.

Morgan turned out to be more than happy to have Carleton join the enterprise. After Wilkinson had outlined the disposition of the British detachment, Morgan proposed that his riflemen, bolstered by Major Henry Dearborn's light infantry and Carleton's Rangers, circle around the American left and climb the heights, from there to fall upon the enemy's right flank. Carleton suggested that General Poor's brigade initiate the action by moving against the British front and left. To this they all agreed, and while Wilkinson scuttled off to secure Gates's approval, Carleton and Morgan went to form up their men.

BLUE SKY STOOD BEFORE HIM, head held high, one hand resting on her swollen abdomen. Forcing a smile, Andrews placed his hand over hers.

"Our son must sleep," he murmured. "He is quiet."

Her smile matched his, but he saw the sheen of moisture in her eyes. "Moneto cover you with his wings in the battle and bring you safely back to us again."

"And you," he said hoarsely, his throat painfully tight. "Both of you."

He felt a hand on his shoulder and turned to meet Carleton's sympathetic gaze. Elizabeth moved past him to slip her arm around Blue Sky's waist.

Andrews glanced beyond the gathering crowd of officers and soldiers to the troops he had left on the open parade ground at the camp's center, standing at attention as they waited to march out with Morgan's riflemen. At the insistent rattle of drums, he embraced Blue Sky and pressed a kiss on the crown of her head. Then he hurried after Carleton, silently echoing her prayer.

WATCHING THE RANGERS file out of the camp, Elizabeth bit her lip hard, a lump forming in her throat. She could not watch Carleton stride away from her and kept her gaze on Blue Sky, who blinked back her tears, her lips compressed.

When the last of the troops disappeared through the camp gates, Blue Sky drew in a deep breath, and turning to Elizabeth, gave a firm nod. "Has not Moneto always watched over them? We have nothing to fear, Healer Woman."

Gratitude for her adoptive sister's faith overwhelmed Elizabeth. She had taken Blue Sky's courage as her example in parting from Carleton, and now she resolved to meet the coming hours with equal fortitude.

"How's Mary doing?"

"She is weak but stronger than last night. I will stay with her until the men return."

Elizabeth gave her a keen look, wondering whether the young widow's difficult labor and delivery the previous day troubled her. "I was so grateful Laughing Otter was with me to help stop her hemorrhaging. She'll be fine with rest," she added reassuringly.

Blue Sky forced a smile, but a slight frown creased her brow. "Her son is small."

"He's strong, though, and he's nursing well, which is a good sign." Elizabeth gave Blue Sky a quick hug. "Moneto will watch over them too. Now, I'll be at the hospital. Send Sweetgrass if you need me."

She started toward the other end of the camp but stopped abruptly when she heard a gasp behind her. Whirling around, she saw Blue Sky clutching her belly and looking down, wide-eyed, at the water that puddled between her outspread feet.

FROM HIS PERCH BESIDE RED FOX atop a rocky outcrop shaded by a thick canopy of trees, Carleton could make out the flash of red uniforms and glitter of bayonets moving through the woods directly below at the base of the precipice. Satisfied that the British right flank remained unaware of his and Morgan's force, he estimated that the entire enemy detachment numbered little more than 1,500 men, not including the artillery.

Clearly Burgoyne had to be not only desperate, but also ignorant of how heavily he was outnumbered if he intended to provoke a battle with such an insignificant force when he still had more than 5,000 men at his disposal. At the same time, Carleton was too familiar with the British army's discipline and professionalism to underestimate the threat the detachment posed.

The sudden roar of cannon and musket fire signaled that Poor's brigade had engaged the British center and left. Immediately Morgan sounded his turkey call, setting his riflemen into motion. At the same instant Carleton and Red Fox raised their rifles and gave throat to the unnerving Shawnee battle cry.

As one, they cascaded down the hill in a torrent, riflemen, Rangers, and warriors sweeping away enemy scouts to collide with the British right in a staggering shock. Between the trees ahead of him, almost obscured by a thick cloud of gun smoke, Carleton made out Poor's New Hampshiremen clambering over a fence and charging a body of grenadiers. Their hoarse screams reached him over the rapidly swelling din of battle.

The British light infantry in their path scrambled desperately to change front, but like a floodtide, the oncoming Americans swept them back in complete disarray.

THE MURMUR OF THE WOMEN'S VOICES stilled. Instinctively they all turned toward the sudden thunder of cannon fire.

Kneeling beside Mary's pallet, her movements suspended, Elizabeth could clearly make out beneath the cannon's deeper boom the roar of musket volleys, punctuated by the sharper crack of rifles. As her glance met Rain Woman's stern one, she forced her hands to steady. With what calmness she could muster, she finished her examination of the new mother, then tucked the blankets around her, while Rain Woman returned the swaddled infant to Mary's arms.

As soon as she realized Blue Sky's water had broken, Elizabeth had taken her to Laughing Otter, then hurried to inform the two assistants left in charge of the hospital. She assured them it would likely be some time before any casualties were brought in and promised to check in on them frequently. After directing them to send for her if necessary, she rushed to the small wigewa the Shawnee women had insisted be built a short distance from the warriors' camp, where they could manage both Mary's and Blue Sky's labor and delivery according to their customs.

By the time Elizabeth returned, Rain Woman and Sweetgrass had joined Laughing Otter. The three women were taking turns pacing up and down outside with Blue Sky while her contractions strengthened.

Struggling to block out the clash of battle, which from the sound was swiftly expanding from right to left beyond the camp's breastworks, Elizabeth again focused on her patient. Dark circles beneath the young widow's eyes heightened her pallor, but as she returned her fretting son to her breast, she gave Elizabeth a wan smile.

"He'll be all right, won't he?"

Watching the infant suckle eagerly, Elizabeth reassured her that he would. But worry still shadowed Mary's delicate features.

"I didn't take into account being laid up for so long. The army'll turn me out if I don't get back to work right soon."

"You have friends here," Elizabeth said firmly, "and you'll always have a place. We'll make sure of that."

Mary clutched Elizabeth's hand. "I felt so alone when my Jimmy was taken, but the Lord give me Blue Sky for a friend, and then these Indian women, and now ye. It's like I have a family again."

Swallowing the lump in her throat, Elizabeth murmured, "You do, and you don't ever need to be afraid of being left alone again."

Reassured, Mary relaxed against her pillow and gazed down at her son with a look akin to adoration. "Ye didn't know my Jimmy, but this boy looks just like 'im—dark headed 'n all. I been missin' 'im so much all these months, but now I got his son it's like he's been given back to me."

When Elizabeth laid her hand on the young woman's shoulder, Mary looked up. "Blue Sky and her baby're goin' to be all right," she said fiercely. "And Colonel Andrews and Gen'el Carleton too. I know yer hearts're entwined," she added with a keen look as the color rose to Elizabeth's cheeks, "and the good Lord'll keep ye both safe."

Impulsively Elizabeth bent to kiss her forehead.

"I warrant ye look right pretty all dressed up in a gown and jewels," Mary whispered, giving Elizabeth a wink.

Stifling a giggle, Elizabeth rose and went outside to check on Blue Sky. She found her and Laughing Otter crouched beside the fire. The day was cool, but Blue Sky's cheeks were flushed, and she rubbed her belly, rocking back and forth.

Elizabeth stooped beside her. "The pains are getting stronger and closer together?"

Nodding, Blue Sky stifled a low moan.

Laughing Otter shook her head. "I tell her she must walk more."

"I grow tired," Blue Sky said with a sigh. But she heaved herself to her feet.

"I'll walk with her for a while," Elizabeth told Laughing Otter, and with Blue Sky leaning on her arm, they resumed the slow circuit of the tent.

STAGGERED BY THE FORCE OF THE ATTACK, the British line was on the point of collapse when an officer rushed forward to rally them. As they began to form up behind a fence, movement off to his right drew Carleton's attention, and he turned to see Arnold gallop into the center of the surging Americans, his eyes wild, hair and uniform in disarray.

Andrews ran up, as fouled with gunpowder and sweat as Carleton knew he must be. "What in thunder is he doing here?" the colonel shouted over the crash of weapons and screams of men and horses. "I thought Gates relieved him of his command!"

"I wonder if Gates knows he's here!" Carleton shouted back, signaling to Isaiah to bring his troop forward.

Sighting his rifle from behind a tree, Carleton fired at the oncoming light infantry and swiftly reloaded. Andrews followed suit, while Isaiah's troop spread out to either side and unleashed a devastating volley.

When Carleton started forward, General Simon Fraser jerked his tall grey horse to a halt a short distance ahead, cutting him off. Renowned as a fierce fighter, the imposing Scottish officer shouted to his light infantry to cover the retreat of the Brunswick troops at the British center, which had once more given way under a savage assault by Poor's New Hampshire brigade.

Before Carleton could order his men to attack, from behind him he heard Arnold shout to Morgan over the din, "Fraser's a fair target for a sharpshooter! Cut him down!"

Carleton glanced over his shoulder to see one of Morgan's men immediately begin to work his way up a tree, his rifle slung over his shoulder. He had just turned back when another of Gates's aides, Major John Armstrong, blocked Arnold's path. The two men exchanged hot words, then, waving Armstrong peremptorily out of his way, Arnold spurred his horse back into the fray.

ELIZABETH RUSHED BACK to the birthing wigewa from another circuit to the hospital. The heavy pall of battle hung over the camp, but each time fearful thoughts intruded, she forced herself to focus on the task at hand. In the past hour she and her assistants had set a couple of broken limbs, dug out several musket balls, and stitched up and bandaged an assortment of wounds.

She found Blue Sky inside, in hard labor, squatted on a blanket and supported by Laughing Otter, while from her pallet Mary murmured encouragement. Panting, her face drenched with sweat, Blue Sky looked up at Elizabeth in mute appeal, a trace of blood on her lip where she had bitten through the skin.

Other than an occasional deep moan or guttural grunt, however, she made no sound.

THE BRITISH CENTER WAS IN FULL FLIGHT, scrambling for the haven of their own breastworks while Dearborn's light infantry threw themselves into the breach. Racing forward in the van of his troops, with the British breastworks in view, Carleton made out Burgoyne amid the press ahead of him, heard him order his soldiers back into the two formidable redoubts that guarded the right of the British fortifications.

Nose and throat burning from the acrid stench of gun smoke, head pounding with the repeated volleys of weapons and beat of drums, Carleton came to a halt as Burgoyne cast an assessing look in his direction. Certain he could not make him out in the press of troops, Carleton ignored the hail of musket balls that sizzled through the air to every side, flicking his fringed buckskin shirt at several points, and raised his rifle to sight down the barrel's length.

Before he could pull off the shot, however, Fraser's soldiers advanced between him and Burgoyne. Feeling a strange sense of relief, Carleton discharged the shot into the roiling mass.

With a wild yell Red Fox, Spotted Pony, and their warriors ran by him to throw themselves into the melee, wielding knives and tomahawks with fearsome skill. As Fraser galloped over, shots rang out from overhead, and the general jerked powerfully in the saddle. Blood spurted from a wound to his abdomen.

Glancing up into the tree Morgan's sharpshooter had climbed minutes earlier, Carleton saw the man lower his weapon, eyes narrowed with satisfaction.

ELIZABETH COULD FEEL THE TOP of the baby's head almost completely exposed now, the surface expanding with each contraction. With a wet towel, Sweetgrass wiped Blue Sky's face. Supported on either side by Laughing Otter and Rain Woman, Blue Sky gasped and grimaced, then again bent her head as another contraction bore over her.

"Push!" Laughing Otter commanded.

Letting out a deep groan, Blue Sky obeyed, and kneeling in front of her, Elizabeth grasped the infant's emerging head and shoulders. "Once more!" she said urgently.

This time the baby slipped free, a boy, she saw as she placed him on the blanket Sweetgrass held out. She tipped him upside down and quickly cleared his nose and mouth. He gave a convulsive kick and let out a lusty wail, warm, dusky color washing away his pallor as he drew breath.

"You have a son, Blue Sky!" she cried, gazing in delight at the squirming infant in her arms, "Oh, how beautiful he is!"

Trembling, Blue Sky echoed her laughter, while the other women happily joined in.

DUSK WAS GATHERING under the trees when Arnold again shouted to the brigades around him to follow, and led them at the British breastworks as though he meant to drive straight through the abatis. Furious volleys from the fortification's defenders dropped wounded across the clearing, and the Americans staggered back.

Rifle in one hand, medical kit in the other, Vander Groot broke through the surge of infantry, with McLeod beside him clearing a path for Caleb and the doctor's assistant, who bore between them a bleeding soldier. "Arnold's a madman," Vander Groot shouted at Andrews.

For a moment all of them stood suspended in astonishment, while, as though oblivious of danger or reason, Arnold galloped the length of the battle line, somehow miraculously avoiding a bullet, pulled up short on the Rangers' right, and peremptorily appropriated command of General Learned's brigade. At their head he immediately drove toward a small force guarding a pair of stockaded cabins between the two British redoubts.

"It isn't only himself he's going to get killed!" Andrews answered, furious.

Shaking their heads, the doctor and his small party disappeared toward the rear.

Andrews ordered his detachment against the British center to cut off the last of the enemy soldiers who still clawed their way toward the safety of their fortifications. But before his troops could turn their front, Arnold was back again. This time he pointed his sword dramatically at the farthest redoubt, by now teeming with a strong force of the enemy. Screaming for the riflemen and Rangers to follow him, he galloped toward the sally port with Morgan's cheering regiment surging along.

To Andrews's dismay, his Rangers instinctively turned and started into motion after the general. Uttering every curse he could think of, Andrews forced his way back through the detachment to block their advance. He reached the van just as Carleton did, and together they reformed the line and advanced against the staggering British.

Andrews looked back in time to see Arnold lying on the ground, clutching his leg and doubled over in agony. Around him sprawled a number of wounded and dead.

By now daylight was failing, and with the abruptness of an extinguished lamp, night cast its dark veil over the forest. The remainder of Burgoyne's force had taken refuge behind their breastworks, and finally, exhausted, both sides stumbled to a halt where they were.

By slow degrees the firing subsided, giving way to the muffled groans and cries of the wounded. After conferring with Carleton, Andrews ordered his weary men back into the verge of the forest to keep watch on the redoubts until they were relieved by fresh detachments.

WITH THE AFTERBIRTH DELIVERED and the cord tied off and cut, Elizabeth and Laughing Otter made Blue Sky comfortable, while Sweetgrass and Rain Woman washed her son and rubbed him with a protective coating of bear grease before wrapping and placing him in Blue Sky's eager arms.

Mary left her pallet to join them, wan and trembling, but her face beamed. "Aye, a big, braw laddie. Sure, he'll make a fine warrior, this one."

Blue Sky's attention was all on her son. With the women gathered around her, she whispered, "Thank you, Moneto. I praise you, for you did not forget me, and you have given me this joy." Clutching the infant to her breast, tears dropping onto his blanket," she added with a sob, "Please now bring Golden Elk safely back to us so our son may know his father."

Sitting back on her heels with a sigh, Elizabeth became aware that while they had been occupied, darkness had wrapped the camp. In the distance, the sound of firing had diminished to the occasional roar of a single cannon or the brief crack of individual musket shots. While she listened fearfully, even this faded away, and at last a tentative hush hung suspended over the forest.

AS THEY STRODE DOWN THE SLOPE toward the rear of the warriors' camp, Andrews made out Elizabeth by the fire in front of the birthing wigewa and lengthened his stride. He was only dimly aware that beside him Carleton matched his steps, with Red Fox and Spotted Pony trailing close behind.

At the first ravine they had come to on the way back to camp, they had quenched their thirst at the creek, then plunged into its icy waters to wash off the heat and grime of battle. Delaying only long enough to devour the hard biscuit and dried venison they carried with them, they had hurried the rest of the way under a cloudless, inky sky studded with the myriad brilliant pinpoints of stars. With every step, a nameless fear for Blue Sky had swelled in Andrews's heart.

As soon as they entered the camp, Vander Groot had hurried off to the hospital, and Andrews had dismissed the rest of the brigade. Coming to meet Stowe, Sweetgrass had directed Andrews to the birthing wigewa with a knowing look. It had been all he could do not to break into a run, mindful of his companions who followed at his heels.

As they drew nearer, the fire's leaping flames cast a flickering glow across the small, blanket-wrapped bundle cradled in Elizabeth's arms. Looking up, she saw them approaching and met his anxious gaze with a smile.

"You have a son, Charles."

His mouth dropped open, but no sound emerged. Laughing, Carleton pounded him on the back, while Red Fox and Spotted Pony grinned broadly as their wives stepped out of the wigewa to join them.

"Blue Sky . . . she's . . . she's well?" Andrews stammered.

"Your wife is very well," Elizabeth answered, "She's sleeping at the moment, but you can go sit with her until she wakes."

"Our son was born while I was gone!" Andrews exclaimed. "I should have been with her!"

Carlton's hand tightened over his shoulder. "You wouldn't have been in any case. The women wouldn't allow it. It's just as well you were occupied with other matters."

"The birth of children is a matter belonging to the women," Spotted Pony said, his mouth twitching with suppressed laughter. "A man is wise to keep out of their way at such a time."

A whimper rose from the bundle in Elizabeth's arms. Suddenly all else faded, and a great joy burst in Andrews's chest. When she beckoned, he went to her eagerly, and she laid the child into his arms. Pushing back the wrappings from the tiny face, he drank in the sight of him as the others crowded around to admire the boy. Pierced to the heart by the child's perfection, he was amazed that after so many months in his mother's womb, known only by Blue Sky's swollen belly and the indistinct movements beneath the flesh, his son was suddenly real and visible, cuddled against his chest.

"I've never even thought what to name him," he said, looking up.

"By our people's tradition, a son is given his name ten days after his birth, and a girl in twelve days," Red Fox explained. "In that time, Moneto will indicate the child's name by an *unsoma,* a notable event."

"So . . . we have to wait for this . . . *unsoma.*"

"That's right," Carleton said, laughing. "In the meantime, Blue Sky will have to stay here. And at the end of ten days, the two of you must throw a feast for everyone at which you announce your son's name." Sobering, he glanced at the others. "Of course, depending on what Burgoyne decides to do, we may have to delay the celebration."

"I'M SO GLAD THINGS WENT WELL for us today . . . and so relieved you're back safely," Elizabeth sighed, leaning against Carleton's chest.

He tightened his arms around her and laid his cheek against the top of her head. Although Andrews was with Blue Sky, giving them a rare moment alone, he longed to stretch out right there on the ground and surrender to the sleep his body demanded. In spite of the deep weariness that sapped him, however, the tension and stress of the day had left him too keyed up to relax.

"Waiting for you to return from battle doesn't get any easier no matter how often I'm forced to do it," she added plaintively. "Were there many casualties?"

"Far more on their side than ours," he assured her. His voice sounded as blurred as he felt.

She gave him a keen look in the firelight and reached to finger the tears in his shirt. "You appear to be unscathed, though it looks like you had a few close calls. Any wounds I need to stitch up—for you or Charles or any of the others?"

He shrugged. "Nothing serious. Don't worry about us, dearest. You've enough patients to tend."

Her eyes warmed, and she smiled up at him. Stepping out of his arms, she retrieved her wig and hat from the blanket by the fire and hastily set herself to rights.

"Then I'd better run to the hospital to see if Pieter needs help—and tell him Charles and Blue Sky's good news."

Placing his arm around her shoulders, he gently drew her down to sit beside him on the blanket. "That can wait. Sit here a while and rest. You're worn out."

"No more than you," she protested, then frowned. "Oh, before I forget, a report came in this afternoon that General Clinton's taken the forts on the Hudson Highlands and driven General Putnam out of Peekskill."

His head bent, he rubbed his temples, light-headed with fatigue. "I wonder how Washington's corps is faring. But no matter. Burgoyne will likely attempt a retreat to Fort Edward, but though he may not know it yet, his surrender's inevitable. And when he finally concedes, we'll have won a notable victory. If this doesn't persuade France to ally with us, nothing will."

He gathered her to him, and she came willingly into his arms. For some moments he stared into the fire, haunted by vivid images of the day's action. As too often before, so much destruction, so many men lying dead or grievously wounded.

It seemed to him all the world was consumed by war. He wondered when the conflict would end and what would be left of their world when it did.

If it did.

Truly, he had been at war so long he doubted he even remembered what constituted normal life. Was there such a thing left or would battle rage inside his heart forever even after the outer war ended?

For even when the Long Knives' Revolution was victorious, as he firmly believed it ultimately would be, yet the struggle of his people, the Shawnee, for their very existence stretched out into unseeable shades, and anguish and grief engulfed him at the portent of that future.

Remembering suddenly the expression of awe in Andrews's face when he had first gazed upon his son, a pang of envy stirred in Carleton's soul that his friend had been given this blessing withheld from him. Yet that unworthy emotion gave way as quickly to something deeper: gratitude that he shared in the joy of those dear to him, pleasure in their delight . . . and hope for his own future and Elizabeth's, and at last his people's as well.

As it had down through the ages, innocent new life had once again been born into this world of death and destruction. Could his parents keep this child safe, Carleton wondered, or would he too be crushed by evil, or in the end corrupted?

Yet as he lifted his eyes to the black bowl of the heavens high above, he felt a quiet assurance steal over him that the great Spirit who brooded over them in struggle and pain and joy would also guard this fragile, holy spark against any hostile force that might seek to quench it.

"THANK YOU FOR OUR SON," Andrews whispered into the lustrous hair at Blue Sky's temple. "Moneto has greatly blessed us."

She smiled sleepily into his eyes. "The Great Spirit has promised us many sons and daughters, my husband. I rejoice in His goodness."

He drew a deep breath and let it out, gratitude and humility filling him in equal measure. "As do I—and in your love and in this child."

After she had drifted off to sleep again, he cradled the boy to his chest, reluctant to let him go. Finally he rose and quietly stepped out of the wigewa. The night was windless and chill, and the sparkling dew that settled on the grass quickly turned frosty.

A faint glow behind the treetops heralded the moon's rising, and overhead, the brilliant flame of each individual star glittered against the velvet-black sky, impossibly far away, yet seeming to him now a very personal thing—the intimate reflection of his joy, the celebration of the deep love that already filled his breast for this tiny, incredibly beautiful being he held, this melding of his and Blue Sky's bodies.

Looking down at the bundle in his arms with an emotion akin to fear, he pulled away the cloths the women had wrapped so tightly around the child and studied him hungrily. The infant's tiny, round face puckered, and he opened his eyes, giving a wail of protest as he flailed his thin, wrinkled arms and legs.

Andrews marveled at how perfectly he was formed, with skin a lighter shade of his mother's dusky tones, eyes dark like hers. And surely the shape of the small face and nose was Andrews's own, while the downy hair that thickly covered his scalp had dried to reveal the rich color of ripe wheat.

A paean of gratitude and praise filled Andrews's heart. "Thank you, Father. I praise you, O Almighty One, for You are good," he whispered, the words repeating over and over in his mind.

He tucked the cloths tightly around his crying son and cuddled him close. Giving a last, shuddering sob, the boy quieted and for a moment looked up intently into his father's face. As Andrews smiled down at him, unexpectedly he felt the leap of something powerful between them that caused his breath to catch and his heart to increase its pace. Then slowly the infant's eyes drifted shut.

Andrews looked up. The dark forest seemed to beckon him, and taking several steps into its mysterious, shadowed aisles, he paused, transfixed. Before him, as the moon overtopped the trees, a pale, silver-gold glimmer fell onto the forest floor, lighting a distinct path that stretched between the misty trunks straight before him, beckoning him into the hazy distance that stretched out of his sight.

In his arms the child stirred, and Andrews saw that he had awakened. As though he followed his father's gaze into the forest, he squirmed around, then flung one arm loose from his wrappings and reached out his hand with a whimper. Andrews caught his breath at the expression of expectancy on the small face, and looked to see what had drawn the boy's attention.

All that lay before them was the muted, silvery path through the trees. By subtle degrees, as the moon imperceptibly ascended, the vision faded until Andrews wondered whether he had truly seen it.

But he had. And so had his son.

He hesitated, suddenly remembering his and Blue Sky's first real talk back at Grey Cloud's Town. She had mourned the loss of her husband, Pathfinder, then, and asked whether Andrews still hoped for love. He had answered that he did, adding, "Moneto has a good plan for all our lives if we only allow him to lead us."

And suddenly he knew: Moneto had given the *unsoma.*

"Your name is He Leads the Way, my son," he whispered, cupping the infant's head in his hand. And lifting him up to the night sky, he said to the heavens, "Bless this child, Great Spirit, for he is yours. All the days of his life may he serve no one but You, and may he lead many to follow Your straight path."

Chapter Thirty

AT THE HEAD OF HIS BRIGADE, Carleton sat his stallion at rigid attention, grateful for the bright sunshine that blunted the chill of the cold north wind. It was Friday, October 17, and to all sides along the south bank of the Fishkill spread the vast American army, both Continental and militia units, clothed in colorful array and bearing a motley assortment of weapons.

Although it was early afternoon, lingering streamers of pale mist still hung over the heavily forested ridges whose flaming autumn colors glanced back from the Hudson's turbulent waters. The land lay quiet now, undisturbed by the clamor of war. The only sounds were the rattle of drums, the tramp of thousands of feet, an occasional shouted command.

On the creek's north shore, long columns of British and German soldiers, wearing worn and faded uniforms of red, blue, or green, filed onto the meadow, colors flying, fifes and drums playing "The Grenadiers March" bravely but with a noticeable lack of enthusiasm. Rank by rank, Burgoyne's entire corps of 5,800 men laid down their weapons, and then marched off as prisoners of war.

Carleton felt no sense of triumph at the sight, nor, judging by the solemn expressions all around him, did any of the American troops. All of them also had experienced failure and defeat and took no joy in an enemy's disgrace. Nor in the sobering British casualties at Bemis Heights, tallying four times that of the Americans—more than half the force Burgoyne had led into battle that day.

While he watched the soldiers stack their muskets and draw their field pieces into orderly ranks, the text of Joel 2:20, from the sermon one of the army's chaplains had preached that morning, came to him: "But I will remove far off from you the northern army, and will drive him into a land barren and desolate, with his face toward the east sea."

So it was.

Images from the past ten days filled his thoughts: At nightfall on October 8, after enduring a day of skirmishes and sporadic artillery fire, Burgoyne's corps had stealthily crept out of their lines, leaving behind tents and fires to deceive their foe, to begin the retreat north toward Fort Edward. A cold, driving rain mired the road in deep mud, and with daylight skirmishers began to harass their rear, slowing the fleeing column's progress to a crawl. To hamper their pursuers, the British force burned buildings and tore down bridges as they went, then began to abandon wagons and baggage, killing their foundering horses and leaving their carcasses to rot along the road, while the bateaux that carried their dwindling supplies bobbed laboriously upstream below them on the turbid Hudson.

On the night of the ninth, the exhausted column waded icy Fishkill Creek and moved onto the heights above the small village of Saratoga, which they had fortified on their way south. They had traveled only eight miles from the battlefield.

By then strong American detachments had circled north of them on the Hudson's east bank as far as the Battenkill. Continental and militia units continued to pour up from Bemis Heights, and American artillery began to bombard the supply bateaux. Surrounded by an army almost four times the size of the one he commanded, Burgoyne yet continued to stall the inevitable for days, waiting vainly for General Clinton to appear from New York to rescue him. On the previous day, with his beleaguered army starving, he had finally given up that hope and reluctantly agreed to terms of surrender.

Or rather, to soften the blow, a "convention." Thinking of Gates's easy acceptance of Burgoyne's terms until the British general's dithering had necessitated an ultimatum, Carleton shook his head.

It was by any standard a staggering victory for the Americans, however. Not even the report received a couple of days earlier of Washington's defeat at Germantown on October 4 could dampen it.

He glanced toward Andrews on his right. Next to him was McLeod, then Vander Groot, and beyond him Elizabeth. Leaving the two new mothers at the Bemis Heights camp in the care of the Shawnee women in order to serve in the Rangers' field hospital, she had accompanied the troops north but kept her distance from Carleton, her identity carefully protected by the doctor and chaplain. Clad in buckskins, with her hair covered by wig and hat, she met his gaze with one that reflected his own emotions, and returned his slight nod with a faint smile.

AN HOUR LATER, closely attended by Colonel Wilkinson, the British commander along with his staff and generals approached the temporary American camp. The Rangers had preceded them and waited at attention just outside the fortifications as Gates emerged from the small, rude cabin where he lodged and rode out to meet Burgoyne.

The two men could not have provided a greater contrast, Carleton thought. Still a dashing figure in his brilliant scarlet uniform despite the privations and humiliations of the past months, John Burgoyne towered over Gates. With his lank grey hair, plain blue frock coat, and spectacles, the American general looked old and shrunken in comparison.

Both men reined their horses to a halt. "I'm glad to see you," Gates said with a smile.

Burgoyne removed his hat and gave a stiff bow. "I'm afraid I'm not glad to see you. It's my fortune, sir, and not my fault that I'm here."

Gates dismounted, and Burgoyne did the same. With a flourish the British general drew his sword and handed it to the older man. For several minutes they exchanged pleasantries, then Gates handed the sword back to Burgoyne. Leading their horses and followed by Burgoyne's retinue, they strode down the line of Rangers toward the entrance to the camp, awash in bonhomie as though they were old friends, rather than merely acquaintances from Gates's years in the British army.

When Burgoyne came level with Carleton, his gaze fixed on Carleton's face. He came to an abrupt halt, his eyes narrowing as a shock went through him. Frowning, Gates directed a puzzled look from one to the other, while Carleton stared straight ahead, giving no sign of recognition.

"So," Burgoyne said hoarsely, "you're alive after all." When Carleton made no reply, he added, his voice thick with contempt, "I'm sure you take great satisfaction in this meeting, Jonnie boy, though it's hardly the one I envisioned."

Carleton turned a steady gaze on him, his expression masked. "None of us takes pleasure in the defeat of a valiant foe, sir. Neither do I."

German general Baron Friedrich von Riedesel stepped forward and in heavily accented English said, "You are the leader of the raids against our foraging parties, are you not? The one they call White Eagle."

Carleton made a graceful bow. "I am, sir."

Von Riedesel motioned toward the Rangers drawn up behind Carleton. "We all admire the manner of your troops on a day that for them should be for jubilation. You make what is a difficult day for us less so."

"Another time our situations might be reversed," Carleton answered, "and we'd hope for the same civility."

He noted that the German general's gaze dropped from his and his face darkened. Clearly, as he had meant him to, von Riedesel remembered the aftermath of the fall of Fort Washington on York Island a year earlier. Carleton had heard accounts of the brutal treatment the vanquished American force had received at the hands of the Hessian troops, and he took satisfaction in the baron's shamefaced response.

WHILE THE COLUMNS of British and German prisoners began their long march to Boston, where they were to be held, Gates entertained his ranking officers, Burgoyne, and the British generals with a dinner at his headquarters. Carleton dismissed his troops and returned to the small farmhouse where he lodged with his officers, relieved that he had not been invited and happily anticipating a transfer back to Washington's corps now that peace reigned in the Northern Department.

To his disappointment, however, the following day brought unsettling news that a large British force was moving up the Hudson. Gates immediately sent messengers rushing ahead to alert the units still at Bemis Heights and issued orders for the army to move out within the hour.

Stowe had just finished saddling Carleton's stallion when he hurried back from Gates's headquarters. The troops had already begun to mount, and he threw a quick glance down the line to make sure Elizabeth was with Vander Groot. Reassured, he handed his pack to Stowe and went to confer with Andrews, Isaiah, and Red Fox.

"Well, well, well—if it isn't my old friend, Jonnie boy."

Carleton swung around to meet Burgoyne's insolent stare. Knowing the vanquished general was also bound for Albany under guard, Carleton concluded he was to accompany the American army south.

"In case you've forgotten," Carleton returned politely, "we were never friends."

"Acquaintances, then," Burgoyne conceded with a sneer. He transferred his gaze to Red Fox and his warriors, then back to Carleton. "I'd heard you'd become an Indian. Pardon my surprise—I expected to see you with a ring in your nose."

Carleton deliberately looked him up and down. "I admit I'm equally surprised. You're looking unusually . . . trim. What happened—outrun your supply lines? Never a wise idea, is it?" he added kindly.

The muscles in Burgoyne's jaw tensed. "I heard Howe came very close to capturing you at Philadelphia."

"Alas, it would seem not close enough." Eyebrows raised, Carleton glanced toward Andrews and the others, who appeared highly entertained by the encounter.

"What a shame I wasn't there. I guarantee I'd not have failed in the attempt." There was real venom in Burgoyne's voice now.

Carleton focused his bemused gaze on his rival. "Unless I'm missing something, John, it appears you have. I've heard you're a middling playwright, but it seems your latest production has sadly met with something less than success. While I admire your bravado, it takes more than flash to win battles. My advice: Go back to the stage and leave the unpleasant business of war to those who have some aptitude for it. War is not a play."

Hearing the others' barely suppressed guffaws behind him, he cursed his propensity to speak before thinking. Would he never learn to keep silent? Cold steel and gunpowder had already said all that needed to be said.

Livid, Burgoyne ground his teeth. "I'll give my last breath, sir, to ensure you suffer the just consequences of your perfidy."

His mouth twitching, Stowe led the stallion forward, studiously avoiding Carleton's gaze. Taking the reins, Carleton swung into the saddle and looked down at Burgoyne.

The general's face was deeply furrowed with anxiety and care. He had aged greatly since the last time they met, when the advantage had been Burgoyne's. Pity flooded over Carleton. Burgoyne knew as well as he that his career in the army was finished, that his words were impotent, and that they would never meet again.

"You have my best wishes for a pleasant confinement and a quick parole back to England," he said, meaning it.

Bending in a slight bow, he urged the stallion forward and left Burgoyne staring after him, his expression blank.

TWO DAYS LATER Andrews met Carleton at the door of their lodgings in Albany with a letter. "This just came in by messenger an hour ago. It's from Washington."

Taking it, Carleton said, "I guess that British detachment we were to drive off heard we were coming. Gates told us they burned down some towns south of here, then withdrew toward New York yesterday."

"I hope that'll mean we're free to head back to Philadelphia."

Carleton broke the letter's seal and scanned the first page. "Here's a report on the defeat at Germantown. It doesn't sound as bad as we'd feared, thank God." He skimmed the second page. "As soon as Washington received news of Burgoyne's intent to surrender, he secured our orders from Congress transferring us back to his corps. He's going to try to relieve Gates of as many of his troops as possible now that they won't be needed here."

Andrews gave an exuberant whoop. "How soon can we leave?"

Carleton looked up, grinning. "I'm sure Gates won't object if we move out tomorrow, though I doubt he'll give up any of his other brigades so easily. Pass the word along, and I'll get the general's approval. I want to ride out before sunrise," he threw over his shoulder as he headed back out the door.

⊛ ⊛ ⊛

AFTER CHECKING ON THE WOUNDED bedded down in a warehouse at the Hudson docks and consulting with Vander Groot, Elizabeth went out into the blustery evening and hurried around the corner to the small house on the next block that she shared with Caleb, Vander Groot, and McLeod. Though a lively fire crackled on the hearth in the larger of the two rooms the men occupied, both were empty, and she wearily climbed the steep stairs to her small room under the eaves.

She removed her hat and wig with relief and began to brush out her long hair, luxuriating in the sensation. If only a hot bath were available, she reflected, she would be perfectly content.

Hearing the door open and someone enter below, she laid down her brush and went to the head of the stairs, expecting to see one of her housemates. Instead it was Carleton. Looking up with a smile, he beckoned her to come down. When she hurried into his arms, he led her to fire.

Perched on the raised hearthstone, reveling in the heat of the crackling blaze, she said, "I didn't expect to see you tonight. I'm glad you were able to get away."

He took a seat cross-legged on the floor in front of her. "I look forward to the day when you'll never have to dress as a man again," he growled.

She gave a soft laugh. "Believe me, I'll be more glad of it than you. Perhaps now with Burgoyne's defeat this war won't drag out much longer."

"There's still Howe to contend with," he reminded her. "And King George and the Ministry. Curse this secrecy! I want to be with you openly, without the constant fear of someone betraying us."

He reached for her hand, and she laid it into his. "I just received Washington's orders transferring us back to his corps, and Gates has made no objection, as I expected. We'll leave early tomorrow morning."

"The baggage train and women too? You'll not ride ahead this time?"

"There's no reason to rush. I want to keep the brigade together." He grinned. "I know Charles and Blue Sky will be happy about that."

"It'll be easier on our mothers and babies," she agreed. "I'm amazed at how rapidly Blue Sky's recovered and how strong He Leads the Way is. Isn't it the perfect name for him?" she added with a smile.

He looked away, frowning. "It is. Someday he'll take Pathfinder's place. And mine."

Feeling as though he uttered a prophecy, she laid her hand on his arm. He looked up, pain in his steady gaze.

"It still hurts that he and Black Hawk were taken from me so suddenly when I'd only just found them again."

She released her breath in a sigh. "On this earth there's much we can't understand. Perhaps someday, when we reach heaven . . . " The words trailed off. After a moment she murmured, "Regardless of war and loss, life goes on, doesn't it?"

"I've thought that often lately." He sobered, studying her for a long moment. "Now that the last British detachments are safely back in New York, you'll leave tomorrow?"

She nodded and bit her lip, an ache tightening her throat. "Caleb's made arrangements for us to travel downriver on a merchant ship to Dobbs Ferry as you suggested, and from there we'll take the post road to Boston."

"It's longer, but an easier journey than riding across the mountains," he approved, "and you shouldn't run into any trouble along the way."

Sensing that he tried to convince himself her leaving was a good thing, she forced a smile. "We needn't have worried that I'd not reach Boston in time to welcome Mama and Papa and Abby home. I'll be able to meet their ship after all."

"Having you nearby these past months has made everything bearable." His voice broke and he stopped, then said gruffly, "It seems we're always saying farewell."

She fought back tears. "I wish you could come back to Boston with me now. Being with my family again will be such joy, but when you're absent, I can't feel at home. It's like there's a hole right through my heart. Promise you'll come this winter."

"I will—that is, if your parents will have me."

"They'll welcome you. I promise."

Her tears spilled over, and he rose to catch her to him with a low groan. "I want you to go to your parents . . . and I want you never to leave me."

When his mouth found hers she returned his kisses with abandon, a wild passion flaming up in her. Cupping his face between her hands, she kissed every part of it, finally buried her fingers in his hair and leaned her brow against his with a muffled sob.

He raised her chin to search her eyes. "What troubles you, beloved?"

"I don't know." Letting out a trembling breath, she glanced fearfully toward the door. "I feel there's darkness all around us, and I can't see what's on the other side."

He drew her back into his arms and held her tightly, his face buried in the tumbled hair at her neck. "It's nothing. You're tired, that's all. Don't be afraid, dearest one. God will watch over us."

He spoke confidently, and yet she had the feeling that her words deeply troubled him. She laid her head on his shoulder, and he gently stroked her hair, his fingers tangling in the silken strands.

"I'll never let anything hurt you, Beth," he murmured. "I swear it. No matter what happens, no matter where you are, you've only to send for me and I'll come at once. Never doubt that. Never."

Chapter Thirty-one

THE SHIP DOCKED AT DOBBS FERRY in late afternoon on October 23, buffeted by a raw east wind under lowering skies. Disembarking hurriedly, Elizabeth and Caleb rode east at a walk through a swirl of sprinkling rain and the last russet leaves blown from the denuded branches of the trees that lined the muddy street.

Joyful images of the coming reunion with her parents and sister after two and a half years brought a measure of surcease to her sorrow at yet another separation from Carleton. The happy anticipation of the past months, so long extended, made her family's return seem almost a dream. That only weeks, perhaps only days remained until they were all together again had her heart brimming with gratitude.

Reflecting on the anguish that increasingly oppressed her because of the deceptions she was forced to practice as a spy, she was suddenly overcome by an unexpected impression of God's nearness and the strong assurance that He would resolve all things in His perfect way and in His perfect time. Her life and the lives of all those she loved were in His hand, and she had no reason to worry.

Had not Jesus said that each day had trouble enough of its own and that tomorrow would take care of itself? God's best would always overcome the worst man could throw at them.

Her heart lighter, she smiled when the Martins' farm came into view at the edge of the town and spurred her mount, eager for a comfortable night's rest before she and Caleb set out on the road to Boston. Glancing warily behind them to make sure no one followed, they turned in at the wagon path that led to the sprawling old house and barn.

Twilight had fallen, and lantern light flickered cheerfully in the windows of the house. As though expecting them, at their approach Martin stepped out the front door onto the porch.

"You won't mind a couple of weary visitors tonight, I hope," Elizabeth called.

She noted that his ready smile did not reach his eyes. "You're both welcome, of course," he responded with what seemed to her forced heartiness.

Instinctively she took in her surroundings. All seemed peaceful, as usual . . . and yet a strange unease suddenly nagged at her. Pulling his mount to her side, Caleb caught her arm in a painful grip and nodded a warning at the ground, his mouth tight.

A trail of fresh hoof prints led to the barn. A substantial party must have arrived not long before.

As she jerked around to face Martin in alarm, the farmer spread his hands, apology and dismay etching his features. "I'm sorry. Warn't nothin' I could do."

Before he could say more, the door behind him opened, and General Henry Clinton stepped into view in brilliant, bloody full dress uniform. He swaggered to the porch steps, a detail of soldiers trailing in his steps, their muskets covering her and Caleb. From the barn another detail advanced rapidly toward them.

They had been betrayed.

Caleb released her arm. *"Ride!"* he hissed.

As they reined their horses around, they saw the detachment of light cavalry that closed in at a trot. Stunned, Elizabeth realized they must have lain out of sight somewhere along the road from the ferry.

Meeting Caleb's alarmed gaze, she gave a slight shake of her head. "Only bravado will serve now," she murmured, her voice trembling.

Thinking fast, she turned back to face the general, masking her dismay with a puzzled expression. "Why, General Clinton, how lovely to see you! And what a surprise! It seems congratulations are in order, sir. On our way here we heard of your triumph at forts Montgomery and Clinton a couple of weeks ago. Coming on the heels of His Excellency's capture of Philadelphia and defeat of General Washington at Germantown, the news is most gratifying to those of us loyal to the king."

Deliberately she neglected to mention the debacle at Bemis Heights.

Clinton's smug look faded slightly, she noted with satisfaction, concluding that Howe must have confided little to him.

"Ah," he said, almost uncertainly, "somehow I doubt your gratification in this instance. I believe I do have the honor of addressing Miss Elizabeth Howard?"

Bowing from the waist, she responded cheerfully, "Of course, sir." Straightening, she tipped her head to observe him as though not comprehending his meaning. "Forgive my dishabille," she continued with a laugh. "For safety and comfort, I prefer to travel in masculine dress. We're on our way to Boston to meet my parents on their return from England."

Clinton hesitated, his frown easing. The hope that rose in her breast was short lived, however.

"If that's the case," he said, throwing back his head to give her a supercilious look, "pray tell me why you come from Albany. That would seem to be considerably out of the way from Philadelphia."

Just then a soldier materialized at her right stirrup and ripped the reins from her hand. At the same instant Caleb flinched and drew hard on his reins, bringing his mount into a half rear as several others sprang to drag him, cursing, from the saddle. He hit the ground hard and rolled, was trying to claw to his feet when one of the soldiers clubbed him hard in the face with a musket butt, sending him prone to the ground.

"Caleb!" she screamed, grasping the pommel of her saddle with both hands to keep from falling as Night Mare curveted, ears laid back.

He lay unmoving, the side of his face covered with blood.

Through her horror she became aware that a handsome, impeccably uniformed young lieutenant now stood at her left. Surveying her with a sneer, he said, "Will you dismount, miss . . . or shall I throw you from the saddle?"

Refusing to show fear, controlling her shaking limbs by sheer force of will, she dismounted. She staggered as the lieutenant tore her hat and wig from her head, releasing her hair in a tangled flood over her shoulders. Trembling with rage and fear, she turned to face Clinton.

"May I demand your reasons for this outrage?"

He gave a chilling laugh. "I'd think that supremely obvious, my dear Miss Howard," he gloated as he leered at her. "It appears I've accomplished what no one else could and clipped Oriole's wings."

SHE PRAYED HER EXPRESSION did not reflect her inward turmoil. Head held high, dirty, sore, and faint with hunger from the ignominious treatment she had been subjected to on the way to Clinton's headquarters in New York City and the three days of abject misery that had followed, she faced General Howe in grim determination.

He must have wanted her very badly to leave his army fighting to clear the American defenses on the Delaware below Philadelphia, while he traveled so far in all haste to honor her with this interview. All things considered, she would not have felt slighted had he spared the effort.

This is how it must have been for Jonathan when they captured him.

The thought braced her. She determined to endure with the same courage he had shown.

"May I pour you a glass of wine, my dear? You look in need of . . . refreshment."

With a hand that refused to still its trembling, she pushed the loose strands of tangled hair from her brow and cheek, hating that her unwashed and unkempt appearance put her at an even greater disadvantage. What she would have given for a hot bath and a pretty gown to replace the shirt and breeches she had worn since Albany, now torn and stained with sweat and blood!

She moistened her parched lips, longing to quench her thirst, to feel the trickle of the wine's warmth through her veins, fortifying her against what was surely to come. "Thank you . . . but no."

"As you wish." A faint smile played upon Howe's face. "You're quite good, you know," he purred. "In spite of my warnings you almost fooled General Clinton. And that's not easy to do."

"Fooled?" she enquired innocently. "I only told him the truth."

He took a long draught of wine, set the goblet on the small table beside him, and wiped his mouth with the back of his hand. Regarding her from beneath half-closed eyelids, he drew on his pipe, then tipped his head back and released a thin stream of smoke into the air.

Deliberately he returned his calculating gaze to her. "Your activities as a spy for the rebels—"

"A spy?" She gave an incredulous laugh. "How absurd! As I explained repeatedly to General Clinton, my cousin, Mr. Stern, and I were traveling to Boston to meet my parents on their arrival from London. Since there are so many highwaymen on the roads, I assumed masculine dress for safety's sake—"

"Come, come, Miss Howard. Do you expect me to believe that? I'm not such a fool, I assure you."

Oh, that I had heeded Jonathan's warnings! she thought miserably.

When he continued to regard her without speaking, his swarthy face inscrutable, she said, "You have proof of this ridiculous claim, of course."

He dismissed her question with a languid wave of his hand. "Does it not seem marvelous to you that intelligence of the most sensitive nature always makes its way to the rebels from any location where you are? First Boston, then New York. And most lately, Philadelphia."

Her mind raced. "Considering that Boston is my home, it would seem natural for me to be there," she said stiffly. "And we sought haven from those wretched Sons of Liberty in New York, where we have acquaintances, then joined the Vander Groots in Philadelphia for the summer. As you well know, we settled in both towns well before the army arrived."

"True . . . but it was a logical conclusion that we'd move against them. In fact, Mr. Washington already had detachments in both locations who were fortifying them against us." Howe gave a conspiratorial smile. "I'd say that getting there in advance gave you and your aunt time to scout out the situation and gain the trust of the local loyalists so that when we arrived you'd already be in the thick of things, with a wealth of intelligence available to you."

"The same could be said of any number of people who've sought the protection of your army," she retorted with a toss of her head. "Not to mention your own officers, who have far more information than I could ever gain."

His smile hungry, he countered, "But you, my dear, have enjoyed *laissez passer* from the very first instant, which has given you virtually unlimited entree to those very same officers. I know my own sex, and few men are a match for the wiles of a beautiful, intelligent, and daring woman, especially if they have no idea of her intent and no reason to question her motives."

He leaned back in his chair, watching her impassively, as a cat watches a mouse. "Let us take Oriole for an example. Or James Freeman, if you will."

The glitter of malevolence lighted his small black eyes, reminding her of a rat.

Elizabeth's head throbbed violently to the beat of her pulse. She lifted her shoulders in an expressive shrug.

"I've no idea who James Freeman might be, and the last I heard, Oriole died on Breed's Hill."

"Indeed—if you believe the rumors planted by the Sons of Liberty."

Refusing to flinch or drop her gaze from his, she narrowed her eyes and studied him coldly. "Surely you're not proposing that I am Oriole?"

He lifted an eyebrow. "An interesting thought. But then, who else could operate with more impunity and less fear of discovery than a woman? Even better, your parents and aunt are loyalists—or so they claim. The perfect cover for a spy. And perhaps the reason Oriole was never discovered . . . until now."

"I'm afraid you flatter me, Your Excellency."

"Oh, I doubt that very much. I've suspected you, dear lady, ever since General Burgoyne first mentioned your close involvement with General Carleton."

"How tiresome!" she snapped. "Nothing could be further from the truth, as I've stated time and again. A relationship between me and that traitor is a figment of General Burgoyne's imagination and vindictiveness, nothing more. There isn't a shred of affection between General Carleton and me—quite the opposite."

"Then why were you seen among his Rangers in Albany not five days ago," he nodded at her clothing, "while in disguise?"

A cold chill fell over Elizabeth, but she forced a tinkling laugh. "If anyone is a master at spying, it is you, sir. But I fear in this case you're too credulous of your informant. If I'd been there in disguise, how would anyone have known my identity?"

"Being a spy, you ought to be able to imagine the answer. I also know that last Christmas, three months after you left New York City, you and your aunt stayed for several days at an inn owned by Jeremiah Wainwright near the rebel camp at Newtown . . . at exactly the same time General Carleton reappeared with Washington at the battles of Trenton and Princeton. The story was that you'd gone to Boston, but when my informant reported hearing you speak the Shawnee language with the Indian maiden who accompanied you—who is evidently Colonel Andrews's squaw—well, I couldn't help wondering whether you might not have gone elsewhere. Might not, in fact, have gone with Colonel Andrews to seek White Eagle. And found him."

She fought to control her trembling, to conceal her shock while he stroked his chin, his hooded eyes never leaving her face. She felt physically ill, tasted the bile in her throat. Into her mind flooded the encounters with Chastity at Philadelphia, and she clenched her hands in her lap until the knuckles whitened.

Her promises to Aunt Tess were all a lie. He'd already bought her services.

"There's no mistake," Howe continued in a caressing tone, "In fact, I've had you followed for quite some time. I have an eyewitness who'll testify quite convincingly to your perfidy—and your aunt's. You see, I pay much better than she does."

A wave of dizziness swept over her at the verifications of her suspicions. But he wasn't finished.

"And I have this."

Flicking open the lacquered box on the table beside him with one finger, he tipped it over. Onto the table's surface tumbled the silver Indian jewelry Carleton had sent her. And the miniature with his portrait.

His voice caressing, he drawled, "These were found among the baggage you shipped to Boston some weeks ago. In case you're wondering, everything—except these items—was delivered safely to your aunt's home, no one the wiser."

She fought back a groan.

He picked up the miniature to examine it more closely. "Unless I miss my guess . . . the young man portrayed here is Jonathan Stuart Carleton. Or perhaps I should call him White Eagle."

She would not cry. She would not shed a single tear, though fear paralyzed her. Her throat was so tight she could not speak, yet still she refused to drop her steady gaze from the one that devoured her.

What does he want? Me?

An even more wretched wave of nausea swept over her. It was certain he would never willingly let her go. But if she offered herself to him, would he allow her sufficient liberty that she might find means to escape?

The hunger of the gaze that raked her held promise he would. Yet her entire being revolted at thought of using her body so, even in such a dire case as this.

No, she would rather hang than sin against the God she revered and betray the man who claimed her complete love and devotion. Even if she could stifle her conscience long enough to commit such a deed, Howe's ruthlessness was abundantly clear to her now. She would only step from the present trap into one more sordid.

She rose unsteadily, her chin tilted at a defiant angle. "What do you mean to do with me?"

Howe got languorously to his feet and stretched, his calculating gaze hardening. "That depends wholly upon you, my dear. If you share your knowledge with us—and I've every confidence it's vast where the rebels are concerned—I promise that you'll receive the kind treatment a woman of your station should expect."

She knew absolutely that he was lying. He had all the evidence he needed to summarily execute her, and sooner or later he meant to make use of it.

There was no point in further pretense. She shook her head.

"I'll tell you nothing," she said, teeth clenched. "Do whatever you will." Her hands clammy, she prayed fervently she would be able to keep that promise.

Howe's mouth tightened. "You forget we have your kinsman—Caleb Stern, I believe his name is."

Swallowing hard, she steadied herself. "You've not harmed him?" She hated the tremor in her voice.

"Not yet. Oh, we can force him to tell us a great deal, especially if threatened by your harm. But he doesn't know as much as you, and finally getting to General Carleton . . . " Howe spread his hands, "now, that's another matter altogether. That'll take more creative methods." With a nod, he directed her attention to the scene outside the window.

Through the spitting rain that streaked the window, she could make out a sweep of lawn bordering the battery and, beyond it, a stretch of harbor. Well offshore several moldering ships swung sluggishly at anchor. As her gaze fell on them, she gripped the arm of the chair beside her so hard the carved wood bit painfully into her palm.

"Remain stubborn, and that shall be your fate. Long enough, at least, for you to dearly regret your lack of cooperation."

She shrank from the view, pressed her hand to the pulse that throbbed in her throat. "Even you'd not be cruel enough to treat a lady so," she whispered through stiff lips.

"Would I not?" Again he smiled, revealing irregular, yellowed teeth. "Then you don't know me well." He cocked his head. "Tell me, how will your parents feel to learn that their daughter is a traitor to the king and a prisoner of war destined for hanging? Perhaps they or your aunt will persuade you to listen to reason."

Her heart contracted and the breath went out of her. Her lips pressed tightly together, she reviewed the current locations of those she loved most dearly: Carleton and Andrews on the way to rejoin Washington by a northern route well out of range of any British force. Tess safely at home in Boston. Her parents and Abby most likely still at sea.

All safe. For the time being.

Thank God they're out of his reach! Please, Lord, keep them safe!

How could she find a way to alert them to their danger, when she was under arrest? And if she could find a way to send warning—or if Howe informed them that he held her—then they would certainly try to rescue her, exposing themselves to arrest. And to Howe's use against her.

Looking into the general's swarthy visage, pierced by the dark eyes under his beetling brows, she told herself she had been wrong. He reminded her not of a rat, but of the devil.

Lightheaded and faint, she fought down a surge of panic, pressed her eyes shut, raging against her folly. How could she have been so careless? And how could she have so underestimated Howe? Of all the enemies who had threatened her, she had discounted him because of his outward indolence of mind, his self-indulgence, his casual immorality. And all along he had been the one most to be feared.

He cannot reach them, she assured herself once more.

But all certainties had fled. Indeed, a message could reach them, and at news of her dire plight they would come. The thought of her father's devastation when he learned of her execution was a punishment more cruel than any other Howe could devise.

Save one.

With a low chuckle, he continued, "But I've an even better plan to make use of you. As soon as you're safely stowed amongst the desperate men left to rot aboard those hulks and subject to the tender mercies of their guards, a message will be on its way to . . . General Carleton."

He spoke deliberately, leaning his ponderous, towering form in close. "All he has to do to buy your freedom is to come to me. Alone. Is that not an offer he'll be unable to refuse?"

The blood drained from her face. She staggered back, gagging on the stench of stale tobacco smoke, wine, and sweat that cloaked him.

"Do you think him so stupid?" she spat. "He'll know at once it's a trap and your promises hollow. You'll never release me. You mean to execute us both."

Fixing her in a calculating look, he sucked in a long, slow drag from his pipe, then released a stream of smoke into the air above her head. The threat in his gaze hung heavy in the room's stagnant air.

"By George, I believe you're right," he drawled reflectively, his lazy smile triumphant. "But then . . . he'll never leave you to die alone. Will he?"

If you enjoyed this story and would like to offer feedback, we invite you to email the editor, Joan Shoup, at jmshoup@gmail.com. We'd love to receive your comments.

We always appreciate positive reviews posted on the book's detail page on Amazon, Barnes and Noble, Christianbook.com, and other online sites. Thank you for telling other readers about this series!

Valley of the Shadow

The American Patriot Series
~Book 5~

J. M. Hochstetler

Coming Soon

Charlotte, Tennessee
37036 USA

THE WORDS SWAM AND BLURRED before his eyes in the lantern's flickering light. Clenched in his hand, the paper shook.

His mind gone blank, Brigadier General Jonathan Carleton stared at the letter, a wave of terror and rage bringing the bile into his throat and squeezing the air from his lungs. By degrees he became aware of the chill sweat that in spite of the warmth radiating from the blaze on the hearth trickled down his brow and back.

He sucked in a shallow breath and forced himself to focus on the letter's signature: *William Howe.*

Knight of the Bath. Commander in Chief of His Majesty's forces on the North American Station.

"Jon, what is it?"

Behind him, Colonel Charles Andrews's voice sounded hollow and far away. Ignoring his friend, Carleton studied the words scrawled boldly above Howe's name as though, if he willed it, they would say something else.

That the American cause was entirely lost. That Washington had surrendered to the British. That Howe's entire army waited outside the door to escort Carleton to the scaffold, there to hang for treason. Anything.

Not this.

Philadelphia
28 October, 1777

Sir,

This is to inform you that I hold Elizabeth Howard prisoner. If you wish her to live, present yourself to me, alone, at my headquarters no later than two days following your receipt of this letter. The guard that bears it has orders to conduct you directly to me, unharmed, with all courtesy due a general officer.

Be advised that if you do not appear or if anyone attempts to follow you, Miss Howard will die in that hour.

I am, sir,
Your most humble servant . . .

Humble servant. If he did not loathe Howe so intensely in that moment, he would laugh.

"Jon, please—"

His expression masked, Carleton thrust the letter at Andrews. Throwing an alarmed glance at Dr. Pieter Vander Groot, the colonel took it and brought it close to the lantern to scan its contents. When he looked up, his face had gone chalk white.

"My God! He has Beth!"

Vander Groot tore the letter from Andrews's hand. He read it, then dropped the page on the table and slumped into the nearest chair.

"It's my fault. I caused this." Taking a shaky breath, Carleton moved woodenly past the two men.

Andrews grabbed him by the arm and spun him around. "What do you mean?"

"When they ambushed me at Gray's Hill," Carleton reminded him, trembling. "I taunted Howe to his face. You warned me he'd move heaven and earth to capture me. Obviously he has." Again he stepped toward the door.

"You can't mean to go to him!"

Carleton tried to wrest his arm free, but Andrews caught him by the other as well and forced Carleton to face him, his fingers tightening like a vise. "This is insane! Think, Jon. He'll arrest you—hang you."

For a long moment Carleton regarded him blankly, unable to make sense of Andrews's plea or come up with a coherent response. "I know," he rasped at last.

"Do you truly think he'll release Beth in exchange for you?"

"No."

"You're right. You'll accomplish nothing but to hand him you head on a silver platter—one of our best officers, the very one who so magnificently fleeced the British of every scrap of intelligence the patriots needed! What you suffered when General Gage arrested you back in Boston will be nothing to what Howe will do now. He'll make a cause célèbre of you to top all others, and then he'll hang you both."

Carleton tore out of his grip, but before he could reach the door, Vander Groot blocked him. "What Charles says is true. I know Howe well enough to be certain of it."

"I . . . cannot . . . allow her . . . to die alone," Carleton said, his voice thick, each word an effort. *"I will not."*

Andrews gripped Carleton's shoulder, his expression grim. "Do you honestly think Howe hasn't thought of that, that he'd allow you to catch even one glimpse of each other, or that he'd give either of you the comfort of executing you together?"

"What could he do that'd be worse?"

"Never allow her to know that you gave yourself up for her! Never allow you to see her one last time and assure her of your love!" Andrews's voice broke. "No, he'll hang you, and then he'll simply let her rot away in misery in some stinking hellhole, knowing full well what would happen if you came, but wondering still whether you ever learned of her fate or, if so, whether your love had failed."

Staggered, Carleton tried blindly to turn away. Vander Groot shoved a chair toward him, and he collapsed into it. Leaning forward, hands gripped between his knees, shoulders heaving, he fought to ride out the tide of agony that bore over him. But it rose all the higher until he feared he must either drown or be swept away to some act of unspeakable violence.

"Dear God, what am I to do?"

Vander Groot pulled his chair next to Carleton's and bent over him, one hand on his back. "First we have to verify that Howe's not lying, that indeed he does hold Beth. I'd not put any deception beyond him."

"I have two days to present myself at Philadelphia before he executes her! A detachment waits outside to take me to him!"

Andrews's face hardened. "They're under guard and will wait as long as we deem fit."

"But Beth—"

His face contorted with anguish, Vander Groot said, "Jon, you know I love Beth as much as you do. To think of her suffering or—" Breaking off, he made a painful gesture, then continued, "But Howe knows full well that if he hangs her, he'll lose any hold he may have over you and gain your undying enmity. As commanding officer, he can't completely secure himself from attack by a determined assailant, and he knows there's no one more determined and capable than you. Despite his threats, he dare not take that course and risk losing you while there's any hope you might be persuaded to voluntarily comply with his demands."

"You have the right to ask for proof of his claims," Andrews approved, nodding, "and that'll buy us time to come up with a plan for Beth's rescue."

Carleton gave a short laugh. Shoving out of his chair, he began to pace the room.

"If that were even possible, how could we rescue her when we have no idea where she's held?"

"He demands you come to Philadelphia."

Carleton rounded on Andrews. "It's certain he'd not hold her there, Charles, not with us on the way and Washington's entire corps near at hand. There'd be too much opportunity for us to discover her location and get to her."

"Then where?" Vander Groot prodded, his eyes narrowing. "New York, perhaps."

Despair shadowed Carleton's face. "Dobbs Ferry!" he groaned. At their questioning looks, he said, "When we left Albany, I sent her and Caleb downriver to take the post road to Boston. All the intelligence we received indicated General Clinton returned to New York after capturing the forts on the upper Hudson. The militias had retaken the area, and I believed that route safer and easier for them than crossing the mountains."

Andrews ran his fingers through his hair and released a sigh. Pulling a map from the rawhide pouch on the table, he bent over it.

"If the two of them were captured at Dobbs Ferry, then New York's where Howe would logically take them, where he'd believe them fully secured from rescue."

Vander Groot sprang to his feet, snatched the letter from the table, and studied it intently. "Judging by their uniforms, the detachment that delivered the letter belongs to one of the regiments under Clinton. And this is Howe's signature, so he must have been in New York when it was written."

Carleton nodded, grim-faced, feeling that they grasped at straws. But in the absence of any other alternative, they had no choice.

He arrested his steps abruptly. Covering his face with his hands, he thought, *No. We have another choice. We are not alone. The One for whom nothing is impossible will help us.*

Drawing in a slow breath, he steadied. Turning to his companions, he said, "Pieter, you're familiar with British dispositions in the city. Where are their prisons located?"

Vander Groot regarded him, frowning. "The North Dutch Church and a number of other churches have been turned into prisons. And there's the Provost's gaol at—"

Blanching, he broke off abruptly, horror coming into his eyes. Carleton strode to him and pulled him out of his chair.

"What is it? Tell me!"

The doctor closed his eyes, sweat beading his brow. When Carleton shook him, he met his alarmed gaze with a hopeless one.

"There's only one place on this continent where he'd be confident we could never get at her," he said hoarsely. "Aboard one of the prison ships in New York harbor. Guarded by the Royal Navy."

A wave of nausea twisted in Carleton's gut. *Oh God, we cannot overcome this!*

"The devil himself wouldn't treat a woman so!" he cried.

Vander Groot's voice echoed the desperation that had taken residence in Carleton's breast. "Perhaps not the devil. But I wouldn't put it past Howe."

Cursing, Andrews slammed his hand on the table, toppling the guttering lantern, which cast dizzying shadows around the room as it fell. Abruptly it extinguished, deepening the chamber's gloom.

Vander Groot hurried to the fireplace and brought a candlestick from the mantel to relight it. When its flame was restored, he said grimly, "If that's the case, how are we to reach her, much less get her safely off a British ship—if we can even determine which one she's aboard? Or, to begin with, if she's held on any of them?"

"I'll board every ship in New York harbor if I have to," Carleton snapped. His shoulders slumped and he let out a harsh laugh. "What am I saying? Foolish bravado won't help Beth. We'd need a navy to even get into the harbor, much less overcome the British fleet."

Lord God, help us! he pleaded silently. Light dawned at the same instant comprehension came into Andrews's and Vander Groot's eyes.

"You have a navy!" the two officers exclaimed together.

"You outfitted half your merchantmen as privateers last summer," Andrews reminded Carleton. "That gives you how many ready for combat—a dozen?"

Carleton shook his head, plummeting from hope back to despair. "Even if every one of them were at hand—and they aren't—what's a tiny fleet of privateers compared to the full might of the Royal Navy?"

Andrews rubbed his chin, giving him a calculating look. "But we won't be going against the entire Royal Navy, Jon. Most of Lord Howe's ships are in the Delaware, trying to break through Washington's defenses and open the sea roads to Philadelphia."

For some moments the three men stared at one another, each calculating the odds. "Lord Howe would never leave New York completely unguarded," Carleton pointed out. "There are certainly enough warships stationed there that the odds would still be decisively against us."

"Do your ships not fly the French flag?" Andrews demanded.

"When they're not flying the Union Jack," Carleton returned wryly.

"Ah, another possibility if the need arises. But are their crews not mainly French?"

"And Spanish," Carleton conceded.

"France is not a party to this war—at least not yet. News of Burgoyne's defeat at Saratoga won't reach London or Paris for another fortnight, and then it'll take a month or more for them to respond. A small convoy of French merchantmen blown off course during a gale at sea and seeking a port to make repairs and resupply should expect to be accommodated."

Vander Groot rubbed his hands together. "Brilliant!"

"Subtlety and deception won't suffice this time," Carleton cautioned, his voice hard. "What's needed is a bold assault and as much firepower as we can muster."

"Deception will at least get us into the harbor, and subtlety may get us aboard the ship where Beth's held," Andrews returned, "then we'll resort to firepower as needed. How many of your privateers are at hand?"

Drawing a steadying breath, Carleton rapidly reviewed the latest reports he had received. "Only three are in port now or due within the next few days. *Liberty* just delivered a prize to Salem, and *Destiny* and *Invictus* were expected at Marblehead at any time. But they'll all have to resupply before sailing again."

Andrews rubbed his hands together in anticipation. "Three will arouse less suspicion than a larger number, and *Destiny* is equal to any British first-rater. Along with the other two, we'll have firepower enough for a bold stroke."

Carleton stopped by the window and stared thoughtfully out into the night. "Even with the fastest post horses it'll take a courier five days to get to Marblehead, then Salem."

Joining him, Vander Groot said, "Write a letter right away demanding proof that Howe has Beth, that this isn't simply a lie meant to trap you. Tell him you'll turn yourself in after receiving verification that she's his prisoner. Then wait until the morning to send the detachment back and have one of your men shadow them to determine whether they head for New York or Philadelphia. Since he's giving you two days to arrive, I wager Howe's currently in Philadelphia. If so, it will take at least four days for an answer to return, two more days for you to be expected at his headquarters. By then your ships will be on their way to New York, and they'll arrive before Howe can send a warning to Clinton."

"What proof will you demand?" Andrews asked eagerly.

Carleton's mouth tightened. "That Howe send Caleb to me with a letter from Beth, written in her own hand."

Andrews and Vander Groot exchanged triumphant glances. "Perfect!" the doctor exclaimed. "Caleb may be held on the same ship as Beth or at least have some idea where she is. And that'll also give us one fewer prisoner to free."

"And also at least four more days while Howe sends a message to Clinton, who then must have Beth write a letter and send Caleb with it," Andrews exulted.

"If Howe agrees to my terms," Carleton broke in. "He may not."

"If he wants you, what choice does he have?" Andrews strode to the door. "I'll send Briggs to Salem and Stowe to Marblehead right away. We must get a message to your privateers with dispatch, ordering them to a rendezvous off the coast where we'll escape detection. And in the meantime, we'll bend every effort to determining exactly where Beth is."

When the colonel had sent a guard to summon his and Carleton's servants, Carleton resumed his pacing. "Even with all my privateers, there's no certainty of success against a large portion of the British fleet. To attempt it will only extend Beth's suffering and endanger her life even more."

"This is our only hope, Jon," Andrews countered forcefully. "Whether we attempt to rescue her and fail or you turn yourself in to Howe, Beth will certainly die. We must make the attempt if there's to be any hope of saving her. Beth's strong," he added as though reassuring himself. "She'll not give up without a fight. We've nothing to lose, and if all goes well, we'll free not only her, but others too."

"All we can do is plan carefully and pray mightily for God's wisdom and favor, then trust He'll guide us," Vander Groot reminded them, his voice breaking.

"Inform your French and Spanish captains of the stakes," Andrews said, returning to the table, "and they'll converge on New York harbor like sharks tasting blood."

Carleton could not suppress a smile, and for the first time on that dark night, a measure of confidence eased the constriction of his heart.

⊛ ⊛ ⊛

Vander Groot clasped Carleton by the shoulders and for a long moment gazed earnestly into his face.

"Thank you, Pieter," Carleton said huskily, returning his look with a grateful one. "With your help, we'll have some hope of pulling off this insane plan."

When he turned away to bend over the map with Andrews, Vander Groot moved quietly to the door. There he hesitated and swung to regard the two men with a hard look. At last he straightened and set his shoulders.

Taking care to make no sound, he pulled the door open and nodded reassuringly to the remaining guard stationed outside. Then he stepped into the dark passage and pulled the door quietly shut behind him.

Appendix

Common Terms of the Revolutionary Period

cartouche box: the case in which a soldier carries a supply of cartridges

gaol: jail

laissez passer: an unrestricted pass

man-of-war: eighteenth-century warship

muffatees: woolen gloves without fingers and palms

picket: detached body of soldiers guarding an army from surprise attack

stroud: a coarse woolen trade cloth or blanket

York Island: original name of Manhattan Island

vault: latrine

Shawnee Characters and Terms

Cornstalk: the principal sachem of the Maquachake, one of the five subnations of the Shawnee, and of the Shawnee tribe as a whole. After defeat in Lord Dunmore's War in 1774, he refused to fight the Whites and counseled the tribe to honor the peace treaty.

Blue Jacket: a Shawnee war chief known for his militant defense of Shawnee lands in Ohio Territory and an important predecessor of Tecumseh.

Hotehimini kiishthwa: the Strawberry Moon; May

killegenico: tobacco mixed with dried sumac leaves

Kispokotha: the warrior sept of the Shawnee who provided the tribe's warriors and war chiefs

Long Knives: the Americans, whose soldiers carried swords

Moneto: the Shawnee's Supreme Being of the universe

Piqua: the Shawnee sept in charge of the worship of Moneto, the Great Spirit, and lesser deities and spirits

Pooshkwiitha: the Half Moon; April

Sha'teepakanootha: the Wilted Moon; October

Shkipiye kwiitha: the Sap Moon; March

unsoma: a notable event

wampum: strings, belts, or sashes made of shell beads used either as ornaments, tribal records, a medium of exchange for goods, or to transmit messages

wigewa: a large rectangular or square dwelling for one family framed with poles and overlaid with bark, woven mats, or animal hides